Deuces Are

Wild

ACES HIGH, JOKERS WILD BOOK 6

O. E. TEARMANN

Amphibian Press
P. O. Box 190
West Peterborough NH
03468

www.amphibianpressbooks.com
www.oetearmann.com

Printed in the United States of America

In these times of great change, nonviolent action should not stay between the covers of a novel. We must lift the story off the page and into our lives.

-Rivera Sun

Reader Advisement

Themes of police brutality and injustice are explored in this volume. Included are romantic and sexual scenes between people whose genders may not fit your expectations. If this offends you, consider yourself warned. If you want to be involved in the kinds of communities discussed in this story, there are resources for the real world in the back of this book and at www.oetearmann.com.
Buckle up for the ride.

Contents

Event File 01

File Tag: Environmental Maintenance...1

Event File 02

File Tag: Reassessment..10

Event File 03

File Tag: Assignment of Duty...21

Event File 04

File Tag: Primary Objective..45

Event File 05

File Tag: Mission Prep..49

Event File: 06

File Tag: Statement of Intent..59

Event File:07

File Tag: Recruitment Friction...73

Event File 08

File Tag: Reclamation...85

Event File 09

File Tag: Onboarding...95

Event File 10

File Tag: Calorie Requirements..103

Event File 11

File Tag: Recruitment Failure..109

Event File 12

File Tag: Site Security..120

Event File 13

File Tag: Operative Security...129

Event File 14

File Tag: Recruitment Pressures..143

Event File 15

File Tag: Hearts and Minds..152

Event File: 16

File Tag: Mission Deviation...157

Event File 17

File Tag: Operative Assessment..167

Event File 18
File Tag: Community Buy-In..181
Event File 19
File Tag: Mission Report...193
Event File 20
File Tag: Strategic Approach..200
Event File 21
File Tag Strategic Withdrawal..207
Event File: 22
File Tag: Mission Compromised...214
Event File: 23
File Tag: Actions On Contact...224
Event File: 24
File Tag: National Strategy..231
Event File: 25
File Tag: Nested Concept..236
Event File:26
File Tag: Personnel Extraction...245
Event File:27
File Tag: Unit Integration..254
Event File 28
File Tag: Measure of Effectiveness 264
Sneak Peek: Book 7..272
Acknowledgements...303
Resources...305
A Wildcard Playlist, Part 6...315
Other Books By O.E. Tearmann..319
About the Author..321

Event File 01
File Tag: Environmental Maintenance
09:00·05·04·2160

"Seriously?"

"Yep."

"You're shitting me."

"Nope."

"Fucking tumbleweeds? F-fucking seriously?"

"Yep."

Tweak stared at the snarled pile of weeds leaning against the slicktarp of Base 1407, interlocked like nature's scrap-yard and just as full of sharp edges. She looked up at Milo; a long, long way up. He was a big guy, and she was short even for an Asian chick.

She still couldn't believe it. This had to be a joke.

"We have to replace. A whole slicktarp. B-because of some weeds. The fuck?"

Milo cocked a brow, his locs swaying in the hot wind. "Some weeds? Some of those things are bigger than you, tech girl. Almost as mean, too."

Tweak snorted. "Like that's anything. Everything's b-bigger than me."

Over beside the tarp, her commander dropped into a crouch, blond hair catching hazy sunlight. "Tweak, can you come check this with me?"

Tweak trotted over and dropped to the dusty ground beside Aidan, pulling out her tab and studying the tarp with narrowed eyes. The windstorm had kicked up two days ago, and their team had been stuck inside since, sheltering from the hot grit carried in it. It felt good to be outside again, but now there was this clusterfuck to deal with. The wind had picked up tumbleweeds along with the dirt, and now a six-foot high wall of the round, brown-grey plants was heaped against the side of the base and the slick-tarp that enclosed it, all their sharp spines sticking through the fabric that masked the base's signature across the visual and electromagnetic spectrum.

She studied the slicktarp, running her tab over it to let it find the punctures her eyes couldn't see. Her tab racked up the damage, and she sighed. "Shit. Yeah. There's holes."

"The kind of holes that are going to get bigger?" Aidan asked. Tweak wasn't sure if the face he was making was worried, but she could figure that out later. She focused on the tarp. The damage the tumbleweeds had done was ridiculous. The bigger spines had worked their way between the carbon fibers and pushed them out of their spots in the weave. The little ones had splintered off in the fabric, interrupting the visual illusion in a million places. Sure, the holes weren't big, but enough small holes could leak an electromagnetic signature that a search-and-destroy drone could pick up. How did a bunch of dry weeds do this?

At least none of the strands in the tarp had snapped. That was a relief. The fiber-optic inlaid mesh was tough; after all, it was made of graphene strands and fiber optics, all coated in heat-deflecting samarium nickel oxide. But patching it when something did manage to snap the strands was a pain in the ass.

Tweak looked up, squinting against the sun. The tarp would make it for a couple hours before she'd need to fill the holes with sealant. Right now there was a bigger problem: the six-foot wall of tumbleweed pushed up against two sides of the base was totally wrecking their visual camouflage. The stupid things were painting a target on the Wildcards.

Tweak checked her tab. "Boss. Weeds. Gotta g-go. No d-drones for another half hour. Em-mitter?"

"Yeah, if you can get it turned on that'd be great," Aidan agreed, blue eyes on the mesh. "How's the tarp?"

Tweak shrugged easily. "Good. Gonna make it, no big. Just n-needs lotsa sealant. Doesn't need a patch," she replied, bouncing to her feet.

Aidan smiled up at her. "Well that's a relief." Carefully, he stood, wincing a little. A twinge of pain cut across Tweak's heart. She hated the way the wounds Aidan had gotten in a corporate interrogation cell still held him up. He moved a lot more carefully these days. Tweak had gotten him out of that cell a few years back, sure. But she couldn't get him out of everything the corporate bastards had done to him. That really sucked, sometimes. She let him get to his feet, and watched him stare out at the mess of tangled weeds.

"And now we have to figure out how to move all that," the man added wearily.

"Think we can burn it?"

Tweak turned at the sound of one of her favorite people, her commander's little sister. Naomi was studying the tumbleweeds with a glint in the eye that wasn't hidden by her long-cut side-bangs.

Tweak cracked a grin. "Yeah, and the whole b-base. That much plant stuff? B-barbecue city."

"Especially when it's kochia," Milo agreed ruefully. "Burns hot and fast, that stuff."

Naomi brightened up. "Yeah, I know. We used to light piles of them up as a distraction when we were kids. Drones went to see what the fire was and left people alone. It's gorgeous. So I say—"

"No go, Omi," her big brother chuckled. "Too dry out there; I don't want to set the whole Region on fire today. We haven't had to deal with wildfires in our backyard for a couple years now, and I want to keep it that way." He pointed at his sister. "And for the record? *We* didn't pile up tumbleweeds and set them on fire; *you* did."

"Yeah, yeah," his sister chuckled. Smiling, Aidan brushed his hands off. "Okay, Tweak, get the big emitter on to cover us while we get this done. Milo, grab Janice and all the exterior maintenance tools. Naomi, grab Liza, she can get everybody organized. We need everyone out here to clear the perimeter, before all this kochia gives our base away to the drones. They may be a lot more erratic these days, but they're still up there. Tweak, I want you inside monitoring the slicktarp through your feed. I don't want us to put a hole in the tarp because we're in a hurry and end up with a bomb dropped on our heads because of it. Make sure it doesn't start degrading when we're ripping weeds off it, and start pinpointing areas of damage, okay?"

"Roger!" Tweak agreed, nodding. She could do that. She was pretty useless outside; the tumbleweeds irritated even Alpha skin, and she was a Gamma. No way she was going to touch the things. But she *was* going to get the damage fixed.

It took four hours, everybody's work, and a lot of sweat to get the base fixed up again. Tweak watched through the cameras as her buddies worked. Liza ran around the whole time with Deliquisha right behind her, reminding everybody to drink water, check the coolant levels on their chill vests and jackets, and keep their hats on. It sucked that this had to happen on the first really hot day of the year, up around a hundred and twelve, but it got done.

As soon as they could, most people headed back inside for a shower, and it was Tweak's turn to be outdoors, going over the slick tarp with a schematic holo hanging in the air beside her, checking it to pinpoint the holes and dabbing every one with sealant. Heat didn't get to her the way it did to Alphas; she kind of liked it when it was hotter.

Teasing out a few dabs of sealant, she watched Milo and Kevin fuss over the mobile planting beds on their big, heavy wheels while she sat, running the fabric between her fingers. The guys were stressing way too much. The covers had been over the base's food plants for the windstorm; they were totally fine. Tweak had already taken a look at her pet plant, the coffee-bean tree; it was the most delicate thing they grew, and it was good. If it was fine, the stupid potatoes would be fine too. But from the way the two men fussed, you'd think their plants were about to keel over.

She glanced up at her baby, smiling. The coffee cherries on the genetically modified tree were half-ripe; she'd have to take some time for a little harvest work pretty soon. It was such a beauty, standing there with red cherries gleaming in the slick-tarp's shade.

Tuning the guys out, Tweak turned her attention to the sound of Janice cussing up a storm as she cleaned grit and dust out of the solar panels that fed the base power up on the roof. Janice didn't sound worried about her tech, the way the guys were worried about their plants. No, she was pissed. It made Tweak grin to listen to her cussing out the whole world, the dust storm, and all the ancestors who'd changed the climate as she worked, mixing Spanish and English and a hell of a lot of stuff she'd probably made up into a long string of cursing.

At one point, Milo raised his head. "Hey beautiful, you got it? Want a hand?"

"What I want is to make the fuckin' sum'bitches who gave us these dust storms eat their own balls!" Janice called back.

Milo shook his head, smiling, and got back to his part of the work. It was good to see that he'd learned how to be a decent partner to Janice. He'd screwed up a lot when he arrived, but he'd gotten his head out of his ass eventually.

By sunset they were safe again, and even Tweak was hungry. The heat and the work must have burned some serious calories. She didn't usually get hungry; after all, it was one of the things they'd been aiming for when Cavanaugh Corporation started the gene experiments that wound up making kids like her. She burned about half the calories of most people. But today, she needed food.

Dinner smelled amazing when she walked into the canteen. Smiling, her best buddy handed her a plate.

"I tried a quesadilla thing tonight. See what you think," Billie offered, a smile flashing like a shooting star across her dark face.

Tweak grinned at her. "I think you're awesome."

Billie grinned, ducking her head. "Thanks, Tweak."

Plate in hand, Tweak grabbed a seat with her family. Her *family.* It still felt weird to say that. But the Wildcards were her family these days; Billie and her guy Topher sharing a quick kiss over there, Liza at the far end of the table, all the kids in the middle. There were Sarah and Yvonne giggling over something on a tab, always around to cheer you up. Steady Dozer was plowing through his dinner. Quiet Jim was fiddling with his mug, and sassy Blake was giving Kevin shit about something. Kevin had a hand across his heart, pretending to be horrified. He was pretty cool when he wasn't being a dickbag. There was Milo talking with his daughter Abbie. He was okay these days; at least he'd pulled his head out of his ass. Abbie was awesome. Beside her, Janice and Naomi, both kickass, were talking over some work they were doing together. Damian and Alice, the first medical people to treat Tweak like a human being instead of a lab rat, had their heads bent together, smiling quiet at each other. And beside Kevin, like always, there was Aidan, the guy who went around like it was no big deal holding them all together and keeping them all going. *Family* was the only word for it.

Of course, having a family meant having people around who gave you the fish eye and told you to do things for your own good. She reminded herself of that when she looked back up the table, saw their doctor staring at her, and had to take a second to fight down the lightning bolt of anxiety that flashed behind her eyes.

"D-damian. Staring."

"You missed three appointments in the last two weeks," the doctor stated, face blank as a bricked tab around his black ocular implants. "If I want to give you a checkup, I'm assuming I have to do it this way."

Tweak rolled her eyes. "I. Was. *Working.*"

"And not avoiding me at all," Damian observed, deadpan. "Sure you were."

Aidan glanced down the table. "Tweak?"

Great, now Aidan was in on this too. If she didn't go, he'd pull her aside and have a talk, and that'd waste his time and hers.

Tweak sighed. "Fine! Fine. After dinner, okay?"

Damian almost managed a smile. "After dinner."

In the last year, Tweak felt like she'd had more medical checks than she'd had in the rest of her life. It was getting really old. She fidgeted in the medical diagnostic chair. "So, is it w-working?"

Damian's ocular implants churred as he raised a brow. "Are you going to give me time to check your nerves, or do you want an answer now?"

Tweak rolled her eyes. This guy. "Fine. Check."

On a tray beside her, the bandages she usually wore to hide the scales on her arms and legs glowed white in the overhead lights, lying like sleeping snakes. The scales on her arm gleamed a pale gold in the glare. Deliberate as always, Damian reached for the electrometer wand. Tweak held out her hands, palms up. She knew the drill by this point.

The doctor ran the wand over the palms of her hands, then her face, noting the readings. He jotted those down on his tab, then pulled out the two long pins. "Eyes closed."

Tweak still hated this part of the test, but she closed her eyes. She hated being blind, and she hated being messed with. But the test made sense, and she could put up with it.

One blunt pin, and then the other, pressed into her forearm. "Where are you feeling them?" Damian's voice asked. Tweak pointed. He'd tried to have her explain it the first time he'd done this, but her stutter had shut that down hard. She pointed at the two spots. Damian did the same thing again on her palms, the backs of her hands, and her leg. The only place she'd put her foot down about was her face. The touch didn't set off zinging sensory storms anymore, but Tweak still wasn't cool with somebody else touching her face.

Methodically, Damian jotted down numbers on his tab. Tweak tried to sit still and watch him, but she ran out of patience.

"So? Is it w-working?"

Damian raised his head slowly, one brow cocked. "You tell me. Does it feel like the sensitivity issue is under control?"

Tweak shrugged. "Yeah, it does. But I want numbers. Feeling good? Could be meds, could be therapy. I wanna know about the n-nerves. For sure."

Damian held her eyes for a moment. He couldn't blink, and she didn't. Then he cracked just the hint of a smile.

"Take a look."

Tapping his tab, he popped out a holographic window and showed her his readouts. She studied them, then raised her head. "I oughta smack you."

This time Damian really smiled. "Well, if you did, it would actually hurt me more than you for once."

Tweak looked back at the readings, grinning. The signals for the pruning and microsurgery nanites running through her body were all a healthy green. Set against human baseline, the readings for the number of nerve endings in her body were almost normal. The nanites had been working their microscopic butts off for months now; when they'd started, the palms of her hands had clocked in at thirty-seven thousand nerve endings. Now they were down to nineteen thousand; still a little high up against an Alpha's baseline of seventeen thousand, but pretty damn good.

"It's w-working," Tweak bounced out of the diagnostic chair, grabbed the tab and spun in a circle, giddy with the thrill. "It's working it's working it's w-working!"

On the holographic window, the numbers gleamed with promise. Grinning, she turned to Damian. "And the s-scales? G-gonna go aw-w-way?"

Damian's smile faded a bit. "Well, that's the question. Have you been shedding a lot of scales these past weeks?"

"Tons," Tweak agreed, "but there's m-more under them." She held up an arm covered in gleaming scales that shaded up from caramel to buff to prove it, like it needed proof.

Damian nodded, slow. "I was afraid of that. The nanites are pruning out the largest keratinocytes to let smaller ones come in, but it looks like the growth pattern of the keratinocytes in your dermis, and how much keratin they contain, is a problem with the genetic instructions. Pruning the cells won't cut it. We'll have to get into your genome and do some rewriting before we can change that, and I don't have the gear to do that on human DNA right now."

"Can you use the p-programs we're using to r-r-rewrite the p-plants?" Tweak asked hopefully. That got her one of Damian's deadpan stares.

"Are you a plant? No. You're an animal. So, that's a no."

"Ugh." Tweak's high wore off a little at the words. Keratinocytes; those were the name for her skin cells, Damian had said. So apparently her genes were telling her skin cells to make scales instead of normal skin, and killing off a few of the messed up cells wasn't going to change that. She glanced back down at the numbers. "Fuck. Kay. Thanks. So, what else?"

"For now, nothing else about this," Damian replied with a shrug. "Though we do need to get that blood draw out of the way for the Western Quadrant's research program."

Tweak sighed. More blood draws.

"Gag. Kay." She dropped back into the chair. "So, other stuff looks good? Besides skin?"

"The tests say your cortisol and norepinephrine are coming in at much better levels," Damian agreed, pulling out his topical spray and the blood-draw kit. He sprayed the spot inside her elbow where her scales were much smaller, and prodded it after a beat. "How's that?"

"Numb," Tweak replied. Quietly, she watched Damian place the blood-draw pad. The hundreds of tiny needles sank in through her numbed skin, and the tube attached to the pad began to fill with red as Damian talked.

"The data on your adrenaline spikes still gives me nightmares, but that seems to be the baseline for your body, so I'm going to let that ride. You've got your fast-acting medication to counteract the adrenaline and cortisol dumps when you feel them coming on. That is helping with the behavioral side of things, right?"

"Yep," Tweak agreed.

Damian nodded. "Good. Noticing any side effects?"

"Nope," Tweak replied. Damian gave a quiet grunt of satisfaction. He switched out the sample tubes as he talked, and she watched it fill as her doctor talked out all her weirdness. She held his tab with the arm that wasn't giving blood, studying the numbers as he explained them.

"I'm still a little concerned with the rates of increased breakdown of estrogen in your body; with the kind of high-turnover system you've got, your birth control isn't a hundred percent, so if you ever get with a partner who could get you pregnant, make sure they've got the birth control up to date, alright?"

Tweak snorted. "Me. With guys. As if."

"Just covering my bases," Damian replied, removing the blood-draw pad, sticking it in a sterilizer, then running a swab over her arm. Tossing the swab and his gloves, he looked her in the eye. "Now I want the internal take. How are you feeling?"

"Great," Tweak replied with a smile, handing him the tab and grabbing her bandages. "Not getting the shakes so much," she explained as she got to work. The white bandages covered the snake-skin of her arms. "Not so bad when I get freaked out or p-pissed an-nymore. Easier to eat. N-not moving so fast on the m-meds; kinda hate that. But hey, don't crash neither."

"Which is the reason to cut down on the hyperactivity in the brain," Damian observed dryly. "I'm pretty happy with the dopamine and serotonin numbers you're coming in with these days, so if your only complaint is that you don't get to fixate and work yourself to death so easily any longer, I'm going to say we're done here."

Tweak rolled her eyes as she pinned the first bandage in place on her shoulder and started wrapping the second around her palm. "Not w-worked to death, drama king. Just like to go fast."

"And do you like to crash?" Damian asked, giving her a look like a hawk.

She sighed. "No."

"Then you don't need to go *that* fast," he replied, like she knew he would. He waved a dark hand at the med-bay door as he grabbed a sterile swab from the wall dispenser and started wiping down the diagnostic chair. "Go on once you're covered up, I'm done with you. Be in here this time next week, or I *will* come find you."

"N-now I'm scared," Tweak deadpanned as she clipped her second bandage in place.

Damian raised a brow. "Out, Tweak. I have real work to do in here." Snorting a laugh, she flipped him off and headed out the door.

Event File 02
File Tag: Reassessment
19:00-05-04-2160

It was late enough now that people were settling in for the night; sound echoed down the grey pre-fab hall from a movie night in the rec room to her left. Somebody was playing their music loud down on the dormitory wing; she'd put money on it being Kevin. She headed straight on, back to her coding room in the office wing. Curling up in her big comfy coding chair, she grabbed her headset, settled it in place and powered up her rig. On every side, holographic windows fizzed into life in the air, cocooning her in the lights of the Net and shutting the world out. With the meds that shifted her Gamma body chemistry closer to the human baseline, she didn't feel like she was diving into the code like a rocket shot into space anymore. But she didn't come down out of the code like a crashing rocket either, and that was a trade she was up to make. Bonus, she didn't have to distract herself so much; the feel of the chair and her own clothes didn't get to her anymore. The littlest touch used to drive her crazy. Now it was just there. That was pretty awesome.

On her left were windows for the authorized internet overseen by TechoCo. Tweak gave them a look over, double checked the bots she'd tasked to mess with the mega-corporation that owned America's technology sector, and let that do its thing, turning her chair to the windows on the right-hand side; the windows showed sites on the decentralized peer-to-peer Wi-Fi they were calling the Mesh. She got down into a project she'd been meaning to get back to, getting a portal put together for the Mesh that worked for people who needed better visibility. The Mesh still wasn't as clean and slick as the Corporate-run internet, but between her and all the other anti-corporate coders scattered around the United Corporations of America's turf, they were making the system look pretty damn good for something that had only been running for a couple years. And when it was a choice between something that was running completely decentralized and peer-to-peer or a slick system that owned all your data, charged you an arm and a leg, and monitored you for one word out of place, she was pretty sure people would put up with the Mesh being buggy once in a while. She was pretty happy with the way the thing had gone together. Now she just had to massage the code for this accessible portal, and send the patch out across the interconnected nodes that used every non-corporate device as a wi-fi hotspot.

She was just starting to settle, when the sound of a knock on her office door yanked her out of her zone. Spinning her seat, she caught her commander's eye. Aidan gave a little wave, pointing at the side of his head.

Tweak pulled down her headset. "Hey."

"Hey Tweak," Aidan gave her a little smile, standing easy with his hands in his pockets. "You focused?"

Tweak glanced at her screen, then back at her commander. "Nah. Just fun stuff. Off-duty. What's up?"

"Just checking to see if you're feeling good about the big inter-Quadrant meet at the end of the week," Aidan explained. "I got a private note from Hall; the command folks want to see you in particular. Sounds like they want to do a consult on the Meshnet system, and probably tell you that you're awesome."

"What, again?" Tweak sighed. That got a little laugh from Aidan; always a good thing. Looking at him, she tipped her head. "I'm r-ready. Got everything I need to talk b-baby talk to the b-brass this t-time."

Aidan held up his tab. "Looks like you may not need to. I just checked the attendance sheet. They're wising up and inviting Regional tech guys from every National Quadrant with them. Your buddy Deniki's coming down from the First Nation Quadrant."

Tweak grinned. "Holy shit, yeah? K-kickass!" Then another thought struck her. "The b-brass. They gonna give speeches? I g-gonna be bored?"

Aidan shrugged. "We'll have to find out."

Tweak considered for a moment. There had been a time when going to talk to the brass had scared the shit out of her. But she'd done it so much in the past year that it barely pinged her nerves anymore. She'd even been on a vid call with a National Command guy who apparently headed tech for the Force, and that had gone okay. It still wasn't fun to have eyes fixed on her, but she could deal with it.

She bobbed her head. "Yeah, cool. Bring stuff to w-work on if I get b-bored. That works."

"Great," Aidan agreed. "Oh, and Regional wants another couple blood samples. Sorry about that."

That really did get to her. "Seriously?" Tweak groaned. "V-vampires! I j-j-just gave blood to West! All these blood draws!" She flopped back in her coding chair, sighing. "I'm a f-fucking pincushion. N-national blood draw. R-regional blood draw. Everybody wants b-blood now."

"Guess that's what happens when you've got the blood that combats bio-weapons," Aidan agreed with a crooked smile, leaning against the wall with his arms crossed. "And hey, you're the first one of us to start getting asked personally to do something at the National Quadrant level. That's pretty cool."

Tweak snorted. "Lucky me. How about I s-stick a n-needle in you, see how l-lucky you feel."

"I wouldn't go that far," Liza's voice remarked from the doorway. Aidan turned to his personnel officer with a smile. "Hey Liza. Anything going on?"

"No sir, I just wanted to go over something with Tweak. May I join the conversation?" The dark-haired woman asked, standing at what the born Dusters called 'parade rest'. And if anybody was a born Duster, it was Liza.

Aidan made a funny sort of face. Tweak wasn't sure what it meant; Alphas were really hard to read sometimes.

"Liza, we're off duty. Do you think you're going to quit calling me 'sir' before we retire?" Aidan asked, and that explained the face he'd made for Tweak.

Liza dipped her head, something that Tweak clocked as an apologetic move. Liza proved her right when she spoke.

"Sorry, Aidan. I guess I'm a little worked up."

"Yeah?" Aidan straightened as Liza stepped into the room, her eyes on Tweak's screens. "I wanted to see how the Good Trouble Bundle is going. Will it be ready for the presentation?"

Tweak nodded. "Yep. All c-coded, all r-ready. The C-common Ground app's good. The b-beta groups of civvies love it."

It still threw her to see Liza grin, sometimes. Even after six years on the base, Liza still freaked her out a little with that whole 'I am the Democratic State Force incarnate' thing she had going. But it was the good kind of thrown when she got a smile out of Liza.

"I hear the unions and the civil organizations are passing it up and down the country, so I wanted to take a look at the ledger," Liza agreed. Tweak nodded. "Sure. I'll get it up. Then I'll get you a p-portal, so you can check whenever."

Tapping up a new window, Tweak brought up the ledger of exchanges for the Good Trouble Bundle. She liked the name; it fitted what they'd gotten together. It had been Kevin's idea first. When he'd submitted it to the Sector commander for approval, it had gone straight up to the National Council, taking off like anything.

Across the country, Kevin and a bunch of history buffs had gone digging around and unearthed copies of books and manuals on nonviolent resistance written before the Corporations took control of what used to be the United States. It had taken months of sniffing around and tapping international contacts; a lot of hard work for the history geeks. But it had paid off bigtime. They'd turned up all kinds of materials. It was all banned stuff, but if you knew where to look, you could still find it, and people from outside United Corporations land had passed along a ton of stuff too. The history buffs had named it after some guy called Lewis, a government guy who'd done this kind of work a hundred years ago. Kevin had talked about Lewis like some kind of saint, but Tweak had mostly tuned her base mate out at that point, so she wasn't real sure what the whole thing was about. Working with history geeks, you had to learn when to listen and when to shut your brain off.

Together, the history buffs had packed all of their finds into a giant five-hundred gigabyte file tree. They'd handed that off to Tweak and coders like her. And that was when things had gotten interesting. The project goals had been a hell of an ask: they needed it to be open-access for the right people, and opaque to the corporate pricks. The file had to be encrypted in a way that let users get to it, but it needed the capability to be wiped completely from their machines as needed. It had to be tracked to make sure it didn't get into Corporate hands, but it had to be easy to access for every civilian who wanted to get in on a Union or a social movement.

Tweak and her coding buddies had put their heads together over the Meshnet, and come up with a decentralized, block-chained library that could be accessed through a Virtual Private Network on the decentralized Meshnet. The Grapevine had been a huge help; the oldest of the civilian resistance groups had given them a ton of tips about what people needed, and looked over the whole plan before they'd started work. The folks up at the hidden community of Coomb Olwen had acted as their first beta-testing team. Between them, they'd come up with something really solid: an app they called Common Ground, where people could create accounts, access the Good Trouble Bundle, and chat about resources. Nobody could download the files from the Good Trouble Bundle directly, but anybody who had the Meshnet enabled on their tab could download Common Ground, talk to others safely and read as much of the Good Trouble Bundle as they wanted. The only complaint they'd gotten was that the app took forever to download once someone activated the QR code they were using as the download portal, but there was no getting around that. The poor app had to jailbreak people's tech so the devices looked normal to the Corps, and hide the secure app on the hardware from corporate surveillance. That just plain took time and CPU. People could deal.

Aidan and Kevin had gotten in touch with international people, and that had gotten them hooked up with one of the National Councilors. It'd worked out: now something with the stick-up-its-ass name of Office of the High Commissioner for Human Rights was working with a group called CANVAS to provide the Dusters with room on international quantum servers, so they could afford to put all of Common Ground on a blockchained ledger and keep it secured the right way. And the Good Trouble library kept growing; every time the history geeks turned up something new, the coders patched it into the file tree. There had to be hundreds of books in there now.

Tweak popped the portal up, and got into the ledger. Enlarging the window, she dragged her finger through the air with the hologram trailing after, placing it between Liza and Aidan. The two officers studied the readings.

Liza caught her breath. "Is that...is that really six million unique user log-ons?"

"Yep!" Tweak chirped. "Pretty awesome, yeah?"

Liza stared at the screen, dark eyes wide. She turned to Aidan, shaking her head. "All these people, getting in to access works on community organizing and nonviolent resistance, I can't... I never thought it'd be so many!"

"Looks like we're on a roll, hunh?" Aidan asked, giving the woman a quiet smile. "And this is just the early adopters. Wait until the Unions release this to their people directly and get them to start using it."

Liza grinned, still shaking her head. "So many people, I... I didn't think it'd take off so fast! I still haven't gotten through vetting all the resources and adding notes on modifications for modern times; I hope that doesn't get someone hurt, I mean—"

Tweak caught Aidan's eye, and rolled hers. That was Liza for you, always worried about something. And if you told her to relax, she nailed you to the wall with The Look.

Aidan gave Tweak a little nod. Stepping in, he took Liza by the shoulder. "Hey. You did good. People are getting something they can use. If there are mistakes, they'll get ironed out at the big inter-Quadrant meeting. This is good, okay?"

Liza focused her eyes back on Aidan. She drew a breath, smiling. "Thanks. I know it's good, it's just happening so fast!"

"The pressure's been building for a long time," Aidan acknowledged. "Once people saw anything that looked like a change, they really went for it. How many users does the Mesh have now, Tweak?"

Tweak see-sawed her hand. "Thirty m-million, about. Americans. Another two m-million, Canada, Sudamerica. Some Asia. Some Africa. They got better systems over there, not really into it. But hey, it gets us around the in-n-ntern-national firewalls, so people are getting out and t-talking a lot more. Good n-news!"

"You bet," Aidan agreed, glancing between the screen and Liza. "So, pretty good news?"

"Yes sir, very good," Liza agreed, but she still sounded shook.

Aidan cocked his head. "Sir, again?"

Liza sighed. "Point. Aidan, can we talk tomorrow? This is a lot, and we're getting all those requests for in-person training again too. The Grapevine can't cope with the number of training sessions they're being asked to do."

"Sure," their commander agreed, a little crease appearing between his brows. That meant he was worried. "After lunch works for me. See you then?"

Liza jerked her head in a nod. "Yes, sir. Good night, sir. Get some rest, Tweak."

"Yes mom," Tweak grumbled. That got her The Look for a second, but Liza's heart wasn't really in it. And then she was headed down the hall, marching as always.

"What's up with her?" Tweak asked, staring after the personnel officer. Aidan shrugged. "She's just stressed. And she's right; this is a lot." For a moment, the guy she thought of as a big brother glanced out into the hall, his eyes far away. Then he seemed to remember she was in the room, and shot her a smile. "Great work in here, Tweak. You're off duty, though; you want to take some down time?"

Tweak knew Aidan well enough by this time to read that; when he said 'do you want to do the thing', what he meant was 'I think you should do the thing.'

Smiling, she pointed a thumb over her shoulder at the holographic displays. "This? This's down time. B-billie's b-busy with Topher, so I'm c-chilling here." Plopping back into her coding chair, she rested her boots on the desk and gave him a grin. "Relax boss, I'm good."

She'd learned to read Aidan pretty well by now; when his skin crinkled around his eyes, he was giving her a happy smile. He did that now.

"Sounds good. Have a good one, Tweak. I'm going to go tell my husband that the whole base is sick of Bon Jovi. Sarah's threatening an oh-three-hundred assault with Ghana Pop if he keeps playing the stuff, annnnd I don't want to get caught in the middle of that."

Tweak barked a laugh. "His music. Sucks balls."

"Yeah, well, that's not an insult in his book," Aidan chuckled. "Fact is, if you do it right, sucking somebody's balls is fun for everybody."

"Gross!" Tweak groaned, grabbing her headset. "Not listening no more! La la la la!"

She just caught Aidan's laughter as she slid the insulated headset over her ears, grinning.

It took another hour for the portal to make her happy. Satisfied, she put her rig to bed and headed down the hall. Tonight was Billie's weekly date night with Topher, and it was a fifty-fifty bet whether she'd be in their shared room or not. Tweak missed Billie on the nights when she stayed with Topher; everything felt a little safer when she could wake up and hear Billie breathing in the middle of the night. But it was so cool to see Billie with a guy after the girl had been sure the crap in her past had messed her up too bad to date, Tweak wasn't saying anything to screw with that.

"Hey," Billie said as Tweak opened the door of their room, sitting on her bed with her arms around her knees and a smile on her face. Something looked funny about that smile, but Tweak wasn't sure if it was anything. She knew Billie would tell her if it was, so she didn't sweat it.

"Hey," she acknowledged, flopping belly-down on her bed, her personal tab in one hand. "Got you the new c-comics! Just got them s-scrubbed; they're safe to read on our gear. Sent. On your tab!"

"Thanks," Billie murmured. She was quiet tonight. Granted, she was always a little quiet, but there was being Billie, and then there was being quiet for Billie. Tweak knew the difference. She rolled over and sat up in one move. "Billie? You okay?"

Billie bit her index finger for a moment, and Tweak's breath caught. Billie did that when she was really worried. She swallowed against the tightness in her throat, controlled her breathing to keep from setting off her stutter, and spoke.

"Billie. What. Gives?"

Slowly, Billie raised her eyes to Tweak's. Nervy as a jackrabbit, she smiled.

"Tweak, I... if I didn't sleep in here anymore, would that be okay?"

Tweak blinked. "Y-yeah? I mean, yeah... but man. B. Wow."

"More wow than that," Billie glanced down, her shy smile brilliant in their room's low light.

"What's the more?" Tweak asked, stepping off her own bed and dropping down beside Billie. Her best buddy twiddled the fabric of her coolant-lined jacket between her fingers, grinning down at her hands.

"Um, Tweak..."

"Yeah?"

Finally, Billie raised her head, and her dark eyes were full of stars.

"Topher asked me to marry him!"

Something lurched inside Tweak. "Uh...wow." There was more she was supposed to say, she knew that. What'd they do in the vids at times like this? She grabbed the first thing that seemed like it'd fit. "So. You say yes?"

Biting her lip to control her grin, Billie nodded. "That okay?"

At least Tweak knew the answer to that. "Hell yes!" she declared. "This's k-kickass, B. Yay! So cool!"

"You sure?" Billie asked.

Tweak rolled her eyes. "I. Said. So. *Genius*." She tipped her head. "Wanna hug?"

"Yeah?" Billie answered the question with what sounded like another question, but Tweak knew she meant it. Now all the medical checks she put up with paid off: she pulled her best buddy into a hug, squeezing her tight. Billie's arms wrapped around her, and these days the emotions and the touch both felt good.

They sat like that for a couple minutes, Billie breathing hard. Was she crying? She didn't make a sound, but Billie had always been scary quiet when she cried.

Finally, the other girl pulled away, wiping tears from her cheeks and grinning.

"Thanks, Tweak."

"Sure," Tweak agreed, matching her grin for grin. "Heads up, warning you. I'm t-telling Topher this at the w-wedding. He messes up w-with you, then I—"

"Break his nose again?" Billie interjected, teasing.

Tweak crossed her arms, sticking out her chest. "Damn. Straight!"

Billie covered her mouth, giggling. "You're so bad!"

"I'm the best," Tweak tossed right back. Leaning in, she gave Billie another quick squeeze. "Seriously, B. Awesome. This's awes-some. Want help getting your stuff over t-to his r-room?"

"That'd be nice, we can do it tomorrow," Billie replied, studying her face with those soft brown eyes. That was her 'I worry about you' look.

"B. What?" Tweak asked, tipping her head.

"You sure you're going to be okay?" Billie asked gently. "I mean, you and me are still going to be tight. You know that, right? I'm gonna be next door, not gone."

Tweak groaned. "Oh gag, Billie. D-don't get all gooey."

"Tweak." Billie was always too good at calling her on crap, and here she was, doing it again. "Gooey is okay. And you're my sis, yeah? I got a right."

"Yeah. You're my sis," Tweak agreed. "And you're r-right here. Just gotta knock on the wall."

"Yeah," Billie agreed. "Either of us need something, just knock on the wall."

"Sounds good." Swallowing around the weird lump in her throat, she flashed Billie a grin.

"One thing?"

"Yeah?" Billie asked, eyes still a little frightened. Tweak knew how to fix that.

"Don't fuck loud, kay?" She asked, grinning ear to ear. "Don't wanna listen to you guys hump."

"Tweak!" Billie covered her face with both hands, losing it in grossed out giggles. "Oh my god, just no…"

Tweak kept the grin up while Billie got some clothes together and headed back to Topher's room. Even after the girl who was her sister in everything but blood was gone, she sat and grinned.

Alone.

In her room. Just her room, now.

Slowly, the smile faded. Tweak glanced around the room. It wasn't anybody's idea of big. But for a second, it felt too large. Too open. Too *empty*.

In the silence, she could hear her own breath. Her heart began to pound.

She closed her eyes, breathing through the moment in the dark.

Event File 03
File Tag: Assignment Of Duty
04:00-05-09-2160

In the mirror, Liza watched her fingers ram home the pins that held her hair in its bun. It was like her mom had always said: do it right, do it tight, and it's done for the day. The efficiency of that saying had always satisfied Liza; the clean, squared-away look the hairstyle gave her was great on any day, but it served her best on the days from hell.

She was really hoping this wouldn't turn out to be one of those days. But Liza couldn't be sure. So she used her special hairpins and followed her mom's rule. Do it right, do it tight. Do the absolute best you can, and then? Well, if it all went to shit, at least it wouldn't be your fault. And the hairpins were a good backup for her knives.

The last hairpin slid into place; Liza worked with it carefully, making sure not to tap the little button on its apex. Opening her hair-cream, she dabbed some out and ran her hands over her hair, making sure no stray wisps would sneak out of place. She checked the hang of her jacket, straightened her unit patch and rank pin, and pulled herself up for one last look in the mirror.

"Okay," she whispered to her reflection, "Let's get this done."

Turning, she stepped through her quarters door and out into the hall. It was quiet this early; only Billie and teams headed out on long-distance runs started work around now. Striding to her office, she checked the clock. Just enough time to go over the communications from National, the unions and their civilian contacts one more time, and make sure she was prepared for the inter-Quadrant Council meeting before she checked with Dozer about the truck they'd use for transport on this early-hours jaunt.

Taking her seat, she brought up her screens and ran over the messages.

> **Message Handle: NationalComm**
> **Message Authentication: 5365645swordfish**
> **Biometrics: Validated**
> **Secure Message, Command Authenticated**
> **Message: Requesting named**
> **Sector commanders and relevant**
> **base personnel for attendance at**
> **inter-Quadrant implementation**
> **talks with civilian groups.**
> **Finalization forthcoming. See**
> **encrypted attachment re coordinates.**
> **Focus: network security, resource**
> **and personnel allocation.**
> **Personnel Requested For Attendance:**

Liza scrolled down the list, which read like an honor roll. The best bases from around the country were going to be at this event. It was going to be a heroes and legends convention. No wonder security had been so tight around it; one good drone blast would knock out the cream of the Duster crop.

Scrolling down to Western National Quadrant, CO-WY Region, Sector 14 (Front Range), she stopped at the entry for Base 1407, marveling nearly as much as she had the first time she'd read the documents two weeks before. All eleven Quadrants and who knew how many of the Regions within them were sending people to this. She'd never seen people from every National Quadrant of the country in one place.

She read the names under her base's number. Aidan, Kevin, Tweak and herself were requested. She still wasn't sure how the ride up was going to be, with the four of them stuck in a truck. All of them had gone up for their own specialties, but they'd never gone all together. In fact, Liza could count on one hand the number of times she'd gone up to the Regional base with anyone else, let alone to a big inter-Quadrant event like this. And Tweak hated early mornings, too. That wouldn't make the ride any more fun.

Liza let herself sit back and think in the early morning stillness. She'd never worked at the National level personally before, so far outside the day-to-day concerns of her own Sector and base. It was part of her duties to go up and represent Base 1407 or sit in virtually when presentations were given on new personnel procedures, new entries to the code of conduct and discipline, or new intake procedures for inducting members of the Force were implemented, but that was the kind of organizational detail she knew like the back of her hand. This was different. This was everyone from everywhere talking over options, and probably getting their hackles up about all kinds of things. That was the kind of thing Aidan was good at settling down and Kevin was good at talking around, at least when he didn't get impatient. And of course the tech people would grab Tweak; they'd want to worship at her feet, then they'd want to work with her on checking everything over and making sure the Common Ground app was ready to go and the security was air-tight. All that made sense. But Liza was an implementation person. She needed a direction to work in. An order to execute. What they thought somebody like her was going to do at a massive wrangling session, she had no idea.

The longer she looked at the list, the more amazed she was. The number of people showing up in person was incredible, and even more folks would be attending virtually. She was seeing names she'd whispered to the other Base kids with awe, telling stories about their work like fairytales at bedtime. And now they were going to be in the room with her.

Liza couldn't quite believe it, so she switched to thinking about the practical things. The meeting rooms at the Regional Hub were going to be packed. Good thing Tweak had gotten work done on her nerves and started getting past her personal-space issues; all the same, Liza made a note to keep an extra eye on their prickly little coder. If anyone set the girl off, Liza would need to step in before Tweak took them apart. Maybe that was why she had been invited.

She opened the first civilian message on her list, then the second, third and fourth. All of them said basically the same thing: all this information is nice, but if you're releasing it to us, send someone who can show our people how to use it.

She sighed under her breath. "People, come on."

"That bad?"

Liza turned at the sound of her friend's voice. She gave Kevin a tight smile. "It's the civilians in the Good Trouble beta group, they all want their hands held, even with all the resources we're handing them. The Grapevine's trying to help with on-the-ground training; they've got the experience, but they don't have the numbers. And the organizers are insisting that in-person training is what they really need."

"Considering the price if they get it wrong, I don't think the organizers should be faulted for that request," Kevin observed grimly, stepping over to drop into her spare chair with a yawn. His red hair was all over the place. It always irritated her when he left his hair a mess like that. It was so pretty when he paid attention to it.

"I know," she agreed ruefully. "That's part of what worries me about all this; if we get it wrong, all these civilians are going to get hurt. And…"

And she didn't really know what to say after that. Saying she didn't want to be responsible for that was ridiculous. But saying she didn't want people hurt didn't make sense either. People got hurt every day.

"You don't need to be up yet," she offered quietly, noting the sleepy eyes behind Kevin's glasses. "You need more rest. We don't head out for another couple hours."

Kevin raised a brow; how he did just the one eyebrow, she'd never know.

"I do believe that's the pot maligning the kettle, Liza."

She gestured at her screens. "I've got procedural details to go over for all this, and I'm not tired."

"Well, neither am I," Kevin tried, but since the sentence ended in a yawn, she felt justified in calling him on it.

"Now say that without falling asleep halfway through."

"Touché," Kevin chuckled. "I was on a call with some contacts on the other side of the world last night, so I may be a little sleepy. We were talking till the wee hours. An early morning trip on top of a late night call isn't a winning combination, but I'll nap on the ride up. Good news though; we're getting more and more international backing, not just the server space for the Common Ground. It seems we're no longer listed as a terrorist organization by any country outside United Corporation land."

Liza's heart leaped. "Really? We finally got legitimacy?"

Kevin nodded through another yawn. "Indeed." He gave her a grin. She glanced back at her screen, staring at it as Kevin went on. "The United Nations officially announced that they took us off the list of terrorist organizations earlier this year, it seems. Shame it took us this long to hear about it; we should have held a proper celebration." He clapped Liza's shoulder. "Congratulations old girl, you're an official freedom fighter now."

Freedom fighter. The words rolled around Liza's head. She'd always known they were doing the right thing. Fighting for the right things. But she'd always known she'd be spat on for a terrorist; it was part of the life she lived. Re-orienting in a world that had changed that assumption was going to be strange.

"Liza?" Kevin asked quietly. "Regretting the loss of your romantic title, by any chance?"

Liza blinked, coming back to the moment. "Being called a terrorist isn't 'romantic', Kevin. What gave you that idea?"

Kevin shrugged, smirking. "Poor reading choices, probably. Bad pulp adventure novels. My greatest vice." He pressed a hand to his heart, affecting a martyred expression. Liza shook her head, smiling in spite of h   e   r   s   e   l   f   . "Of course I'm glad. Everything that's happening is great, it's just..." She paused, lost for words.

"A lot to take in?" Kevin suggested, laying a hand on her shoulder.

She glanced up into his eyes. "Yeah. A lot. I mean, earlier this week I was worrying about tumbleweeds, holes in our slick tarp and ranking requirements for new specialists, and now we're talking about National-level meetings with all the Quadrants in the country. I've never worked at the National level before, not personally. I mean, all of it's good—great—but it's a lot. It feels... unreal."

"I can definitely sympathize with that," Kevin agreed. "Though I will add, it still irks me that they use the term 'quadrant' improperly. Quadrant means one fourth, and there's eleven of them, I mean it's practically language abuse!" Liza gave him a look, and he held up his hands, grinning. "I know, I know, I'm a pedant, but it's still poor usage!"

She couldn't help but smile at that, shaking her head. "You're a geek, Kev honey. And you're trying to cheer me up by being a geek."

"Guilty as charged," Kevin agreed with a little-boy grin. Sitting up, he sobered. "But in all seriousness... when I begin to think it's implausible, everything that's happening... I consider what we've sacrificed. It seems well-earned then."

"You're not wrong," Liza sighed. She gave her friend a weak smile. "Lazarus would have said something about them demoting him from 'terrorist'."

Kevin's sad smile mirrored hers. "I know how I would have bolstered his ego, too."

"Oh?"

"I would have told him that he was still a terror."

Liza gave a little laugh. Reaching up, she squeezed Kevin's arm. "We're doing good."

"Indeed we are," the younger man agreed.

At that point, Liza couldn't resist anymore. "Hold still a second, okay? We've got a big meeting, and I've got a comb in my desk; I'm just going to get your hair neat real quick, okay?"

Kevin was out of his chair like a scalded cat. "You are never going to stop trying to nanny me!" He exclaimed, laughing. "Not 'okay' at all! I'll go back to my own room and brush my own hair with a mirror, thank you very much. You *yank* when you do it."

He stepped to the door, just in time to give Deliquisha a quick high-five as she stepped into Liza's office. "Watch out, she wants to brush someone's hair," Kevin quipped.

The seventeen-year-old gave her a jaundiced look. "Yeah, no, you were bad enough doing that when I was little. Besides," she tapped the crown of Bantu knots she wore for today's look. "No loose hair to brush?"

"*She* takes care of her hair, I don't *need* to brush it," Liza shot at Kevin's back. That got her a wave of the hand and a chuckle out in the hall, along with Deliquisha preening just a little. The girl really did do a good job with her hair; around fifteen, she'd gotten into figuring out Black hair, and now every day her hair was on point in some amazing style. She'd come such a long way from the scared six-year-old in fuzzy pigtails that her big brother had arrived on base with. They'd all come a long way, really; Damian had been delivered to their base unconscious, his eyes destroyed by the chemical bomb he'd found in his home office. The twin six-year-olds in the truck with him had been staring and silent, traumatized. Now Damian was one of the most respected Democratic State Force medical officers in the Western

Quadrant, and you could barely see the scared child in the face of this confident young woman with her hair in Bantu knots and her eyes on the work screens.

"You're up early," Liza observed.

"Yeah. I wanted to double-check stuff before you went out on the big trip," Deliquisha agreed as she dropped into what had become her seat in the last year. "So, you guys leave at oh-eight-hundred. What do we have going on while you're gone?"

"Mainly getting the trade and barter shipment ready to go out. Kevin was cleaning their room, and he bumped into Aidan's old binders in the back of a drawer; add a note that we've got chest binders for anyone who's dealing with dysphoria," Liza suggested. Deliquisha nodded, typing. "Got it. I'll check with Aidan and get the binder size." "And we've got to file everyone's annual Statement of Consent To Serve," Liza added, bringing up the files, and sighing. "Actually, chase everyone down to sign their Statements, *then* file them."

"People haven't signed? It's been a month!" Deliquisha tapped the air around the screen, enlarging it, and rolled her eyes. "Oh *of course* my twin forgets to sign. And *of course* Yvonne and Sarah haven't done it. I'll corner them today, sound good?"

"I like this plan," Liza agreed with a smile for the kid. "We also need to check everyone off on their hand-to-hand training for this week, and on their physical health tests. Alice got us the paperwork last night."

"Got it," Deliquisha agreed, tapping at her screen. "Do you have time for a homework question?"

"Shoot," Liza agreed.

"Our assignment to write up the history of the eleven Quadrants and their Regions." Tapping her screen, she brought up the table of contents for her paper. Liza ran her eyes over it. There were all the Quadrants: Freshwater Quadrant and New Netherlands, the Midlands, Tidewater and Appalachia, the Gulf Quadrant and El Norte Quadrant, Cascadia, Western Quadrant, New France and the First Nation Quadrant. Under each, Deliquisha had meticulously noted the Regions, abbreviated by state grids they covered, and the Sectors inside each.

"Do you want a quick historical summary of each Sector in each Region, or just an overview at the Regional level?" The young woman asked, glancing up.

"I think you'd end up writing a book if you did all that, so let's not go down to the Sector level," Liza replied, keeping her eyes forward. "Maybe just talk about why we partition things the way we do; that's plenty. Why Sectors are designed to encompass three population centers each, things like that."

Del nodded. "And you want to give the official state names for the Regions as well as the handles? So, Colorado and Wyoming for our Region, not just the CO-WY Grid?"

"Yep," Liza agreed. "The Corps still label things by state, so it's important to know how their system corresponds to ours. Besides, if you interact with civvies, they know states, not regions."

"Kay," Deliquisha agreed. "Thanks."

"No problem," Liza agreed. Excitement bubbled under her skin, but she got the words out casually. "Keep it around ten pages and go over how the history of a National Quadrant and Region affects decisions made by people raised there, and you're good. Oh, and we need to make a schedule change for next week. Put something in after the time that's blocked out for debriefing after the big meeting, okay?"

"Okay," Deliquisha brought up the unit's schedule. "What are we putting in?"

"Add a Ranking Ceremony for one Ms. Deliquisha Oshun Coson, noncombatant, to be raised to the rank of Specialist In Training, Command Division."

Deliquisha's eyes shot wide. She turned in her seat. "I made rank?"

Liza grinned. "Turned the paperwork over to Aidan last week. We got the approval yesterday. You made rank."

"I made rank! *I made rank!*" with a whoop, Deliquisha jumped out of her chair and glommed onto Liza for the hug of her life. Liza returned it, grinning. "You earned it," she added, holding Deliquisha out at arms' length to smile at her. "Honestly, we should have gotten it for you a year ago, but Regional didn't want to rank a sixteen-year-old. You've been so much help since you started doing stuff with me. I never could have kept up during the MACHA disaster, if you hadn't been helping out. I couldn't have asked for a better Specialist."

Deliquisha beamed at her, bright as a sunflower in June. "What call sign should I pick?"

"That's up to you," Liza replied, straightening the girl's jacket where it had been rumpled by the excitement. "Right now, let's get everything prepped and settled for you to watch the shop while I'm gone, kay?"

"Kay!" Deliquisha enthused, still a little bouncy. She took a deep breath, composed herself, and straightened up. "Ready for duty!"

Liza pulled back and saluted her, heart swelling with pride as her second in command returned the salute. Then let herself smile. "Let's get after the people who are late on their papers."

Deliquisha grinned. "You got it!"

The CO-WY Regional Base was beyond packed when Liza and her team got in, and there were more people in line behind them. The organizers had taken down some of the module walls between two rec-rooms and one of the base canteens to make a gigantic meeting space, and people were everywhere; clusters of folks from the same base chatting among themselves, people with the lean, quick look of Logistics comparing notes over here, people with the bright eyes of Technical over there throwing their hands around. Liza guessed they were telling stories to impress each other. That definitely looked like an 'I can top that' conversation.

Beside Aidan, Tweak squeaked. "D-D-Deniki!" The little woman took off like a bullet in a black leather jacket, racing across the room to glom onto a huge guy with skin like South Colorado soil and hair long and dark as vulture wings. The man had to be six-four, built like a bulldozer, and Tweak was hugging him.

Liza had to repeat that phrase in her head. Tweak. Was. *Hugging.* Somebody.

"Well will you look at that," Kevin murmured. "Will wonders never cease."

"Pretty cool, hunh?" Aidan observed quietly, dividing a smile between Liza and his husband. Liza gave him a small smile. "Our little girl's all grown up?"

Kevin gave her a dry look. "And you say I'm a sap."

Liza saw his dry look and raised him a patient expression. "You are."

"Attention!"

The conversations around the room snapped off. Everyone faced forward with the precision trained into them as the Regional and even Quadrant Officers filed up to the front of the room, along with a number of civilians and, holy crap, three members of the National Command Council.

Liza blinked, staring at the insignia on the collar of the magnetic woman in front of the room, and the two men who flanked her. Holy crap. *Holy. Crap.* Three of the thirty-three people who met to create consensus policies for the Democratic State Force and stand as an alternate government in negotiations with international press and allies. Were standing in this room. With her.

"Welcome, everyone," the woman at the center of the gathering stated. "I am Councilor Williams, standing for the Cascadia National Quadrant. With me are Councilor Hernandez, standing for the Western National Quadrant, and Councilor DuValle, standing for the Tidewater National Quadrant. We're pleased to see this gathering come together; everyone standing in this room represents a new phase in this fight." She gave the gathering a tight smile. "Today, people, we turn a page. Today, we welcome our civilian friends, and begin to work together towards a better future."

Turning, Councilor Williams stepped out of her place in line and shook the hand of the woman Liza had known as a sick refugee in a bed, gasping as the gene-tailored disease called MACHA attacked her from within. That monster of a disease had been unleashed into the water supplies of dissenters across the nation by Cavanaugh Corporation, and it had cost them all. But today, the head of the Denver chapter of the Writer's Union stood tall, perfectly coiffed and proud in a cream pantsuit. She shook Councilor Williams' hand firmly, then glanced over the crowd. Liza stayed at parade rest, as protocol dictated, but she caught Aidan giving the woman a little wave out of the corner of her eye. Up at the front of the room, Phyllis smiled and returned the discrete wave.

Councilor Williams shook hands with the rest of what must be Union leaders. "We are glad to work with you going forward. If you'll excuse me, for a moment I'm going to address my Force directly." When she turned back, her mahogany face was sober in its lines. "People. I'm going to get to the point here: our mission has never wavered, and it never will. But from now on, our tactics change. If you don't like the direction the Force is going by the end of the week, get out now. You'll have the support to make a new life in a new country. But this change in tactics is happening. Period."

There was a stunned quiet. Liza caught Kevin's eye, giving him a 'what the hell?' look. He shrugged, looking just as confused.

Up at the front of the room, Williams thawed out a little as she went on. "The National Council has been reviewing our tactics, with reference to success rates and effective actions. And we've come to this conclusion: our most successful actions didn't involve a weapon. They involved the informing and the empowering of civilians, and they involved the removal of Corporate power structures. So, this week, we make a change. This week, we will be presenting our civilian allies with a new set of digital tools and resources that will make it possible for them to resist Corporate control and begin to erode the Corporate power base, on the civilians' terms. We will be offering possible options for the Unions to vote on implementing. We will be refocusing on a new aim: gaining the participation of four percent of the American population in orchestrated *non-violent* movements of resistance."

A quiet rumble made the rounds of the room, a summer thunderhead of unease. Williams talked through it. "Why four percent? Research. Data from three hundred and twenty three violent and nonviolent campaigns in the nineteenth and twentieth centuries, and a hundred and seventy seven such scenarios in the twenty-first and twenty-second, were collated and analyzed jointly by the Council and two independent international bodies, CANVAS and the World Court For Human Rights. The findings accorded across the board. A complete file of the research will be on everyone's tabs after this meeting. What we find is this: nonviolent campaigns are *twice* as likely to succeed as violent campaigns. The research shows that a nonviolent campaign led to political change fifty-three percent of the time, compared to twenty-six percent for the violent protests. I *like* the sound of those numbers. Anybody else like the sound of those numbers?" There was some quiet clapping, and a few whoops, but Liza was pretty sure the rest of the crowd was still trying to catch up with the conversation mentally.

"Nonviolent campaigns are more likely to succeed because they can recruit many more participants from across the social strata," Williams continued, "and when all those people act, that *freezes* normal urban life and the functioning of a city, even a country. If we get four percent of the population behind us—and I mean four percent of everyone; grandparents, kids, everyone—then the Corps are *done."* She paced the room, obsidian eyes boring into them all. "People. We've been trying things the old military way since our grandparents' day. And we're still out here eating prairie dogs and ration bars. It isn't working. This is the time for a new way to do things. The population is *sick* of Corporate atrocities. One of our most impactful actions to date was the release of the Folder. Everyday people saw babies and the poor being made into *dog food.* And now the Corps are openly using bio-weapons. People are *disgusted.* If we offer them a real, a *viable* alternative? They'll grab it with both hands. If we can reach thirteen million out of the three hundred million people in this country—four percent—then we win."

She clapped her own hands together. "So. This week, we run discussion groups, as well as break-out sessions that will allow each division to discuss your areas of expertise in detail with our civilian contacts. Schedules are available on the screens around the room."

She swept her eyes around the space. *A real speaker,* Liza thought. *She knows how to make us feel like she's talking to every one of us.*

"We in the Democratic State Force commit today to providing the resources, support and protection the civilian communities need to assert their human rights and demand a government that supports them." Williams continued, her voice ringing around the room. "The days of fighting in the Dust and the shadows are at an end. Together, *all* of us are going to work towards a new way of reclaiming this country. Our country. Together, we're going to shine a light over this nation. And in that light, something new will grow."

This time the clapping in the room was incredible. It went on until Liza's hands hurt.

And then it was time to check schedules, and move to assigned rooms, and really get to work.

Two hours later, Liza was in the Command-division breakout session with heads of Unions, legendary Commanders of the Force and a National Councilor. And she'd never wanted out of any place more. Had it only been two hours? It felt like two days. The leaders for the new Unions just would *not* let go.

"Yeah, we *understand* that you're giving us all this information," the Packing and Shipping Union's head guy was saying for about the fourth time, "but what do you want us to do, hold up a bunch of books we've read when EagleCorp goons come to bash our heads in?"

"What do you expect us to do, be the ones who keep on taking the beating?" the Commander from a Base out East demanded. "What, you want us to die for you some more?"

Liza worked to repress a sigh. She knew that only the best of the best commanders were here; only the people with the highest success and innovation rates had been invited. But it was depressing how often the best of the best didn't get along when you put them in a room.

"People," Aidan cut in, pitching his voice in that sharp tone that always cut the chatter back home. The two men went still. Aidan spoke into the silence he'd made. "Nobody wants anybody to die around this table. Don't start that. It doesn't get us anywhere good."

At the head of the table, National Councilor Hernandez sighed, running a hand over his salt-and-pepper hair. "I think we all need a break. Ten minutes, everybody."

With a lot of side-eyes and grumbles, people got up and took their breaks. Liza turned her head and watched Aidan deflate a little in his seat. He caught her looking, and gave her a crooked little smile.

"You want to go home yet?" He asked in an undertone.

For a moment Liza froze, the idea of being unprofessional in this setting grinding the gears in her brain. But most people had left the table, and after all, this was Aidan.

She gave him a tight smile. "Been wanting to get out of here for an hour," she murmured. "You?"

Aidan leaned back in his seat with a tired grin. "Wanted out pretty much since we got in."

They shared a quick laugh, resting up for what was starting to feel like rounds of sparring. Liza had thought the civilians would be excited about the Common Ground App and all the information it handed them. But the leaders of the Unions' reactions ran the gamut from unimpressed to intimidated. None of them seemed even a little excited. It was kind of a letdown.

In the corner, Hernandez was having a quiet conference with Commander Hall and Commander Magnum. For a moment, Magnum flicked dark eyes up, and Liza watched him and Aidan share a look. Then Magnum swept that searchlight look over Liza, and away. She breathed out. Her sector commander was great, but that said, he was *intense*.

"Okay," Hernandez began when everyone had taken their seats

again, "new plan. How does this sound: the Force puts together dedicated training teams, people with experience in organization and operations, as well as dealing with Corporate backlash. They'll travel between Union setups within their Sectors. We'll give day-long classes—"

"A day?" The guy from the Denver chapter of the Union of Health Workers demanded, voice shrill. "Are you kidding?! That isn't enough!" Liza repressed a frown. Trust a Cavanaugh guy to feel entitled to more.

"It would need to be longer than a day to cover the material," Phyllis agreed with quiet calm.

"They're not wrong, sir," Aidan agreed. "There's a lot to go over."

The adobe-skinned man considered for a moment, tapping his knuckles against the table. "What about this? We kill two birds with one stone and send out tech personnel with these training personnel. Techies add VPNs for the Meshnet. At each gathering, they'll get everyone's tabs cleaned of Corps surveillance and set up with Force encryptions and a copy of the Common Ground app, while trainers teach. That way, our new friends know what they're doing and have the tools to do it with. Thoughts?"

"I like the sound of that," Commander Magnum agreed.

Thoughtfully, Hagge nodded. "I don't like this long-term personnel depletion on our bases; it could bring down mission effectiveness." She tipped her head. "But it could work. Let's talk about a core curriculum for these teach-ins. That'll tell us how long they need to be."

Four hours later, they had a bare-bones outline for a set of classes that nobody hated. That would be refined and expanded later, but it was a start. And they had a plan for week-long training sessions given to each Union gathering. They took dinner and reconvened, going over a plan that was looking less and less awful.

"Last thing we need is a name that people want to say for these classes," Commander Seattle suggested, their dark eyes dancing. "You name something, you give it spirit. And this needs a hell of a lot of spirit to get off the ground."

"Good point," Hernandez agreed, nodding at the commander. "Floor's open, people. Throw out ideas."

And people started putting things up. Revolution Academy, 1776 School, Dandelion Academy, Mustard Seed School and Matrix Training all got suggested, in honor of old history and old stories. None of those were quite right. The Democratic State Force-Civilian Coalition Joint Training

Groups got offered up. Everyone agreed to drop that one; too much of a mouthful. Someone suggested the Democratic Army Training, and that got the man the stink eye and a comment of 'yeah, if you want to get us shot', from the guy standing for the Grapevine. He wasn't wrong.

An uncomfortable lull fell over the gathering. Liza glanced around the room. Was nobody going to say the obvious?

She cleared her throat. "Permission to speak freely, sir?" she asked, addressing the National Councilor. She was actually addressing a National Councilor. If she wasn't a professional, she'd be giddy.

Hernandez gave her a patient look. "The floor's open, Officer Carlan. We're not standing on protocol tonight."

He knows my name! The little girl inside Liza exclaimed. She gave a polite smile. "Thank you, sir. What we've been sending out is called the Good Trouble Bundle. So the logical follow up is to call this training program the Good Trouble Training, or Good Trouble Camp, or something along those lines. It connects the dots for people intuitively."

For a moment, the room was quiet. Liza's heart seized. Were they all writing her off? Fine. If they were, let them. At least she'd tried.

Then Commander Seattle clapped their hands. "Now that's the spirit!"

"Good Trouble Training. I like that," the guy from the shipping union put in, mulling it over out loud.

"I'd suggest Good Trouble University?" Phyllis offered. "It gives a touch of class."

"Even better!" The Medical Union guy agreed, nodding enthusiastically. The more they talked, the more concrete Good Trouble University became.

"Okay, everyone in favor of the name, hands up," Hernandez offered. Out of the twenty people at the table, eighteen went up. Liza didn't want to be seen voting for her own idea, but she had to smile at the sight. Glancing over, Aidan gave her a quick, proud grin that made her heart swell.

"Now that's settled," the National Councilor stated, "I've got work for my Regional and Sector Commanders. List out your best people where it comes to structure, personnel placement and organization. If they know tactics, even better. Get me a list by tomorrow. Base Commanders, day after tomorrow you'll meet with your Sector Commanders to discuss the assignments and give your feedback. Everyone, expect to see finalized lists by day three of this event."

"Yes sir," the Dusters around the table replied automatically. The civilians looked a little freaked out.

It was amazing how fast the days went by, considering that individual meetings never seemed to end. Liza sat in with the logistics teams to talk over how to liaise with the civilians and get them hooked up with more tangible resources; sound boxes and slick tarps for securing meeting spaces were the first thing on everyone's list. She sat in on two more discussions to finalize the core curriculum for the Good Trouble University; the trainers who went out would have to use every moment of their seven-day trainings effectively, and that took planning. She sat in with the Union leaders to help them clean up their charters and draw up effective policies and codes of conduct that pushed citizens in the direction of becoming the kind of people the movement needed. They worked up a list of solid nonviolent actions that could be carried out on a city-wide basis, as well as some bigger campaigns that could be orchestrated across the country. The assembled groups of Dusters and Union members voted on the actions that would go out across the nation, and Liza was impressed with the list they ended up with. The union leaders would have plenty to take back to their organizations for further discussion and voting. Liza sat in on the on-boarding talks too, discussing how to balance recruitment and security. The talks were mostly productive, though everyone was still stumped on the question of preventing infiltrators and informants from getting in with everyone else. That conversation set off some arguments, but it could have been worse. Liza was glad to see that people had worked out most of their bravado on day one. By now, you mostly got quick fizzles of irritation from the tired and the frustrated, but that was easy to deal with.

She was grabbing breakfast and checking her daily schedule on the third day, when Kevin's voice pulled her out of her thoughts. "Got a moment, Liza? I've got something I think you should take a look at."

"Hm?" Liza looked up from her tab, oatmeal dripping off the serving spoon. "Something wrong?"

Kevin shook his head, smiling his 'I've got a surprise' smile. Times like this, it was hard to remember he wasn't the teenager who'd arrived when she was twenty.

"I'd say something's very right, personally. Come on, put the spoon down and come see this."

Wondering what the catch was here, Liza put the spoon down and followed her friend. Kevin wasn't usually the type to pull tricks, but he got up to something every once in a while. He usually had better sense than to do anything during important events, but Liza had learned to keep an eye on everybody in her team. Love them? Sure. Trust them to behave? Not so much.

She followed Kevin across the room, where a handful of projectors were throwing lists up on the wall.

Good Trouble University Teams, By Sector

Kevin gave a ceremonial little wave of the hands. "My lady, your superior nature finally receives the recognition it merits."

Liza gave him the side-eye. "Kevin, we're at a high-level meeting. Tone it down."

He gave a sigh of defeat. "Yes, nanny."

"That's not toning it down."

Kevin rolled his eyes. "You are absolutely no fun sometimes. Read the bloody list and let me be proud of you for five minutes, Liza."

Taking her eyes off her basemate, she scrolled down through the Regions and Sectors, all organized by Quadrant. Kevin kept talking.

"Tweak will be thrilled, though I'm surprised the brass is sending her out, given the situation with her DNA. On the other hand, her skills are salient and she is the quickest hacker in our sector, so I suppose..." Liza barely heard him. Finding Western Quadrant, CO-WY Region, Sector 14, she read the names.

Technology: Officer T., 1407

Training: Officer L. Carlan, 1407

Security: TBD

She turned her eyes to Kevin, and his smile fell off. "Liza?" He reached out, touching her shoulder as if she was fragile. "You alright, my girl? I thought you'd be pleased?"

Liza didn't know what to say to that. "Yeah, um... Where's Aidan?"

"Not sure, last I saw him he was having a shave in our quarters," Kevin replied, eyes worried behind his glasses. "Liza, I... shall I call him for you?"

Mutely, Liza nodded. She couldn't talk to him about this. Not now.

Kevin pulled out his tab and brought up his call app, stepping away for a moment. Liza stood at parade rest, staring at the list. She'd straighten this out. She had to.

"Hey Liza," Aidan offered a few minutes later. Liza breathed again.

"Commander, can I speak with you in private?"

"Sure," Aidan agreed. "They lent me a spare office. C'mon."

Liza followed her commander to his temporary workroom, stepping inside as he shut the door. Keep it together, keep it professional. That was the key.

"Commander, can I speak freely?"

Aidan gave her a cockeyed look. "Liza, nobody's listening to us. Relax. What's going on?"

Aidan was a good Commander for the most part, but he never understood the value of procedure. It kept things clean and clear and professional. It kept emotions under control.

Liza kept it professional. "I'd like to give feedback on the assignment for civilian training. I'm honored to be suggested, but I don't believe I have the qualifications to fit the position."

Aidan blinked at her for a moment. "Hunh. Why don't we take seats?"

Liza followed the order. Aidan watched her, eyes calm, chin in his hand. He should not be this calm right now.

"So, what qualifications are you missing?"

Keep it professional, she ordered herself. "I don't have the required on-the-ground experience for coordinating a civilian group and instilling structure."

"And what makes you think that?" Aidan asked quietly. Liza just stared at him. How was he asking this?

Keep it professional. "Sir, I have no experience in giving training effectively outside a Force paradigm."

Aidan smiled, just a little. "I don't know about that. I mean, you do most of the training for the Wildcards. And we're not exactly following the Force paradigm, are we?"

"We are adhering to Force structure," Liza replied, feeling like a block of wood.

Aidan watched her for a moment, quiet. "You think so? Because I kind of think you and Del file paperwork to keep Sector off us whenever they bug you, and the rest of us stick on rank pins and use them when it's going to get us somewhere. The rest of the time, I like to think we act like a team." He tapped his collar. "I mean, sometimes this Command pin means I can get assholes off our backs, and that's great. And you and Kevin can pull rank if somebody's being a shit, sure. But the most experienced person on our base keeps telling me she doesn't want to be an officer on paper, because she wants to be on base with her machines, not sent out all over the place. I figure, that's because we're not here to earn rank badges like the handbook tells us we should want to. We're here to be a team."

Aidan's blue eyes were gentle, but they were stripping the one thing Liza was holding onto away. She felt her heart rate rising. Swallowing, she tried to get it through to him again. "Sir…"

"Liza. Breathe. You're talking to me. I'm just Aidan. Just talk to me, yeah?"

Liza fixed her eyes on a spot over Aidan's shoulder. It made it easier to get the words out. "There's no structure to this. No rules. I wouldn't even know where to start. I can't do anything without a direction to go in. And if I don't get this right, then… then I'll get people killed. Again."

Aidan's voice was gentle. "Yeah. I get that. But I want you to hear something: people we love have died; that doesn't mean you got them killed. And you're going to have a direction, yeah? Think about all the books you've been reading and annotating for everybody. All these resources. The core curriculum you just helped plan. That's your direction."

Liza shook her head. When she spoke, the fear quavered in her voice. She hated the sound of it. "It's too theoretical. It hasn't been tested."

"And you don't want to be the one who tests it and gets people killed if it doesn't work," Aidan suggested. Liza's throat tightened.

"It feels premature," she offered. "We need more research. More experience."

Slowly, Aidan shook his head. "Sorry, Liza. We don't get to wait till this doesn't feel like a gamble. It's *always* going to feel like a gamble. Everything's a gamble right now. And if you're scared, you're not the only one. But I thought about this last night. Can I tell you what I came up with?"

Wordless, Liza nodded.

"I think it's better if we go in there and say to the civvies, 'look, we're all scared, but we're in this together, so we're going to show you what we know and get you everything we can.'" Aidan offered. "I figure, that's got to be better than leaving a lot of scared civvies all alone and telling them to figure it out. Sure, maybe they won't like finding out that we're not heroes or monsters, that we're just scared people too. But maybe that's what they need to know. And maybe that's what we need to be. Scared, sure. But still... there's that word Kev uses, 'resolved'? Yeah. We're still resolved, even if we're scared. And maybe we can show everybody that they can be scared and still stand up for what's right. I think that's what you're best at."

Liza swallowed hard. "I'm... Aidan, I'm a behind-the-scenes person. I *can't* lead. I don't have the presence. Nobody will listen to me." Staring at the wall, she got the words out. "They don't listen to me at home. They think I'm a joke. When I lead, everything falls apart. I remember what happened when I tried to fill in for Commander Taylor. It's just...it's not my place. I belong in the background, keeping things organized."

Aidan laughed softly. "Liza. Hey. Liza. Look at me, okay?"

Screwing up her courage, Liza turned her head. Aidan was giving her a tired, commiserating smile. Reaching over, he put a hand on her shoulder. "You think you didn't keep your family together? Way I see it, you kept them *sane* through some seriously messed up shit. And they don't listen to you? That's because they're all brats, and you're either their *sister,* or their kiddo. Of course they treated you like somebody in the family and not somebody with rank. I mean, come on, our team? They're nuts. They're a bunch of off-the wall punks and freaks and geeks and geniuses. And you kept the lid on all of them—and I'm gonna cut you off right here, because I know you're going to tell me you couldn't keep them from pranking Commanders into relocating and fighting with each other." He had both his hands resting on her shoulders now, his eyes holding hers. "And I'm telling you right now Liza, *nobody* could have stopped our family from going off the rails after they lost Taylor, and then got shit on by two pissants waving their rank pins around. These days, I know the crew, and I've heard all the stories. And I'm going to say you're the *only* one who could have kept Lazarus or Kevin from shooting Commander Quinn. After what he pulled, you did an amazing job getting them down to the level of covering him in glue and a pillowcase full of insulation. You say you're in the background? I say you're the foundation that holds us all up. And if you can get the Wildcards through the worst year of their lives without any friendly-fire incidents, you can handle *anyone,* hear me?"

Liza opened her mouth, but Aidan held up a hand.

"Still don't believe me? Okay. Here's some more proof. Look at the way you took care of the base when I was in a fucking cell and Kevin was on the grid, running like hell and going out of his mind? And after that, look at how you handled a whole base of refugees when your family was sick in bed last year? That wasn't me running things and you taking orders, Liza. I was in bed choking on MACHA. I know that for a fact. I was flat on my back and so was Blake, and Kevin was a lot sicker than us, so don't tell me we were running things. *You* kept us going. *You* kept a bunch of civvies who were freaked as hell calm and working on base chores. And it was *you* who kept the Wildcards who were still up and running feeling like we were going to be okay, one way or another. I was pretty woozy, but I remember that."

Liza shook her head. "That's... that isn't the same."

"I'm going to call bullshit on that," Aidan parried quietly. "The people you took care of then are the same kind of people you're going to be taking care of on this trip. You're the person to teach them. You're the best one there is at making people feel grounded, and secure, and cared about."

His words boxed her in. She didn't know where to go from here. He'd already seen all her arguments and refuted them, and his logic worked, damn it. But everything inside her was still screaming 'I can't do this!' She shook her head, helpless. "The base. It'll be a mess... they need me..."

Aidan watched her as she trailed off, running out of words to wrap around the frantic terror in her gut. He gave her shoulder a squeeze. "Yeah. They do need you. And they'll get you back. But remember, this is a National decision. Everyone knows our Personnel officer isn't on base, and they'll cut us slack for that. Deliquisha can handle a couple months if you're gone that long, filing basic paperwork. She's ready to step up as a trainee. We'll help her with everything." He smiled, holding her eyes. "I won't let them go downhill while you're gone. Promise. Kay?"

Liza felt her muscles tense like wires under her skin. "You really want me to do this?"

"I don't want you gone," Aidan offered. "I'm going to miss you like my right hand, and I don't know how I'm going to straighten Yve and Sarah out without you around, honestly. But I want you doing this work. Because you're the right one for it."

Liza caught her breath. Finally, she forced herself to nod. "Okay. Okay. We'll... we'll make plans back on base. We'll make checklists. We'll make sure everything's running smoothly. And then... okay."

"So you're going to accept?" Aidan probed.

Liza nodded. "Yes, sir. I accept."

Aidan nodded. "Thank you. How long do you need to prep before you feel confident heading out?"

Confident?! Liza's mind yelped, *how am I supposed to ever feel confident about this?!* She squashed the thought. "I can have Deliquisha ready to take over pro-tem in two months, if that works."

Aidan nodded. "Sounds good to me." For a moment he paused, and a little worry came into his eyes. "Um, you did see Tweak is going along too? Is that going to be a problem?"

Liza gave a weak laugh. "Aidan, it's Tweak. Of course it's going to be a problem. But she's the only one I'd want protecting the civilian tech."

Aidan gave her one of his smiles that said 'I get it.' "Okay. Then let's get out there."

Event File 04
File Tag: Primary Objective
14:00-05-13-2160

"I do this? We n-need s-secur-r-rity? I want Omi."

"Yeah?"

Tweak shot Aidan a grin as the crowd of Dusters heading out eddied around her and down the hall. She bobbed her head as they walked. "Yeah. She's cool. D-don't want to be stuck with L-liza and some m-m-meathead. 'Sides. Omi gets me. We click. Sound good?"

Aidan gave her a small smile and a shrug. "I'll have to get clearance to have that many people from the same base going out for an extended run, but hey, we're the Wildcards. They like to clear our crazy ideas; most of them pay off."

"Damn s-straight!" Tweak agreed with a grin, "Wildcards rule!"

It felt good to say that. It felt good to have a name for herself that she wanted to claim. The gang and the last few years had been good to her. It felt good to be doing something that gave back. Even if it was giving blood—*again*—and taking care of a million clueless luds' tech for them. And it wasn't just the civvies; some of the Dusters were seriously dense with tech, and that was just plain embarrassing.

She and the other techies had to give a whole presentation on how ArgusCo was changing algorithms at one point, and they shouldn't have needed to spend nearly so much time on pointing out the obvious. A kid should have noticed that the infrastructure-building and management corporation had started working with the shipping and merchandising monster that was ZonCom to spot the vehicle identifiers for traffic appearing on a road using an IP that hadn't entered the traffic at a legitimate spot upstream. The two corporations had used those anomalies to triangulate points of origin for any traffic outside established patterns of shipping and travel, pinpointing Dusters and Fringers. But the Corps weren't as slick as they thought they were; it had taken Tweak and some other hacker types she'd been working with all of five minutes to hop on a group call, talk it through, and start working on programs to inject tracking signals into the Corps' monitoring platforms, creating a false record of Duster wheels entering a given roadway any time they needed to get on a monitored road. It'd been such an easy fix that Tweak had wondered if some Corps coders secretly wanted them to win.

Aidan glanced at his tab. "Kev says we're all packed, so let's—"

"Headly?"

Tweak tracked her buddy as he turned and saluted. "Commander Hall, ma'am."

The old woman gave him a nod. "If you'd send your team a delay alert and you and Officer T. can accompany me, I'd appreciate it."

Aidan blinked. "Yes, ma'am." Tweak tried to catch his eye, but he was looking straight at his boss. What was up? No clue. But Aidan would have her back if it was sketchy. It was probably just more procedural stuff. There was always more of that.

She stuck close to Aidan as they worked their way back up the hall. It didn't bother her so much to get touched anymore, but she still hated being in the middle of busy crowds like this. It just didn't feel *safe.*

Commander Hall led them to one of the smaller meeting rooms and shut the door. Pulling two sound boxes from her pockets, she placed them in the corners of the room. Then she turned.

"I'd like to present Base Commander Headly-McIllian, and Officer T."

Tweak didn't crack a grin, for Aidan's sake, but it was hard work. She'd gotten all kinds of requests to give a last name for the records. When she didn't, the brass had given up and started calling her Officer T. It still made her laugh that they couldn't *stand* to mix a street handle with the super-special ranking system they all loved so much. But hey, that was the Force for you. They talked democracy, sure, but they walked military.

She glanced around the seated people. Okay, there was Magnum, that was good. Hall was tough, but pretty cool. And there were those three National-level people. Tweak pegged them as bigwigs; that could be good or bad, no way to know yet.

What she wanted to say was 'Yeah? What?' but she'd learned that letting Aidan talk to the brass at times like this turned out better for everybody. So she stood still, and watched them, and let Aidan do his thing.

Aidan glanced around the room. Tweak heard him gulp. "Um... Commanders and Councilors. It's an honor."

"At ease, Headly," Hall added, and Tweak realized she was smiling at him. "We'd like to address your subordinate directly."

Tweak blinked. "That's me, yeah?"

"That's you," Commander Magnum agreed in his deep, patient voice. "Councilors, I'd like to present Tweak, Technical Officer for Base 1407, leading member of the Inter-Quadrant Technical Solutions Committee, and—"

"The savior of the Democratic State Force, from what we hear," the old white guy on her left cut in. DuValle, that was his name. He'd been in on a couple of the tech talks. Not a moron, so it could be worse. But what was this crap?

"S-savior?" Tweak asked, cocking her head.

"It was your DNA sequences that allowed us to create the vaccine that neutralized the MACHA attack?" the man suggested, smiling a little. "And that DNA has saved us from two more bio-attacks in the last year."

Glancing down, Tweak shrugged. "Wasn't anything I d-did. Just what I am."

"No need for modesty, Officer. Your contribution saved lives across the country, and for it we're grateful. We want to make that clear at the outset."

Tweak raised her head to glare at the guy. Modest? She was talking straight, and here was this guy thinking she was faking it for brownie points? Fuck that.

"It saved my guys," she snapped. "My crew."

"And hundreds of other crews besides," Commander Magnum agreed smoothly. He glanced up and down the table; Tweak guessed it was either a look to ask if he could talk, or a sort of 'I got this, chill' look to get everyone else to give him the floor. Whichever it was, they let him continue. He turned his heavy head, slow. Magnum moved like a vid with a bad lag problem, but his voice always made Tweak feel like things were being handled. Not 'going to be okay', exactly, but 'not totally out of control', which she'd take.

"That's why we'd like to speak with you, Officer Tweak," he continued. Cutting her eyes, Tweak noticed DuValle trying not to make a face when Magnum said her name. Hah. Sit and spin on it, asshole. She snapped her attention back to Magnum as he spoke. "I want to make it clear, we're meeting with you to discuss a possibility and reach a consensus. It will be your decision whether to accept the mission. We are giving you an option. Not an order."

Tweak crossed her arms, black leather jacket creaking. Having all these people looking at her was making her scales shiver under their bandages. "Yeah? Whatsit?"

Aidan coughed. "Could you present the proposal, sir?"

Magnum gave that little grunt that Tweak took to mean 'nice job, you got us both out of trouble.' She wasn't sure what the trouble had been, but she'd probably said the wrong thing. Talking to Alphas was a pain sometimes. It was worse when they were Alphas in charge. They got so damn picky. And *touchy*.

"Given the fact that Officer Tweak's DNA has provided us with vaccines and cures that have saved millions," the older man went on, "we'd be very interested in looking at the DNA of other Gammas. But we realize how delicate that could be, as a project."

Tweak tapped her foot. "I don't get it." She considered it for a moment, and tacked on another word. "Sorry."

Magnum gave her a small smile. "Let me get to the point. Gamma blood and Gamma DNA from just one person—that's you — has given us the material to fight three gene-tailored bio-weapons. If your blood saved us three times, we want to get more samples of Gamma DNA, because more biological weapons will be made in the future. We have to prepare for that. If we want to be ready, we need more Gamma DNA samples. However, people like you have a historical reason to be cautious of strangers, and to resist requests for samples of their DNA."

Tweak barked a laugh. "Got that r-right."

"Which is why we're talking to you," Commander Hall cut in. "You're going to be on the Grid for this civilian solidarity operation. We'd like to offer you, along with a very small selection of other operatives across the nation, the option of a secondary mission: we'd like you to try to contact other Gammas, explain our situation and offer them a place in our ranks. Failing that, we're authorizing funds. We want you to offer them money in exchange for a blood sample."

Tweak blinked. "You. Want. Gammas. In the Force?"

"As we see it, your community has been marginalized far too long," Williams' voice continued in her smooth tones. "It's time they were welcomed into the fold, as partners in the future."

Tweak shot her a look. "Don't do that."

The woman looked like she'd gotten slapped. "Excuse me, Officer?"

"I said. Don't do that," Tweak repeated. "Don't use fakey n-newscaster talk to make it sound pretty. People like me get n-nervous when you try to make it p-pretty. Means there's s-something ugly undern-neath."

She turned back to Magnum and Hall. "You need Gammas. Our blood saves lives. Doesn't need to be a lot of blood. S-samples. Like I've been g-giving. And you trade cash, or a place to be. Their call."

"An excellent summary," Hernandez agreed with a nod.

Tweak glanced up at Aidan. He gave her a quiet smile. "Tell us how to do this without screwing it all up, okay Tweak? That's what we need."

Heart pounding in her ears, Tweak nodded. She realized her hands were hurting, and glanced down. They'd balled into fists. She took a deep breath, the way her psych training had taught her. Unclenched her jaw. Relaxed her hands. Straightened her spine.

"Okay. If I d-do this, there's gonna be rules. Rule. One. These people. They c-come on as Force m-members. Or as r-refugees we're getting out of the c-country. But they come on as *people*. You sign them up l-like anybody else. They get to hold the pen and s-sign. You don't t-tell them what happens. You *ask*. Don't treat them l-like lab rats. Fuck that."

Aidan cleared his throat, and Tweak looked up. He tipped his head in the direction of the table, giving her a 'watch it, okay?' look.

It must have been saying 'fuck that'. She glanced back at the seated people. "Sorry. Cussed. N-not supposed to cuss with the brass."

Commander Williams cracked a smile. Commander Magnum chuckled. So maybe it wasn't too bad.

Well, she was already pretty far into this. She might as well keep going.

She swallowed. "Rule. Two. You *ask* how the Gamma shows up. And then you *help*. S-somebody got m-muscle problems? You get them spoons that d-don't spill when their hands shake. Somebody got problems with skin? You get them meds. Got problems with their brains? You help them deal. You want one part of somebody, you give *all* of them cred. You don't t-take what you w-want and make fun of what you don't. Not. Cool."

"Anything else?" DuValle asked dryly. Tweak pinned him with a look. "Yeah. Rule three. Anybody f-fucks with a Gamma, they get writ up. Charged. We always get shit, and it's always our fault. Fuck. That. Noise. You want us here, you treat us like p-people in the rules and regs." She ran her eyes up and down the line of older people. "Those are the rules. You say yes, then I do this. You say 'm-maybe', we're done here. People like me go through enough shit. No putting them through more."

There. She'd said everything. Now she just had to see.

"While I don't like your tone, Officer—" DuValle began, but Hernandez held up a hand. "I got this, Chad." Standing, he came around the table, and walked to stand in front of Tweak. A smile creasing his weather-beaten face, he held out a hand. "You have a deal, Officer. We'll bring your people on as equals, and we'll treat them right. And they'll help us save lives. Just like you did."

Tweak stared at his hand, thoughts racing. Bracing herself, she raised her eyes to his face. "I want it in writing."

"You'll have the document within three weeks," Hernandez agreed. "If the new regulations protecting Gammas aren't in our Force protocols by the time two months are up, we'll make any recruitments non-binding. Anyone who doesn't get what they were promised doesn't have to stay."

Tweak nodded, eyes drifting back down to his hand. Either this was going to make a lot of people's lives better, or a hell of a lot worse. And she had no way to know which it'd be.

But the Force did try to do the right thing. They were always trying, even when they screwed it up. That was already better than the Corps.

She glanced up at Aidan. He gave her a quiet smile. He'd helped her so much. Maybe if she did this, she could get other Gamma kids to commanders like him; people who could help the broken pieces fit together. Aidan had done that for her. Maybe, just maybe, she could make sure other Gammas met the person who'd do that for them.

Gritting her teeth, she reached out and shook Hernandez's hand.

"Okay. I'm in."

Event File 05
File Tag: Mission Prep
17:30·05·21·2160

"What's on the screen?" Liza asked, glancing at the scrolling list Tweak had projected in front of herself while she ate. The light reflected blue from her black hair as the little woman munched her burrito.

"Copy of the old Blacklist," Tweak mumbled around her dinner "Saved it b-before we took down the Citizen Ratings. Tryna' get ideas about the g-Gammas in the Metro."

"You can read it when it's going by that fast?" Yvonne asked, glancing down the table.

Tweak blinked, burrito halfway to her mouth. "You c-can't?"

The top half of her burrito flopped over onto her plate, soggy casing giving way. Billie bit her lip, glancing at Kevin. "I don't think amaranth flour is going to work for these burrito casings. Can we get wheat flour this month?"

"We can certainly try," Kevin agreed, poking at his burrito with a fork. "And you're not wrong."

Liza glanced from Tweak's face to her plate. "It might be a better use of time to focus on eating right now, and then focus on work."

Tweak rolled her eyes. Around the table, all kinds of people gave her looks like teenagers tired of getting a lecture. She really hated that look.

"Yes, Mom," Tweak grumbled, tapping her tab. The window

fizzled away on the air.

Liza supposed this was better than Tweak's early-days response of 'fuck off', but now she'd started copying Sarah and Yvonne and saying 'yes mom' whenever she got reminded not to run herself into the ground. Worse, Naomi had picked the habit up too. Getting called 'mom' got really old. You'd think someone would show some gratitude when you went out of your way to make sure they took care of themselves, but no.

Well, at least Tweak was actually coming to dinner. Liza had thought that she'd have to threaten to shut down the little coder's rig again. Tweak was working even harder than Liza herself to prep their team for the big training run in two months.

Two months. The departure date was like a rockslide, rolling down on them way too fast. Less than two months now, really. And there was *so much* to do.

"Hey, Tweak," Don piped up, breaking through Liza's mental fog, "if you can read that fast, can you do me a favor?"

"Yeah?" Tweak asked distractedly, playing some kind of game on her tab with one hand and eating with the other.

Don dropped his voice to what he *thought* was a conspiratorial level. "We gotta read about the eleven Quadrants of the country and write up their history and name their regions an' states for the education app."

"So?" Tweak asked through a mouthful of burrito.

Don gave the coder his best puppy-dog look. "So can you read it and then tell us the important bits?"

Tweak blinked once. Twice. Then she shook her head. "Hard pass. Your homework. Not mine. You're the one 'sposed to l-learn. Sides. I don't work for free. You don't pay, you don't get."

"And on top of that, there's no 'we' here," Deliquisha added hotly. "Don, that is such bull; this is stuff we need to know!"

"Besides," Abigail added from Tweak's other side, "this stuff is cool!"

Donovan raised his head, bewildered and cranky. "You guys weren't supposed to hear me!" When he whined, he sounded years younger.

The two girls looked at each other, a look that so clearly said 'this boy' that Liza had to push down a snort of laughter.

"You weren't supposed to talk about a secret at the dinner table, maybe?" Tom suggested. The boy was developing an understated sense of humor that Liza really appreciated. Given the pair of nutcases who had adopted him, it was surprising how calm and sensible the fifteen-year-old was growing up to be. Donovan, on the other hand, had some growing up to do yet, seventeen or not. He was the polar opposite of his granite block of a big brother, all brashness and big, impish grins. He hadn't said anything yet, but Liza had a hunch that he was going to choose either munitions or food-prep for his vocation; he liked to make people happy, and he liked to make things blow up. They'd have to see which one took over with him. Liza mulled the thought over as she watched Kevin quietly leave his seat and sidle up behind the chattering kids. She'd known he'd be Logistics in his first month on the base; it was all there in the way he moved and the way he thought. She had a knack for spotting who would be in what division as adults; she'd known Topher would be in the motor pool before he was sixteen, and she'd spotted Deliquisha's talent around thirteen. Liza was pretty sure Tommy was going to end up as a Command adjunct; he enjoyed order and he liked to be helpful. His girlfriend Abigail would, no question, be out in the gardens and down in the gene-modification paperwork with her dad one day. But some kids, like Don, were harder to pin down. Yvonne had been like that too.

"Come on guys," Don sighed, "I got things to do besides read this stuff, give me a break!"

"And what would these all-important 'things' be?'" Kevin asked. Liza had been watching him patiently work his way to standing right behind the kid, but the boy hadn't noticed a thing. Kevin's cat-foot act paid off; Don jumped a mile.

"Jeez, how'd you *do* that?"

"Practice," Kevin replied arily. He rested his hands on the boy's shoulders. "So, let's hear about all these 'things' are for. Or should I say *who* they're for?"

"Whaaat?" Abigail leaned against Tom's shoulder. "Don, are you *with somebody?*"

"Oh man…" Don groaned, giving Kevin a look like a kicked puppy. "Seriously?"

Kevin smirked. "Do tell us more about this person who's so much more interesting than your studies, she must be fascinating. After all, she was definitely more interesting than the work we were doing when you came to 'help' me with picking up deliveries over at 1520."

"Wait, you actually *did* meet somebody? For *real*?" Deliquisha chimed in, grinning even as she crossed her arms. "And that's why you've been dumping Education and not caring that you're missing your Ranking Requirements, isn't it? For real, man? I wanted us to do our ranking ceremony together, and now you're *way* behind me!"

Don ducked his head. "Aw Dill, I didn't think about that, I'm sorry."

"Yeah, I know you didn't think," Deliquisha snipped, rolling her eyes. "Okay, give. Who are they?"

Don grinned, white teeth bright in his dark face. "Her name's Callie, she's non-com 1520, we met at one of the inter-base Dust Survival trainings, and we've been talking on the Mesh since it went up. Somebody set up a recreational forum for non-coms, and... well yeah." His smile was even goofier now. Liza sighed. She'd never felt even a hint of what Don was experiencing, but she'd seen it often enough to recognize the signs. Another romance in the making. Joy. Hopefully this wouldn't be one of the messy ones. Given how often being allosexual had made her friends either brainless or completely miserable as they all grew up, she'd always been happy that she wasn't wired to end up in the middle of that drama herself. And now it looked like it was the next generation's turn.

Damian looked up from his tab for a moment and cocked a brow at his siblings, but he didn't say anything.

Liza glanced down at her tab as it buzzed in her hand.

> **Message Handle: KingOfClubs**
> **Message: PSA for every adult Wildcard: if anyone says a single word about a Touchdown Party, I will find a valid medical reason to prescribe weekly colonoscopies. And enemas.**

Liza choked on her water. Up and down the table, she heard more splutters and a few snorts. Deliquisha cut her eyes around the table, catching that something was going on, but getting more details on her twin's girl kept her from asking about it.

Watching her family rally around Don's first romance, Liza felt her heart swell. This was love for her; sitting and watching her family with a full heart, bathed in their happiness. Don was glowing, Deliquisha was nodding and grinning now that she had gotten her word in. Tommy was quietly happy, Abigail beaming and practically bouncing in her chair. All her kids were doing so well.

If there wasn't an empty space where one of her kids ought to be, everything would be perfect. Henrietta ought to be right there in the middle of this. Liza glanced down the table at Jim, the warmth running out of her heart as if someone had put a hole in the bottom. The man was studying his plate, keeping his eyes averted from the gathering of kids. No wonder; his daughter had always been in the middle of their conversations, chattering away and shining like the sun. Fucking MACHA had taken that little light away from them all.

She reminded herself to check up on Jim later. He still wasn't doing so good. There was so much to do in getting ready for this training mission that it was easy to drop the ball on her base responsibilities, but her duty to a comrade in mourning had to come first. She'd catch him tonight during off-duty hours, or tomorrow if she got too wrapped up this evening. She made a note to add checking in on him to her to-do list.

That list was the first thing she saw when she sat down at her work console, waiting for her like a mountain lion ready to spring. The list of everything she had to check before she left her family and headed out to try to teach strangers was exactly that terrifying.

That feeling of everything bearing down on her swept back in with a vengeance. To distract herself from the frozen panic of the moment, she opened up the Good Trouble Bundle. And that was the *wrong* move. There was so *much* that still needed annotating in here. How the hell was she ever going to learn it all in two months, annotate it for the modern world and make something like a decent lesson plan out of it all?

She sat frozen in her chair for a moment. Then the cursor on the screen moved, and a little note was put in the margin. For the longest time, Liza stared at the notes, feeling her rabbit-racing heart begin to slow.

She kept forgetting. She wasn't alone here. Tons of commanders and officers of all levels were in here with her; annotating, taking notes, and working together to make this information useful.

Liza clicked, and the Good Trouble University curriculum and teaching schedule opened up, around fifty people annotating, cross-indexing and adding references to it in realtime. A couple of the Union heads were currently writing a Workers' Bill Of Rights, using something from a twenty-first century organization as the template. She stared at the discussions going on in the margins of the texts, trying to get it through her head. She might be the teacher for her Sector, but she wasn't alone in this. She was part of a country-wide team. She repeated it in her head: *I'm not alone. I'm part of something. I'm part of the Force.*

Her fingers thawed out. Her pulse stopped pounding behind her eyes. She let out a long breath.

"Okay," she whispered. "Okay."

Carefully, she read the comments on the curriculum, and added a few thoughts of her own. Slowly, her fingers began to move.

The weeks slipped away like sand through her fingers. Liza kept her head in the game for the most part, though the sense of the responsibility bearing down on her still froze her like a rabbit at the beginning of some editing and work sessions. At least the crew was around to snap her out of it; someone was always poking their head into her office, asking for a check on paperwork or procedure. She normally helped Kevin oversee the kids' education regime, so she had to take some time to work out a curriculum he could run solo as a sideline to his base and Sector duties. It meant the kids would miss their fitness and hand-to-hand combat training, but since Deliquisha could practically run those herself by this point, Liza and Kevin agreed to delegate reminding the other kids to do phys-ed and defense training to the girl. Having just a little authority to boss her twin around would be a perk of the job for Del. Liza looked forward to hearing how *that* went over when she got home.

But before she could even think about coming home, she had to get out there and do this. She'd been assigned ten union chapter meetings around the Denver Metro. A bunch of unions had cropped up in different industries under Zoncom, along with a couple in different industries owned by ArgusCo and Cavanaugh. Even EagleCorp had a couple unions for different job capacities. Only the poor bastards at AgCo had scraped just a single union together. Liza had gotten handed a mixed bag of ten unions within her Sector to train, which meant twelve weeks away from home, if everything went well. If it didn't... well, there was no planning for what that'd look like.

She only had a week before they headed out now, and she was down to writing up her speech notes and roleplaying possible scenarios and the kind of questions Grid-born citizens might ask with Blake, Kevin, Aidan and Naomi on a rotating schedule. And she *still* felt completely out of her depth. Was this feeling ever going to pass?

The thought about schedules flicked a switch in her brain, and Liza double-checked Naomi's orders. It had taken forever for them to clear, but they'd come in the day before. Reading the orders over, she nodded to herself. Naomi was approved as their on-Grid security detail. That was great; Naomi was the best possible fit for this project. And she could act as a buffer when Tweak got annoying.

"Knock knock?"

Liza turned in her seat, and Kevin gave her a lopsided smile.

"Kevin. Come on in."

"Am I interrupting?" Kevin asked, standing easy in the doorway. Liza smiled and pulled out her extra chair for him. "No, I'm on double-checks and details at this point. Grab a seat. I thought we did our last scheduled roleplay? Did I miss it?"

"You know you never miss anything," Kevin replied, lounging into the chair. It still made Liza smile to watch the grace he'd grown into. As a teen he'd been all sharp edges, whiplash-fast movements and awkward angles; these days, it looked like he was part cat when he moved. What a change fifteen years made. If she'd taken care of a little orange kitten that turned out to be a tiger, she couldn't be more proud. Except when he got cocky and made stupid decisions, of course; then she got frustrated, because she knew for a fact that he could do so much better.

Kevin met her eyes warily. "What? It can't be my hair; I just brushed it this morning. And you cut it last week."

Liza managed a laugh. "Sorry, I'm just zoning out. My brain's so full of stuff it's coming out my ears. Oh, that reminds me, Blake said he'd take care of haircuts while I'm gone."

"Oh that will be *fun*," Kevin replied dryly.

Liza gave him a look. "Cut him some slack, alright, Kev?"

Kevin sighed, raising his eyes to the ceiling. "It is not, nor it cannot come to good; but break my heart, for I must hold my tongue."

And now he was quoting. Liza stared at him. "Are you going to be like this all day?"

Kevin chuckled, straightening up in his seat. "Sorry, couldn't resist." Adjusting his glasses on his nose, he studied the screen. Then he turned and studied her instead. "And how are you doing?"

Liza made a point to keep her eyes on the screen. "Not bad. The curriculum's set now, and I've drilled Deliquisha on her pro-tem duties. She's ready to handle routine paperwork for a few weeks; it's faster than I want her to take it all on, but she's excited. We've got our travel itinerary set, and it looks good."

"And that's your duties," Kevin pointed out mildly. "That's not you. I want to know how *Liza's* doing."

Liza glanced away, checking things off her to-do list.

"Liza," Kevin cajoled. "Come on, old girl. Talk to me, or I'm going to worry. I don't like to see you get so brittle."

"You don't need to coddle me, Kev," Liza stated quietly. "I'm the one who does that to you, remember?"

Her friend was quiet for a moment. When he spoke, his voice was gentle. "This isn't coddling, Liza. This is a boy checking on his big sister. So, in all seriousness. Are you okay?"

The tender note in his voice got right through her defenses, the way it always did, damn it.

"Liza?" Kevin pressed quietly. Liza closed her eyes.

"Okay," she managed eventually. "How am I? Totally inadequate, is how I am. They should be sending you, not me. You're the one with all the charm and the public speaking voice. You're the one with the presence. I'm the one who chases after people and tells them to eat and cuts their hair." She smiled weakly. "Remember you showing the twins Peter Pan during their first week on base?"

"Oh yes, and then they wouldn't stop watching it." Kevin agreed with a weary smile.

Liza nodded. "Yeah. I thought they'd corrupt the file, they loaded it so often. How many times did they watch that and Hook back to back?"

"I don't want to remember," Kevin chuckled. "A hundred, at least. I had such fun teasing Peter about it; the kids kept asking him to play pretend with them and be Peter Pan."

"Yeah, I remember the green tights you scrounged," Liza added, hiding a grin behind her hand. Kevin outright laughed at that. "Oh good God, those tights. One of the biggest mistakes of my life, picking them up. I had the devil of a time getting Peter out of them!"

"TMI, Kev honey." Liza suggested.

Kevin gave her a cockeyed grin. "Mind you, I still love Hook. But I could do without having every line etched into my brain by repetition."

"Yeah, well," Liza sighed. "This is the thing. I brought it up because... I know you said it was your ex, but that was just because he's named Peter and he's cute and full of energy. Really it's you who's Peter Pan. You've got charisma, Kev. Everybody gets inspired by you. And I'm Wendy. I'm the one nobody wants to follow."

Kevin's smile faded. For a moment, he studied her with sad grey eyes. Then he reached out and put a hand on Liza's shoulder. "And do you remember the scene in the movie when everyone was exhausted, and over-excited, and hurting one another?" Kevin asked, voice quiet.

Liza glanced at him. "Yeah, but—"

"Wendy's the one they need then," Kevin continued, gently surfing his voice over hers. "Wendy's the one who wipes off the war paint and makes the boys look at each other and themselves like people. She's the one who gets them to act more like human beings than beasts. She's the one who's needed to *end* a battle. Peter can only *start* the trouble."

Before Liza could put together an answer, Kevin leaned his elbows on his knees, steepled his fingers, and rested his chin on his fingertips as he went on. "And do you know what people would see if I did take this mission? I'll tell you. They'd see another member of the elite; stamped with the genetic markers of the ruling class, trained in the art of speeches and persuasion, giving another set of orders and platitudes and propaganda. They'd see more of what they've been forced to swallow all their lives. And if they see that, we'd lose them before we begin."

"But you're *not*—" Liza started. Her friend held up a pale hand. "I *know* I'm not like that, Liza, but I know for a fact that I *look* like that and *sound* like that, to those who don't know me personally. I've got no illusions about that. Now, what do they see when they look at you?"

Liza stared at him, mute. How the hell would she know? "Tell me."

Kevin's silvery eyes held hers. "They'll see someone up there who could be their sister or their co-worker. Authentic. A little worried. Very real. Speaking to them as equals and partners. They'll see a person who's competent, and good, and *just like them.* And that will tell them that this movement isn't just for the fanatics, or the Fringers, or people from the top of the food chain. This is *for them.* And you will speak with knowledge, but sometimes you won't know the answer and sometimes you'll be exasperated, and that will make you *authentic.* We don't need perfection. We need authenticity and connection. You can give that; I can't. I default to being a performer, and people can see that I'm hiding behind a performance, whether they can articulate it or not. You default to being a competent organizer. And people want that right now. They *need* it. Because the world is changing, and it's a bit terrifying. And in that situation, people want to see one person stand up and say 'okay, we're all scared, and I'm scared too, but here's the plan.' See what I mean?"

Liza stared at her friend, biting her lip. He stared right back, earnest and patient and so sure of her.

Finally, she shook her head. "I don't see what you do, in me. But if you see it, then I guess…"

"You don't have to guess. You can assume," Kevin quipped, leaning back in his chair with an elaborate show of relaxing. "After all, I do have impeccable judgment."

That deserved a side-eye. "About other people, sure," Liza acknowledged. "How about when you should eat? Or sleep? Or take breaks?"

Kevin snorted. "That's it. You're not Wendy. You're Nana the Sheepdog."

The comment was so ridiculous that Liza couldn't help but laugh. "You are such a pain in the ass."

"Only selectively," Kevin replied with a wink. He barely blushed when he made jokes like that anymore.

Liza rolled her eyes. "Definitely TMI, Kev honey." Kevin gave a gracious tip of the head. "Touché."

For a moment, they smiled at one another. Reaching out, Liza squeezed his shoulder. "Thanks, Kev."

"Any time, Liza my girl." For a moment, Kevin just smiled at her. Then he pulled her into a hug so tight that she squeaked.

"Kev!"

"I need you to be careful out there," he murmured into her shoulder. "Promise?"

And that was when Liza realized that he wasn't playing around.

She put her arms around him in turn, holding him tight. "I'll be careful, Kev hon. I will. I promise."

"And you'll come home. Swear?"

"I swear."

Event File 06
File Tag: Statement Of Intent
19:30-07-27-2160

The heat pump ticked over, blowing erratically cool air over the gathering.

At the front of the space, Liza stood, and stared, and listened to herself sweat. The lazy fan squeaked as it turned overhead.

Oh god, oh god, what am I even doing?!

The chapter president had introduced her already and taken a seat. Now, she was all alone at the front of this oven of a room, with the whole audience's eyes on her.

In the back of the room, Naomi put two thumbs up, pale flesh on the left and black plastic on the right. She gave Liza a lazy smile. *It'll be fine,* that smile said.

Easy for her to say, she wasn't standing up here.

Liza snapped her eyes back to the crowd of Zoncom citizens who'd joined the Denver chapter of the Zoncom Warehouse Workers' Union, crammed into this makeshift little meeting room during what little down time they got from the Zon. Liza ran her eyes over them. Stringy, tired women. Haggard men. Teenagers with eyes that said 'please give me a future that's better than this'. Those kids should have been in a real education program, not here.

These people needed so much. And she had to figure out how to give it to them.

She cleared her throat, checking that her speech was projecting on a discreet window above her tab.

"Good evening, everyone. Thanks for leaving your tech with our officer upstairs; it'll be returned to you at the end of our meeting tonight, with new programs on it to ensure everyone's safety and give you access to everything we'll be talking about. We appreciate the trust you're putting in us."

The eyes bored into her. "Now give us a reason to trust you," the silent crowd seemed to be saying. The fan squeaked above. Liza's mouth was dry as the Dust in summer. She swallowed, glancing at the speech she'd prepared. The holographic words glowed.

"Okay. Thank you for attending the first meeting of the Good Trouble University. The intent of these classes is to give you the tools to…"

And she froze.

The tools to do the impossible. The unbelievable. How could she tell this room full of exhausted people they were going to knock over the Corps?! They'd shout her down when they heard that kind of canned trash. They'd laugh her out of the room.

She stared at the words on the screen. Reading them now, in front of all these people, they sounded fake, and not just fake: trite as hell.

Murmurs started in the back of the room. Liza closed her eyes.

"Okay. Let's be real." She opened her eyes. "We all know why we're here: we all want to get the Corps off our backs and start living in a country that treats us like people, not raw material for their products. You want to be treated like you're worth something, and asked what you think." She glanced around the room.

Silence. Then, slowly, tentative murmurs of assent began to rise. People looked at one another, and nodded.

"You want to be able to choose what happens in your life. Right?" She asked. The agreement was a little stronger this time.

"And you want a government that cares if you have food on the table and some dignity, right?"

This time, there was a rising note of 'yeah!' and a few quiet whoops from the gathering. People were starting to smile. Liza managed a bit of a grin.

"And that's why we're here. Because that's what we all want. What I'm here to do is start showing you how we get it. It's not going to be something that happens overnight, and it's not going to be easy. Some days, you're going to wonder if it's worth it to chase this kind of thing. But when this country has a democracy again, it'll be on account of the work you're doing now."

This time there was an honest to god cheer. Liza felt her spirits rise. They were listening. They were buying in.

Tapping her tab, she brought up the schedule she'd prepared. "So, for the next seven days, anyone who has time off will come and be given notes and techniques to share with the rest of the Union chapter. Your union chapter leadership will ensure that everyone is trained on everything, when your contracted work hours allow it. The Force and your union heads decided on this approach together, in order to make sure nobody is under too much of a burden to attend the entire training and put themselves in danger." She drew a breath. "So. On Day One and Day Two we'll go over the theory of effective community action and unionized organization. Day Three, we'll go over effective union structure, organization, and structural philosophy. Days Four and Five, we'll go over what works and what doesn't out on the street, in terms of nonviolent action and tactics. And Days Six and Seven, we'll roleplay scenarios and go over applied tactics. We'll also get everyone signed up for their first inter-union vote, deciding on what the first large community action will be. Officer Henderson-Adler in the back will be giving everyone a lot of tips for nonviolent self-protection and defense." She nodded at Naomi, who waved at the room. Liza ran her eyes around the gathering.

"By the time we're done here, we intend to make sure you feel confident about planning and doing a nonviolent action that will weaken Corporate control over the way we think, receive information, and act in this country. And remember; none of us are in this alone. I know this is all scary as hell, but you need to remember this: we're going to stand together, all the way through this work. The Corps are big, and they're rich, and they're powerful. But when we're together, we have power too. They've tried to tell us there's nothing we can do. And you know what? They *lied*. When we don't let them isolate us, distract us and scare us, we the people are stronger than you can believe. You don't have to believe me yet. I haven't proved it to you yet. But I'm going to. Just watch."

For a moment, the room was completely quiet. Then the teenagers broke out in cheers, and everyone else followed suit.

That evening, their safe house was a tiny apartment on the fiftieth floor of a housing block.

"You kicked ass in there," Naomi observed once they'd gotten the sound boxes in place. Naomi poured the phage nanoids into her hand, blowing the dusting of tiny machines into the corners of the room.

Liza gave her a smile. "It did turn out okay, didn't it?" Then she glanced at her tab. "But tomorrow the real work starts. That was just the warmup. Tomorrow's when we find out how this is really going to go."

"Liza. Quit," Tweak interjected as she flopped onto one of the beds. "Stressing. Won't help."

"Easy for you to say, kid." Naomi parried with a smile. "You got to sit nice and quiet with their tech tonight."

"You call that easy?" Tweak exclaimed, rolling her eyes. "Buncha asshats! No maintenance! Junk files and v-viruses everywhere!" She threw her hands in the air with a little 'ugh!' of frustration.

Naomi smirked. "Poor *baby*."

"Oh. Fuck. You." Tweak shot back, grinning. Naomi chuckled. "Yeah, no thanks. Not my thing."

"Let's get ready for bed and get some sleep, guys. Tomorrow's going to be a long day." Liza cut in before the sassing could really ramp up.

Tweak and Naomi looked at each other. Then they both looked at Liza, and grinned. "Yes, mom," they chorused.

Liza sighed.

In the morning, Liza started the group off with theory; this area was still academic enough to let her ease in before they hit the really deep waters.

"Okay everyone, please get out your tabs. We're going to start with learning to open up the Common Ground app and access the Good Trouble Bundle."

She walked them through the signing-in process to get on the Mesh and into Common Ground, then into the Good Trouble Bundle. Tweak zipped around the room like a hummingbird, taking a minute with the folks who got stuck here and there.

"At the top, you'll see a file marked Good Trouble University: Principles Study Guide," Liza continued. "Let's get that open." The group complied, though Liza was starting to see a few bewildered looks thrown her way. Well, hopefully the conversation would move them on past whatever they were worried about.

"Great," she went on, "So, let's get started on the first day's materials: myths and truths of nonviolent work, followed by a history of attempted movements against the United Corporations to date. First we'll draw from the work of Rivera Sun, an activist of the twenty-first century, who describes—"

"Uh, miss?"

Liza broke off. A man with a black-and-blue hat shoved down over his thatch of ashy hair had a hand up.

"What's up?" She asked. The man cleared his throat uncomfortably. "Look, I don't want to be rude, but... I thought we were showing up to get trained to get rid of the Zon and break our Corporate Contracts..."

"Yeah?" Liza asked, though she was pretty sure she knew what came next.

The man gave her a helpless look. "So... where's the stuff? The invisibility stuff? The guns? I mean... I thought we were getting stuff."

Oh boy, here we go, Liza muttered silently. But she'd roleplayed her way through this with Blake. She knew what to say.

"That's a really important question... I think I missed your name?"

"Jeff," the man offered eventually, fear in his eyes. Liza nodded. "Thanks for asking that, Jeff. I think a lot of people in here have been thinking exactly what you just said," she began carefully. "Last night, our technical officer got you digital tools to protect your anonymity. The thumb drives we've handed out can be passed to anyone joining you in this work; they'll automatically clean your tabs of corporate surveillance programs, and get you connected to some basic apps for communication and self-defense. They will also introduce a small subroutine that vets individuals for corporate connections, so you can feel a little more secure; if we detect people infiltrating the organization with unsavory ties or strangely large bank accounts, the tabs will send alerts. Once someone is fully vetted, new subroutines will be unlocked that connect you to the entire suite of subroutines and apps." She drew a breath. "Our officer has also gotten you hooked up with a form of internet that the Corps can't track and don't control. For starters, you'll be able to speak freely there. And we've brought devices that you can use to keep your meetings and homes secure. These sound-wave modulation units work to mask the sounds in the room and overlay them with white noise and something inane; a talk about vids or sports, for example. We also have ported units we'll be giving out, which can plug into your cars and other devices. They find all the sound-detection tools that are used for surveillance and do the same masking trick on them. The 3-D printing instructions for these are part of the Good Trouble Bundle. They can be printed with a consumer rig." She drew a breath. Now for the hard part. "But we won't be giving out weapons. We're not going to be using weapons. Not anymore."

A rush of whispers scurried around the room. People shot each other panicky glances, cynical glances, terrified looks. Liza stood still, waiting it out.

"To explain this well, I need to divert this lesson a little bit and talk about history first. Raise your hand if you're okay with that."

The room was still, but Liza recognized this kind of mute tension. She ran her eyes over the sitting audience; looking people in the face, giving people her attention and her connection. This was what you did with scared new trainees who wanted to do their best and didn't know how.

"It's okay, everybody. Take a deep breath. I know you've been taking union chapter votes on a lot of things; voting with me isn't any different. I'm not in charge here: *you are.* I'm just a resource. When I ask you to raise your hands, it's because I want *you* to make the choices. I'm here to ask you what you want to learn, and then teach you." She smiled, holding up her empty hands. "I promise, I don't bite. Nothing bad will happen if you raise your hands. If you do, you're asking to learn about history and why it matters to the decision to stop using conventional warfare. If you don't, you're asking to continue the lesson plan according to what's written down. Nothing bad will happen if you vote for either of those things."

She let that sink in for a couple seconds. "Okay. So. Raise your hand if you'd like to hear the history behind the decision to try removing the power of the Corporations without guns."

Slowly, hands raised around the room. Liza counted. "Okay, so, more than half the room wants to hear this. With that in mind, I'm going to talk about it."

Turning off her screen, she relaxed into parade rest.

"In 2085, the Great Shutdown happened. So by the middle of the year, the Dissolution Riots were raging, and twelve corporations were consolidating power and beginning to create the Citizen Contracts to protect their investments. The American Army was mostly absorbed into EagleCorp and a rival security corporation that Eagle beat out and took over a few years later. But about twenty percent of the Army broke away back in those days, and they rallied around leaders who formed a National Democratic Defense Council. The first Council was really just a handful of generals sitting in a tent, talking. But it grew from there."

She tipped her chin up as she spoke, standing tall. "These people knew they were outgunned and outmanned, but they also knew they'd sworn an oath to defend the Constitution of the United States of America. And they were going to keep their word. They were the people who named my Force for what we were fighting for: the Democratic State Force.

"They tried to fight head on, at first. That's what you probably learned in school as the Ugly Eighties. Problem was, the Force members were up against the eighty percent of the Army who were standing with the Corps, and they didn't stand a chance. After their troops were massacred in a couple fights, they drew back and started planning. The intelligence folks in their ranks stepped up, and they started working quietly.

"For the next twenty years, the Force went to ground; using their contacts, getting the soldiers and their families resources to escape tightening Corporate controls, and finding ways to live that would leave them free to act. We lived as a resistance force in an occupied nation, scrounging and stealing supplies from the Corporations where we could. It's written into our code that we will never steal resources from the tables of individual citizens, but the news vids don't lie: we take what we need from the Corporate shipments directly on a pretty regular basis." There was an uncomfortable rustle at that, but Liza talked through it. "We built a network of people fighting for democracy across the nation, link by link and contact by contact. After twenty years, we were strong enough to start making actions. And that's when your grandparents started hearing about terrorists pretty often.

"We did a lot of covert work to erode, undermine and delegitimize the Corps. The problem is, we thought like soldiers, and we were up against plenty of people who know how soldiers think. The Corps just worked us right into the fabric of their control system. We never meant for that to happen, but that's what they did. They made us the bogeyman in the shadows. They made us the ones who would come and get you if you weren't good. We hate that trash, but it's been more than fifty years, and we're the third generation born in the Dust. I'm saying that because we're the generation that's looking back and understanding where the people that started the Force went wrong."

She took a sip of water. "If we keep on acting like a military Force, we'll be trapped in this forever war until... well, forever. And that doesn't get us what we're fighting for. That doesn't get us democracy, or human rights, or a safe place for our kids to sleep at night."

The crowd was hanging on her words. Hunh. Maybe she wasn't as bad at this as she thought.

"You guys have kids?" a very young teen asked. Liza smiled. "Yeah, we have plenty of kids born into Force families. There's four kids on my Base right now. I was born on the same base they're growing up on."

She raised her eyes from the teen's face. "This's the thing; we're not just soldiers anymore. We have ex-Corporate families in our ranks, from every Standing level and all seven of the Corporations. We have people from other countries in our ranks. And we're all just families trying to take care of our kids, and our parents, and our friends, whether we're out in the Dust or stuck in a warehouse. We're all just families. The Corps are trying to wall us off from one another, and for way too long, we let them do it. So now that we've figured it out, we're going to try something new. The Democratic State Force is going to try to become a security force *for* the people, nothing else. We want to get to the point where *you* call *us* when your life and liberty is at peril, and *we serve you.* That's what a 'security' force should really be about: making everyday people secure."

Tapping her tab, she brought up a new set of windows.

"To do that, we're going to try a method with a lot of research behind it. This method is twice as effective as violent campaigns. The research in the section marked 'Reasons for Resisting Without Violence' shows that a nonviolent campaign led to political change 53% of the time, compared to 26% for the violent protests. There's three hundred years of proof in there; three hundred years is a pretty solid test of a hypothesis, I think."

Her little joke got a few tiny chuckles, and that was really all she'd expected. It was definitely a start.

"Okay, so let's get into the material. Riviera Sun wrote a very solid study guide; we'll be using it as a framework, and going over the works of Srdja Popovic today as well. These are twenty-first century sources, but their advice works really well in our situations. If you can open the first file…"

It was amazing how the days after that speech flew by. Between them, Liza and Naomi walked the union members through what they needed to know. Together, the members learned about the Workers' Bill Of Rights that their Union leaders had crafted, and the principles of acting in concert. They started with phone trees, the panic buttons and rescue measures they'd be using, and contact triads, making sure that everyone had at least two other people checking on them after any given event. "This is something we're big on," Liza explained, "and we do this with all our on-grid operatives. Always check on each other. We never leave our people behind. Nobody just disappears."

After those first couple days, the union members started to really perk up and get into events. They handled a surprise confrontation really well, which was great given how shocked they were by it. Liza had them roleplay as they tried to think out how to engage other workers, bystanders, and the general public. She walked around the room, listening in on the conversations and getting pleasantly impressed by how well everyone was engaging.

"So, those were great talks," she offered, "but don't focus so big. Don't talk about freedom and democracy and human dignity; talk about things people get really engaged in. Like 'isn't it stupid that you can only walk into stores marked for your Standing?,' or 'why don't you get two days off in a row? Isn't that unfair? Don't you deserve a break?'"

Naomi was absolutely in her element when it was time to explain weapons and evasion methods for everything from tear gas and fear gas to being grabbed. She laid a few air mats on the floor as she spoke, letting them fill as she walked the room, showing various methods of wrist holds, pinching nerves, and how to take a blow without too much damage. She pointed out the largest man in the room half way through her talk. "Hey, bud, you up to roughhouse a little?'

The big teddy bear of a guy gave an awkward little smile. "I mean, sure, but I don't wanna hurt you…"

"Forget that, the Corps definitely want to hurt me, and I deal," Naomi stated flatly. "Come up here and grab me from behind, okay?"

Warily, the man did. Seconds later, Naomi had flipped him over her shoulder and laid him spread-eagled on the mat.

"And that, friends, we call ju-jitsu," she announced with a feral grin.

Seconds later, the union members were scrambling to stack chairs and lay out mats Naomi passed out, inflating them, eager to learn. For the rest of the day, the room was full of laughter and the sounds of backs thwacking into mats.

It wasn't all fun and games of course; they talked the union through some courses on first aid and how to handle bones or skulls broken by Peacekeepers, what to do about fear gas, tear gas, and people hit with batons. They described the exact steps that would happen to arrestees. If anything, it calmed the union down. And that made sense; after all, it was what you didn't know that scared you to death.

Liza could hardly believe it when her seventh day with the warehouse workers' union came. She grinned at the room full of participants. "You've done great things. You've got the tools to get started, and to teach others. So today, let's take a break from the training and do some democracy in action. Your Union leaders have come up with a set of actions. Every chapter of every Union is going to vote on what they're comfortable participating in, all across the country. Let's get involved." Tapping her tab, she brought up the list, each action displayed with a description and a bar beside it.

"If you open your Common Ground app and click 'votes', you'll see this section. Let's talk about the options you're comfortable participating in. The voting is anonymized and blockchained; the only point is to make sure nobody votes more than once." She pointed up at the screen. "Our current objective is to get everyone of every Standing an eight-hour, five-day work week, paid overtime, a list of workers' rights they're entitled to, and paid time off. And—"

"I thought it was to take down the Zon?" someone called. Liza nodded. "It is, eventually. But this is the first step. We have to start winning victories, one after another. And every time we win, it'll be easier to win the next time. Remember the pillars?" she switched screens, bringing up an image of a CEO standing on top of what looked like a Greek temple. "The point of these actions is to start pulling the pillars of support out from under the Corps. Those pillars are big, and they're heavy. Right now, we just have to get them to shift. But eventually..." she flipped to the next picture, which showed the CEO falling from his perch as the pillars crumbled. That image got a bit of clapping, and even a few whoops.

Smiling, she flipped back to the voting screen. "Okay, so, these are the actions. You'll see that they're broken into Loud and Quiet. If you've got reasons to avoid Loud situations, you're a great candidate for the Quiet actions. And if you get an idea, there's a section to submit them. They'll be added to the National list of possible actions and become part of the vote."

"Really?" an older lady with the bent look of someone who'd been beat down too long asked.

Liza nodded. "Really." She tapped the holographic screen, enlarging it in the air. "So, there's a lot to choose from. You could paint 'Good Trouble' on walls, anywhere people will see it. You could vote to start a general strike. That would mean you'd stay home and refuse to provide your work; it's a great way to show the Corporation that they are nothing without your labor, and they ought to act like it. You could vote to work together on the Move Slow, Break Stuff campaign. The point here is to slow your work down as a group, lose orders and paperwork, and generally act like you've lost your energy. Anytime a manager gives you crap, explain that you're tired and hungry and need a break. The key here is that the managers have to get the same exact answer from every person they try to yell at. If blocs of workers do this together, it can succeed. And there's these other, more public stunts too."

She moved her pointer down the list. "For quieter movements, you could put up Walk In My Shoes displays. Get a bunch of old pairs of shoes, type up labels with the stories about people who have gotten the short end of the stick, been worked to death, been denied medical aid, whatever really sticks with you and breaks your heart. Label each pair of shoes with a story. Day by day, everybody leaves a pair on a street corner, at the top of a set of stairs, or somewhere else really showy. We want to drive home that this stuff impacts people.

"For people interested in gardening, we can get you hooked up with unpatented food seeds and security measures to protect your garden.

"And perhaps most importantly, you folks have the chance to create an open facility where anyone can get food, get them set up with Common

Ground, secure their tech, and receive vaccines against MACHA, DARA and BEAST. And here's the thing: there won't be any checks on Citizen Standing. This will be a free space, a Common Ground space. If that's what you vote on, we will get you the resources to build it. But you have to man it. And you have to move it regularly, and make sure people know where it's moving to." She turned her eyes to the crowd. "These are things that are being voted on and put to work across the country. But I can't choose for you which ones you're going to do. That's up to you. It's your vote."

For the longest time, the attendees stared at her in tentative awe, fingers hovering over their tabs. Then, the screen registered a vote. And another, and another, and another. Excited murmuring went up around the room.

"C-can I put something up for a v-vote?"

Liza blinked. "Uh, sure Tweak. What is it?"

The little coder held out her hand. "See this?" In her hand was a tiny white sticker, with some kind of emblem. At first glance, it looked like a Citizen Standing logo... but no, it was a blue bird, rising above the silhouette of a strand of barbed wire.

"Take a picture," Tweak suggested. Warily, Liza shifted her tab, and did as Tweak said. The emblem turned up on her screen.

"Click the pic," Tweak offered, grinning. Liza gave her a look that she hoped the little coder read as 'you better not be making fools of us both', but she did it.

A window popped up, showing a loading bar. 'Loading Freedom.exe,' her tab remarked pleasantly. Then a red X flashed across the screen. "Error," the tab's modulated voice bleated, in time with the flashing words on the screen. "Problem loading Freedom.exe. Please uninstall Corporate Control.exe and try again."

The whole room burst out laughing, and Liza right along with them. "What the...how did you..."

"It's a QR code, encodes a little pop-up that hides itself in the boot s-sequence." Tweak replied, bouncing on her toes and grinning like a cat. "It'll s-stick around for a m-month on any s-system, then delete itself. You g-guys c-can't get in trouble for t-taking a p-picture of a s-sticker, yeah?"

"Yeah!" the crowd agreed in a cheer. "We could put it on the system computer at the work station!" someone crowed, and that got an even bigger cheer. "We could put it in messages and send it all over!" someone else enthused, and that got applause and whoops of encouragement.

"Pattern's in the b-bundle. Prints on n-normal agar-plastic." Tweak remarked with a shrug. "Have fun!"

They left the hidden gathering on a high note that night. "I love the trick," Naomi offered, examining one of the little blue and white stickers as they took turns scrubbing off the synth they were using, putting on a new genetic identity, and changing their clothes as they prepped to move on. "And they did too, that's for sure."

"Yep!" Tweak agreed, still bouncing. "That was easy. Hey, hey, m-maybe it's gonna be easy after all!"

Looking up, Naomi made a face. "Kid, cross your fingers when you say stuff like that. You're gonna jinx us."

Event File 07
File Tag: Recruitment Friction
24:30-08-2-2160 / 15:00-08-3-2160

"So we're trying this after all?" Naomi asked, walking easy at Tweak's side down the crowded club-strip.

Tweak nodded tightly, hands stuffed in her pockets. "Said I would. So I'm gonna." No way she was going back on her word. But if she was real, she was regretting everything about this deal she'd made. This was *so* asking for trouble.

Sleazy ads and slinky music oozed out of clubs, coating them like grease. Tweak flexed her fingers around the knuckle duster in her pocket, giving anyone who dared to glance at her a blank stare until they backed down. She'd always avoided the Five Points. She *hated* slimy meat markets like this. Places that sold bodies like they were junk food played on the same marketing that junk-food subsidiaries of AgCo did. When it was sex and bodies they were selling, it bugged her. It was that kind of thinking that let people treat each other like shit. It was that kind of thinking that let them do the math on messing up people's genetics.

Well, no choice this time. She was going to suck it up, get in, talk to this lady, and get out. It was the only thing to do. She'd made a promise. And she didn't go back on that.

Another pissy thought crossed her mind as she watched holos of naked people dance in a window. Liza was going to throw a total fit when they came back to the room coated in who-knew-what from being down here. They'd left the personnel officer back in the room prepping for her next week of teaching, and now Tweak wished they'd all stayed up there. This place was gross. She was definitely going to change her bandages when she got back. And scrub her coat, maybe.

"This's the address." Naomi tipped her chin at a building painted in garish purple neon.

The music inside was a heavy base beat that made the air throb. On stage, a woman was swinging around a pole upside down, her long hair tumbling like a waterfall of ink. Naomi gave a sigh. "Performance art. The file said 'performance artist.' Annnnd it just has to be stripping."

Tweak tipped her head. "It bothers you?"

"A bunch of hooting, horny dickweeds who show up at the kinds of places putting on strip shows is what bothers me," Naomi replied, shrugging. "I hate the way people treat each other in these places. The customers and the workers, they look at each other like things. So yeah, anyway," she continued, nodding at the stage. "Info says the woman you want lives upstairs. Look for a stairway or something."

It took them ten minutes to find the narrow stairway in the back and bribe their way past the single guard keeping people off the stairs. The second floor of the club was barely quieter than the dance floor, but it was better lit. Three doors lined the hall, each with a name plaque on it.

"We're looking for Circe. She owns this place." Naomi murmured, eyes narrowed. "Legal name changed to Circe Dare from Mercy Otieno. Okay, Tweak, let me scope and—"

"Oh for chrissakes." Pushing past her, Tweak knocked on the door marked 'Circe'.

"I told you not to interrupt me while the club was open." The voice was smooth and cool, but there was an edge on it. The door swung open to reveal a slender Black woman with a long face and a red chemise Tweak could see right through. A puff of some perfume that made Tweak's nose itch rolled out to enfold her.

The dark woman stared at them, nonplussed for a minute. A slow smile spread across her face. "And what's all this? Are we into threesomes?"

Naomi just blinked.

Tweak looked up at the tall woman. "This's business. Good deal. Could make you cash. We come in?"

"Don't do business in my bedroom," Circe responded, switching gears smoothly. She leaned against the doorjamb, showing herself off with every breath.

"You like talking about stuff in the hall? Stuff that gets you in deep?" Tweak demanded sharply.

"If we could find a place that might be a little less public, then—" Naomi began, but Tweak interrupted, her eyes still on the woman's.

"Blacklist stuff?"

Circe's eyes widened. For a moment, fear flashed across her face. About time. Tweak didn't have the patience to play word games.

Circe swept her long braids off her shoulder. "I've got an office downstairs. I'll join you there in five minutes." The door swung shut on another wave of that perfume. Tweak rubbed the back of her hand across her nose.

"Wow, she's hot," Naomi muttered. Tweak blinked, glancing up at her buddy. Since when did Naomi care about hotness?

The blond woman was staring, her eyes a little unfocused. She blinked, swallowed hard and glanced down. "And you just freaked her out, Tweak."

Tweak shrugged, feeling prickles of frustration running under her skin. "Gets the job done."

The office was actually nice inside, plush. One of the cocktail waitresses brought them neon-colored martinis as they settled into the dark leather chairs, Tweak tucking a sound box under her chair.

A few minutes later, Circe slipped into the office dressed in a red skirt-suit, her braids pulled back in a high ponytail. She sat smoothly behind her desk and steepled her fingers together. Even in business clothes, she moved like a model on a catwalk.

Tweak shot a look at Naomi, who was acting weird. She kept swallowing hard and fidgeting.

"Now," Circe said, her voice strong and crisp, "What was this about business? How'd you get ahold of the Blacklist?"

"That was m-me." Tweak chirped. She thrust out a hand before she could chicken out. "Hacker, me. Figured I needed a copy, before I wiped it. And the Citizen Ratings. I w-wiped it all. You getting less trouble since then?"

Circe turned her deep brown eyes on Tweak for a moment, but she didn't touch Tweak's hand. Tweak knew it was supposed to be an insult, but it was a relief all the same.

"Yeah. I owe you one," the woman stated, every word grudged. "What do you want?"

"Long story." Tweak stated. "Short story is, help. For us. Dusters. Good people out there. Me, I'm on that list too. That Blacklist. But out with them, I'm a p-p-p-person. Straight up truth. Thing is, Corps have s-started using bio-weapons. MACHA. DARA. BEAST. Been hearing about it?"

"Plenty," the swanky lady agreed, sounding like she didn't like this talk much.

"Great," Tweak went on. "Those bugs? They're evil. But us, we can stop it. Something in our blood kills the b-b-bugs. So, Force wants to see more Gamma DNA. And they trade. For a blood sample, money. G-good money. Or we can g-get you off the g-g-Grid. Out of here." She smiled. "You get loose, and you s-save lives. Inter-r-rested?"

"Not a bit," Circe replied mildly, sitting back in her chair. "No offense, kid, but I don't have anything to do with the Dusters. Thanks for taking the Blacklist down, but I think we're done here."

Naomi leaned forward. "We don't have to be. I mean... can we talk?"

Circe turned to the pale woman with a smile that Tweak really didn't like. It looked hungry. "Oh, yeah? What're you asking, hot stuff?"

And Naomi grinned. She actually grinned, goofy as anything.

Tweak's eyes narrowed. She studied Circe for a moment. Then she leaned over and smacked Naomi across the back of the head. "Hey. Wake up." She shot an irritable glance at Circe. "Pherom-m-mones, yeah? C-covered with all that p-perfume. And you didn't w-warn us. Not. Cool. Dick m-move."

Circe snorted, giving Tweak a look like she was dog shit on her shoe. "I'm not going to out myself if I can help it. And I owe you people nothing. We have no contract. Now, was there anything else, or can I get on with my night?"

"Even a blood sample would be useful." Naomi put in, trying a little smile. Yep, it was official. She was on a chemical high. "It'd help a lot of people... please?"

No wonder this bitch could get to the place where she owned a club, if she could even make *Naomi* get all goofy for her. That was just plain creepy.

"No offense," Circe sighed, leaning back in her seat and showing off one gorgeous leg, "but I'm not really in the business of helping everyone who drops by with a sob story." She leaned back in her chair, looking down her nose at them both. "In here, we may be renting our looks by the hour, but we do it on our terms. I'm not selling my talents or my boys and girls wholesale; not to the chop shops, not to the work stations of a factory or an office. And not to people like *you*. I'm not a germ line to be experimented on. I take care of my girls and boys, and that's more than enough for me."

"You could be doing something a lot more." Naomi pleaded. Actually pleaded. "You could be helping to save our country. Our world, for that matter."

Circe snorted. "Just like you Dusters to be dramatic to try and get someone to help you. I said no. You're not one of my people; I don't owe you anything. And I would really like it if you left my club."

Naomi opened her mouth, but Tweak grabbed her sleeve and tugged. Her buddy had been embarrassed enough. "Omi. Cut it out. This one? I get her. Doesn't do anything that doesn't get her something. Don't give a shit about anyone else. Forget her." Pushing herself back, she stood, tugging her taller friend's sleeve. "Done here."

The hot, throbbing street wasn't exactly a great place to clear your head, but Naomi started coming back around after a couple lungfuls of air outside the club. When she growled and hissed "that *bitch*!", Tweak knew the pheromones had worn off. She nodded. "Yeah. Knew a girl like that in j-jail. Real p-piece of w-work. Could turn anybody on. Traded it. You ok?"

Naomi ran both hands through her hair. "Uh... I guess? I mean I'm shook, but yeah... still, that fucking *bitch*..."

Tweak shrugged. "She c-can't help it. Makes pherem-mones."

"Yeah, but she doesn't have to play on it!" Naomi grumbled. She sighed. "Okay. Okay. Now what?"

"The room," Tweak replied, shrugging. "N-nothing else to do."

"How'd it go?" Liza asked as they stepped inside their safe-room.

"L-like shit," Tweak muttered. She was glad she'd hacked in and turned off the room's TV before they'd left. Her ears hurt, and it was good to be somewhere quiet.

"You can say that again. That sucked." Naomi remarked, sitting down and pulling her few necessities from her pockets; pocket toothbrush, folding comb and deodorizing wipes. "Bitch," she added under her breath.

"What happened?" Liza asked, standing. "Are you two—"

"Yeah, we're fine," Naomi reassured before Liza could get started on freaking. "The Gamma bitch had a pheromone trick that made her pretty much impossible to look away from, and I ended up looking like a complete dipshit, but hey, that's life. Tweak had my back, like always."

"Yeah," Tweak agreed for the look of it. But it hadn't been like always, had it? She'd been just like Circe a couple years back. She'd been a Gamma bitch too. Give nothing to anybody, keep what's yours, take what you can. Yeah, that was how you survived. And she would have done exactly what Circe had.

She was no better than that.

"Got a plan for the next try?"

Naomi's voice made her jump what felt like a foot. She looked up into two sets of startled eyes.

"Tweak?" Liza asked carefully. Tweak gave herself a shake. "Yeah, sorry. Plan? There's five g-Gammas in a travel r-radius of here. Least, there were. If the addresses still work. So..." she shrugged. "I guess we just go down the list." Dropping onto the bed, she glanced at Liza. "How 'bout you? Plans r-ready?"

"I think so," Liza agreed carefully, switching off her tab. Sighing, she lay back on the bed. "I hope so, anyway."

Tweak smiled bleakly. "I hear that."

Naomi kept an eye on Tweak the next day. The night before had deflated their little coder a bit; some of that dynamite spark was missing when they left her with all the tech for this TechoCo Writer's Union chapter. Heading down four concrete sets of stairs after their guide, they stepped behind a shelf full of cleaning supplies and into a room where the brickwork was an awful lot older. Probably a forgotten cellar, Naomi guessed. It hadn't been opened all that long either, based on the damp-concrete smell of the room.

All sorts of TechoCo types were sitting huddled in their chairs, watching with wary eyes as Liza was introduced by their chapter president. Naomi chose a spot to lounge against the wall, and gave what she had for a friendly smile every time one of the desk jockeys shot a nervy look her way. They had good reason to be on edge; after all, it was their union chapter that had gotten cracked down on so hard, not that long ago. They'd probably seen some friends go down under the batons on the vids. Not fun.

Liza got them all going with her talk about their rights, and someone raised her hand. "So... what rights are we talking about?"

"I'm glad you asked," Liza smiled at the woman. "Let's talk them over." Clearing her throat, she pulled up the statement, letting the screen hang in the air for everyone to read with her. "The Union heads have worked together to write a statement everyone will be using, if you and the other Unions vote to approve it. Here's how it goes right now:

"We, the members of your workforce, respectfully require that the following Workers' Bill Of Rights be instituted.

"One: Employees will be treated with honesty and respect.

Our workplaces must be free of verbal abuse, threats, sabotage, and bullying. Our jobs should maximize the fulfillment and development of the people doing them and should minimize drudgery. Employers that make promises to their employees about pay, benefits, promotions, and responsibilities must honor those promises.

"Two: Working full-time should guarantee a basic standard of living.

People who work 40-plus hours a week must be able to afford safe and comfortable housing, nutritious food, adequate clothing, quality health care, retirement security, education, reliable transportation, and at least some leisure activities and savings at any Citizen Standing.

"Three: Working people should be able to afford healthcare for themselves and their families.

Every individual under contract with a Corporation should have full and comprehensive healthcare to allow them to continue a fulfilling, healthy, and productive life. Denying or withholding these rights cannot be permitted.

"Four: Working people of all Standings should be able to retire.

Employees, no matter their Standing, should be paid enough that they can afford to save for and enjoy retirement. Companies that defer some of their employees' compensation in the form of pensions must honor those obligations.

"Five: Employees have the right to leave a job with dignity.

We must abolish the tyranny of supervisors and employers over the lives of their workers. When firings or layoffs are justified, they must be carried out with as much notice, dignity, and support as possible. Housing must be decoupled from the status of Corporate contracts and Citizen Standing. Petitions to move from one Corporation to another must become accessible to all. Meaningful job training, career counseling, severance pay and benefits, and unemployment insurance must be available to all who need them.

"Six: Every workplace should be as safe as possible.

Having a job shouldn't be a matter of life or death. Employees must be provided with any and all protective equipment and training required to minimize their chances of getting hurt or sick on the job. Enforcement of health and safety laws must ensure that it costs more to break the law than to follow it, and employers that willfully put profits before people must be punished. Those employees who still get hurt or sick, even with the best precautions, deserve adequate workers' compensation.

"Seven: There is more to life than work.

Our entire society is better off when people are able to spend time with their families, be active in their communities, and participate as citizens. Businesses that encourage their employees' lives away from work find that those employees are more productive, more satisfied, and more loyal. Employers should have no control over their employees' time off-the-clock; they should respect the privacy and autonomy of their employees.

"Eight: Employees are entitled to work together.

For those workers who wish to pursue traditional union organizing ingrained in this country's history, or other collective action, employers must continue to honor that established right.

"And finally, Nine: employees should be able to stand up for their rights.

Employees should never be afraid to stand up for their rights or face punishment because they have done so. Employers should not be able to force employees to give up their rights to get or keep a job. Employees need fair and accessible means to pursue justice when their rights are violated."

You could have heard a pin drop in the room.

"How *do* we get them to give us *all that*?" Someone quavered.

Liza cracked a wry grin. "Well, that's where tactics come in."

She was pretty well into her shtick about the big public actions they could vote to participate in, when a big guy started heckling her about why they weren't getting guns. Liza handled it pretty well, explaining all the research, but the guy wasn't having it. He got out of his chair, right on cue, and took a couple steps towards Liza, ranting about 'you don't get to tell us to be nonviolent when you people have been blowing up the country for decades, if you want us to fight you better arm us'.

That was when Naomi decided it was time to step in. She sauntered to the front of the room, hands in her pockets, and put herself between the beefy guy and her basemate.

"Okay buddy, show's over. Take a seat."

"You think you're going to intimidate me, do you?" the guy demanded, trying that looming thing that guys always thought they were good at. One or two people were saying quiet things about 'isn't that enough?' in the back, but nobody was doing much.

"Dave, this isn't any help," one of the man's coworkers suggested, but when he turned and growled 'keep out of it' she wilted.

"Look," Naomi stated calmly, "move back, or I'm moving you."

"Oh, now you're gonna get tough and move me? What happened to nonviolence now?" the man in front of her taunted. He stepped in. Naomi put her cybernetic hand in the middle of his chest, grabbed a fistful of shirt and lifted him off the ground. Her servos strained, but her arm was good for it.

"Last chance," she stated, ice cold. Someone in the crowd whimpered.

And Liza clapped her hands. "Okay, okay. Everybody relax. Thanks Dave, Naomi."

Over her head, Dave grinned and waved at Liza. Naomi set her fellow Grid operative on his feet and gave him a quick side-armed hug that he returned, both of them chuckling. "Nice acting," she offered. He grinned. "Nice lifting, you been working out?"

"Stick working out up your ass, I'm always this tough," Naomi laughed.

Grinning, Dave turned and opened his arms to the coworkers who thought they knew him. "Okay everybody, relax. What you just saw was a surprise confrontation roleplay. Sorry I told you off, Ellise. We gotta get used to surprise confrontation, because we're gonna go up against it out there. And this's the thing: you're gonna learn how to react if somebody starts razzing, starts throwing their weight around and making trouble. Because dollars to donuts, we're gonna have people try to join us just to burn shit down."

"And worse, you're going to have agents provocateurs; plain clothes members of EagleCorp, contractors, and basic paid thugs coming in looking like everyday people," Liza picked up the thread smooth as butter. "That's why I schedule a random confrontation for every training. So, let's workshop what you could have done as bystanders, how you could intervene to de-escalate the situation, and what actions it makes sense to take to protect your friends while staying nonviolent."

Once the union realized that the thing was a game and they were invited to play, they really got into it, and the roleplay went great from there. Naomi nodded to herself. Liza hadn't been sure that doing this on Day One was great, but it turned out that she had read the group right; they were ready to get things going. They weren't as tentative as ZonCom's union. They'd already been in the fire.

Naomi settled back into her slouch against the wall as the group went over assigning someone to record altercations on the spot, de-escalation tactics and basic personal defense, and she got on with her job; watching the exits and listening for any trouble. All she heard was the usual. She checked her tab regularly for any alerts from the security Tweak had helped her set up around the building perimeter, but it looked like they were in the clear.

They let the Union members file out in ones and twos to get their tech from Tweak and head out through the building's five exits. Eventually, Liza and Naomi headed up themselves. "Not too bad," Naomi offered with a smile. "This stuff is coming out really well, Liza. You got a knack for it."

"You think so?" The dark-haired woman asked, biting her lip. "Think I scared them off?"

"Are you kidding? The way they were interacting, I think what you did was get them to sit up and pay attention. And that—"

"Hahaha dead! You're d-dead!" Tweak cackled from her little tech station down the hall.

Naomi glanced at Liza. "Any guesses?"

"With her, no clue," Liza replied patiently. "We'll find out."

"Fry!" Tweak was crowing when they stepped into the repurposed cleaning closet she was sitting in. She glanced up, grinning like a kid. "Two secs. Gotta finish the l-level."

"Sounds like some game," Naomi observed, leaning against the wall and watching the younger girl do her thing.

Tweak bounced to her feet. "Omi, g-gotta see! Lookit lookit

lookit!"

"Chill, Gurgi, breathe!" she laughed, and the kid really did look like the cartoon character she'd gotten nicknamed for, hair flopping as she bounced. It was kind of incredible how cute Tweak could be once she took the armor off around you and let you see her kid side. You wanted to buy her ice cream and kill anyone who'd ever hurt her when she looked up at you with laughing eyes.

"Lookit!" Tweak enthused, shoving the tab into Naomi's hands.

On the screen, a big black bird was... yeah, he was electrocuting a cartoon of Bob Walton, CEO of ArgusCo. The fat little caricature did a ridiculous dance, all his bones outlined every time the lightning struck.

"Oh my god!" Naomi laughed, "what is this?!"

"D-deniki and the First Nation c-coders! Made a game! 'S called Raven's Revenge!" Tweak's laugh pealed around the room. "They want us to start passing it out. Get people l-laughing at the Corps, not s-scared. Fun! You get to use l-lightning to get rid of toxic d-dumps, d-drones, p-peacekeeping stations, and you p-plant trees and flowers, and when you do a level you get to c-chase CEOs around and *fry* them with l-lightning! We play together in a bit, kay?"

"Okay then," Naomi agreed, laughing at the kid's antics. Tweak was absolutely in love with her new toy, and it was adorable. She wouldn't stop playing it all the way down the hall. Even out in the street, she went on electrocuting little cartoon CEOs with delighted whispers of 'yes, fry!' and 'gotcha!'

Liza was giving the kid the eye, but Naomi let her have her fun; after all, plenty of people played on their tabs in the streets. It actually made their group look more like part of the crowd. And Naomi knew that she could keep an eye out for all of them. Besides, Tweak didn't have fun very often.

A Peacekeeper was starting to look their way, and Naomi watched him carefully as he did his little patrol of the open-air shopping area they were passing through. Finally, he was out of sight. Naomi had just started to turn, when Tweak gave a little kitten-squeak of outrage.

"B-bastard! Gimme!"

A scrawny guy danced back with Tweak's tab in his hand, his lip split and dribbling blood. "Too slow," the man replied as if she hadn't hit him at all, grinning as he dangled Tweak's tab over her head. Turning, he took off through   the   crowd.

With a snarl, Tweak went right after him.

"Tweak! Don't!" Naomi called. Shit. This was all going south faster than a bullet train. She turned to Liza. "I'll go after her, go back to the safehouse, okay? I'll meet you there once I wrangle her."

The personnel officer nodded sharply. "Good luck." Turning, she walked away. At least one person in this team wasn't crazy.

On the other hand, one person in this team was an absolute batshit bonehead who was probably going to get herself killed.

Naomi didn't run after Tweak. She knew better than to run. Running people got tracked on cameras. But she did move fast.

For the next hour, she tromped the streets, looking for the little idiot. She must have pinged Tweak's tab a hundred times. No answer.

Finally, hot, thirsty and pissed, she headed back to their room. Screw it. It was too hot to be schlepping around the streets. They'd agreed on the hotel room as a meetup location in case of separation or tech failure, and a backup at a local statue. The little nutcase had probably gotten her tab back and headed to their room without thinking about how her stunt had affected anyone else. Typical.

She was angry enough that she didn't wait to get cleaned up before she ripped into Tweak. She just shut the door and made sure the room was secure. "Tweak, if you ever do something that stupid again—" she started before she even turned around.

"You found her?" Liza asked, standing from her perch on the bed. Naomi looked around the room.

The girl wasn't here. She hadn't come back.

She leaned against the wall, and let her eyes close. The exhaustion washed over her. The frustration. And then came dread. She smacked the wall behind her.

"Fuck. We fucking lost Tweak. Fuck!"

Event File 08
File Tag: Reclamation
14:10-08-3-2160

Tweak snarled and launched herself after the bastard who'd snagged her tab. *Nobody* took what was hers. She was faster than any damned Alpha pickpocket. She'd catch him, and she'd show him.

He was faster than she expected. That dark body was already out of sight. She only kept up by looking for the drops of blood from his split lip on the concrete, but that wouldn't work for long.

Skidding into an alley, she vaulted for a fire escape, and made it onto the roof's maintenance catwalks. She peered down into the streets she could see from her perch, spotted the running body, and took off, shadowing him from above. Sure she had to scramble in one or two spots, but no big deal. Hopping roofs made the tracking a lot easier than the street did.

The thief was slick. He was quick. But he wasn't so smart. She waited until he stopped to catch his breath in an empty alleyway, the white outlines of feather tattoos shining dimly on his arms. Quiet as she could, she scrambled down the fire escape, timed it, waited for her moment…. and leaped down, bowling the thief to the ground and raining punches as she straddled him. "Give. It. Back. Or. I. Take. Out. Your. TEETH!" she spat, grabbing a fistful of his blue hair.

Something beeped as she did, and the air fizzled. Tweak froze, fist raised, and stared.

The slim Black man under her didn't have blue hair; that had been a holo image. But he did have ears like nothing she'd ever seen.

On second thought, she had seen those kind of ears in vids, on deer and llamas. But these were hairless, as dark as the rest of the guy. And they were sinking down to press against the sides of his head and throat, the way a dog's ears went down when they were in trouble.

"Fuck," the guy whispered. Grunting irritably, he squirmed and shoved at her. "Beat me up, fine, just let me cover!"

He squirmed until he could work one hand up to touch the silver circle implanted in his neck, just under his ear. "Look, I'll give you your tab back and all the cash I got," he panted. "You can even take another shot at breaking my face if you want. Just don't tell nobody."

"Holy shit." Tweak breathed. Another Gamma. She'd been trying to reach people for weeks, and here another Gamma just dropped into her lap. Okay, maybe she dropped into his, but still.

"Okay. Chill. N-not gonna beat you n-no more. I'm going to let you up. Don't run. You and me, we got something to t-t-t-talk about."

"What, the fact I just jacked your tab?" the man asked with as much sarcasm as he could scrape together, but Tweak could hear it when his voice shook a little. She knew the sound of that fear.

"Nope," Tweak corrected. "More like a list we're both on. A b-black list?"

The guy's eyes widened a little. He looked Tweak up and down as best he could, from his spot pinned to the concrete. It had to be pretty easy to work out now that she'd said it; her arms were wrapped in bandages from the shoulder down. Most Alphas couldn't keep up with a healthy, running Gamma, but she'd done it like it was nothing. If that didn't tell him she was telling the truth, nothing would.

"Yeah... sure," the guy she was sitting on agreed, sounding dazed.

"I mean it," Tweak repeated. "Don't run. Wanna talk. Sides..." she gave him a grin. "Gotta fix your holo. Can probably do it here. Five minutes. Gonna let you up now..."

Warily, she released her hold, sliding off.

The thief sat up and scrubbed his fingers through his hair. He wiped his nose, making a face at the blood that came away on his fingers. "You break my holo *and* my nose? Dammit."

Tweak blinked. "You just noticed? I cracked you good. When I punch people, they notice."

The guy shrugged uncomfortably. "I got a thing. Is it really fucking broken?" He pushed at his nose, harder than most people would have, wiggling it from side to side. "Nah. Just bleeding. Good. Can't afford another hospital."

Tweak winced. "Fuck, you got balls... Anyway, turn your head. Lemme see the holo. Name's Tweak, m-mech and tech. Dumb move, by the way," she added, peering at the thumbnail-sized button below one ear. This close, she could see the little fizzle in the air that gave the illusion of light away. "Cameras gonna catch you some d-d-d-day, you keep stealing. Happened to me once, I t-t-t-tried this shit."

The guy snorted at that. "No one cares any more. Not since the Blacklist and the Citizen Ratings keeled over. These days, they gotta catch me if they wanna arrest me."

Tweak didn't bother saying anything to that. "This holo's good stuff," she murmured, checking its casing. "But you never m-maintain it."

The stranger gave her the side-eye. Was that a pissed look, or just annoyed? She listened to his tone of voice; that was easier to parse than his face. When he spoke, he just sounded tired.

"You think I can afford that? 'Sides, it's still working. And it's better than handkerchiefs and shit. Not much'll hide my stupid ears."

Tweak didn't say anything to that. After all, he wasn't wrong. She pulled a roll of micro-utility tools from her jacket pocket, and lifted out the micro-electrometer. "It's got a short. It shorted when I hit y-you."

"Yeah? Tried not hitting people?" The dumbass threw out. Tweak took the casing off the holo-emitter as she shot that down.

"F-fuck you, you s-stole from m-me."

He shifted under her fingers, shrugging. "Point."

Carefully, she worked her tools into the wiring in the man's throat. "Want some cash? I got something going. Better money than s-stealing. Hold still. Gonna find the wire that's s-shorting. This can hurt. Where's the b-battery?"

"My heart. Got it hard-wired in," her companion replied. Tweak froze. "Are. You. Fucking. C-crazy? What if it shorts *at that end* and the el-lectricity s-stops your heart?"

The guy shrugged. "Hey, they see my ears, I'll die *for sure*. Power source's more stable this way. Can't afford the thing crapping out on me."

"Stupid!" Tweak snapped. "This setup's stupid, and s-s-stealing with a j-janky holo w-w-wired to your heart? Even s-s-stupider! I said. Hold still. Tip your head. Lemme get a good l-look. You can do b-better'n this shit, asshat."

"Yeah? Better'n stealing? Try me," the guy retorted, tipping his head to let her work on his holo. "I tried every damn gig on the planet, and I got kicked out soon as they learned what I was. Name's Inyoni, by the way. Friends call me Bird. This gonna take much time? I don't wanna sit down here all day."

"Whiner," Tweak shot back, fiddling. Then she grinned, and tapped the little device's casing back into place. "There. Good." she chirped, sitting back.

"Thanks." Inyoni straightened his head. For a moment, they stared at one another.

"I got some friends." Tweak stated after a breath. She had to say it now, before he ran off or she chickened out. "Need extra hands. Get you cash. Wanna talk terms? Buy you lunch."

Inyoni hesitated a moment, considering. Then he nodded. Tweak could almost see the thought behind his eyes: a free lunch was a free lunch.

"Yeah… sure." The man darted his eyes between her and the ground. "But don't… your friends, don't tell them about my ears, okay?"

Tweak flashed a smile. "Won't matter. C'mon."

She turned away, but turned back and held out her hands. "One thing. My tab. Give. It. Back."

With a sheepish little smile, the man pulled her tab out of his jacket pocket and passed it over. "Sorry girl, if I'da known, I woulda left you alone and gone after a norm."

"Yeah well," Tweak shrugged. "But hey. I got a name. Tweak. Use it. Come on, lunch."

The CAS café Tweak found did decent Chinese food; more importantly, they left you alone in the booths, and there weren't any dynamic pop-up ads in the walls or the tables; just some stationary stuff hanging up that could be ignored, and the news playing in the background. Tweak grabbed her seat and pulled the holographic menu up out of the table. "Pick stuff. Gotta m-message my friends. N-need to tell them where I am."

Naomi had blown up her tab with messages, moving pretty fast from worried to straight up pissed. You'd think she'd chill. Tweak wasn't a baby. She could handle herself on the Grid.

She tapped out an answer.

> **Message Handle: DeuceOfDiamonds**
> **Message: Hey. I'm fine. Meet me here. Got somebody you want to meet. Wants to come in out of the storm.**

She put in the address of the restaurant, and stuck her tab in her pocket. "So, lunch. Whatcha getting?"

"How much cash you got?" Inyoni asked, eyes riveted on the menu. She guessed he hadn't eaten in a while. Even Gammas got hungry if you didn't feed them.

"Plenty," she offered. "Order anything."

Inyoni tore his eyes away from the menu to stare at her. She glanced away, his eyes too much to handle.

"Wow. Seriously?" His voice asked.

Tweak shrugged. "Yeah. Sure."

"Okay then." The excitement in his tone made her smile. He had to be hungry.

She ordered egg-drop soup and baozi with a side of mochi, and put her fake card through the system. Once that was done, she glanced at her companion, sizing him up. She put her card into the dispenser and bought a dollar's worth of napkins. Pulling them out, she thrust them at Inyoni.

"Your lip. Bleeding."

Inyoni glanced at her guiltily. His left eye was starting to swell, and he looked like he was trying to check his teeth with his tongue to see if any were loose. "Thanks," he mumbled, taking them and dabbing at his face. "Anywhere else bleeding? Any cuts?"

Tweak blinked. "Can't you t-tell?"

Inyoni glanced at her quick, put a finger over his lips. She nodded. "Sorry."

"S'cool," he mumbled through the napkin, shrugging.

Tweak stared at the man across from her, until the silence started feeling weird.

"So... what's with Bird?" She asked, gesturing at the tattooed lines of feathers showing white down the dark skin of his arms. "Tattoos, nickname. What gives?"

Inyoni shrugged. "'S'what my name means, in Zulu."

"Where's that?" Tweak asked, tipping her head.

Her companion gave another shrug. He did that a lot. "Somewhere in Africa, from what I hear. Couldn't point at it on a map, but my mom was from there," he offered. Their food arrived, and he dug into his plate of bouncy chicken with a fork. The cheaper kinds of vat-meat were always a little rubbery, but when you fried it up in Chinese food it was pretty good. And it was affordable; natural-born meat was priced for CES types. Tweak unwrapped her chopsticks, wondering how out of practice she was these days. Turned out she could still hold them just fine. She started on her soup, watching the guy across from her chow down. His lip had come open again, and blood dribbled down his chin as he ate. She wondered if she should say something. That had to hurt.

The bell over the door rang, and Tweak glanced up, spotting Naomi and Liza. She stood, waving a hand. "Hey, guys."

"Where. The hell. *Were* you?!" Liza demanded, every word coming out shaking with anger and nerves. Looking her in the eye, Tweak shrugged. "Getting my t-tab back. Met a guy. Liza, chill. We're having lunch. Out of the storm." she added pointedly. "This's In-n-ny-y-y..." And now her fucking stutter kicked in, because of course it did. She massaged her throat.

"Inyoni," the guy finished for her. "Bird works too."

"D-d-don't w-worry about the blood." she added for her friends' benefit, taking her seat. "Sorta hit him."

Inyoni smiled sheepishly and wiped his chin with the third napkin. "She hit me a lot, matter of fact."

Naomi blinked. She glanced between them. "I think you're going to need to say a little more than that."

Pulling a sound box from her pocket, she let everyone at the table see it, then set it in her lap. Tweak could feel it inside her ears when the box was turned on. Inyoni twitched.

"Okay, explain everything." Naomi leaned back in the seat and casually put in a food order.

Tweak grinned. "He's. Gamma."

"He's bleeding," Naomi observed. "Tweak did a number on you, pal. And you don't seem to care. And what's up with the hair? Way to stand out."

"Plenty of people have cosmetic holos on their 'do around here," Inyoni defended. "I got a reason to wear a holo. Blue hair gives me a good excuse."

Liza looked the guy up and down. "So, you're pretty tough, I guess...you should put something on that lip, before it gets infected."

Tweak rolled her eyes. "Lame."

Liza shot her The Look. Tweak gave her a cheesy smile and a shrug. Sometimes it was fun to jerk her chain, just a little.

Inyoni watched them as he ate. "Tweak says you people can pay, if I work for you. How much cash you guys got?"

Naomi glanced from Tweak to Liza. Then she shrugged. "Enough."

"And better than cash. W-work. Good work." Tweak added quickly. "What you good at?" If she could hook him with the work first, maybe he'd come along. Maybe that had been her mistake with Circe. Nobody liked hearing about being a lab rat. Maybe this would be better.

Inyoni looked up from the menu to blink at Tweak. Then he snorted. "Not much. Stealin' shit, 'cept when fast freaks like you catch me at it. Sneakin' 'round the Corps, sometimes."

The word 'freak' stung, but internalized stigma was a bitch. She let him slide with it, this time.

"You're still alive. Means you're good, right?" Tweak asked.

"Guess so." Inyoni shrugged and leaned back, studying her. "Never been caught yet by anything but the cameras, an' my Citizen Standing Score's already shit. Don't care if I go down a couple points. Sides, these days even that kind of point drop doesn't happen."

Tweak grinned. "You're welcome."

"That was you?" Inyoni straightened up. You were the one who got the Citizen Ratings detached from the Scores? You're the Golden Dragon?!"

In the air, Tweak thought she saw just the hint of the tip of one of his ears above his head, poking past the holo's projection area. So they went up like a dog's too. She kind of wanted to see that when his holo was off.

"Careful, champ," Naomi cautioned, "higher-amplitude noises can go through the sound modulation. Keep it down."

Inyoni gave her an uncomfortable look. "Yeah... sorry. Never had one of those around before."

"Don't worry about it," Naomi reassured. "So yeah, Tweak?"

Tweak tapped her chest with two fingers. "Dragon. That's me. How'd you know the name?"

Inyoni glanced around the little café. When he spoke, he'd lowered his voice. "Folks talk about The Golden Dragon sometimes. Folks say he took down the Scores and turned every TechoCo screen saver across the country into a gold dragon when he did it, to rub it in their faces. Folks say he's the one who took down the Grid that time everything went nuts. And they say he took down the drones. Folks say he can unlock any Corporate code and get into anything, undo anything. Some folks say that if you can get to the Dragon, he can rewrite your whole Citizen Contract and your profile, and get you a whole new life. And that's...you?"

"That's me," Tweak agreed, a little bit thrown. She knew she'd been doing big things, and she had flipped TechoCo the bird by changing all the screensavers to a Luck Dragon. She hadn't realized she'd changed all the screen savers for the country, though. But she had been in the source code, so it made sense.

And yeah, she had taken down the Grid, basically. But she didn't know she'd become an urban legend. That was.... well, kind of awesome. Weird as hell, but yeah. Kind of awesome. Except the word on the street had made her a guy, because of course that's how they'd tell the story. Yay, patriarchy.

Inyoni leaned in. "So... can you do it?"

"Do what?" Tweak asked, pulled back into the moment.

"Rewrite somebody's whole life in the Corps' books," Inyoni explained, eyes full of wonder and worry. "Can you?"

"We can definitely change your circumstances, if you want to work with us," Liza cut in smoothly. "If you want it, Mr. Inyoni, we have a contract to offer you. We're interested in your skills, and in some specific abilities related to your being a Gamma. If you like the work with us, it could become permanent. Otherwise, we'd be happy to work up a refugee contract and get you out of the country as soon as it's filled. Interested?"

"Depends on what kinda work," Inyoni replied carefully, looking at her sideways. "And what kind of abilities." He sank lower in the booth. "Can't really take on fightin' stuff, on account of my thing. Don't really know when I'm hit. Been a problem before. Learned my lesson. Cash ain't worth dyin' for."

"We don't think there'll be fighting," Liza stated carefully. "Basically, it's a two-part contract. We need your help to help us research disease immunity—don't worry, it's only taking a couple blood samples, nothing else—and we need your help getting in touch with other people with your attributes. In exchange, we're offering—" she pushed her data tab across, and Tweak watched the man's eyes widen. "And, if you'd like, we can also offer safe passage off-grid."

Inyoni stared at the numbers on the data pad for another long moment, before looking up at the three people watching him. His dark eyes slid from one to the other. That look made something funny happen inside Tweak. She remembered when she'd gotten her own offer, that same terror and hope fighting for space in her chest.

Inyoni drew a breath. "What if, say, I want in, but I don't know any other Gammas? Never met another one, 'cept this chick." He motioned to Tweak.

Liza nodded. "Well, I'd say that's a shame, but we can't fault you for that."

"Question is," Tweak put in, "You want in?" For some reason, she was hoping this funny guy might say yes. Her heart jumped when he grinned.

"Hell yeah, I want in," Inyoni replied, eyes bright. "This's more money'n I've seen in my life, and a chance to get off-grid? Where do I sign?"

Tweak could never read Liza's face real well, but she'd learned to look at Liza's shoulders when she wasn't sure. Liza's shoulders got more and more square, the more tense she was. Tweak watched her shoulders ease out of rectangle shapes and into rounder, easier slopes. Okay, she was relaxing. That was good.

Her tab buzzed with a message. Sticking it under the table, Tweak read.

> Message Handle: QueenOfClubs
> Message: Can you start a background
> check on him as soon as you have a second?

Sighing, Tweak typed.

> Message Handle: DeuceOfDiamonds
> Message: Well yeah, duh.

The taller woman shot her a warning look. Then she held her hand out across the table. "Shake on it, for the moment."

Inyoni gripped her hand, shaking without hesitation.

"All right." Naomi added, glancing from Liza to Tweak. "To start with, you'll probably want to cut any ties around here; it makes tracking easy. Where's your digs? Anything in it you want? One of us can come with you and help you get things settled, help you wipe the place down. We've got some tricks for making you untrackable."

Inyoni stared at her for a moment, blinking. He snorted. "Lady. I been shelter-hopping for years. Far as the Corps're concerned, I don't exist."

Tweak grimaced. She'd been there. Oh boy, hadn't she. The shelters were better than jail, but not by much.

"Do you need—" Liza began, but Tweak snapped her fingers in front of her face, cutting off the next lame thing she knew Liza was about to let out of her mouth.

"Liza. You don't. Leave stuff. In shelters. Gets swiped. Poof." She glanced at the stranger, noting—with a little satisfaction, to be honest—that she really had done a number on his eye.

"Where's your stash?"

Inyoni waved a vague hand. "Down by the river, under one of the bridges. Good folk down there keep an eye on it for me."

"Great," Tweak agreed. "We finish eating, we go. You and me. Liza, Omi, see you back at the r-room, kay?"

"Only if you answer your tab when we message you this time, Gurgi," Naomi replied, lips canted in a tiny smile. "And don't let this guy borrow it again, maybe?"

Tweak rolled her eyes. "Yeah, yeah."

Event File 09
File Tag: Onboarding
16:30-08-3-2160

"Over this way," Inyoni murmured, gesturing vaguely as his long legs carried him down the walkway beside the river. Tweak trotted at his side. She glanced behind them as they slipped under the shadow of the high concrete embankment. Nobody watching. Good.

The scent of the river rose up to meet them like a coiling snake. Everything got dumped in the water, and it showed. Tweak had forgotten how bad it could smell; like an uncleaned public bathroom doused in chemical solvents. Which, if you were real about it, was what the river was.

"Watch your feet here," the man suggested. Inyoni slid down the slick, muddy path that led under the massive bridge. It was dark underneath the concrete, but a small fire crackled beside one of the huge pillars. Inyoni headed for it, calling out, "Hey Macky! Got a friend with me!"

A grizzled head under the stocking cap raised painfully, and the rheumy eyes squinted. "Friend isn't named Johnny Walker, is he?" the broken voice demanded with a laugh tacked on the end.

"Yeah, no luck there," Inyoni shrugged.

Out of a nest of old blankets, the tattered guts of a sofa and a cardboard box, faces peered, then broke into slow smiles.

"We got raided!" a man who looked like he was made of wires and brambles proclaimed, jumping out of his nest like an angry pop-up ad. Then he got a good look at Inyoni, and whistled. "Shit man, who'd you tangle with?"

Tweak smiled. "Me." She jerked a thumb over her shoulder in Inyoni's direction. "This shithead? He screwed up. Tried to pick my p-pocket. Guess who won?"

The man stared between them for a second. Then he started laughing, doubling over with it.

"Ain't *that* funny," Inyoni muttered under his breath.

"You know it's kinda cheatin'?" the old man creaked. "Birdman can't feel no pain."

"Hunh?" Tweak blinked, turning to stare up at the man.

Inyoni shrugged uncomfortably. "Told you I had a thing."

"Cool thing. Lucky bastard." Tweak remarked in admiration, but a croak from Macky cut her off.

"Think again, girlie. Bastard nearly bled to death an' didn't notice jack shit first time he ended up down here. That sound 'cool' to you?"

Behind them, there was a giggle, then the sound of something banging. Tweak's brow creased as she watched a pale man smack his helmeted head against the wall monotonously.

"Aw crap, Spazz," Inyoni muttered. Tweak watched as he knelt in the mess of blankets beside the skinny, rhythmically moving figure. "Bad day today?" Inyoni asked quietly, reaching out to hold the sick man's hand.

"Yeah, he's freaked 'cause we got raided," a big man in a ruined t-shirt muttered. "Lost most of' the food we'd stashed, an' Jeany got nabbed. She an' Spazz were fuckin' for a while; he's takin' it bad."

"Fuck," Inyoni muttered, glancing around himself. "Guys..." He trailed off, leaving whatever he was thinking unsaid.

Tweak cleared her throat. "Bet I can getcha food. Good at it." Liza would probably get after her for running an off-the-books op later, but what the hell. People were hungry.

She caught Inyoni's eye. "Better at jacking food than tabs, 'bird'?"

Inyoni shrugged. "Food's easy. Tabs're easy too, usually." Inyoni's eyes went to Spazz, and then to the guy he'd called Macky.

"Sorry," he stated, the word coming out awkward. "Sorry."

"Yeah, well, go do what you're good at if you wanna make it up," Macky wheezed. "You two got better places to be."

"Sure," Inyoni agreed. "When I get back, I'm gonna grab my stuff, kay?"

The old man leading this little group narrowed his eyes for a moment. Then he grinned. "You gonna fly, Birdman?"

"Yeah, yeah," Inyoni muttered. "I'll go get you something to eat."

Tweak nodded. "We'll be back like—" she snapped her fingers. Spazz giggled again. "Get him some pills too." she added quietly. "Try, anyway. What m-meds is he on?"

The group looked at each other, puzzled.

"None?" the big guy by the fire offered. Tweak looked at Inyoni, who shrugged.

"And get me some damn bourbon while you're out," Macky groused. "My hands are shaking something bad; need the bourbon to make it stop."

Tweak shrugged and made no answer to that request.

"Damn bourbon gonna kill him," she muttered as they climbed the slope again. "Seen that b-before. The shakes. Not getting booze. Not en-en-en-nabling."

"He ain't gonna survive withdrawal out here," Inyoni muttered back as they slipped onto the streets. "Might as well make him happy 'fore he goes."

Tweak didn't say anything to that. It was probably true. Then she glanced up at Inyoni, studying him. After a moment, she flashed a smile. "You're pretty c-cool. For helping them." Then she lengthened her stride. "C'mon. Got an idea."

Inyoni had no trouble matching her steps. "Whatcha thinkin'?"

"Big warehouse depot," Tweak offered. "Deliveries in and out all the time. Lots of contractor-c-c-couriers. You got a code, you pick up deliveries and go deliver. And guess what?" She glanced back, grinning. "I got all the code."

"Sweet to know a hacker," Inyoni said with a grin. "What don't you got?"

"A normal life," Tweak threw over her shoulder. "Also, tact. Keep up."

The streets were full of Go cars and people grabbing boxes around the depot. Tweak was glad they were both dressed in nondescript working clothes, though she shot an irritated look at Inyoni's hair. Pulling out her tab, she put it on Do Not Disturb; no sense in that going off and getting them in some kind of sticky spot while they were in there. That done, she dug in her pocket and pulled out a gimmie cap. "Bird. Hair. Fix."

Inyoni looked at the cap she held out, snorted and reached up to tap the holo-projector implanted in his neck three times. The air shimmered over his hair, and it turned a normal shade of brown. "Better?"

Tweak considered for a moment, then nodded. "Cute. Anyway..."

Two hours later, they lugged a cart marked 'Cleaning Services' down the hill and under the bridge. "Merry c-c-Christmas!" Tweak declared, throwing the cart's door open to show off the haul.

The brambly guy stared, slack-jawed. "That's a crapton of food!"

"Nice job, Birdman! And girlie, too," Macky chuckled.

"Mostly me," Tweak replied. "This guy? He carried stuff. It helped." Tweak agreed with a shit-eating grin. "Good mule, for a bird."

Inyoni shrugged. "Hey, being a jackass ain't all bad." Tweak had to smile at that.

They celebrated by eating the cake on top of the stack. It tasted like sugar and glue, not nearly as good as Billie's cooking back home. But it worked.

The guy in the old t-shirt pulled a duffle-bag into the circle of firelight. "Here's your stuff, man. This mean you're not comin' back?"

Inyoni was quiet for a beat. Then he nodded. "Think so."

The old man leading this little group narrowed his eyes for a moment. Then he grinned. "You gonna fly for real, Birdman? Took long enough. Get off your ass and fly already. I had wings, I'd fly."

Inyoni didn't say anything to that, but he reached over and gave the old man's shoulder a squeeze.

For a long time after they left the river, Tweak and Inyoni walked in silence.

"Good guys." Tweak muttered eventually. "Crazy as shit. But good guys."

Inyoni nodded. "Only guys I trust. Helped me get my holo put in. And that's not mentionin' all the times they stopped me gettin' killed on accident."

Lights flashed in their eyes as cars snapped past. A jingle for some shaving cream blared out of a loudspeaker, and they both covered their ears.

The noise ebbed and flowed as they moved through neighborhoods. Inyoni cleared his throat. "Hey. You... uh, might be a weird question, but... you want to get a drink or somethin'? Before we go back?"

Tweak glanced up, holding his big brown eyes as long as she could. The guy was asking her out for a drink. That felt... well, weird. But kind of good. She should probably wait until after she'd vetted him for something like that, but...

She shrugged. "Yeah. What the hell. Sure."

Inyoni nodded. "I know a place. Come on."

The 'place' was a small, cozy CPS hole in the wall, with faux wooden paneling and fewer news feeds than most. Tweak ordered them drinks, and Inyoni led her to a little table in the corner, where the shadows made the white tattoos around his elbows pop and no one would notice if they set up a soundbox.

Tweak studied the tattoos under the low light. "What Macky said. You give yourself wings?" she asked as they took their seats.

Inyoni shrugged, staring at his glass. "Seemed right, y'know? Being 'birdman' and all."

"Right," Tweak agreed. "Zulu. Your mom. She from there?" She asked, head cocked, taking a sip of her tequila.

Inyoni hesitated. The news jabbered on about fires eating their way up the West Coast as he stared at the tabletop. "Don't actually know. She didn't talk 'bout it at all, and then she was gone 'fore I was old enough to pick up much."

Tweak heard the bad story in the tone of his voice, so she changed the subject.

"Your ears. Cute. But your holo's shit. When we got time, I'll fix it right." She took a sip of the fiery tequila. "Llama," she added. "The gene splice. They used llama for some genes. Water retention. Don't drink so much. Great idea. When it doesn't screw up."

"So I got stupid llama ears," Inyoni grumbled, propped his chin on his fist. "Great. Always assumed it was a jackass, you know? Mule or donkey. I mean, people tell me I'm a jackass often enough."

"You give them a r-reason?" Tweak asked.

Inyoni shrugged. "Kinda. Sometimes. You know what else they used? I ain't really met other Gammas before, and research was never really my thing. But it's interestin'. Knowin' what the Corps did to fuck us all up."

Tweak nodded. All the things she'd read, all the stuff she'd seen, it was bubbling to get out now. She'd barely ever met another Gamma either, and talking about all this with someone who *got it* didn't feel like it did when she explained things to Alphas, even her buddies. It didn't feel like outing herself; it felt like her words had gotten free of a cage.

"Lots of stuff," she offered. "They used l-lots of stuff. Llama, camel, some birds, l-l-l-lizard. I found out lots."

Inyoni blinked. "Yeah, I noticed. How come you got so read up on us?"

Tweak glanced down. Her words worked their way out as her fingers drew circles in the condensation. "My b-baby brother was born with two s-s-s-stomachs. I was t-trying to figure out how he could get b-b-better."

"Man," Inyoni murmured. "He okay?"

That old ache throbbed in Tweak's chest. She shook her head. "He died. Four years old. Built all wrong. Couldn't m-make it."

"Damn." Inyoni shook his head. "Wonder who thought all this shit was a good idea in the first place. I mean, our parents looked okay yeah, but the Corps must've known DNA mutates on its own and screws shit up, right?"

Tweak smiled, quick and brittle. "Too many people. Not enough food. Had to do something."

Inyoni snorted and shook his head. "I'd start fucking with the food 'fore I fucked with people. But what do I know?" He swirled his drink. "Um. So. You're a Duster, yeah?"

"Yeah," Tweak agreed. Inyoni raised eyes full of hope and fear.

"How'd you get off-grid?"

Tweak shrugged, glancing away. "Made some friends. Helped me out. I do their tech now."

"And you... you think they'll have a use for me?" Inyoni asked, sipping his drink. "I mean... I ain't exactly a genius or anythin'."

Tweak nodded. "Give it till after we're done here. It'll work. You'll see." She opened her mouth to say something more, but closed it, unsure. She wanted to tell the guy it'd be okay. But she couldn't promise that.

Inyoni nodded. He took a long sip of his drink.

Tweak glanced up, and gave him a quick smile. "Hope it does work."

This time, she worked to hold his eyes when he looked at her. Slowly, he smiled, weak and still a little scared. "Yeah, me too."

Something funny and fluttery happened in Tweak's chest. She glanced away, grinning. But the grin fell right off when she read the time on the table's clock and menu display.

"Shit. Guys are gonna skin me. Chug it," she added, downing the rest of her drink in a swallow. "Gotta move."

"We on a schedule?" Inyoni asked in surprise, though he downed the rest of his drink in a single go.

"Out too long and L-liza freaks. Thinks we got picked up. We been g-gone five hours!" Tweak pocketed her white noise filter. "Got talking. D-didn't check my t-tab. Too much talking. Shit. Gonna get yelled at. Again." She yanked out her tab and glanced at it. Yep. Another metric ton of messages from Liza. Fuck.

Inyoni bit his lip, standing with a sigh. "Blame it on me. I said we should get drinks. Got carried away. I can take a bitching out."

Tweak shook her head. "Not like that. L-liza's a helicopter mom. You'll see. We're n-not in big trouble, just big talk. But... hey, thanks." She flashed him a grin. "Let's move."

Liza was on her feet, and had obviously been pacing, because they caught her in the middle of her circle. She whirled and stamped over to them. "Where have you *been*?!"

"Getting Bird's stuff," Tweak replied easily. "Cool it. We're good."

"Didn't get nabbed," Inyoni put in, offering the words like an apology. Tweak felt for the poor guy, stuck in the middle of a family fight like this. Liza was a lot to get used to.

"Yeah, you just left us wondering if you had! Just left us freaking out!" Liza exclaimed, throwing her hands in the air. "I messaged you a hundred times! I almost called home I was so freaked! And you went against protocol, Tweak. You ignored your messages, you didn't write in, you didn't give us any time table. I'm writing you up for this when we get home! You scared the shit out of us!"

"Yeah, Omi looks scaaaaared." Tweak dropped onto the bed, unlacing her heavy boots. "It's all good, Liza. Relax. No hovering."

"No hovering?!" Liza demanded, voice pitching up another notch. "No hovering?! God damn it Tweak, will you grow up?!"

Tweak ignored her. With Liza, you just had to wait her out.

"For the record," Naomi added from her lounging spot on the bed, "Liza's only overreacting a little. Dumb move, kiddo. The second one today.

And it's not cool." She sat up carefully. "We need to know when you're safe. Not because we're hovering. Because it's basic security. I need to know if I need to call my brother and tell him to write your death certificate. And I really don't want to make that call. So keep us in the loop, you got me?"

Tweak sighed. "Yeah, Omi. I got you. S-sorry."

Liza blew out a breath of irritation, turning to Inyoni, a shaky professional smile in place. "Sorry. Family fight, you know how it goes."

Tweak snorted, tossing her boots in the direction of the bed. "So. Plans. Tomorrow. Bird. Grab a seat. What'd we m-miss?"

Inyoni dropped into one of the hard chairs by the window.

"Common sense?" Naomi suggested where she lounged on the bed. Tweak flipped her off. Liza was still breathing hard through her nose, but she was calming down. "I've got some condolence notes that you can add a signature to," she stated crisply. "Aidan sent them along. The Force is holding a commemoration ceremony before we get home," she added, her voice dropping. "Half of base 707 died from BEAST before we got the new vaccine put together, 745 all got wiped out, and 758 lost a third." Liza held up the tab she'd been looking at.

Tweak nodded, staring at the scrolling names. "Yeah. Okay." She remembered when it had been them getting notes of condolence from across the country, because of fucking MACHA. The idea of more bases going through that just plain sucked. "Bastards." she whispered, fingers clenching into fists.

Inyoni cleared his throat. Tweak shot a look at him, fingers flexing in stifled anger. If they'd known sooner where the newest disease had come from, they could have gotten a vaccine out sooner. If they'd had more DNA samples from more people like her…

But at least they knew now. And they could save lives from now on, if they didn't alienate the people who could help them first. People like Inyoni.

"Hey. Your holo." she stood, crossing the space between them. "Lemme work on it? Make a better fix, maybe."

Inyoni studied her for a long moment. "Whatcha gonna do?"

"Depends. But first, gotta turn it off... that ok?" Tweak asked quietly, holding his eyes.

Inyoni swallowed hard, glancing between Liza and Naomi. In a whisper barely more than a breath, he asked Tweak, "They gonna care?"

Tweak shook her head a fraction of an inch. "Don't mind me. Won't mind you. It ok?"

Inyoni's dark eyes shot to Tweak's bandaged arms, then back up to her face. Taking a deep breath, he nodded. "Yeah."

Tweak flashed him a grin, and pulled out her tools. "Hey, Liza. Don't be a shithead." Reaching up, she gently tapped Inyoni's holo.

"A shithead about wha—ah!" the question ended in a yelp as Liza jumped. "Holy...you could've warned me!"

Under Tweak's hands, Inyoni flinched. She rolled her eyes. "Said don't be a shithead, Liza. Bird, whoever put this in, he sucked balls. Quality model. Wired it bad. You got electrical burns in the s-skin around it. Hold s-still."

Inyoni sat like a stone, his long ears pressed flat against the sides of his head. He gave a barely perceptible nod to Tweak.

After a minute, Liza cleared her throat. "Hey um... I didn't mean to... I mean, I'm sorry."

"She can't help it." Tweak added dryly. "L-liza was born freaking out."

"Not cute, Tweak," Liza sighed.

Inyoni shrugged with one shoulder. "'S'okay," he mumbled. "Most people freak."

"But I imagine most people don't apologize afterwards." Liza added, and there was a softness in her voice. Good. Liza being decent would help.

Turning, Tweak dug in her bag, pulled out a handful of parts, and began to dismantle a flashlight and a broken tab. On the table beside her, solder spat as it warmed up.

Ten minutes later, Tweak sat back with a nod of satisfaction. "Try that."

Inyoni carefully reached up and tapped at the holo-projector in his neck. It didn't jolt and hum this time. He glanced at Tweak with the eyes of a dog that isn't sure what it's going to get, a slap or a pat. "It workin'?"

Tweak grinned. "Perfect. Not gonna go bad on you either. Even if it gets smacked. You're all set."

Inyoni glanced between the three of them. Then, very slowly, he smiled. "Yeah. I guess I am…"

Event File 10
File Tag: Calorie Requirements
12:30-08-17-2160

"In here," their guide offered, taking the stairs down to the sunken doorway. Not a great spot to be, in Naomi's mind. If there was trouble somewhere underground, you were fish in a barrel. But Liza was already following, and the area was vetted. Technically, it should be okay.

Crossing her fingers in her pocket, she took up the rear, keeping Tweak and Inyoni in the middle; one because she didn't know him and couldn't count on him yet, and two because she did know Tweak and she knew better than to take her eyes off the kid. Tweak was good at a lot of things, but situations like this weren't one of them.

The man led them down into an industrial basement, and Naomi prepped herself as they turned the corner. She knew spaces like these; all barren, grey concrete dotted with pillars to take the weight above. They were hell on the nerves for an operative; all hidden corners and shadows, no clear sightlines at all.

Then she got a look at what the civvies had done with the space, and started to smile. The whole area had been turned into a big indoor café, with bright mismatched umbrellas, scrounged folding tables, and a bunch of people sitting together. A hand-lettered sign by the door greeted them with the words 'leave your Citizen Standing here, this is Common Ground!'

"You eaten yet?" The young man that the Financial Justice Union had sent to guide them asked.

Liza shook her head. "No, and we'd love to join you."

"Great," Niles agreed, gesturing. "line's over here."

They joined the line of folks waiting for a free lunch, Liza chatting with their contact. Naomi got down to doing what she'd been brought here for, going over what she could see of their security setup. Plenty of exits, that was good. Looking carefully, she spotted soundboxes stuck to the ceiling. Good call. She'd have to recommend a few things to reinforce their security culture, but for the most part, this gathering was being run pretty well.

She grabbed a plate when her turn came, and got a pretty damn good meal; a panini stuffed with protein cubes and cucumber, sliced peppers on the side, and even a chunk of melon.

"One of our members started a really big garden with all the seeds we got," Niles explained. "The compost is feeding a cricket farm for our protein. Pretty efficient setup, isn't it?"

"Yeah," Naomi agreed, biting into her panini. The rich, nutty cricket protein was a perfect complement to cucumbers and the sauce the whole mix had been blended into.

"Fuck, this's good," Inyoni muttered between bites. Even Tweak looked happy about her meal.

"And how's the movement schedule going?" Liza asked, leaning in towards Niles. "You haven't had any trouble, have you?"

Niles shook his perfectly-coiffed head. "Not so far; as long as we message everyone on the Common Ground, they get their groups and neighbors the new address, and we've been using NatBank's property ownership records to track what buildings are vacant. Once we make sure that the security systems are handled, we move in. It's been working pretty well so far." He smiled at a knot of laughing kids running past. "We fed just a couple kids breakfast that first day, but after a while we were feeding about three hundred families with kids breakfast, lunch and dinner. Another setup like this does an open kitchen for adults without children; we lay everything out, and they pick out what they need and cook it for themselves, or take it home. We give a few classes on cooking for the adults. Everyone's really careful about getting in and out; if it's not safe to gather, we send people out with food boxes. But we've been okay for the most part, and people seem to like getting together to eat meals."

Inyoni turned back to their guide, brow creased. "Wait, I thought you guys were NatBank. What's a bunch of bankers doing feeding people?"

Niles gave him the kind of smile he must use when clients signed gigantic loan documents. "Who would expect a bunch of bank employees to be running a free food program for school kids? We're assumed to be 'too good for this'. Nobody expects us to be running anti-corporate free food programs in our free time. We put that privilege to good use. The Grapevine's been a lot of help in getting supplies to supplement our garden. A few nutritionists from the Healthcare Union came and checked over our menu. We keep a food prep and serving roster, as well as a venue-moving roster, and everyone lends a hand where they can. But for the most part, we get away with this because NatBank doesn't think we're the type to do it." He toyed with a slice of cucumber. "There is a question coming up, though. Since I'm here, maybe I should ask it for my friends. We keep getting asked..." He trailed off, taking a contemplative bite of the vegetable. Naomi checked his body language over, but the threat here was internal, if there was one.

"Getting asked what?" Liza asked, leaning in.

Niles swallowed. "We've been getting asked what the endgame is. Where this is all supposed to end up. Where we want to be when this is all done. Someone who was... let's just say they were skeptical, and they said some fairly rude things. But it boiled down to 'if all you're doing is giving out free food, it's not going to help.'"

Naomi watched as Liza nodded, her body language shifting. Now she was thoughtful, easy in her skin. She'd lost that high-strung worry she usually carried in her shoulders.

"It's a really good question. So, when will we know that we've won?"

"I think that's a good way to phrase it," Niles agreed. Liza nodded slowly.

"Well. We'll know we've won when communities in this country have the ability to make decisions at the local level, based on what's going to make our neighbors thrive instead of what will turn the highest profit. We'll know we've won when human dignity is something you're born with, not something you have to earn. When everyone has access to sustainable food and water in their community. We'll know we've won when everyone has the right to speak and be heard in their community, their state, and their nation. When everyone has opportunities and agency in their lives." She gestured around the room. "We'll know we've won when rooms like this are everywhere, and they're normalized. We'll know we've won when we're organizing the nation based on what creates the greatest public good, not the biggest private gain." She gave a little smile. "Which means we're a long way from winning. But when you send a kid to class and they're not falling asleep in class or crying with a stomach cramp? When you feed a pregnant mom so her baby isn't underweight? That's the first step to winning. And you're helping in another way too."

"I am?" Niles asked, rapt. Liza nodded. "You are. If the Corporation tries to say your unions are a bunch of disgruntled employees or anarchists or terrorists, or whatever they try to say? The people who sat here and ate a good meal will say 'No, they're not. They're the people who fed our kids.'" She pointed across the room, where a doctor was giving shots. "When the Corps call Dusters terrorists, people will look at each other and say 'No, they're not. They're the people who held free clinics for my grandma and got my nephew his shots. They're the ones who gave me the vaccine against the newest bio-weapon.'" She shrugged, smiling gently. "And that's how we win. We show the people that we really care about them, by being here for everyone. We make sure everyone makes it. And some people will be cynical about that. But you'll give them breakfast too. It's not what we say that wins us anything. It's what we do."

Once again, Naomi watched stars light up in someone's eyes when Liza spoke. Liza might not believe it, but man, she was good at this. This NatBank guy who spent most of his life knee-deep in financial papers and deals that favored the high-Standing clients looked ready to wave a flag and hit the Dust after a couple minutes listening to Liza. That was power. Liza bit into a slice of her cucumber. "But that's a lot to say to somebody in the lunch line. So, when somebody asks you 'What's the endgame' tell them 'Getting you the right to have a say in your life and your world. And that starts with getting you fed.'"

"I'll remember that," Niles agreed, sounding a little dazed.

After a second's silence, Naomi cleared her throat. "So, you got a food service roster. You want a hand getting lunch on plates?"

Niles blinked. "Wait... aren't you the security specialist?"

Naomi cracked a grin. "Buddy, if your food isn't secure, neither is anything else."

It was good to take a break from the constant teaching and just do something physical to help people out. It was one thing to talk about all the ways they wanted to serve and uplift and help, but all that was abstract. Handing kids plates, on the other hand? That was real. And so were their smiles.

As they worked, Naomi kept an eye on Inyoni and Tweak. After all, she might be relaxing, but she wasn't getting soft.

Inyoni looked a little out of his depth wearing an apron on the serving line, but he spooned sliced peppers onto plates with a smile for everyone. It was Tweak that really surprised her. Not only had the girl jumped right into going around the tables of kids with their parents and serving them cookies and boxes of electrolyte-reinforced juice, she was actually chatting with all the kids, especially the little ones. That was something to see. Naomi even spotted Tweak playing peek-a-boo with a baby at one point.

The lunch rush didn't so much end as slide seamlessly into the dinner crowd, the serving platters changing from paninis to tamales and the melons switched out for applesauce.

"You folks have done plenty," a motherly woman with the body of someone who spent too much time behind a desk assured Liza eventually. "Why don't you go sit down, and we'll take a turn?"

Naomi was glad to agree; her off-hand was starting to click every time she turned her wrist. Using the tongs one too many times must have gotten to it.

"That's c-clicking," Tweak remarked as Naomi reached for the pitcher of iced tea on the table. "I'll fix it l-later."

"Thanks," Naomi agreed, pouring herself a cup of tea. Out of the corner of her eye, she spotted a kid staring at her with wide eyes.

Setting the pitcher down, she gave the little girl a smile, waving with her off hand. The girl couldn't be more than four, and she watched Naomi's hand as if it was a rattlesnake.

"It's okay. I don't bite," Naomi reassured. She glanced up at the man who was probably the grandad. "Is it okay if I get her a cookie?"

"Sure, thanks," the old man agreed, giving the little girl a reassuring squeeze. "It's okay Amy. You don't need to be scared."

Naomi reached into the basket on the table using her off-hand, and held it out to the little girl. The kid stared at her black plastic fingers for a second. But the cookie did the job eventually. The little one took the treat with both hands, staring up at Naomi.

"Thank you," she lisped.

Her grandad gave her a little squeeze of encouragement, and smiled over the top of her head at Naomi. "Thanks. She's a little shy."

"No problem," Naomi offered with a smile. "This is a lot to get used to."

"So, uh... Liza?" Inyoni asked as they settled into their room for the night.

"Yeah?" Liza asked as she carefully removed those neat tactical hairpins she wore. While she studied the mirror, Naomi studied Inyoni. He fidgeted like a teen, looking from Tweak to the wall.

"Uh...you guys mean that stuff? What you said at lunch?"

Slowly, Liza set down her hairpins and turned. "You mean about what our goals are?"

Inyoni nodded.

Liza smiled. "Yes. That's what we're all working for. I think it sounds like it's worth it. How about you?"

Inyoni ducked his head. When he looked up, it was at Tweak. "I mean... all that? Can that even happen?"

Holding his eyes, Tweak nodded. Naomi could see what it cost her to hold eye contact in the set of her shoulders, but she was doing it.

"We do enough. It can," the girl offered. "You'll see."

Event File 11
File Tag: Recruitment Failure
18:30-09-2-2160

"Alright everyone, please pull up the file on effective tactics. Today, we're going to walk through different nonviolent actions. At the end of the session, we'll take a break on training so you folks can vote on what actions you'd like to participate in. If you'd like to add a thought or a comment, please put up your hand and state your name for the group at the beginning of your remarks."

Obediently, the infrastructure designers' union turned to the page on their tabs, dust floating in the air caught in the beams of the holograms and the sunlight streaming through the ancient warehouse's windows. There wasn't as much discussion with ArgusCo people as there had been with the TechoCo people in the writers' union, but the questions that did get asked were smart, incisive and worth remembering. It had gone pretty well, all things considered. The site left something to be desired, but it could have been worse. She'd been telling herself that for two days now: it could have been worse.

Liza walked up and down the lines of folding chairs the union had brought with them, checking in with folks, though she didn't need to help many of these people figure out the Common Ground app or its file trees. ArgusCo might work its people to death, but it educated the hell out of them too. It had been so strange switching between different sets of norms and cultures since she'd started teaching these classes. She'd known in theory that all seven Corporations had different social norms, but experiencing it realtime still took some adjusting to. She was starting to get curious—and nervous—about her first EagleCorp and AgCo classes. That EagleCorp class was next week. It was coming up so *fast*.

She brought a large window into life in front of the room, showing the list of possible actions. "So, all of these actions build on what we've already discussed. Whatever you do, you'll want to keep in touch with your contact triads and move in starling formations, also known as murmuration. This style of movement will keep both the Peacekeepers and the AI systems off balance. We borrow this maneuver from the works of Rivera Sun. So, there's four basic rules: Keep moving forward, whoever is in front is the leader. Leadership changes when the flock turns. And never leave your wing mate out on a limb." As she spoke, Liza flicked a clip up to play in the air. On the screen, a great flock of birds flew in mesmerizing undulations. "You'll see the lead bird outlined in yellow by us; notice that it changes in each turn. That's what you want to do. All of you can lead when you're out there."

A hand went up. "Bob Percell, and I'm wondering who's going to say when it's time to change?" a beefy guy asked. Liza gave him a smile. "You are. When the group hits an obstacle, some traffic, anything that gets in the way, then you flock. Keep the three people nearest to you in your sights at all times, and move together. You turn in the same direction as the people around you. If we move like this, we'll drive the AI in surveillance cameras bonkers, along with the Peacekeepers trained to rely on the camera feeds. So, we'll be effectively blinding and confusing them by moving in ways they don't expect."

"So what stops them from beating the hell out of us if the Peacekeepers are there in person?" A skinny guy in his sixties demanded. "Daniel, sorry. Thing is, I'm not going to be able to make a living—hell, I might not even live—if a Peacekeeper beats the crap out of me when we march."

Liza nodded at him. "It's a good point, Daniel. Don't forget that, if you're not built for Loud actions, there are plenty of Quiet actions that need participants just as much. For those who do want to participate in Loud events like marches, we've got a lot of plans to help defend you; the first step is making sure the Peacekeepers are too confused to form the kind of blocks that can beat a lot of people. The Force plans to disrupt and complicate their communications, disable their vehicles, and make their lives hell while you're in the streets. All our ideas are described in the Civilian Security section of your notes. If it does come to a physical altercation, we've got a lot of physical trainings tomorrow and the next day; that's going to get covered. The notes on all the material are in sections Five, Six and Seven of your Bundle."

She flipped her tab off. "And that's the end of today's discussion. Let's go over questions and thoughts. Once we're ready to go, remember our safety routines. Break into six groups. Take six exits. Message your contact triads when you get home to let them know you're safe."

"I got a question," a hard-muscled woman in the front began. "Name's Marla. I got kids at home. What's stopping some schmuck from knocking on my door in the middle of the night and putting black bags over our heads? I don't want my kids to disappear into a detention center... or a bag of dog food."

The room shifted uncomfortably.

Liza nodded. "I hear you, Marla. It's hard to stand up and it's hard to be brave when a black van could drive up in the middle of the night. Our Grid operatives live that way every day, and it isn't fun."

These folks were easier to talk to in some ways; she didn't have to sugarcoat it, like she did for the writer's union, or simplify things as she did for the warehouse union. "It's a good question, I'm glad you asked it," she continued. "On your first day in these classes, you gave your devices to our technical officer for jailbreaking and loading with a VPN that makes your device a part of the Mesh. The Mesh is a nodal meshnet made up of interconnected VPNs, it doesn't connect with the traditional internet." She pulled out her own tab, displaying it.

"The next step is something you'll choose. For our own operatives, we've created a counterspying system. When one of our people is grabbed, we do all we can to launch a rescue. To do this, our apps have a subroutine that builds a profile of any given participant's expected activity and then alerts a human in the case of sudden deviation from those routines. So, if someone walks home the same route at more or less the same time for four nights in a row, and on the fifth night they move in an unexpected direction at a much higher rate of speed, an alert fires off and the Force looks into it. Now, we do have some funny false positives sometimes; one of our folks on the Grid was dating a new guy, and a rescue team knocked on the door of his apartment just when things got interesting." She winked. A nervous chuckle ran around the room.

"And that's why this is an opt-in feature," she went on, walking up and down the line of chairs with a smile for everyone. "Mistakes will happen, and we might see something awkward, but that won't be used against you. If you have plans, you can go through your Common Ground app, open the Plans Today tab, and add it ahead of time to avoid flagging. And we *will* shield this private data from human interface. I know that's hard to believe, but you have to trust us if you want to get rescued." Liza projected her tab. "Most importantly, there's a Panic Button here on the app. If you have even a second, you can hit it, and the Force and everyone else who's opted in within the local Union chapters will be notified. This way, you can protect each other, and the Force can work to protect all of you. If the worst happens, please know that the Force has created a stipend system to support the families of our people. Your families won't starve if you're taken in. That's a promise the Force will stand by. Forever."

It wasn't the last question she was asked by a long way, but with every question Liza answered, the people around her seemed to ease a little more into the idea that they really were doing this. Soon enough, it was time for the day's session to end. This was another time that the cultural differences really showed. ZonCom people had swarmed her after the official lesson, eager to talk. Cavanaugh people had pulled her aside quietly every day in groups of one and two. NatBank people mostly sent her private notes with their thoughts. Here in an Argus community, people packed up and moved out, efficient and quiet. That was probably a good thing, but it did feel weird.

"Don't forget, homework tonight for those coming back: think about stories that could be effective for use during Quiet actions," Liza called as people filed out.

Once they were gone, Liza glanced to the little corner that her people had claimed. Tweak was visible again now that the stacks of tabs she'd been taking care of on Day One and Two had been reclaimed by their owners. She sat with her headphones on, buried eyebrows-deep in something that really had her interest. Inyoni wandered over from his round of Raven's Revenge with the kids a few parents had brought along as the attendees took off. He watched over Tweak's shoulder, his face a funny mix of emotions.

The air around his head flickered, reminding Liza of what lay beneath the holographic screen. Llama ears. If she hadn't nearly had a heart attack when she'd seen it, she wouldn't believe it. Honestly, when his holo was off, the boy looked like something out of a vid.

Inyoni glanced up at her, and got to his feet. "Uh... you wanna go?"

"It's about that time, yeah," Liza agreed. "With any luck, we'll catch the man on our list as he comes off his work cycle, and see what he thinks about our offer."

"Uh... yeah." Inyoni mumbled, reaching a hand towards Tweak.

Naomi intercepted it neatly, catching him by the wrist. "We don't touch Tweak, buddy. Especially when she's focused. Good thing to remember if you like all your bits and pieces where they are."

Inyoni blinked at her, nonplussed.

The commotion over her head did the trick; Tweak looked up, and slid her headphones off. "Go time?" she asked, bouncing to her feet.

Liza nodded. "Yep. How's security?"

Tweak made a face. "Total. Shit."

"I'm with Tweak on this one," Naomi added, throwing a pack over her shoulders. "Trying to secure this place is like trying to carry water in a paper bag. No door sensors, no clear lines of sight, and windows everywhere. I straight up hate this site."

"Would a physical security check of the building help? A circuit once an hour, maybe?" Liza asked, sidestepping the crankiness in her base-mates' voices and focusing on what she could do something about. Naomi snorted a laugh. "Sure, if you want us to get caught. If the area's surveillance drones pick up some random chick walking around and around a building, they'll get curious and we'll get screwed. No go."

"What if Tweak disabled the drones in this area?" Liza asked. Almost immediately, she shook her head. "No, that alone would give us away..."

After a beat, Naomi shrugged. "I'll do an interior wall-walk, and Tweak's watching all the feeds for any signs of drones, but yeah, I still hate this site. Wasn't there anything else?"

"The other sites the chapter president suggested were worse." Liza replied, glancing around the rotting warehouse. "At least this place is out of the way, and we're sure it doesn't have its own monitoring system. So, what can we do to improve security for tomorrow?"

"Fuck. All." Tweak grumbled. "We don't have the g-gear. I didn't c-come here thinking I'd have to w-wire a whole w-warehouse."

Liza kept her professional expression in place. Fine, so she'd put them in a site that wasn't ideal. And they didn't like it. That was to be expected. And dealing with it was their assignment.

"Can we print more security material on a consumer rig?"

"If you want us n-nabbed, sure," Tweak groused, stuffing her oversized headphones and tab in her pockets. "S-stupid idea."

Liza really wished the kid would learn to express her anxiety in a way that wasn't snarking other people. It made it really hard to show any sympathy.

"So," she went on, maintaining her cool, "are we ready to go meet with the next Gamma on our list?"

"Probably f-fuck that up too," Tweak muttered. Liza felt the barb hit home, but she wasn't rising to Tweak's bait.

After a breath, Tweak turned and actually looked her in the eye. "Sorry, L-liza. I'm freaked. Being a b-bitch."

"Thanks for saying something," Liza acknowledged, letting her breath out slow. "Let's move."

"Looks like he was working as a late-shift janitor when the Blacklist clocked him," Naomi murmured as they worked their way along the street, out of the warren of last century's warehouses fanned out around the MLK and the highway. "Least he doesn't live far away. Poor bastard," Naomi added, shooting a jaundiced look around the neighborhood. It had been single-family homes once, but now most of the houses in the area had been turned into cot-squats where people rented a cubicle with a cot in it, just big enough to lie down in. Every one of these low, rectangular homes held fourteen or fifteen people, sometimes as many as twenty, squashed under the oppressive heat.

These places were the bottom of the barrel, and they looked it, with broken shutters, sagging roofs and weedy trees cracking open the sidewalks. Nobody had paid for shade-cloth to reflect the sunlight pounding down on these streets; the air sizzled over the pavement. The houses sat cooking quietly in their weedy lots. The people on the street didn't look much better than the buildings.

"Oh hey," Naomi added, "remind me later, I got an idea about tying the general strike to the Workers' Bill Of Rights in a snappy way."

"Mm. Great," Liza agreed distractedly, feeling like cringing as they walked down the street. She still couldn't believe cot-squats existed; even a printed pre-fab dormitory wing on a Duster base was nicer and more liveable.

On the other hand, making those involved getting a printer and permission. And these people couldn't do either, it looked like.

What a mess. One more mess in a seriously messed up country. Some days Liza wondered if it could ever get fixed.

But it'd be so damn easy to do, and that was what drove Liza nuts. All the people in this neighborhood could fix it up in no time, if they were just given the tools. All they needed were some hand tools for the weeds and the demolition, an affordable way to get some building printers, some time to do the work and somewhere to dump the debris from these run-down wrecks of houses. And presto. New neighborhood. It wouldn't take much. But if they couldn't get even that much, they got stuck with this shit.

"Earth to Liza?" Naomi's voice tugged her out of her reverie. She glanced the other woman's way.

"Yeah?"

Naomi nodded forward. "Let's keep an eye on Tweak, 'kay? The kid's really tense."

Liza glanced forward, and repressed a sigh. Tweak was stamping along the street like she had a grudge against the ground, glaring at anyone who looked her way.

"How bad was the last trip to meet a Gamma?" She asked.

Naomi rolled her eyes. "The guy called Tweak a snitch and a sell-out. So far out of these four meetings she's tried, she hasn't gotten a good one. Biggest break she's had was snagging Inyoni. The kid's taking it hard."

"I see that," Liza agreed, watching Tweak. The little coder didn't handle frustration well at all, and that got on Liza's nerves pretty regularly, but she could feel for her on this. The poor kid really hadn't had any luck. And what 'luck' she did have so far, Liza wasn't very happy about. She glanced back at Inyoni, who was trailing them in his long-legged slouch of a walk. Out of this whole teeming city-filled Sector, the person who *just happened* to try to rob Tweak *just happened* to be a Gamma, and one interested in leaving the Grid. That was too many coincidences for Liza. It was too much of a good thing. Tweak had run a check on the guy, and she'd cleared him. Tweak was the best, there was no question about that. But Liza still didn't feel right about it. They'd run a basic check on that bastard who'd stolen the name Ezra too, and Aidan had almost died because it hadn't dug deep enough. After what had happened to Aidan the last time they'd been too trusting, she wasn't letting this 'lucky' find of theirs out of her sight.

Tweak stopped in front of a woebegone grey house set in a brownish lawn full of kochia, vape canisters and puncturevine. "Here."

"Okay," Liza agreed. "Inyoni, Naomi, hang back. Tweak, let's go knock on the door."

The man who opened it had the heavy, puffy look of an average-built guy who'd eaten too much of the wrong food, for too long. He scratched a grey-stubbled cheek distractedly, looking them up and down.

"Yeah?"

"Good evening, we've come about a job opportunity for Sebastian Tesfaye?" Liza stated calmly. "Is he in?"

The guy who either ran or bounced for the cot-squat gave them the fish eye. "You seriously want to hire that crazy fuck? Your problem, lady."

Liza didn't have time to respond before the guy turned and hollered into the cot-squat. "Tesfaye! Out here now!"

There were a few thumps from the gloom inside, and a spidery man scrambled into view. He looked at the door-guard with wide eyes. The beefy man poked him in the chest. "Don't start fucking around again. House rules, remember?" He waggled the door meaningfully, and Liza got a good look at the sign plastered to its inner surface.

Notice To Residents
Peacekeepers Called
Automatically In Case Of Voices
Raised Above 60 Decibels.

With a last skeptical look their way, the big guy stepped back into the relative cool of the house.

Sebastian stared at them, eyes wide and darting. His words came out like startled mice. "I don't know you. Who are you?"

"People with a j-job offer," Tweak suggested with a quick smile. "Heard you w-were the g-guy we should hire from a f-friend. Wanna go t-talk about it?"

The guy's eyes froze on Tweak's face. "Job offer? Job offer?" His breathing picked up into a sort of pant. "I heard about people like you! Say it's a job offer, get guys on their own, and pow! Dead on a meat hook!" His voice quavered up into a shout. "Meat in the organ market! Organ traders!

You're organ traders! They're after me! They want my liver!" He wobbled on his feet, his eyes frantic.

"Officer En Route," a harsh warning blatted from inside the house. Liza's breath caught in her chest.

"And we're leaving," Naomi called from the sidewalk. "Tweak, Liza, come on."

"No!" the little guy snarled, grabbing Tweak. "You! You think you can—" Tweak clocked him in one clean move and backed off, rubbing her jacket where the man's hands had been.

On the ground, the little guy pulled a gun. "I'll kill you! Thieves! Organ thieves!"

"Run!" Naomi ordered as bullets sprayed into the air.

"What the fuck did you *say*?" Inyoni shouted as he scrambled after the three women.

"Talk later! Run now!" Tweak yelped as the wild-eyed man stepped out, yelling incoherently as he sprayed bullets into the street. Liza yanked her by her jacket as the other woman stumbled, and pulled her around the corner.

Sirens blared somewhere. One more problem they didn't need. She skidded down another alley, Naomi hissing, "In here, cover!"

It was a dumpster. But it was better than nothing. Hidden between it and the wall, the four people gasped for breath. Tweak unzipped her pack. "Infrared-bounce." she panted, doling the packets out. "In c-case the c-c-cameras s-saw us."

Liza took hers and sat listening, eyes wide, as guns went off. Then there was a loud, final thump. A moment later, the wail of an ambulance rattled the air.

Tweak gritted her teeth. "Just got him killed. We just got him killed. Fuck."

"Don't know that," Inyoni muttered, though it was a weak protest. "He might've killed someone else and ran."

Naomi gave him a long, slow look, but she said nothing.

Tweak snorted, staring at her feet. Just when Liza had begun to try to figure out what she could say to give her some comfort, the coder blinked. She looked up with a start, staring at each of her friends in turn before her eyes fixed on Inyoni. "Fuck. Need an auto-pad. N-now."

Liza glanced down. A long red ribbon of blood was unspooling on the pavement. She raised her eyes to Inyoni. "Wait, did you get hit?"

Inyoni blinked. "I... maybe?"

Tweak gave a snort of frustration. "Shithead! Omi, l-look at him."

"Roger," Naomi agreed, leaning over and starting on a cramped check. She looked up. "Well okay champ, I guess you were serious about the pain thing. You've got a graze all down your arm."

"Aw fuck," Inyoni winced. "Is it bleeding a lot? Is my ink okay?"

"I'll say it's bleeding," Naomi agreed. "Tweak? This sucks, but if you can take the bandage off one of your legs, under your pants, we can put that and your jacket on him and get him to the hotel. Can you do that?"

Tweak was completely still for a moment. She gulped. "Tweak, take a deep breath," Liza suggested. "You can do it behind me, where he can't see."

Tweak glanced between the three of them. Naomi gave her a fierce little smile. "If he looks your way I'll smack his head."

"You don't gotta," Inyoni grumbled. "I ain't gonna look if she says not to."

Tweak's black eyes flicked to his, riveted. The world froze for a moment. Liza could taste the tension in the air.

Then Tweak nodded. "Kay."

It was a rotten ride back to the hotel they'd claimed, everyone on edge and jangling with nerves. Liza thought she'd relax when they got inside, but it wasn't much better in the room. The air tasted of frustration and dismay as they sat, Naomi working on Inyoni and she and Tweak avoiding one another's eye.

"Why'd the crazy bastard start shooting, anyway?" Naomi finally asked, breaking the quiet. "We didn't do anything different with any of the others."

"He was scared." Tweak muttered. "Scared we were g-gonna t-t-take him."

"Organ market, yeah," Inyoni muttered, his voice quiet. "He kept saying that."

Naomi snorted. "If he thought we looked like organ-fixers, he's never seen any."

Inyoni turned his head on the pillow, looking up at Naomi. "Don't matter. When you're like us, the whole world's out to get you."

"His brain. Wired wrong," Tweak muttered, chin in her hand and black eyes far away. "Couldn't tell the difference. When you get grabbed..." she shook her head hard. "Worth being scared of."

"Not worth shooting at people trying to do some good," Naomi grumbled under her breath.

Tweak shot her friend a glare. "What do you know? You n-never been so s-s-scared you c-can't think. You n-never been there. You *can't* get it."

Naomi raised her head, taking on Tweak's glare for a minute straight. She said nothing. The backing came off the autopad with a snap. Liza had a horrible moment of wondering who would come out on top if Tweak and Naomi ever got into it.

Finally, the blond woman looked down at Inyoni, smoothing the autopad into place. "Okay, that's the best I can do. At least you won't get an infection. You really didn't feel that? At all? Don't move it for a bit."

"Nah," Inyoni agreed. "Felt something hit, but I didn't know it was a bullet."

Naomi stared at him for a moment, shaking her head a little. "Lucky son of a bitch." Then she glanced at Tweak. "So, how many is that off our Gammas To Visit list?"

"Three no, one hell no, one c-crazy." Tweak replied blankly. "Four names left."

"Any of the other people in the Gammas program have any luck?" Liza asked. Tweak shrugged, looking like a kitten left in the rain. "Dunno."

"Four. That ain't much," Inyoni muttered, frowning at his hands. "What'll you do if they all tell you to fuck off, too?"

"Be a pincushion," Tweak muttered quietly. "Again."

Nobody seemed to know what to say to that.

When the silence had stretched too long, Liza cleared her throat. "Let's get some dinner and some rest, everyone. Today was long, and tomorrow will be too."

Event File 12
File Tag: Site Security
12:30-09-4-2160

"So, today we're going to talk about possible actions," Liza began, bringing up her window. She pointed to the options that had been worked out months ago. "Our first action is the Make Good Trouble Campaign: we're aiming for an eight-hour, five-day work week or paid overtime for lower-Standing citizens, and paid time off for everyone at every Standing. So, we have a lot of ways to approach this."

In the back of the room, pops and giggles from the game circle Inyoni and Tweak were running for kids brought along by parents who didn't have any childcare options rose to fill the quiet. It sounded like they were playing Raven's Revenge again; they must be handing it out. At this rate, every kid in the Sector would have that game on their tab pretty soon.

"Yesterday, I asked everyone who was here to do some homework, and I sent the request to the attendees who weren't with us in person. Let's talk about Quiet actions, and the kind of stories and slogans that reach hearts and minds. Does anyone have an idea from the list that felt particularly right for them? If you do, please raise your hand, state your name, and let's talk about what you're thinking."

She let the expected moment of hesitation pass. Then Marla spoke up. "Hey folks. I'm Marla. I'm really attracted to the Walk In My Shoes display. It just *feels* right; telling people the story about what's really going on."

Liza nodded. "Put up in the right way, it's a really powerful display.

Who's read the entry about the Walk In My Shoes displays?"

A smattering of hands went up. Liza tapped her tab, displaying the Good Trouble entry.

"Here's the details, drawn from the work 'Beautiful Trouble' by Boyd and Mitchell—a book in the Good Trouble Bundle—and expanded on by collaboration with the Seattle Tech Workers' Union and the Cascadia Quadrant Command.

"The idea is to bring the issue home. People care, they do. But that abstract caring isn't usually enough to act on until they understand what's at stake in their gut. So, the point of this action is to make that happen." Liza enlarged an image of a little girl's shoes with a name, an age, and a cause of death written on a card laid across them.

"It originated with a protester during the Middle Eastern Conflicts lining up shoes with the names of those who had died in another country, to make the war real for Americans. Marla, what do you think we could do in the same way?"

The muscled woman held up a pair of little flip-flops. "I'd be up to copy that. Here's one to start with. A little boy named Jamie, just thirteen. When his educator told him he couldn't take the exam to go on with school because his family had too low a Standing, he went home and killed himself."

"That's really rough," Liza murmured. "Do other people have stories they want to share?"

An old man stood. "Samson, ma'am. I'd like to share a story."

"We'd like to hear it," Liza agreed.

The man swallowed. "My brother was a site compliance man, CSS Standing. He was a good worker, a good member of the team. A beam dropped on him on a jobsite, crushed his pelvis. Instead of getting him a new spinal cord and pelvis, Argus accused him of negligence and dropped him to CAS. He's still in a wheelchair."

Liza nodded. "That's a powerful story. I think it would have a real impact."

Another storyteller came forward, and another, and another. Liza let people talk out their trauma together.

"These are all really powerful stories," she offered. "So, let's talk about where we display them and how." Bringing up a new window, she titled it 'Sites For Walk In My Shoes.'

"What about the Fort Collins Old Town Square?" a man named Tim suggested.

Liza jotted it down. "Great idea. I just made this doc available on your tabs; type up ideas."

"Ma'am? Joyce, ma'am," a woman with close-cropped hair offered. "The shoes are a nice idea, but the street cleaners will only remove them. What if we did decorative drone swarms? The consumer-grade micro-drone swarms aren't too pricey. They could spell out the stories and display images of a line of shoes against the sides of prominent buildings, and whenever security drones show up, well, they'll scatter and do it again somewhere else."

Liza's eyes lit up. "Oh that's great! Joyce, let's get that written down in the National database, that's really—"

The tab in her hand cut her off, snapping to an alert that sent Liza's heart into overdrive.

Drones Incoming. EVACUATE.

Liza gulped down a breath. "Okay, everyone, this is faster than I want but let's put the starling maneuver to the test. There are security drones coming this way. Break into six groups. Take six exits. Keep moving forward, whoever is in front is the leader, leadership changes when the flock turns. And you don't leave anybody behind. Also, don't run, because—"

KA-THUNK.

Dust poured from the windows as they rattled. A recorded voice sounded.

"This is an Eaglecorp Automated Crowd Control Message. Please exit the building and accept detention by the drones. Non-compliance is a breach of your corporate contract. Non-compliance will be met by force."

All the careful calm Liza had been trying for shattered. The ArgusCo people broke, scrambling out of their chairs.

"Six groups! Six exits!" Liza called, "remember, murmuration!"

"And that goes for us too," Naomi muttered, stepping to the front of the room and grabbing Liza's arm. "Come on, let's—"

KA-THUNK

The sound rattled the panes of the warehouse's windows, raining more dust. Naomi cocked her head. "Fuck."

"What?" Tweak snapped.

"You don't want to know," Naomi replied tightly. "Let's move. Fast.   Where's   Inyoni?"

"Behind you," the lanky kid muttered, sliding out of his spot behind some boxes. Naomi nodded. "Okay, and we are moving, we—"

BOOM.

The explosion didn't rattle the windows; it blew them out. The world dissolved into glittering shards of sight and noise.

Liza had trouble remembering the next half hour in any sort of sequence; it was running, and it was raining glass, running and air that tasted of dust and copper. And all the time, there was the thought screaming in her head: *I led all these people into a deathtrap. I probably got them all killed.*

They moved hotels as quick and quiet as they could, changing their clothes and layering infrared-reflecting compound over their faces as they went to confuse the cameras. Only when the new room was secured and the door was locked did Liza's heart stop racing.

"So, let's make a deal," Naomi stated quietly. "When we know a site's not safe, we choose another site."

"Agreed," Liza mumbled numbly, bringing up the Common Ground app and the affinity groups for the ArgusCo union. Slowly, she breathed out.

"Okay. We just got the numbers from the chapter."

"How many did we lose?" Naomi asked, still as stone. Liza raised her head, and gave the other woman a smile.

"Only three people arrested. Thank god"

"Good," Naomi murmured. ". Still…"

"Yeah. Still," Liza agreed.

An awkward silence filled the room.

Inyoni cleared his throat. "So, uh... what the fuck?"

Liza glanced up at him. "About what, exactly?"

Inyoni waved his hands. "About all this. I mean... what, you think we're really gonna... I dunno, knock over the Corps? I mean... seriously?" He glanced between them with an expression that said he was looking for the punchline. But nobody in this room was laughing.

"Seriously," Tweak stated simply. "Yeah."

Inyoni let out a long breath, dropping back against the bed. "Shit man… I mean… shit…"

"If you want out, say it now," Naomi threw out casually, but Liza heard the sliver of an edge to her tone.

Inyoni glanced at her with what Liza was coming to see as his signature 'wait, I'm confused' look. "Hunh? No, I just mean... shit. Seriously?"

"Seriously," Tweak repeated. "Sounds c-crazy? Sure. But we got the skills. We got the gear. We got the way. Now, we just gotta get the bodies."

Liza sighed, feeling the words tighten like nanotube shackles around her ribs. "Tweak, can you not say it that way? It makes me think of body bags."

"Annnd we're not going there," Naomi cut in, pulling up a window on her tab. "Okay, next meeting, we need new venues. Let's get to work finding them. I say we take two days off, let things die down, and then we start again at the new site."

Liza thought it over, and nodded. "Sounds smart."

Naomi shot her a little smile. "Now let's talk about something that'll cheer us up. I got an idea for the protests."

"Yeah?" Tweak leaned in, interested.

From her pocket, Naomi pulled her tab and tapped up the window for a note-taking app. "Check this."

Liza studied the image. Naomi had doodled the TechoCo logo, and added devil horns and fangs. Around it, she'd written the words 'I Deserve Rest. I'm Taking It. Send Them The Bill'.

The thing was so goofy that Liza couldn't help but smile. "Hunh!"

"Skip the horns and fangs, of course," Naomi explained, "but what if we used this as the tagline for the general strike that people are going to use to get the Workers' Bill Of Rights paid attention to by the Corps?"

"I like it!" Liza exclaimed, looking over the little image. "It's quick, it's snappy, and it's amusing. Perfect. I'll enter it in the options pool and put it up for a vote; I need to write in Joyce's idea anyway. At least we got one good thing out of today."

Liza spent the next two days collating and annotating a report on what went wrong at the warehouse, sending it to Aidan and the union leaders as a tool to glean new approaches from. When she wasn't doing that, she was checking on the running of the free breakfast and dinner programs in the Equal Standing Kitchens of the area, or working through ideas with Naomi on choosing a site, while Tweak checked and double checked the security on the Union tabs remotely and tried to look for chinks in their tech armor.

"Wish the r-rest of the people would opt in already," the little coder grumped on her spot in the bed. It had become a technological sparrow's nest of tech, all her gear fanned out around her. "Too many holes. Maybe moles. C-can't tell. Pissing me off."

"Mm," Liza agreed, though she only heard Tweak with half an ear. She pointed at a picture. "What if we meet here, pretend to be a mindfulness and yoga club?"

"That could work," Naomi judged, studying the building schematic. 'It's got enough exits... yeah, actually, let's start doing this. Write it up, can you? The unions need to start covering the meetings by looking like something else, not by being sneaky enough to go undetected. Better to pretend to be all kinds of things; less obvious that way. Cooking clubs, book clubs, whatever; that'll give them some breathing room."

"I'll send it in as an idea, I like it," Liza agreed, jotting the note down. Her stylus skewed as Inyoni jostled it in passing.

"Sorry," he muttered sheepishly.

Liza repressed a sigh. "You're pacing a lot. Something wrong?"

Inyoni blinked at her, looking like 'system processing' was written behind his eyes. He shrugged. "Nah. Jus'... kinda small in here. Nothing to do, yeah?"

"Hey," Tweak offered, "got a game. Come play?"

Inyoni perked up. "Yeah, sure."

"Hunh," Naomi murmured. Liza shot her a look, brow raised. Naomi waved her away. "Nothing. So this site, yeah?"

Walking to the new meeting, Liza spotted a few Good Trouble stickers on utility boxes and light posts. The words 'good trouble' were sprayed on a wall down an alley, and she couldn't help but smile.

Only half the expected participants for the ArgusCo chapter had returned to the next meeting, but the ones who did had a kind of fire in their eyes. Before they did anything, Liza got them hooked up with the mental health section of the Common Ground, making sure they had plenty of tools for recovering from the shit they'd just gone through, and everything they were in for. After that, they got back to it.

"The national vote on the first large action is due tonight, so tomorrow, your chapter president will announce what's prefered across the country," Liza finished at the end of the day. "Be safe going home, everyone. Don't forget, message your affinity triad when you get back to your place."

That night, she went over numbers and possibilities again and again. Around seventy percent of the Unions she'd spoken with had opted into what everyone was calling the Safety Net, pledging mutual aid for their Union members in case of Peacekeeper intrusion along with the support the Force could offer. The numbers from other instructors didn't seem to be quite as high as Liza's, but everywhere people were signing up to take care of each other and work together to make sure nobody disappeared. It was a step in the right direction.

"Liza. Hey."

"Hunh?" she managed, raising her head.

Tweak was staring at her. "You got the union, right? Got classes. Here. Another three d-days."

"Yeah, they're doing okay," she conceded, "why, Tweak?"

"You need me?" the younger woman asked. The tone was neutral, and Tweak's expression wasn't any more telling.

Liza froze for a moment, not sure where things were going. "The tech side of things is done for right now, but if you mean do we need you on the team, then of course we—"

Tweak waved a hand. "Nah. Not that. I wanna go out. Down to Aurrora. Be a couple days."

"You what?" Naomi and Liza said the words almost in chorus, the blond woman's head snapping up so hard her hair swung away from her face. Tweak shrugged. "Bird and me. Talked. The next g-Gammas. We want to meet with them. On our own. No Alphas."

Liza blinked. "Tweak... this is so many levels of 'bad idea'. Think about how high you are on the wanted list, and how much you're needed. We can't risk you as an asset by sending you out solo."

And that was the wrong thing to say. Tweak's tiny jaw set. "I'm n-nobody's asset. I'm a g-goddamn p-p-person."

"It's military lingo, Gurgi," Naomi sighed. "And Liza's right. This idea stinks. Sorry, but it does."

Tweak crossed her arms. "No. It. Doesn't. Alphas. Scare. Gammas. We want more Gammas, we need. To go. Alone. Got it?"

"Then we need to set up a perimeter, secure the area, and do prep work," Naomi explained with something like her big brother's patience. "We can't just send you into some place you've never been, alone and blind. That part stinks." She tipped her head. "That said, maybe the part about you going up to them alone works."

"What?!" Liza exclaimed, turning wide eyes on Naomi. So much for her being sensible! "Naomi, are you kidding me? She's the hacker who kneed the Corps in the balls. And she's a Gamma on top of it. She's got a target painted on her!"

"And that's why she's wrong to want to go up to them alone without any prep work," Naomi agreed, holding her eyes. "But Tweak is a Gamma. With a compelling story and a decent pitch. And that's why you're wrong to shoot it down on reflex."

Liza threw up her hands. "This is all kinds of against regulation! We don't send non-grid operatives into liaison, and we don't leave operational teams without backup, and—"

"And and and," Tweak yapped. "Chill, Liza. Sides, won't be alone. B-bird's going with me."

Liza couldn't believe what she'd just heard. She spoke slowly, hoping to get through the coder's mile-thick head. "Tweak. Think about what you just said. You want to enter an unpredictable situation with a recent ally who we barely know?" *A contact who looks to me like he could be a corporate mole?* She repressed the words, barely. "What kind of sense does that make?"

"Hey uh," Inyoni started, but Tweak held a hand up in his face.

"Bird. Shush. L-liza. What you just said. I w-walk in blind, not sure, with p-people I don't know. Yeah?"

"Yes, exactly. Can't you hear what a bad idea that is?" Liza asked, trying not to sound frustrated.

Tweak blinked twice, very slow. When she spoke, every word was measured.

"L-liza. That's what. I. Did. With you. With the W-wildcards. That's. Exactly. What. I did."

Liza opened her mouth. But damn if she could find a single word to get out of it.

After a moment, Naomi cleared her throat. "Okay. This is what we'll do. We'll send the idea back to Aidan. He can decide to approve it or not, and work on it with Kevin, get us a vetted route and approach. In the meantime, we focus on how the Corps found the last meeting, and we patch the leak if we can. How's that for everybody?"

Tweak tipped her head first to one side, then to the other. Then she bobbed a nod. "W-works for me."

Naomi turned to Liza. "How about you?" Liza glanced between the three people, feeling the cage closing in around her. She sighed. "Fine. Fine! But we do this by the book.*" She glared between the two women. "And if either of you say 'yes mom' right now, so help me God…"

Naomi held up her hands. "Wasn't going to."

Tweak snorted.

Event File 13
File Tag: Operative Security
20:30-09-6-2160

They talked deets and plans until they were all beat. At some point, Inyoni had curled up in the hotel chair and sacked out. He looked like a puppy that way.

Tweak got into bed, but she stayed awake for a long time, staring at the ceiling.

Turning her head, she could just make out the silhouettes of Naomi and Liza in the other bed, and Inyoni in the chair. His holo must have gotten turned off; in the dark, he had the silhouette of a sleeping deer.

Another Gamma. Even his silhouette in the dark made her grin. She'd never been around another Gamma like this, in a safe—well, okay, safe-ish—space where they could really start to talk. The things she wanted to ask him were fizzing under her skin, bubbling on her tongue. But they weren't the right things to ask when Liza and Omi were around all the time. If she got what she wanted, if they let her spend a couple days alone with him, then she could ask all the questions.

She hadn't trusted this feeling at first; it was too good, too fizzy; a sugar rush for the brain. Liza was kind of right, too; Inyoni had just dropped into their laps. And that was always a red flag. So Tweak had done her thing; she'd spent a couple nights digging and vetting. She wasn't as dumb as Liza thought; she wasn't going to walk into a trap just because the bait was shiny.

But it looked like Inyoni really was legit: he had a full Citizen Standing Profile with ZonCom, and it was a seriously shitty one stamped with 'Antisocial Citizen' and a score to match. Digging a little deeper, she didn't find any sign of a bounty-hunter's profile anywhere, or any under-the-table contracts for him in all the dark little places where ZonCom and EagleCorp hid things like that. Lying in bed, she ticked off all the boxes. Yeah. She'd done all her checks right. It didn't mean he might not be getting paid as an informant, but that just didn't jive. He didn't even have his own tab, so if he was checking in with somebody, it was by messenger pigeon or some shit. And she wasn't seeing that happening. Besides, an informant would be asking questions. And Inyoni wasn't.

She watched him breathe in the dark, feeling herself smile. She'd done all her checks. For now, she was going to let this good feeling be there.

Another Gamma. Maybe he would know how it felt for the whole world to get too loud. Maybe he would know a fix. And if he didn't, at least they could bitch and moan about it together. Just talking with somebody who *got it* was going to be the best.

She passed out somewhere in the middle of that thought.

In the morning, they had the first half of what Tweak wanted waiting on their tabs.

> **Message Handle: AceofSpades**
> **Message: we're going to need to run security on this, but since we've had crap luck so far on the recruitment side of things, let's try it. I give approval. Omi, start a security sweep. Stand by for an operation plan from Logistics.**
> **Take care of yourselves.**

"What was he doing up and working at this time of night?" Liza muttered, running a finger over the message timestamp. "He should be getting his sleep."

"Aidan never was a heavy sleeper," Naomi offered through her own yawn. "That was me. Pass the caffeine, yeah?"

Inyoni passed across the coffee pot. As Naomi poured herself a cup, she glanced at Tweak. "Okay, so we've got approval. You sure about this, kid?"

Tweak shrugged. "Pretty sure. C-can't get a lot b-better out here."

"Isn't that the truth," Naomi chuckled as they downed their protein bars and synth-java.

Tweak made a face at the first mouthful. "Eugh. This's s-shit!"

"Hotel coffee isn't going to be gourmet," Liza came back, but she was smiling, so it probably wasn't a telling off. "You'll live."

"Still shit," Tweak grumbled.

"Bring your own next time," Naomi suggested through another yawn. Tweak sighed. "W-wish I had. Miss my b-beans."

"Spoiled."

"Yeah..." she agreed wistfully. Inyoni made a funny little sound, and Tweak glanced up. He swirled the coffee around in his mug, looking puzzled. "So... what's wrong with it?"

She couldn't help but crack a grin at the sight. He was just so hopeless.

"It's g-garbage," she offered. "When you c-come home, we'll show you the g-good stuff. We've got—"

"—secure information you're about to spill to an unapproved contact, pretty soon," Liza cut in just when Tweak was going to brag about their coffee tree. This time, it *was* a scolding.

Tweak rolled her eyes. "Lame, L-liza. Seriously."

Liza's Look was on full force. "Stick to protocol, Tweak. It's there for a reason."

Tweak snorted and stuck the rest of her protein bar in her pocket for later. So much for a nice morning. Liza was such a killjoy sometimes.

They didn't have another class until the afternoon, so Tweak killed time collating the intel on everyone who'd opted into the Safety Net Program and double-checking the Common Ground app. She and the other coders had worked out a plan to track problem messaging that might be an informant feeding the Corps; they'd built a behavioral analysis into the Common Ground to look for users who uploaded weirdly large amounts of data compared to other users. Since that was the best way to tag a compromised device being used for exfiltration, it was a good way to make sure they weren't feeding a mole. There'd been a whole ethics debate about it, but Tweak hadn't seen why they got so worked up. This solved a problem in a smart way. It wasn't like they were looking at people's messaging; just how much stuff was going in and out. No big.

She worked until a new message showed up on her tab

Message Handle: KingOfHearts
Message: a route and schedule
attached for your contact
meeting, taking into account
Liza's classes, which, of course,
will take precedence.
Post Script: Do be careful, will
you? Everyone here is biting their
nails about you ladies.

Tweak snorted at the 'ladies' comment. The guy still talked like he'd just walked out of another century. But her lips quirked as she tapped up a screen and hung it in the air. "Hey! Kev sent us deets!"

Naomi leaned in to read the holographic words, and snorted "Ladies. That guy."

"Right?" Tweak agreed, grinning. "Dweeb. Who talks l-like that?"

"The people in his vids," Naomi replied, smiling as she shook her head.

Liza gestured the attachment open, reading over the plan. She drew a breath. "Okay. Okay. This looks like it can work... according to this plan, you two get a room near the contact's location for one night. Naomi uses that room as a base and vets the area. Once she approves, you two enter the area for the... I really don't like this bit about you and Inyoni staying somewhere by yourselves for a night, Tweak, but if Kevin thinks..." She glanced up, biting her lip and staring at Inyoni like he might bite. Inyoni met her eyes with a 'what's going on?' look.

Liza looked her way. "Tweak, are you okay with this?"

Tweak shrugged. "Yeah. Sure. Why?"

Liza blinked at her. "Tweak... look, let's message. It'll be easier that way."

Tweak cocked her head. What the hell was going on with Liza? She was being weird. Watching her, Tweak grabbed her tab.

What gives, Liza?

Liza didn't type as fast as she did, but the message came back eventually.

Tweak, this guy might seem
harmless, but we don't know him.

> Are you really sure you want to
> stay alone in a room with him for
> a night? It would weird me out. I
> don't like putting you in a position
> with a complete stranger who could be anything.

Tweak's nose scrunched as she typed.

> Seriously, Liza? I vetted him like
> day one. Plus, I can beat the crap
> out of him! What are you worrying about?
> I'm worried about what happens
> if he decides to pull something in
> the middle of the night when
> you're asleep, Liza's message read
> when it blipped on her screen.
> Tweak, I know how good your
> vetting is. But I just don't like it.

Tweak rolled her eyes.

> Jeez Liza. I can handle myself. I
> did a full vetting on him already. I
> TOLD you I did; I looked around and
> made sure he's not using a dead
> Duster's identity, and he doesn't
> have a Corporate contractor's
> profile anywhere. I did all the
> things we normally do to vet a
> contact. I know the drill. I'm not a
> baby and I'm not an idiot. I checked him out.

When Tweak glanced up, Liza was biting her lip again. She paused for a moment. Then she typed.

> I trust your vetting skills, I do.
> Don't get me wrong. But this? It
> feels all wrong. This guy just got
> dropped into our laps. Doesn't that
> feel weird to you?

Tweak stared at her screen. Then she glanced up, fighting the urge to look Inyoni's way. No sense freaking him out.

"Feels lucky, Liza. I know weird. I know lucky. I got this."

Liza stared at her until she couldn't take it. Tweak glanced away. Looking at her hands, she heard Liza sigh. A new message popped up on her screen.

> Tweak, I'll admit, I may be freaking out here. But when we relax, bad things happen. The truth is, I don't want what happened to Aidan to happen to you, okay? You can call me Mom if you want, but that's what scares me. I don't know if

The cursor flashed a few times, but when the next words appeared, they were a new sentence.

> Just be careful.

Tweak raised her eyes, offering Liza a smile. After all, she was trying to watch Tweak's back. She cared. She showed it in the most awkward way ever, yeah, but she did care.

"I got this, L-liza. Really."

Liza nodded, though her shoulders didn't relax. She sucked in a breath. "Okay. Okay."

The train to their next stop was packed, filled with people getting off shifts and crowds headed out for the first parties of the night.

"Naomi will message later tonight. You'll call us if anything goes wrong?" Liza asked for what had to be the hundredth time. "If you've got trouble, call us."

"I got it already," Tweak snapped, exasperated. She flashed a small smile at Naomi. "Don't let her keep freaking, kay?"

Naomi gave her a cockeyed smile. "I'll do my best, but no promises."

Inyoni smiled weakly. "We'll be good. No worries."

That got him The Look off Liza, which wasn't really fair. What did Liza have against this guy?

"C'mon, Bird," Tweak muttered, stepping onto the train. "Let's go."

They were practically invisible in a train full of party-goers. LED lights flashed in hair and on clothes, and glow-in-the-dark lips glimmered whenever they went through a tunnel. These were the cheap seats, and the train stopped way too hard. Tweak hung on to the guard rail and fixed her stance, trying to keep clear of the people all around them.

The train shifted, and she stumbled. A hand grabbed her arm, and a bolt of panic raced through her. She whipped around. Inyoni gave her a smile. Tweak tried to smile in return as she pulled her arm away. "Nobody touches me. Okay?"

Inyoni held his hand up apologetically. "Sorry. Just trying to help."

"Don't. I can handle it," Tweak replied, shaking the moment off. She didn't really need to protect herself that way anymore; the feel of his fingers hadn't imprinted themselves like burning lines across her nerves, the way they would have a year ago. There was no electric shock on contact; barely even a residual tingle now. Maybe it was time to start getting used to being touched. And he couldn't feel her scales through the bandages and the coat. Or could he?

What felt like hours later, the train slammed into their stop. It was a dark part of town, a lot further from the center of the city. A few blocks more and they'd be in the warehouse district. Tweak pulled her leather jacket tighter around herself as they left the station. "C'mon."

Inyoni said nothing, but shoved his hands in his pockets and followed, head down.

The room Tweak had paid for was pretty crap; two small beds, clean for a given value of clean, and a bathroom that would just about fit her, but nobody average-height. It sucked, but it'd work for now. Tweak flopped onto one of the beds, pulled out her tab, and got to work on a code she'd been trying for a new kind of application tunneling. She kept her eyes on the screen, and off Inyoni, with some work. *Don't jump into all the questions,* she told herself over and over. *Don't freak him out. Play it cool. Don't jump all over him the second you're alone with him.*

She heard the mattress foam let out a whuff of air as Inyoni sat.

"Place sucks, doesn't it?" She asked, raising her head to flash him a quick smile.

He nodded. "It's a roof over my head, so I'm not complainin', but yeah."

"Easy to secure," Tweak explained. "So yeah." *Play it cool,* she reminded herself again. *Just be cool.*

"Reminds me of a holding cell." Tweak muttered after a few minutes. "Sucked."

She heard Inyoni shift. Glancing up, she noted him sitting up straight.

"You were in a holding cell? You got nabbed?"

"Yeah," Tweak agreed. "TechoCo Special Holding. Sucked balls."

Inyoni whistled. "How'd you get out?"

"Lucky," Tweak explained. "Made a friend. Billie. Without her, it wouldn't have w-worked. She got a keycard off a guard, I copied code off it. She got us food, I got us c-cash, we used the keycard we made and booked it."

Inyoni stared at her for a moment, nodding slow. "That's a solid pal, huh? Lucky."

Tweak glanced up for a moment, smiling slightly. "Real lucky. I was a stupid k-kid, though; n-needed some luck. 'Lleven, when I got c-caught. Took five y-y-y-years to get l-l-loose."

"Glad you did, though," Inyoni muttered with a little smile.

Tweak glanced at the clock, frowned, sighed, and stood, pacing as she coded. "How 'bout you?"

Inyoni shrugged and looked back down at his hands. The harsh room light showed through his cosmetic holo, making the blue cover on his hair look weirdly translucent. If she looked close, she could just see the outline of his long ears.

"Picking pockets, last few years," he offered with a shrug. "Like I said, I tried everything else. Worked in a shop for a while, 'fore they fired me when my holo got turned off. Did trash work for a bit, 'fore Argus did a background-check on me and said they didn't want no Gammas workin' for 'em. Bounced around a lot. You know."

Tweak glanced at him with a wry smile. She did know. "That's what got me nabbed. Taking stuff."

"Yeah? What'd you do?" Inyoni looked up warily, his fingers twisting around themselves. "You don't mind sharin', I mean."

The look on his face made something go funny and soft inside her. She flipped off her screen, dropping onto the bed in front of him. "Don't mind. K-kinda wanted to talk. Just us. N-no Alphas, y'know?"

Inyoni glanced down, smiling. "Yeah. I know. Never talked this much before. To somebody who gets it, I mean."

"Same here. Somebody who knows where I'm coming from. And isn't batshit," she added ruefully. Inyoni chuckled weakly. "Yeah, I get that. It's... hard, ain't it?"

Tweak nodded slowly. "Hard. Yeah." She straightened up. "So. What I did. This's it. My baby b-brother. He got sick. System. All fucked. Right? Two stomachs. It caught up with him. My m-mom got sick from the s-stress a little l-later. So, I d-d-decided to make some c-c-cash. Started stealing stuff outta the TechoCo dumps. Fixing it up. R-refurbish, you know? All kinds of stuff. Tabs, players, anything. Rew-worked them. J-jail-broke stuff, if they paid me to. Sold them cheap. Made good money... pissed Techo off, though. Fast." She snapped her fingers. "Got me nabbed. No time at all. Then they f-figured out I was g-Gamma. Hello, special holding. Met Billie because they made her b-bring the meals to the freaks."

And there was Inyoni's whistle again. Tweak looked up at his face. He looked... was that impressed? "That'd do it, yeah," he offered. "Corps don't like people steppin' on their turf, 'specially if you can do it better than they can."

"Always could," Tweak agreed, trying for some of her usual sass. But it didn't stay long. She glanced at the clock again, and sighed. "I suck at waiting. Wish it was t-tomorrow."

"I hear that," Inyoni sighed. "I get all fidgety, with nothing to do and nothing to think about."

"Same here," Tweak agreed, feeling a funny little thrill in her belly. He reacted the same way she did.

She gave the man across from her a smile. "Our doc. He says some of us make too much of the stuff that keeps people sharp. Adrenal-l-l... ugh."

"Adrenaline?" Inyoni suggested.

Tweak nodded. "That."

"Hunh," Inyoni considered the words. "Yeah, that makes sense."

Tweak shrugged. Then, after a moment, she dug in her jacket pocket, and pulled out a deck of hand-printed cards the Sanctuary Station had started making. "You play?"

Inyoni blinked. "What the...you got analog cards? Seriously?"

"Yep," Tweak agreed, riffling the cards between her fingers. "Nice to take a b-break from a s-screen. So. Play?"

"Which game?" Inyoni asked, staring at the cards. "I know a few, but I ain't any good."

Tweak considered. "Mmmm... Blackjack." she declared eventually. "Blackjack's cool."

Tweak had fun with blackjack. Once Kevin had taught it to her, it had become her favorite game. It was all about thinking fast and counting fast; stuff she was good at. Besides, the analog cards kept her hands moving, which felt good.

"You want your c-cards to add up as close to twenty-one as possible without going over. That's c-called b-busting," she explained as she pulled the joker cards out and set them aside. "Cards with numbers are worth that. C-cards with faces, worth ten." She dealt them each two cards. "You get to twenty-one, say 'blackjack'.

Inyoni lifted his cards, studying them. "So, how about the aces? What're those worth?"

"Either one or el-leven," Tweak replied, staring at the six and eight in her hand. Damn.

"Uh... Blackjack?"

Tweak raised her head at Inyoni's voice. "Seriously? L-lucky bastard! Lemme see."

Inyoni turned his cards, showing her, yep, a ten of clubs and an ace of hearts. She grinned. "B-beginner's luck! Go again."

Shuffling, she dealt them both another two cards. "Say 'stand' if you d-don't want another c-card, and 'hit' if you do."

"Why?"

"Rules."

"Kay. Hit."

"Grab a card."

Inyoni made a face at his cards. "Twenty-four. Bust."

"I win! N-ninteen," Tweak grinned. "Discard, n-next."

Tweak pulled two. But at the moment, she was a lot more interested in Inyoni's face.

"B-bird? Can I ask s-s-something?"

"Yeah?" Inyoni agreed distractedly, looking at his cards. "Stand."

"What's it like?" she asked. "Not feeling p-pain? You still feel, right? Heat, cold, stuff? Touch? Hit." She drew a card.

"Some stuff," Inyoni admitted, eyes on his cards. "I can feel pressure, when someone's touchin' me. I feel hot and cold, but not much.

Never really feel hungry, either; had to set a timer to remind me to eat when I was little. Hit."

Tweak nodded. "Think that's a g-Gamma thing. If Billie d-d-doesn't t-tell me to eat, I forget. For d-days sometimes. So, if I touched you. You'd feel it."

"Yeah. Wouldn't feel it if you cut me or somethin', though." Inyoni shrugged.

"You like it?" Tweak asked carefully.

Inyoni hesitated. Then he shook his head. "Hate it. Can never tell when I'm fucked over, 'till someone tells me. Got a pop in my wrist from breakin' it too many times. My leg didn't heal right once, and it sometimes goes all sideways an' pops out an' someone's gotta tell me not to walk for a day or two or I'll fuck it up worse. Not worth it."

"Shit..." Tweak grimaced. After a moment, she glanced down at her cards nervously, and forced out a laugh. "Funny. You and me. Wish we could t-trade. T-twenty," she added, laying down the cards.

"Seventeen," Inyoni offered, laying his cards in turn. "Trade, how?"

"Touch." Tweak muttered. "P-pain. I win." Cards riffled in her fingers. "I feel everything. Skin's weird. Too many nerves. And other stuff."

"That why you don't let people touch you?" Inyoni asked mildly, watching her shuffle.

"Yeah," she agreed. "It's g-getting b-better though. The doc on my base is doing some stuff for me. Pruning the nerves down. Helped a lot."

"Your doc's decent?" Inyoni asked.

Tweak nodded. "I mean, he's freaky. Real hardass vibes. Good guy, though."

"Cool," Inyoni murmured, playing disinterestedly with his cards. "What's pain feel like, anyway? I mean... I know it's bad, but... you got any other words for it?"

"Feels like hell," Tweak replied offhandedly, dealing him his cards. "Think lightning under your skin. That won't stop."

"Huh." Inyoni murmured. He picked up his cards. "You don't mind me asking... what've you got under the bandages?"

Tweak's mood dropped as if a switch had been flicked. She fought down a snap of fury with three slow breaths. "Arms. Hit." she stated simply, and flicked the cards, drawing another. "Shit. Twenty five. Bust."

Inyoni glanced up, studied her for a moment, then grinned like an idiot and tossed his cards down. "Blackjack. Twenty one. On the nose."

Tweak grinned. "Lucky. So, do you have t-trouble r-r-reading people? Like, they think you should get all these little things you don't?" Inyoni glanced at her. "Like what?"

"Stuff on their faces," Tweak offered. "Stuff in their voices. Alphas want you to r-read minds, like."

"Oh that!" Inyoni exclaimed, nodding. "Yeah, that's a pain. Mostly for me, it's a filter thing, you know? The world's huge and loud, and Alphas filter it some way I don't got, I think. They expect me to pick up all these details and I'm like 'in this noise?' Honestly, can't tell if it's my brains or my ears there."

Tweak glanced up at him. "Hey, um... can I see your ears again?"

He met her eyes. "Can I see your arms?"

She dropped her eyes. "Okay yeah. Sorry."

Eyes on her cards, she heard him sigh.

"Yeah, me too. It's just... yeah."

The cards flipped with their whispery little snaps.

"Hit."

"Hit."

"Fifteen."

"Damn. Nine. Deal again?"

"Yeah," Inyoni agreed.

Tweak's tab blipped, and she grabbed it, tapping up her messages.

Message Handle: QueenOfSpades
Message: Security sweep's done.
Map of the area with everything
you need attached. You're clear
for tomorrow. Luck. Message if you get in deep.

"What's up?" Inyoni asked. Tweak gave him a quick smile. "Omi. Says we're c-clear for tomorrow."

"Uh... good?" Inyoni offered after a moment.

Tweak bobbed her head. "Yeah. Good. Okay. Cards." She picked hers up again.

"So... where's your fam out of?" Inyoni asked as he drew another two cards.

"China," Tweak replied. "Dad got a c-contract job over here. Was supposed to come in, make really g-good money, g-go back. 'Cept, Mom delivered too early. Got took to the wrong c-clinic. Bao Li—my brother—the way he came out got us caught. Dad was Beta. They ar-r-rested him for lying on his c-contract, his im-m-migration papers. Threw us out of our n-neighborhood, dropped us to CPS. Couldn't get to the c-consulate. They wouldn't let us. C-couldn't get back to China."

"Shit," Inyoni murmured. Tweak nodded. "Yeah." She raised her eyes. "You know what, though? In C-china, they don't call us Gammas. They call us Deltas. 'Cause that's the s-symbol for change, r-right? And over there, we're kinda s-special. They do all this gene therapy stuff so we come out our best, not our worst. They took the tech C-cavanaugh made for them, and they kept g-going with it. They think it's us who're gonna save the species. Our genes. We're how so m-many people survive without so m-much food and w-water."

"Yeah?" Inyoni asked, staring at her. Tweak nodded. "Yeah. Mom and Dad told me. It like that in Africa?"

"No idea." Inyoni laid down his cards. "Mom was Beta; Corps came callin' and she ditched me to keep me safe. Said she'd come back to get me later. Didn't. She didn't have a lot of time to tell me about where she was out of."

Tweak nodded. "How old for you? Hit."

Inyoni looked up at her over his cards. "Huh?"

"How old were you?" Tweak asked again, then rolled her eyes at his blank look. "When you got cut loose?"

"Oh." Inyoni looked down again and sighed. "Seven."

Tweak cocked her head. "Seven? Serious?"

Inyoni nodded as he drew a new set of cards.

"Shit." Tweak glanced down at her cards again. "Seven's bad."

Inyoni shrugged. "Heard of worse. Made it out okay, for the most part."

"The guys under the bridge, right?" Tweak asked, laying down her hand. "It was the guys who took c-care of you, wasn't it?"

"Nah. Was on my own for a long time, 'fore I met 'em." Inyoni groaned as he saw the hand Tweak laid down this time. "You cheatin' or somethin'? Jeez."

"You kidding?" She shot back with a laugh, "this's Blackjack. Don't need to cheat. Game was any easier. I'd fall asleep." Tweak tapped the side of her head. "This brain. Runs fast."

Inyoni gave her a half-grin. "Yeah well, this one does too. Still think you're cheating."

"Then you're a j-jackass."

"Well yeah, you seen my ears? 'Course I'm a jackass." He grinned. "How much is the ace worth again?"

"Depends, what's your other card?"

"Why's it depend?"

"'Cause I'm gonna cheat and t-tell you a n-number that'll make you lose." She glanced up, caught his eye, and grinned back at him. He snorted a laugh.

"How'd you make it?" Tweak asked as the cards moved.

Inyoni shrugged and focused on the shuffle. "Luck. Quick learner. Had the cute factor goin' for me for a while."

"Still do," Tweak remarked quietly. Inyoni made a sort of 'erk' noise in the back of his throat. She raised her head, meeting Inyoni's eyes with a flare of nerves. "What?"

"You think I'm cute?" Inyoni asked, a surprised grin on his face.

"Yeah," Tweak admitted grudgingly, "I do. Got a problem with that?"

Inyoni's grin widened and he looked back down at his cards. "Nah. I like it. No one's called me cute before."

"Don't push it." Tweak replied with a smirk. "It's the ears. Look like a puppy."

"Damn. Guess the holo's kept me from picking up girls, then."

After a moment, Tweak glanced up, a little smile tugging at her lips. "Still cute with normal ears. And you lose again," she added, laying down another winning hand. "Twenty."

"Not sure if I should be happy or mad 'bout all that," Inyoni muttered, though his lips quirked up again as he tossed his cards down. "Both, I guess. I really suck at cards."

"Yeah you do. A program wins more'n you do." Tweak agreed, shuffling the cards. Hanging out with this guy was almost like hanging out with Billie, but not quite. And that was just plain weird, considering how long it had taken her to relax with Billie; it had been almost two years of daily meal deliveries before they started to be friends. But this guy just felt... *good* to talk to. She was saying stuff she barely told the team back home, much less some guy. It felt like somebody had turned all her warning systems off with him. All that stuff that normally sat in the closet of her brain was just pouring out.

Was it because he was another Gamma? She studied her cards, trying to decide. That was part of it. It was nice to be around someone she didn't have to slow down and watch herself for. And sure, he was nice. But the Wildcards were nice too, and they were good to her, and she didn't go spilling her guts to them. It wasn't their problem, and they didn't need to hear it.

Tweak set the thoughts aside. Whatever was going on, it felt good. Weird, but good. She was going to just let it feel good for a bit.

"Should've bet money on this; would've cleaned up," she added with a quick, teasing smile. "Really glows. Cool."

Inyoni glanced up at Tweak. "No clue what you're talkin' 'bout."

"Your tats. They glow. Am I being weird or are you being slow?"

"Oh." Inyoni twisted his arm to look at the feathers curling around his elbow. He shrugged. "You went from bettin' to glowin'. Didn't know what the change was. But, yeah, they do. Bio-ink. Don't glow much when I'm inside all the time, but runnin' around today, they should light up plenty tonight."

"Kickass." Tweak grinned. "Worth turning the lights out for." She grabbed her tab, checking the time. "We should do that. Getting late. Need some sleep. Lots to do t-tomorrow."

Inyoni wasn't kidding. In the dark, his tattoos shone white. Tweak watched them shimmer until she fell asleep.

Event File 14
File Tag: Recruitment Pressures
05:30·09·8·2160

They ate without a lot of talk in the morning; Tweak still had a million things she wanted to say, but it looked like Inyoni was one of those people who didn't wake up until the day was half over.

"Why're we up so early?" He asked again. Tweak sighed. "Look. This woman. She works nights. We go now, we c-catch her on her w-way home. Got it?"

"I guess," Inyoni grunted into his mug, swilling down his shitty coffee. Tweak tapped up a screen of her tab. "Girl's name is Jillian Jones. This's her," she offered, setting the screen at Inyoni's eye level and flipping it so he could see the picture. "How we gonna do this? Walk up, c-call her by her name and say hi? Don't wanna freak her."

"What're you asking me for?" Inyoni blinked, bewildered. "You're the super-operative Duster here. I gotta say, if it were me, some stranger said my name, I'd book it. Strangers knowing my name ain't no good."

Tweak sighed. "Yeah, well, the super-op sucks b-balls at g-getting other g-Gammas to listen. So yeah, I want help. And if I don't say her name, what am I supposed to say?"

Inyoni bit his lip. "Honestly? No clue. I ain't real fond of outing ourselves, but... that's what's gonna make her feel safe, right?"

"Hit your holo? In a corner?" Tweak suggested with a 'it could work' gesture of her hands. "Best proof we got? Omi marked all the c-cameras and we got the drone schedule. We can d-do it when n-nobody'll see."

Inyoni grimaced at that. "Can't get you a DNA reader to show her or somethin'? That'd work, right?"

Tweak cocked her head. "You believe that? Could be faked. I wouldn't buy it."

"What if I turn the holo off and she sells us out?" Inyoni asked, and Tweak heard the snap in his voice.

"Hey. Chicken. I got your back," Tweak threw out, giving him one of her quick, razor sharp grins.

Inyoni glared at her, his shoulders hunched as he slumped in the chair. "Good. 'Cause you can feel pain if you fuck it up."

"Thanks a lot." Tweak snarked back. She checked her watch and let out a sigh of relief. "Time. C'mon."

Inyoni stood slowly, stretched, and put his head into the bathroom. He touched the side of his neck, and Tweak realized he was double-checking his holo. It had to suck to have something even harder to hide than her scales. It had been a dick move for her to say he should show his ears, hadn't it? She'd've smacked anybody who said 'hey, why don't you show off your scales to prove that you're trustworthy?'

"Ready?" She asked when he joined her. He shrugged.

"Hope so."

"Stay close," she added as they got within a block of the tenement where the woman they wanted was supposed to live. "Look for grey overalls, kay?"

"Kay," Inyoni agreed as their feet shushed against the concrete. A few steps later, he nodded ahead. "That her?"

The woman walked with her head down, her brownish-yellow hair nearly hiding her face. Tweak glanced up at Inyoni, showing him her crossed fingers and a grin. Then she picked up her pace.

"Hey, Jillian?"

The woman spun when they spoke as if she'd been punched, green eyes gone huge. Tweak smiled. "Hey. Can we talk?"

The lady turned on her heel, and took off running. "Shit," Tweak grumbled, and took off after her. "Bird, c'mon!"

The contact wasn't a challenge to keep up with. Tweak ran easy, hoping they weren't making too much of a scene and knowing they were. If this didn't put them on the Corps' map, nothing would. Shit. But there wasn't anything else to do.

"Hey! Wait up!" Tweak shouted as the woman cannoned down an alley, knocked over garbage bins in front of them, and jumped onto a chain-link fence. "Seriously, WAIT! We're gonna HELP! HOLD STILL!!!"

The woman didn't look back as she careened around a corner.

Tweak leapt over the fence and came right after. This was *such* a pain in the ass. She skidded around the corner, and ran face first into the barrel of a gun. That stopped her.

The woman holding it was breathing hard, her face red, her hands trembling. "What the hell do you want?" Jillian asked, her voice hard.

"We're friends," Inyoni replied quietly over Tweak's shoulder. Tweak glanced up at him as he glanced around. He looked down at her, his eyes so wide. "We're clear?"

"Clear," she agreed, feeling like a bitch for putting him in this spot now that they were in the middle of it.

Inyoni swallowed hard. "Okay. Jillian, I'm gonna reach up to my neck. Be cool." As Tweak watched, Inyoni slowly reached one hand, and carefully tapped the holo. Now his hair was brown, and his long ears were down like a scared dog's. "We're like you, Okay? We're like you. Just want to help."

"That was a holo," the woman with the gun snapped, her voice quivering. "You're faking."

Tweak breathed slow and steady, trying to calm her racing heart. Reaching up, she gently tugged one of Inyoni's ears out from his head. "See? I can t-touch it. These're his ears. Real. The holo's for l-looking Alpha. N-not faking you out. We're here to do a thing. To help. By g-Gammas. For g-Gammas. Okay? We wanna talk." She swallowed hard against the fear choking up her chest. "W-w-we wanna help. B-b-but we c-can't do that standing in trash down here with a g-gun in our faces. R-r-relax, l-let's go in, we'll t-talk, kay?"

Jillian's green eyes shot wide. She gulped. "Both of you? Both of you are Gamma?"

"Yep." Tweak chirped. "Kept up with you, didn't I? Whatcha run for?"

The wage-slave gave her a look that was half panicky, half pissed.

"Strangers walking up to me and saying my name? I'm supposed to be okay with this?"

Inyoni gave Tweak a half-glare as he reactivated his holo. "Told you not to use her name."

"Yeah, you did. My bad." Tweak agreed with a shrug, smiling at Jillian. "So. Got a place? We can talk?"

Jillian looked at both of them for a long moment. Very slowly, she lowered her gun. "You're not being tracked or anything, are you?"

Inyoni held up his hands. "We made sure. If I thought we were tracked, I wouldn't have turned my holo off. Seriously. We just want to help."

"Birds of a feather." Tweak agreed with as reassuring a grin as she could manage, working not to fidget from foot to foot. She wanted out of this alleyway so bad her muscles were starting to shiver.

"Inside? Please?"

Jillian swallowed hard, and put her pistol away. "Okay. Follow me. But if either of you say a word about what you see, I swear I'll make you regret it."

Inyoni glanced at Tweak with a 'please tell me we aren't fucked' sort of look as he nodded. "Promise. We'll keep our mouths shut."

Tweak crossed her heart, a little pissed with the whole thing now that she was calming down. "Quit freaking. We're on the same side here. Get it?"

Jillian looked at her for a moment, and Tweak saw the terror in the green eyes. She needed to chill out if she was going to help her, she reminded herself.

"Okay. Okay," the woman agreed. "Come on in."

They trekked up six flights of stairs in the dark. Tweak stepped on a couple things that crackled and something that squished. She really didn't want to know what it was.

Jillian's hands shook as she unlocked the grey-painted door.

"Cam?" she called as she opened the door, "It's me. I've got people with me, and—"

Tweak took a step back, because there was a gun pointed at her head. A much. Bigger. Gun.

Very slowly, she held up her hands. "L-let's c-c-c-cool it..."

"Jill?" The man holding the gun blinked dark little eyes at them, his hands steady as a rock. "You okay?"

"I'm okay," Jillian replied in a whisper. She put a hand on the guy's wrist. "And they're okay. That's what I was gonna say. I think they're okay. They'... they're like us."

"Cept we're not batshit with guns," Tweak added, letting a little of the snark out. "Goddamn, trying to help here. You p-people want to talk about this in the hall? I don't?"

The man's eyes flicked to Jillian questioningly.

"Let them in," Jillian muttered, squeezing the guy's wrist softly.

Slowly, the brick wall of a man stepped back from the door, though his eyes never left their faces. Tweak stepped inside with all the slow and easy she had. Spooking either of them looked like a seriously bad idea.

The room hadn't been redone in a long time, and it hadn't been redone well then. Now chalky wooden slats showed in some places where the plaster had flaked away. The pre-fab floor felt uncomfortably springy.

The place was a dump. But it was a clean dump; swept and neat. Somebody had even tried to make it cheerful with window curtains and bright-painted furniture. It hadn't worked, but it was a nice try.

Tweak turned an irritated glance on her 'host.' "*Seriously,* big guy. Put. The. Gun. Away." She spread her arms. "Look at me. I'm a matchstick. You got more m-muscles than me in your l-little finger."

She glanced down at his hands, and blinked. He didn't have a little finger. He only had three fingers and a thumb on each hand. And it wasn't cut off, either.

She blinked. "You too? Both? Wow." This guy hadn't even been on the Blacklist. Holy crap, two Gammas living together. That was a surprise.

A thin squall rose from the back room. The big man squeezed his eyes closed. The woman gasped. At first Tweak thought it was a cat screaming. Then it clicked, and her eyes went wide. "Holy..."

Jillian cursed under her breath. She gave the guy a desperate look, and hurried into the other room. Inyoni shot a quick look at Tweak. She held up her hands in a 'do I look like I know?!' gesture, and the big man tensed, gun raised again.

Tweak rolled her eyes. "Christ. Look, I'm Tweak. This's Bird. You?"

For a moment, the man stared at her, his little eyes wild. Then he blinked. "Cameron. Cam, to most." Then he did the first human thing she'd seen him do, reaching up to brush his heavy, brownish-red hair out of his eyes in a nervous gesture.

"Okay, great. Names. That helps. Less gun helps too." Tweak added, starting to get sick of this whole thing.

After a moment, the gun was lowered. Tweak let out a breath she hadn't realized she'd been holding. She heard Inyoni's sigh of relief.

Jillian showed up again, a fussing baby held to her chest. The look on her face dared Tweak or Inyoni to say something about it. "Now, tell me what you mean by you want to help."

"Sure," Tweak agreed, perching on the edge of a sofa whose days were numbered. "First, I'm g-gonna do something. R-relax." From her pocket, she pulled a white-noise box, turned it on and set it down. "Okay, now. Safe to talk. That means n-nobody can hear. White n-noise filter. Okay. I'm a D-duster. Don't freak. Chill. We need Gammas. Offgrid. Corps are doing bio-war. But our DNA beats their bugs. You get the free v-vaccines for MACHA? DARA? BEAST?"

"We got them from one of the street doctors," Jillian agreed warily. "They said they were free. Said they were from... Dusters."

In her arms, the baby twisted their head. For a moment, bleary little eyes peered at Tweak. Bleary, bright yellow eyes, Tweak noted. There was something weird about the shape too. She looked a little closer when the baby turned her way again. Holy crap, the kid had goat eyes.

"Pretty." she managed after a moment. It was nicer than saying 'why the hell did you have a kid?!'

"Boy? Girl?"

"Jenny's a girl," Jillian said quietly, fussing with the kid.

Tweak bobbed her head. "Okay, so. And all those v-v-vaccines. Were made. From my DN-n A. So. If my code. Fought all that. My people. Want to see. What other Gamma p-people's code. Looks like." She splayed her hands. "That's why we're here. We're paying for your help. Just blood samples. That's it. We pay good. And then we're gone. If you want us gone, we're gone. But if you want. If you need to get off grid, we can do that." she added, with a nod in Jillian's direction. "If you want to get off the grid, want to work w-with us, or leave the United c-Corps land, we can do that. Whatcha think?"

The room was dead silent for what felt like a decade. Tweak tapped her foot to burn off her fear.

Cameron gave a bark of laughter. "Right, you're going to come in offering us the exec seat for a blood sample. Do we look stupid?!"

"What's the catch?" Jillian asked coldly, adjusting the baby drinking from her breast. Her green eyes were hard.

Inyoni shook his head and shifted his weight from foot to foot. "No catch. 'S'what they want. Dusters, just tryin' to stay alive."

Jillian glanced at Cameron and shifted closer to him.

"Trying to change things." Tweak amended with a quick shrug, watching the little family thoughtfully. "Point is, you want to get the baby girl out of here? Off grid? Get yourselves off? I would, if it was me."

"We're getting by," Jillian replied warily, her shoulder brushing against her man's. "Getting off-grid is… it's suicide."

"Yeah? And what do you call staying here?" Tweak asked, throwing a little shade this time. "Couple Gammas, one don't work; you not on a Corporate contract? You freelance? Yeah, I guessed." she added when Cameron started. "And a double-Gamma baby. And you think here's safe? Get real."

Cameron glared at her, his words rumbling out. "We're fine."

Tweak met his eyes, and she refused to look away. "Yeah. Right."

"At least we've got food and a home," Jillian replied, though her voice was thinner this time.

"Home don't do you much good if the Corps finds it." When she said the words, Tweak saw the woman wince.

"Home isn't home if you're scared." Inyoni added.

Jillian looked between the two of them with the eyes of a pigeon caught in a wire trap, collapsing into one of the brightly-colored kitchen chairs. "We've been okay here," she fidgeted with the baby in her arms as she eked the words out. Tweak could hear the pleading in them.

"For how long? Couple months? And when she gets big?" Tweak asked.

Cameron's body tensed. "You don't talk to my wife like that."

Tweak snorted. "Save it. You two stay here, all three gonna die."

"And we won't die off-grid?" Jillian demanded, green eyes hot when she raised them. She cursed quietly and looked down as the baby started wailing again. Taking a seat on the ratty couch, she rocked the child. "Shhhh. Jen, stop… please… it's okay…"

Cameron glared at them, then stepped to kneel beside his wife where she sat, looking like a dog who wasn't sure whether his master was threatened or not.

Jillian looked like she wanted to cry as she gently bounced the baby. "Cam... what do you think?"

Cameron looked down at her and the baby with frightened eyes. Tweak noticed that his hands were shaking. That couldn't be good.

In a split second that spiked her heart rate through the roof, the man spun up and away, slamming his fist into his own leg a couple times. For a few minutes, he paced like a caged animal. Tweak shot a 'what are we getting into' look at Inyoni. He shrugged a fraction of an inch, just as lost as Tweak.

"Cam, stop," Jillian said, her voice cracking over the baby's cries. "I... we... if they were followed, we're screwed anyway...."

That got to Cameron. He froze, his eyes pinning Tweak to the wall. "Were you followed?"

Tweak shook her head. "'Course not. We're not stupid." But she felt her heart sink. They *had* been stupid; running and making noise in the middle of a CPS multi-unit area, the kind of place the Corps watched most? The kind of place where they *expected* trouble? They'd been shitheads.

But there was nothing to do about that now. After a moment, Tweak hopped off her seat. "Want to see where we'd go? Lookit." Pulling out her tab, she brought up a locked and encrypted file, putting in three of her fifty rotating passwords. It opened into a photo collection. "Look, this's my base. Here." she added, passing the tab to Cameron. He took it slowly and knelt beside Jillian, flipping through the images. Tweak glanced back as Inyoni craned for a better view.

After a moment, Cameron raised wide eyes. "Wow..."

"You have a garden," Jillian whispered in awe. "A real garden. With real food."

"Yep. And the food's the best." Tweak carefully knelt beside them. "That kid's Tommy. Born on base. Sweetheart. That's Abbie. She's cool. The twins. Good kids. Motor pool guys. Real cool. This'n's our Commander, he's great. Logistics Officer. Here. There, Munitions. I'm Tech Officer. Got the spot two years ago. This's our cook, awesome. This's our m-medical people. The best. Great gang." Tweak smiled down at the picture, her heart doing something funny and floppy and irritating. "Best ever."

Man, looking at this made her want to go home.

Jillian stared at the picture for a long moment, before looking up at her husband. "They've got kids, Cam... Jen could have friends..."

Cameron stared at the image, his brow wrinkling, hands pleating the fabric of his pants. Then he looked up at Tweak, spearing her with his eyes. "Is it safe?"

"Is it here?" Tweak asked as gently as she could.

"Makes you feel any better," Inyoni put in carefully, "I ain't never been out there, either. But I'm goin'. Worth the risk, to me."

Jillian looked at him, then back down to her baby, swallowing hard. "Maybe... maybe it is for us, too. Can't be *that* much worse than here... right? And they got real food?"

Cameron stood, pacing again, but it was less panicky this time. Finally, he stopped, staring at his family. Then he looked at Tweak. "If we say okay, what happens next?"

"We s-stay here and chill 'til my t-team l-lead gets done for the day," Tweak explained. "Then her and me, we g-get on a c-call. Touch base w-with my boss. He gives me and l-logistics the go ahead. And we g-get you an out.

Cameron swallowed hard. "How?"

Tweak grinned. Bingo. "The how? That's my job. And me? I *kick ass* at my job."

Event File 15
File Tag: Hearts And Minds
15:30-09-8-2160

"Okay everyone, the votes are in," Liza announced to the room full of teachers. Technically they were ArgusCo employees, counted as part of the country's infrastructure, but this group was assigned to teach the curriculum that EagleCorp wanted to see taught and live in EagleCorp neighborhoods, so exactly what culture they acted in line with was a little weird to figure out. Liza had okay luck with them so far; at least, she'd been getting some good interaction during the first day, so she crossed her fingers and hoped she was on the right track.

"Our first national action will be the Send Them The Bill Campaign. From September seventeenth to September twenty-fourth, we're going to help you run a general strike. The point of this action is to remind the Corps that they have nothing we don't give them. So, we're going to stay home for ten days. Not just stay at home either: be very publicly at home. Take a nap right in front of the window. Read on your front porch if it isn't too hot. Make it obvious that you're staying home, and if you are in a safe place, print and hang this sign—" She pulled up the cleaned up, nicely done version of Naomi's scribble— "in your window. We'll be sending the design for the poster out."

The letters blazed on the screen, a playful font surrounding the ArgusCo logo.

"I Deserve Rest. I'm Taking It. Send Them The Bill."

For a moment, there was quiet. Then laughter burst out of the gathering. Teachers looked at one another, equal parts hope and amusement in their eyes. Liza held her smile for the ones who looked her way.

"For the weeks leading up to your big vacation, this is what we need you to do. Fill your corporation's Contact Us and Make A Complaint forms out with this statement; across the country, millions of people will be doing the same thing." Clearing her throat, she pulled up the statement and started to read. She almost knew the thing by heart now.

"We, the members of your workforce, respectfully require that the following Workers' Bill Of Rights be instituted."

She read through the Workers' Bill Of Rights, and finished it with, "pursuant to these rights, we demand that the wages of all workers be raised to twenty-five dollars an hour within the next thirty days. We demand all shifts be scheduled for eight hours only, including time for physical needs. We demand that all petitions by workers to change Corporations be addressed. We demand that all Morality Executions be canceled. And we demand that Workers' unions be formalized.

"If these demands are not met, we the workforce will take steps to make our needs understood, respected, and met by Management.

"The decision is yours.

"Your Workforce.

"You'll all send that," Liza finished. "Their inboxes will fill up with that. And when they try to ignore you? Well. You'll stay home. We've got stipends ready for folks on survival wages. You won't be starving. And you will be showing the Corporations that if they don't listen to you, they don't get your labor. Period."

Liza waited out the moments of awe and consternation.

"I know this is a lot," she offered quietly, "but the Corporations have done so much damage to so many lives. Isn't it time they paid for what they've done? Isn't it time to send them the bill and make them pay it?"

The room stared at her as if she was the voice of God for a few heartbeats. Then the excited questions came flooding in.

Liza was exhausted by the end of the teaching session, but elation had her walking on air.

"We're really starting to get through," she laughed, flopping into a chair. "It's really starting to work."

"Yeah, I think it is," Naomi agreed. For a couple seconds, they just grinned at each other.

"Has Tweak checked in yet?" Liza asked once she came down from her high a little.

Naomi nodded. "She said call her when we're done. Big news, she said."

Liza nodded, feeling a little knot in her consciousness smooth out. "Okay, that's great. Good that she's checking in. Let's give her a call."

Tweak gave a little wave when she came on the screen. "Hey guys. Need some help. G-gonna patch home."

"You get someone to say yes?" Naomi asked, leaning over Liza's shoulder.

"Got that," Tweak agreed, bobbing her head, "and got trouble. Lots. Need a plan for offgridding a family. With a baby. Fast."

"A *family?*" Naomi asked, sounding surprised for one of the few times in her acquaintance with Liza. "What the hell, Tweak?"

"Just w-wait, I'll tell everybody." Tweak sighed. "Calling K-kevin now. He p-picks up faster than Aidan."

A beat later, the screen bisected into two windows, and Kevin distractedly waved at it while peering at another window. "Afternoon, ladies. We didn't have a call scheduled. Something up?"

Tweak gave the screen a lopsided cynic's smile. "Yeah, I'll say something's up. Kevin. Focus. Lookit." The angle of the camera in her window flipped, and now they were looking at a gigantic man with three fingers, a woman, and a baby. The man glared at the camera.

"Found these folks," Tweak's voice chirped. "And they need off Grid. Yesterday."

Now Kevin was paying attention. He stared for a moment, blinked, and whispered something about the Virgin Mary under his breath. "There weren't any babies on the list. It'll take us at least two days to make arrangements for that. Can you guys hold out that long?"

Tweak had flipped her tab back around, and she glanced off-screen for a beat. Then she nodded, and shrugged. "Guess we gotta. 'Cept, Kev? The b-baby and the guy. They're freelance. And the l-lady's CPS."

Kevin nodded, jotting down notes. "Alright, we'll have to work up false identities and synth for everyone, that will be interesting, and are we dealing with any physiological divergence that needs to be accounted for?"

"English," Tweak snapped.

Kevin sighed. "Does anyone have anything like your arms?"

"Are you even l-looking at the c-camera?" Liza could hear the bite in the coder's voice.

Kevin gave back as good as he got, of course. "Tweak, don't start with me. I'm not in the mood."

"Guys," Liza cautioned. "Let's chill."

There was a heartbeat's worth of quiet, the chastised kind Liza was used to getting from these two when they were coming out of their snits.

"Cam's got three fingers 'stead of four," Tweak offered the words like an olive branch. "And the baby. Goat eyes."

"Me too," someone added off-camera. "I'm wearing contacts."

Tweak sighed. "The baby and the l-lady. Yellow eyes. Pupils like a g-goat."

"That's easy enough to deal with," Kevin mused. "The gentleman's hands... give me a few ticks, I'll think something up. In the meantime, how hot are you?"

Tweak shrugged. "Cool. I think."

"You think, or you know?" Liza asked, feeling herself tense. Tweak glanced down at her hands. "I kinda had to r-r-run through this place. Might've sent up some red flags. We'll see."

"Oh lovely," Kevin grumbled. Liza caught his eye and shook her head. He sighed, but when he spoke again he'd softened his voice. "Are you alright, Tweak?"

"Fine," Tweak bit the word off. "I'm. Fine."

"Alright. Let's get Aidan on the line, we can get this talked over now and he can start the paperwork."

The screen quartered, and now Aidan's bent head was on-screen as well.

"Got a moment, love?" Kevin asked.

Aidan started, sitting up. "Um... hey guys."

"Hey big A," Naomi offered, leaning in to give her brother a quick grin.

Aidan returned the smile, a little bewildered. "What's with the tab party?"

"We've got a bit of a situation we need the commander in on," Kevin began.

"Three adults and a baby," Aidan repeated once they'd explained it to him. "And that's not including getting our team home safe."

"I'm dropping everything to get on this," Kevin offered. "Tweak, we're going to talk it over here, and we'll be in touch tonight. Can you and your new friends go to ground?"

"Say what?"

Liza could practically hear Kevin telling himself to be patient. "Can you keep your heads down?"

"Will do." Tweak chirped.

"Good," the redhead agreed, "then I'll be in my office getting to work. Probably for the foreseeable future. Take care, all." His window fizzed out.

"Does this change any of our planned educational actions, sir?" Liza asked. Aidan's far-off look came back into focus. "Hunh? Oh. No, Liza, go ahead with your part of things. Tweak, you and that family be careful."

"Duh," Tweak grumbled, flicking a new window into place. "What about—"

A sudden pounding on the door rammed through her sentence. In the image, Liza could see it rattle on its hinges.

"Peacekeepers! Open up!"

"Fuck," Inyoni hissed. Tweak squeaked. She jumped to her feet, and her screen flicked out of existence.

Liza stared at her commander, seeing her panic reflected in his eyes. "Oh fuck."

Event File 16
File Tag: Mission Deviation
17:00-09-8-2160

Tweak's heart jumped into her throat. Peacekeepers. Shit. Running in this place *had* alerted them. And now they'd had a whole day to get around to watching the tape, and deciding to call in a squad. Shit!

Inyoni looked at Tweak, then the little family, and back to her. "Gimme a gun. I can draw fire. You get them out safe."

Tweak shook her head hard enough to make her black hair swing. "Bull. Shit." As the pounding got louder, she turned fast. "Back way out? Fire escape? Anything?!"

Jillian shook her head, trying to smother Jenny's cries, though it didn't help much. "Fire escape rusted off last year and no one's fixed it. Only way out is through the front door."

Tweak spun, eyes darting. Her pulse hammered behind her eyes. She couldn't get taken by Peacekeepers again. She could *not*. Think think think... yeah. That'd work.

The sound of splintering wood underscored the pounding of her boots as Tweak darted down the hall, ransacked the galley kitchen and the bathroom, grabbed what she needed, tossed the whole mess in a mixing bowl, messed with the innards of one of her white-noise filters and dropped it in. She spun the bowl across the floor to slide into the door, turned and dove. "Everybody behind the c-c-couch! C-c-cover ears and eyes!"

In a scrambling second, the bowl exploded.

When Tweak dared to raise her head, it was powdered with plaster dust sifting down from the ceiling. The blast had taken out the cushions of the couch. It had also taken out the door and the officers on the other side.

She took a moment to double check. Good, everybody had listened and gotten behind the couch. They all looked freaked and the baby was screaming, but they were all okay. Cool.

"Naomi taught me that," Tweak declared with a grin. "Good trick. C'mon."

Inyoni gave a little laugh as he vaulted the remains of the couch, making sure there weren't any other peacekeepers waiting for them around the corner. "Man oh man...you gotta show me how to do that!"

"Our things," Jillian murmured. Something about that voice was off. Tweak turned. The woman was moving like she was in a dream, blinking at the room. "What about our things?"

"Whatcha need?" Tweak asked, one hand massaging her throat to keep her stutter from kicking in. "Pack fast. Before we hear s-s-sirens."

Jillian just stared at her, shaking her head. And what was worse, Cameron was still in his spot behind the couch, hands clutched over his head, moaning softly to himself.

Well great. She'd broken the civvies.

"Tell me. What. You need," Tweak demanded. "We pack. You t-talk to him."

Slowly, Jillian looked down at her husband, and nodded. "Okay. We need diapers. And Jen's bear. And two changes of clothes each. Toothbrushes and... stuff."

"On it," Inyoni walked into the bedroom, flashing Tweak a smile and hefting his backpack.

Tweak grabbed another pack that was hanging on the wall and hit the bathroom, then rifled some drawers.

"Where's your c-chill vests?" she snapped out.

Jillian had been whispering soft things to her husband, their baby between them in the cover of their ruined couch. Both adults started.

"We don't have any," Jillian managed finally, her eyes far away. Tweak sighed. "Fuck. Kay."

Her chill vest and a spare were both hidden in her jacket, but if the family didn't have any vests of their own, there'd be no running out of town and hoping to make it home. The heat would cook them to death without the coolant-lined vests keeping their body temp in survivable ranges. So that option was out.

Fuck.

Tweak stood still for a moment, running through a breathing exercise. They didn't have much time, but if the panic took over they were all dead. She had to keep it together.

Her meds. That would help. Reaching into her pocket, she pulled out an anti-anxiety tab and slipped it under her tongue. *Okay. Breathe.*

Out in the corridor, one of the Peacekeepers started to come around. Tweak stepped out, kicked him in the head, then hopped back in with her brain going a mile a minute. The adrenaline was fizzing in her blood, making her throat tighten up. This was so not her thing! Herding civvies wasn't her job!

But if she didn't do it, they were all dead.

She closed her eyes, and forced herself to be still. Okay. She could do this. She just needed to get them somewhere safe, and call home, and hand it off to the gang.

Get somewhere safe, call home. Hand it off. Yeah. Good plan.

"Okay, okay, okay," she panted. "We're going. Now. Follow. Me. Stay. Close." Digging in her pocket, she caught Inyoni's eye as she spilled glittering dust into her hand, and threw it into the air. "Nanoids." she explained. "Eats d-d-dead skin, anything with our d-d-d-d-dna on it that isn't attached." Then she came back around the couch and nodded at Jillian. "He ready?"

The big man gave a shuddering sigh, and stood. "I'm okay."

"Good," Tweak replied, "'cause we gotta m-move."

They picked their way across six groaning or unconscious men, Tweak digging in her bag. "Put. This. On. Now." she rapped out, passing out tubes of infrared-reflecting compound. "And don't run. N-no m-m-matter what."

Feverishly, she checked the drone schedule and the camera feeds on her tab, tapping in parameters for a building she wanted and instructing the tab to sort for candidates, choose the best and find them a safe walking route. It blipped as they hit the last set of stairs. Okay, an old garage, that'd work.

"Kay, here's the plan. We split up, two groups of two." Tweak stated quietly. "Bird, here's the addy. Gonna r-remember?"

Inyoni squinted for a second, nodded. "Yeah."

"Kay. Jill, you're with me, and—"

"No." Cameron put in. Tweak rolled her eyes, "Look, we're too showy as four. We gotta—"

"I said *no!*" The man's voice was a low roar.

"Keep your fucking voice down if you wanna live!" Tweak snapped, glaring up at the gigantic asshat.

He glared right back, fists clenching and unclenching. "No. I'm staying with her."

"Cam..." Jillian turned to him, tears in her eyes. "If it gets us there safely... just go. I'll... Here, take Jen. I'll see you there. You take care of Jen, okay? Promise."

Cameron stood rooted to the spot, body swaying, head shaking from side to side. "No...no, I've gotta stay with you." he muttered, sounding as if he was thinking aloud.

Tweak groaned. "We don't got time for this shit! There's men with guns c-c-c-c-coming, g-g-g-get it?!"

"Just go!" Jillian pleaded, pressing the baby into her father's arms. "Please, Cam. Just go."

Inyoni grabbed Cameron's arm. "Come on. We gotta go before they find us."

Cameron made a low, animal noise in the back of his throat. But he did move.

"See you there." Tweak waved a hand at Jillian. "Follow me, keep up."

"Where are we going?" Jillian asked behind her as Tweak moved.

"Somewhere safe," Tweak replied over her shoulder. "A little ways from-ack. This way." she added as three Eaglecorp cars screeched to a stop in front of the old building, sirens blaring. "Don't. Run. I mean it."

She could practically feel Jillian vibrating behind her. She wasn't a lot better off. If she let it, her brain was just waiting to play a highlight vid of every shitty Peacekeeper who'd ever smacked her around. If she let that get started, she'd curl up in a ball and melt right down. And that *couldn't* happen now.

"Play cool. Play cool. Play cool," Tweak whispered, not sure if she was talking to Jillian or herself. "Just play cool..."

Sweat trickled down her back as they walked past the mess of officers and security, looking like any other hopeless people in this community. "Don't look up," she muttered. She heard Jillian swallow.

"This-a-way." Tweak muttered, darting down a side street, then through as many alleys and back ways as she could find. They dodged down into a drainage ditch. Ahead, bars blocked the entrance to a concrete culvert tunnel, but they were old and rusted, and the cutter from Tweak's mech'n'tech gear didn't have any trouble with them. Slicing through the joists, she let them fall and slipped between. "In."

Jillian opened her mouth to protest, but closed it without a sound. Thank god. Tweak so did *not* have the bandwidth to argue.

They came out on the other side with nothing worse than filthy pants, and in Tweak's book that wasn't bad at all. The safehouse, an abandoned garage, was right next to the culvert.

They were the first in, and Tweak grabbed a seat on a stack of old tires, frowning at her boots.

Jillian slid down the wall, ending up in a heap on the ground and trying to wring muddy water out of the leg of her jumpsuit. Tweak could have told her that was a waste of time; it'd just get her hands dirty.

She didn't say anything as they waited, the silence stretching out into what seemed like years before the door opened. She tensed, expecting more trouble, and relaxed when Cameron ducked through the door. "You good?" She asked.

Inyoni sidled in after the heavier man and shut the door. He looked freaked, with hunched shoulders and wide eyes. Cameron crushed his wife to him for a moment, which set off more squalling from their baby.

"She wouldn't stop crying," Cameron muttered, voice cracking on the edge of panic. "Why won't she stop crying?"

Jillian muttered under her breath and took the baby, leading Cameron back to the corner she'd claimed to look after Jen. "She's dirty, Cam."

"Lucky she's alive," Inyoni muttered, glaring at the couple. "Cried the whole fuckin' way, and then he freaked and took off running; got us shot at, nearly nabbed."

"Damn." Tweak looked him up and down. "You guys take fire? Hurt?"

Inyoni hesitated for a moment. His shoulders slumped as he sighed.

"Don't know. Didn't feel anything, but I was tryin' t'keep that guy alive…"

"Want me to take a look?" Tweak asked carefully. "Um… nothing weird."

Inyoni seemed to think it over, looking from her to the family in the corner, and back. He swallowed hard, and nodded. "Uh. Yeah. Probably best if you do. Just… can we go somewhere they won't see, you think? Don't… don't really want everyone to know."

Tweak nodded. "Got it. Over here." she added, gesturing at a bunch of piled tires.

Inyoni ducked behind them with her, and sighed as he flopped down to the floor.

Tweak studied him, frowning when she saw red. "I see blood. Shirt off."

"Dammit," Inyoni muttered under his breath. All the same, he did pull his shirt off. Tweak took in the sight. Inyoni's skin was the color of expensive wood. Gigantic white wings flared across his shoulder blades and upper back. Wow. The feathers she'd seen on his arms were just a little bit of the design. He hadn't been kidding; he really did have wings.

And they're gorgeous, she realized. *He looks amazing.*

Scars crisscrossed the tattoos, under and over the shimmering white ink, some faint and others gnarled. But they made the wings look like they had texture, blending into the feather design beautifully.

I wonder what they feel like.

Tweak blinked. *Shit, what did I just think?! What the hell?*

Inyoni sighed. "How bad's it?"

Tweak snapped herself back to the moment. *Get it together.*

"Where'd you get the cash for all this?"

"This what?" Inyoni asked. Then he got it. "Oh, the ink?" His shoulders rose and fell in a shrug. "Scraped it together. Might have picked some pretty deep pockets now and then."

"Picked some fights, too." Tweak observed wryly, eyes studying the lines and curves of his back. All those scars.

And then she spotted the trickle of blood. "Shit. Here. Some kind of gash. In your side. Not deep. Just b-bloody. Got the kit here. Two secs. Easy fix." Tweak muttered, pulling on surgical gloves and squeezing out antiseptic. "Really like your name, huh?" she asked, spreading the paste and smoothing a basic autopad over it.

Inyoni shrugged, which made the tattoos rise and settle. "Like the meanin' of it. Birds've got this freedom we don't. Wish I could really be one sometimes."

Tweak glanced up, and grinned. "You're close." she remarked, pointing at the tattoos. "Nice look."

Inyoni smiled weakly over his shoulder. "Thanks. You got any ink?"

Tweak's smile morphed into a smirk. Tattoos. Yeah, right. Like you could tattoo over snake scales.

"Me, I hate needles," she deflected. "Too many n-needles in my l-life." For a moment, she looked at Inyoni, and his smile made her want to keep smiling too. Then she turned, scooped his shirt up and thrust it at him. "On. You're good."

"Thanks," Inyoni muttered as he slipped back into his shirt. He tugged it down "So. What now?"

What now, that was the real question. What the hell now.

"Now. Yeah." She flopped down on a tire.

The panic was starting to rise again, now that she wasn't moving. She drew a breath that came a little hard. "Okay. Okay. I'm gonna c-call my people. They'll fix this. Keep them busy, kay?" She nodded at the little family in the corner.

Inyoni glanced that way, and gave her a smile. It looked a little weird; nervous, maybe. "I'll try?"

"Cool," Tweak agreed. Scooping up her tab, she trotted into a corner, and tapped in Aidan's call sign on her tab.

The guys would fix this. Of course they would. She repeated the words in her head as the Mesh connected her through who knew how many people's devices, all the way back home. The guys would fix this. She just had to get ahold of them, and it wouldn't be her problem anymore.

When the window came up, Kevin and Aidan were both crammed into it, almost squeezed into the same chair. Kevin let out a long breath. "Oh thank you Lord Almighty," he murmured fervently. "Tweak, are you alright?"

"Yeah," Tweak agreed.

Aidan looked freaked. "The Peacekeepers at the door, what happened with that? How hot are you right now?"

"They're not. Alright." Tweak tacked on, to make sure the two

Alphas got it. Was Kevin technically an Alpha? He was a gene mod too, just a fancy one. So did that make him an Alpha, or was he... Shit. Her mind was playing with ideas that weren't here and now. Bad sign. Okay, breathing exercise. Here and now. Focus.

"We're hot," she finished on a breath. "It's bad."

"Give me details," Kevin replied tightly, bringing up three new windows. "We'll get this worked out."

Tweak swallowed. "I'm gonna type it."

Kevin nodded. "Go ahead, that won't slow me down."

So Tweak typed out all the details of the situation, and Kevin typed on his end, whispering little things to himself under his breath now and then. After a while, he sat back, sighed, looked at Aidan with some expression Tweak didn't get. Then he looked at the screen.

"Alright, Tweak. You're probably not going to like this. Brace yourself."

Tweak rolled her eyes. "Seriously? Give."

Kevin glanced at Aidan again. That wasn't good. Kevin looked at Aidan a lot when he was scared. Not good at all.

"Alright," the CES man explained, "I've collated the Force and union plans with the reports on your actions—a Peacekeeper died, so you've officially pulled the buzzards' tails—and I've indexed available Force safehouses. Working in the fact that we have to make up four identities, their associated documentation, and synth for all of them from scratch, which is a bit of work, and factoring in our own transport and logistical parameters... I'm sorry Tweak, but the plan with the highest likelihood of success is this: you and your new contacts stay in a safehouse near a reliable egress for three weeks. Liza and Naomi join you, and you can all get out easily when the stay-home action begins; the Corporations will be distracted then. Someone from the base acts as a courier and brings your documents and synth to you at the end of the safety period. And then you can—"

"Three weeks?!" The words ripped themselves out of Tweak like shards of glass, crow screams of terror and anger. "Three weeks?!"

Kevin held up his hands. "I'm sorry, all right! I'm sorry! It's the best I can safely—"

"Roll your best up and stuff it up your ass!" Tweak snarled. "We need fucking out K-k-kevin! Yesterday! Fucking yesterday! Fucking three w-weeks?!! Fuck that!"

"Tweak, please, if you'd just calm—"

"And fuck c-calm too! Up the ass!" Tweak yowled. "The P-p-peacekeepers n-n-nearly had us, and you want to leave us out here for three w-w-weeks? You w-w-want us f-f-fucking d-d-dead?!" The tab in her fingers shook.

On the other end of the connection, Aidan leaned in, holding her eyes. "Tweak, listen. Take a breath. Come on, breathe with me."

"N-no! I'm g-g-gonna get caught! I'm g-g-g—" She had to gasp for air. "I'm g-gonna d-d-die!"

"You're not going to die," Aidan murmured, his voice quiet. "Come on. Breathe with me, okay? In for seven. Out for seven."

Tweak's lungs weren't as big as Aidan's. She breathed in for five and out for five a couple times, until the tab in her fingers wasn't shimmying anymore.

"You okay?" Aidan asked. Tweak shook her head. "N-no. But I'm n-not l-losing it."

"Good enough," her commander replied quietly. "Okay. So. This plan is what we've got. We're working to find something else, but this is it for now. We've sent Liza and Naomi your coordinates. I know it sucks and I know we're putting you in more danger, but this is how it is. We've got faith in you, Tweak. You can do this."

"You're gonna get me k-k-k-killed!" Tweak groaned. "Aidan, the p-p-Peacek-keepers... I c-c-c-can't—"

"Yes, you can," Aidan interrupted. "You've done tons of shit harder than this. You took down the entire Citizen Standing system. You took down the whole fucking CO-WY Grid. Listen to me, Tweak. I know what you can do. They call you the Dragon for a reason. You *can* do this. You can lie low and survive for three weeks. Like I said, we're sending help. Liza and Naomi are on the way. And I'm trying to get ahold of grid contacts who can help you, too. You *can* do this."

Tweak shook her head. This time, her words sounded so small, as small and as scared as she felt. "Aidan. Please. If they g-get me I'll d-d-die. They'll d-d-d-dis-s-sect m-me. P-p-please! I g-g-gotta g-g-g-g-get outta here."

Beside Aidan, Kevin winced as if he'd been slapped.

"We're doing everything we can," Aidan replied, and his voice was little too. "I'm sorry, Tweak. I really am. We'll let you know if we can come up with anything better as soon as we can."

Tweak sucked in a breath. If she let this fear get any bigger, it would kill her. No more fear. She glared at the two men staring at her like she was a pet cat in the vet's office, all worry and love. Fuck that. They deserved to be just as scared and hurt as she was.

"Fine," she snapped. "Fine. But this's your fault. If I die, it's your goddamn fault."

"Trust me," Aidan replied quietly, "I know."

Tweak didn't know what to say to that. So she hung up.

"Three weeks?"

Tweak winced at the sound of Inyoni's voice. Slowly, she drew a breath. "Three weeks. Gotta wait."

"If it's near an out, why d'we have to wait?" Inyoni asked as he leaned against the wall beside her. "Why not just get out?"

Tweak raised her head, studying him. "How much did you hear?"

Inyoni shrugged. "With these ears? All of it. The family missed the words, but they heard yelling. They're kinda freaking out. Asked me to come check on you."

Tweak dropped her head into her arms. "Fuck."

Inyoni slid down until his knees were level with his nose, giving her some kind of sad little smile. "So it's three weeks 'fore they can send anyone for us. So much for us being important, hunh? Thought we was s'posed to help people stop dyin' and shit."

That brought Tweak's head up, fury snapping through her. "You shut the fuck up, you hear me?!"

Inyoni's eyes went wide. He held his hands out defensively. "Sorry." If anything, that made her angrier; where did he get off acting like she was going off the rails when he'd just dissed her friends like that?! What right did he have to talk that way and then act like she was the one scaring him?!

"They're doing what they can!" She snapped. "They'll get us out soon as they can, safe as they c-c-c-can. They c-c-cc-can't go any faster! G-g-get that straight. Isn't about who's imp-portant. It's about g-g-getting us out alive. We *are* a p-p-priority. D-d-don't say d-d-different." Turning on her heel, she stamped away.

Event File 17
File Tag: Operative Assessment
02:30-09-9-2160/09:30-09-10-2160

The hiss of the train's wheels skating over the rails filled the baggage train with white noise. Tweak listened to the train whisper to itself and shifted in her rail-worker's jumpsuit. The thing was way too big, it was itchy, and it was starting to piss her off. But the jumpsuit was actually the worst thing about this whole plan, and that was fucking amazing. Kevin had sent her all the details for the plan to get them to the safe house, along with a little note that had said 'I really am sorry'.

Maybe she should send him a note back. She had kind of ripped into the guys. Sure, she'd been scared... but so had they. And she knew she'd taken a chunk out of Aidan with that crack about dying. That wasn't right.

The train shushed the dark. Tweak had offered to take the first watch, because there was no way in hell she'd sleep, amped up as she was. She stared into the safety-light accented dark. Sprawled over a couple of pieces of luggage, Jillian and her family slept like nesting dolls: Jillian curled up on Cameron, their baby curled in her arms.

Tweak still couldn't believe they'd had a kid. Who'd give a kid a life like this?

At least the baby hadn't cried when they'd gotten aboard. Following the directions Kevin had sent, they'd snuck the uniforms and key cards out of a maintenance workers' closet in the middle of the night and used them to walk over and hop onto one of the slow baggage and freight trains that ran by night. The freight cars took forever to get anywhere, but traveling this way was safe. In a couple hours, they'd be in a house where they could hide out. Kevin had made a plan for her that worked out great. That meant he cared about her, didn't it? Yeah. Of course it did.

Her fingers tapped on the empty screen of her tab, counterpoint to the whisper of the wheels.

Of course the guys cared about her. Screw Inyoni, the Wildcards did care about her. She knew they did. Aidan had spoken up for her more times than she could count. He'd let her stay after she fucked up in her first year on the base. And Alice had knitted her a sweater for Christmas two years back. She only did that for people who were really part of the crew. Kevin had sat with her and talked her around when she'd felt like trash about being a gene-mod last year. They *did* care about her. They *would* come for her. That's what families did. Wasn't it?

Restless, she turned her tab on and re-read the plan again. Re-read the note at the bottom.

> 'I really am sorry, Tweak. We'll get
> you out of this morass as quickly
> as we can. My word on the Good Book; I'll fix this.
> -Kevin.'

Beside her, Inyoni cleared his throat. "Everything look okay?"

Tweak just about jumped out of the baggy railway uniform. "Fuck!" she hissed, forcing her hand to relax out of the half-cocked fist she'd folded it into. "Don't s-s-scare me! You're s-supposed to be passed out!"

"Sorry," Inyoni muttered. "Couldn't sleep…"

For a moment, they sat in silence. The safety lights outlined Inyoni, cutting through his holo and giving him the outline of a deer cut from black paper.

"Look, I… I'm sorry 'bout last night," he murmured into the dark. "Didn't mean to get to you."

Tweak stared at him for a second. But that was weird. She didn't want to be weird. So she stared at her feet. Damn. She wished she was better with people. She hadn't cared a few years ago. Fuck the world, that had been her motto. But now there were people worth caring about. Things had changed.

And if Inyoni was one of those people...

Tweak let out an explosive breath. "Look. What you said. When I got mad. Wasn't you. The guys... the base. They're my guys. My gang. They care about me. I *know* they d-do." Her fingers tugged at the bandages near her right wrist, checking them. "Not a lot of people cared about me. Not before. Care about. *Me*. Not cared 'cause I *code*. Cared 'cause *I am*, you get it?" She swallowed. "Sometimes, I get scared. Why do they c-care so m-much? What if it's fake? I think about that. So, what you said. S-scared me, y'know?"

The soft sound of the rails filled the silence. Tweak cleared her throat. "So... sorry, ok?"

When she turned her head, Inyoni was watching her. He smiled weakly. "Call it good. And you know... I think they do care. Wouldn't have made such a fuss getting' you back if they didn't. Those guys on the screen looked really worried about you, too. Handlers don't get worried. Friends do."

Tweak gave him a small, bleak smile. "Lady at my base. She told me the same thing, when I t-told her what I was s-s-scared about. She cussed more, but yeah." Glancing away, she sighed. "I gotta tell the guys sorry. Those two guys. Who you saw. Commander. Logistics. Good guys." She shrugged. "What I said. No fair. They're gonna freak till we're home." After a moment, she glanced up. "You'll like them. Good guys. The blond guy. Sweet. The carrot, he acts stuck up. Ignore it. He's okay."

"Good to know," Inyoni offered quietly.

Tweak smiled at him. "Hey. Turn your holo off in here. Save the power."

That was bull, but it made her feel good to see his ears. It made her feel like she wasn't alone, and right now, away from Billie and all her people, she really wanted to feel less alone.

Inyoni hesitated. In the safety-lights, the whites of his eyes gleamed. "'S'okay. Powered on my heart, yeah?"

Tweak made a face. "Still don't l-like that. Bad for you."

"Better'n getting seen," the slim man suggested.

Tweak sighed. "Yeah. There's that."

Overhead, the wind whistled beyond the train's skin.

"We're cool, right?" Tweak asked quietly.

"Yeah." Inyoni's teeth gleamed in a quick smile. "We're cool."

"Cool." Tweak repeated. "Glad. Gonna need help, keeping those three alive."

Inyoni snorted. "Can't promise nothin'. Man…"

Tweak nodded. "I get you. Won't shut up, won't take orders, no streetwise. How they're still alive, I d-d-don't know."

"Some folk get all the fuckin' luck," Inyoni agreed with a sigh. He leaned back, closed his eyes, and reached up to tap the silver circle in his neck. His holo flicked out.

Tweak glanced over, and gave him a quick grin. "Y'know, I wasn't lying. Cute. The ears."

Those ears lowered as he shrugged. "I think they're stupid. But… thanks."

"Could get them fixed. Doctor?" Tweak asked curiously, then rephrased her question to make it easier for other brains to parse. "Ever tried to get them fixed?"

Inyoni shook his head. "Got looked at once, when I was little, but the doc wanted too much cash. The docs we could afford would've reported us. Mom wasn't gonna risk it, and I can't afford shit like that on my own."

Tweak nodded. "Yeah. I wondered," she added, leaning back. She watched his ears droop. She really wanted to see those funny ears perk up again.

"Could be worse," she offered.

"Yeah," Inyoni agreed with a sigh. "Could have somethin' a holo couldn't hide. Like that poor bastard." He motioned vaguely towards Cameron. "Three fingers… how's he managed like that?"

"Yeah," Tweak agreed, her mind on her own arms. Then she shot the guy beside her a sidelong smirk. "Could be a *lot* worse. Could have a llama dick."

Inyoni busted out laughing, his ears springing up in amusement. It took him a long moment to compose himself enough to add, "Then no pretty girl'd let me near her."

"Yeah," Tweak agreed. "You'd look like you had a r-r-rifle in your c-crotch. Imagine that!"

"Don't make me, that sounds fucking awful," Inyoni laughed.

"Or you c-could have camel balls. Hang down past your knees," Tweak suggested. She grinned wickedly, watching his ears wobble with his laughter. This was fun.

Inyoni bent over, he laughed so hard. "Oh shit, man. That's raw!

What other things they mix in to fuck us up?"

"Lizards, some snake. Some cat. Waterbear; kinda bug," Tweak ticked off, grinning. "Could have a w-waterb-bear face. Shit, babies'd scream!"

"Lizard eyes—poppin' out of your skull and wrigglin' all over," Inyoni tried with a grin.

"Lizard tongue that goes across the table," Tweak offered, sticking out her own tongue.

"Whiskers!" Inyoni suggested with a grin. "Or a tail. Imagine a cat tail, huh? That'd be hard to hide."

"No shit," Tweak agreed, grinning. "Other hand, could join a kinky strip joint. Real pussy. Meow!"

Inyoni laughed until he had to gasp for air.

Behind them, a thin wail rose, along with a pissy rumble out of Cameron. "Will you two shut up?"

Inyoni's ears flattened against the sides of his head. Tweak glanced over her shoulder, frowned, and resisted the urge to flip Cameron off. He really knew how to kill a mood.

"Gonna be a long three weeks," she grumbled to Inyoni, once Cameron had put his head down. "Too long."

"No shit," the man beside her muttered. Tweak closed her eyes and listened to the train chanting itself through the night.

Getting off the train was hell. Tweak's heart nearly stopped three times; once when Jen started to fuss inside Jillian's baggy jumpsuit, once when two security types eyed them, and in the moment when she slipped into the darkness of the streets outside the station behind the rest. Anyone could have seen them in that moment. Anyone could have walked by.

"Where are we going?" Jillian asked softly.

"Somewhere safe." Tweak replied. She considered her words, then added, offhandedly, "I think."

Silence.

Tweak frowned. Maybe she shouldn't have said that last bit. She was no good with people, she never had been. She sighed, and checked her tab for directions.

"Somewhere safe," Cameron repeated, a whisper in the pre-dawn silence. "Somewhere safe..."

The house the coordinates led them to wasn't great. But it'd work. At least, Tweak thought it would, until Jillian spoke behind her. "You're not serious."

"Oh, right, like the shit hole you lived in was better?" Tweak snapped, staring up at the concrete block house. She had to admit, it didn't look great. But she'd shoot herself before she'd say that out loud.

Inyoni sucked in a deep breath. "Well, it's what we got, right? Stop whinin' and get inside 'fore the Corps drive by."

Tweak shot him a quick grin. "You heard the guy. C'mon."

The little house wasn't as bad as it looked from the outside. It was small, but there was a hallway with four doors off it; a bathroom and three bedrooms, it looked like. There was decent furniture, and food was already stocked in the kitchen. Inyoni whistled in appreciation. "Woah. So the outside was a fake-out, hunh? Your guys got some pull. This's better'n any place I've lived b'fore."

"AC's screwy." Tweak remarked irritably, dropping down beside the wall unit. "Freezing in here." Then she glanced up as Inyoni stiffened. "What?" she asked, watching him stand. He stayed right where he was, still as a statue. Something about his body language told her that if that holo was off, those long ears would be standing straight up.

"What?" she hissed again. Then she heard it too. A rustling. Someone in the next room.

Cameron shoved his daughter into his wife's hands, and ran into the next room like a rockslide. There was a yelp, a thud, then a curse Tweak recognized. "Shit!" she groaned, and darted into the room. "Hey, asshole! Put her down!"

Cameron had Naomi by the throat and was holding her off the ground. He'd just raised a fist, when Tweak kicked him in the back of the knee. "D-d-dumbass! She's part of my team!"

Cameron lost his balance and let go with a strangled yelp. Naomi tumbled to the floor and landed in a fighter's crouch, hacking curses. Once she got enough air to speak a full sentence, she stared up at the big Gamma.

"Okay, so far I don't like you much."

Cameron, sitting on the floor and massaging his knee, gave her a glare.

Tweak gave her an apologetic smile. "Sorry Omi. You okay?" she asked as the taller woman stood.

Naomi straightened her jacket, jerking a black plastic thumb at Cameron. "Long as this jackass don't try to choke me again, I'll be fine."

"Thought you were Corps." Cameron muttered sullenly, turning his face away as he got to his feet. For a moment he stood still. "Sorry," he grunted.

Naomi studied him for a long, cool moment. Then she turned to Tweak, looking her up and down. "You look okay," she judged, and Tweak was pretty sure she sounded happy about it. "Glad you guys made it."

Tweak crossed her arms, grinning. "What, don't think I can hack it?" she demanded teasingly.

Naomi rolled her eyes. "Don't start. So, who's this guy?"

"Cameron," the big man muttered. "You kicked me," he added with a dirty look Tweak's way.

She stared him down. "You choked. My pal. We're even."

Ten minutes later, the six people sat around the small parlor as Naomi explained what they were up against. "So, we've got a bunch of problems here; you guys need papers," she nodded in Cameron's direction. "And since you've never had them before, we have to parse and clean the DNA that will go into the card's read to make it look Alpha. We're doing the same for you," she added with a nod for Inyoni, "And that takes a long time." She drew a breath. "The real problem here is Jenny. Tell me you've got a birth contract for her?"

The kid's parents glanced at each other, and back at Naomi, like convicts told they were going down for life. Jillian shook her head.

"We hired a neighborhood lady to help. She was born in our bedroom."

Naomi looked Tweak's way, and blew out a breath. "Well fuck. Okay, so we need to fabricate everything for her from birth contract and documentation down to a record of her birth in a hospital. It's a lot of work. After we have the papers, then we can safely move you people around enough to get you off the Grid. But it's just too risky otherwise."

In Jillian's arms, Jenny cooed and turned over.

"Then an operative has to deliver the packet with all the synth and new Citizen Cards we need; probably best if somebody here meets them halfway," Naomi continued. "It'll stop a tracker following the courier right here."

"Couldn't they mail it to us?" Jillian asked. Naomi gave her a patient look. "Who owns and checks the mail? ZonCom. Not a good idea." She glanced down at the baby Jillian held. "And then there's the fact that the Corps are on high alert right now, and your little Exploding Apartment stunt didn't help. So, this is where that leaves us: Liza's got to finish her class, and then she's going to join us. The big general strike starts in three weeks, so that times out. We'll lay low until the strike. Aidan sent word that he wants us to post a watch every night until we're out of here, to be on the safe side. Then we'll get our packet, and Tweak and I will escort you folks back to our base. Tweak, since you're hot you'll stay there. We're getting somebody lined up who can do the basics on securing the civilian tech for the rest of Liza's tour."

"Seriously?" Inyoni asked. "Stand watch? I thought this was supposed to be a safe house."

"Doesn't mean the Corps can't find it," Naomi replied levely.

Tweak nodded, then shot a grin at Inyoni. "C'mon, if I can hack it, you can."

Inyoni huffed dramatically, but he shrugged. "Guess so."
Tweak glanced at Naomi, and realized that the other woman was staring at her. "What?"

"Hunh." Naomi blinked. "Nothing important. Okay, so it's probably best if the new folks do the watch with one of us. In two person shifts. So the rotation will be Tweak and Inyoni, then me and Jillian, then Cameron and Liza. So, what you do is, you turn on the house's security feed. It'll project on the wall, with a full view of the house surroundings and a count of people and vehicles for the surrounding six blocks. Keep an eye on it and do something that keeps you awake. Sound good?"

Inyoni glanced at Tweak, flashed her a grin, and shrugged. "Fine by me; made a good team so far."
And there it was again, that weird, irritating flip-flop feeling in her chest. "Yeah," she agreed, "so far. Good team."

Naomi leaned back in her chair, stretching. "Okay, so now we just sit back and relax. The rest of this is up to the team back home."

Relax, Tweak thought, looking around the table full of worried faces. *Yeah, right.*

An image of the safehouse glowed on Kevin's main screen, keeping company with readouts, algorithms and timetables that he'd brought up and scattered around him. Blue Oyster Cult kept him company on the headphones.

Burn out the day,
burn out the night...

The words couldn't have been more apt.

He turned up the volume on the song, checked his current snippet of code and ran a hand through his hair, eyes blinking themselves back into focus. He ignored the clock, and the messages on his personal tab. Later. He could look at that later. At the moment, he had work to do. All of it was intricate, from the forged documentation—which was turning out to be hell on their systems and his nerves alike—to the abysmal planning process of getting all this to his people, and then getting them out. He had to get it done, and it had to be right. And he was running out of time.

"Time ain't on my side

Time I'll never know," he sang under his breath.

He started when a warm hand rested on his shoulder, and glanced up. Aidan smiled down at him. "Hey."

Kevin smiled sheepishly, pulling out his 'buds. "Hey. Sorry. Is it late? I'll be along in half an hour or so, once I get a few more of the details planned out."

"Kevin, it's two in the morning," Aidan replied, his voice gentle. "The route'll wait a few hours. Besides, you're more accurate when you've had some sleep. Come on."

Kevin blinked, looked up at the clock, then sighed and ran a hand over his face. When had it gotten so late?

"I hadn't realized...do you think Damian would give me a StayWake tonight? I need to finish this and... oh." he trailed off, looking at Aidan properly for the first time. His eyes had the hollow, haunted look they took on the nights when he'd awoken from a bout of nightmares. Kevin had come to know that look too well in the past few years.

He stood. "Can't sleep?" he asked quietly, taking Aidan's hand.

"Yeah," his husband agreed. "It's, um... it's not a good night. I... it isn't so bad, when you're there. So, maybe both of us could use some sleep."

Kevin sighed, pulling away to tug out his kerchief. "You're right," he muttered, pulling off his glasses. "But as I'm the one who landed Tweak in this morass and failed to see the complications until they ensnared her..."

He polished the lenses, letting his thoughts sort themselves out. The sound of Tweak's pleas were like struck gongs in his head, impossible to ignore. He slipped his glasses back on, and gave his husband a smile. "And I'm being unrealistic again. And a martyr. Aren't I?"

"A little," his husband agreed quietly.

He worked up a smile. "Well, enough of that, then. At least I'll cheer her up a bit," He patted the package sitting on his desk. "I got into the system and made this look like a legitimate purchase, and it doesn't have anything in it that will set off the ZonCom sensors, unlike the new credentials. I'm hoping to provide a silver lining to the situation for the moment, at least."

"What is it?" Aidan asked, glancing from the package to him. Kevin gave him a crafty little smile. "It's the most recent batch of coffee beans, and that little personal grinder she cobbled together. That should ameliorate some of her anguish until we can get her home."

Aidan gave a little chuckle. "Yeah, but Liza may strangle you for it. You know Tweak bounces off the walls when she's drinking real coffee."

"True; we've commiserated on that little issue once or twice," Kevin acknowledged. He glanced at his screens. "In fact, maybe I'll just brew some coffee and do a few hours more; the least I can do is keep at it until I've planned her way out."

"Kev?" Aidan murmured. Kevin turned to him. Holding his eyes, Aidan shook his head, a slow gesture laden with his peculiar sort of solemnity. "I'm the one who sent them. If anyone should be up and trying to make this right, it's me. But if there's one thing you and Damian have drilled into my thick head over the last few years, it's that we *all* need rest." Reaching out, Aidan took his hand. "Come on. I'll set an alarm. A few hours of sleep won't make much difference."

Kevin glanced at his desk, and sighed. "All right. A few hours."

His thoughts were still far away as they undressed, and he lay in bed staring at the ceiling. If only he'd planned this operation better. If he'd made plans for more possibilities, they wouldn't have operatives in this mess right now.

Operatives. Liza, who'd saved him from himself more times than he could count. Naomi, who meant so much to Aidan, and was a good friend in her own right. And Tweak. Poor little Tweak, with terror in her eyes and a stuttering series of pleas on her tongue. The way she'd sounded on that call still echoed in his head. She was absolutely *distraught.* She'd trusted them to keep her safe. And now…

Tweak's words rang in his head. *"If I die, it's your fault."*

Aidan snuggled in close, and draped himself over Kevin. The sweetness of the gesture tugged a smile out of him. Softly, he rested his arms around his husband.

In the dark, Aidan's voice was a murmur. "Hey. We'll get them home."

Kevin kissed the top of his head. "Trying to read minds now, love?"

Aidan gave a quiet snort. "I'm your husband. I don't need to read anything; I know you."

"That you do," Kevin sighed, eyes closed. "But if I hadn't made a hash of this, we wouldn't have to worry whether they'd come home. If I'd planned for more contingencies…"

Aidan propped himself up on his elbow, and Kevin knew he was looking down, waiting for Kevin to open his eyes. When Kevin gave in, that patient look was in Aidan's face, tired as it was.

"I'm doing it again, aren't I?" Kevin admitted quietly.

"Riding the Blame Train right to the last stop? Yeah," Aidan agreed. "We do what we can with the information we have, Kev. You can't plan for everything. And nobody can plan for the kind of crazy Tweak gets into."

Kevin gave a small, bleak laugh. Leaning up, he kissed Aidan. "You're absolutely right, on all counts. Thanks. It's…it was the tone in Tweak's voice. It's stuck in my head; I've never heard her beg like that before." He looked into his husband's eyes, warmly lit by the faint night-lights. They cast the hollows of Aidan's cheeks in shadow, making him look haggard. His poor love was so tired. They both were.

"It terrified me, frankly, to hear her so vulnerable." He continued quietly. "She's petrified, Aidan. I didn't know it was possible, but she sounded like an abandoned child in that call, begging to be rescued. And I'll admit, it pushed all the guilt and responsibility buttons in my brain. She's depending on me. I've got to get her out of there. She rescued us once," he finished, brushing his lips across Aidan's. "It's up to me to return the favor."

"And you will," Aidan replied. "In the morning, when you're fresh." Aidan shifted, laying his head on Kevin's chest. "Right now, try and sleep, kay?"

Kevin let out a quiet breath. Then he nodded. "I'll give it a try, love. Thanks." he murmured. Finally, he closed his eyes, and let his soul grow quiet.

He was up a little later than he would have liked in the morning; no real surprise there, given the hours he'd kept the previous night. And Aidan had been right; the work did come easier now that he was rested. The man really did know what he was talking about. He was scrutinizing seven birth contract records, trying to decide which one would be easiest to forge, when a knock on the office door pulled him out of his reverie. He raised his head. "Morning, Jim. Anything pressing at the moment? I'm a bit busy, but I can spare a few..." Then he really looked at his base-mate. The tall man looked like Aidan on his worst nights; like a man who was sparring with nightmares.

Kevin turned away from his screens, giving his fellow logistics man his full attention. "Anything the matter?"

Jim sighed. "Mind if I shut the door?"

"Of course," Kevin agreed, pulling out his flimsy extra chair. "Here, take a seat."

The way Jim sat reminded Kevin of someone decades older. For a moment, the man stared at his hands.

"Jim?" Kevin asked quietly.

His subordinate sighed. Then he stood, undid the gunbelt around his hips, and set it on Kevin's desk.

"I need to turn this in for a while."

Kevin could almost hear the whimper of his own heart. But Jim wouldn't thank him for getting sentimental, not now. He nodded his understanding. "Looking a bit too friendly these days, is it?" He asked quietly.

Jim raised his head, and the look in his eyes was breathtaking. So much sorrow. So much weariness. If Jim was a different sort of person, Kevin would have tugged him into a hug. Instead, he smiled his commiseration; the bleak smile shared between men who'd lost too much.

Jim returned the smile weakly. "Truth is... I'm tired these days. And a dirt nap's starting to sound good."

Kevin nodded. "I imagine so." There was no need to ask why. Kevin knew all too well. The little girl they'd lost to the bio-weapon made in his own family's corporate labs had fueled the fire in Kevin's gut; one more innocent death on the heads of the Corporations. A death he *would* hold them accountable for. But though he'd loved the girl as a part of his base family, he hadn't lost his own daughter. And the loss had turned this sanguine, capable man to ashes.

Well. Kevin might not be able to fix this, but he could certainly help.

"Have you talked to Damian? I'm not going to give you any orders, but I'd like to see you have a word with him."

Jim lowered his eyes. "I'm starting to think I need more than what Damian's got."

Kevin's heart ached. Slowly, moving with careful deference, he put the gunbelt in a desk drawer. Reaching over, he put his hand on Jim's shoulder.

"Would taking leave up at a Rest and Retirement base be a good idea?"

"Think so," Jim agreed in a hoarse croak. "Sorry, man."

"None of that," Kevin demurred gently. "You owe no apologies here. I'll drop by Aidan's office. We'll get the paperwork filed. Okay?"

His friend took a deep, shuddering breath. "Okay." Slowly, he raised his eyes. "I gotta tell you this; I don't know how long I'll be gone. But I kept thinking that dying on duty wouldn't be a bad thing, on the last requisition run... and Yvonne was with me. I'm not doing that again."

Kevin caught his drift, painful as it was. Of course, he wouldn't have expected any less from a man as admirable as Jim. He might not care if he lived or died right now, deep in grief as he was, but he was actually stepping back to avoid the danger he could be to his team. That was integrity incarnate.

Kevin squeezed his shoulder. "I hear you. And don't worry about it."

For a moment, a flicker of Jim's old manner surfaced in his dark eyes. "You're getting somebody to fill in after I leave. You running ragged waiting for me to get back won't fly."

"We'll get the position filled, pro-tem," Kevin agreed, feeling the words weigh him down. Pro-tem. Would it be pro-tem? Or was this another friend he'd never see again?

No, this was about Jim, not himself. He smiled at the man with all the authenticity he could muster. "I'm on it. We'll get you up there by the end of the week."

Jim gave him a smile that made his heart bleed. "Thanks, man."

"Any time," Kevin agreed, trying for a blithe manner and failing.

Once he was alone, he took a moment to compose himself. He brought up a Request For Recuperative Leave form and got it filled out. Usually he'd send it to Aidan's tab. But today, he allowed himself the small luxury of walking down to his husband's office.

"Got a minute?"

Aidan glanced up. "Hey Kev. Sure... you okay?"

Kevin gave him a brittle smile. "Not exactly." He closed Aidan's door, dropped into his husband's extra chair, and pulled up the holographic screen. "I'll need your signature on this. Jim's suffering. He's going to need to be put on recuperative leave."

"Oh. Shit," Aidan murmured. Closing his eyes, Kevin nodded. "Indeed."

After a beat, a warm hand rested on his. "Good call on you, getting him what he needs."

"Good call on him, telling me what was going on," Kevin corrected quietly.

He really shouldn't. They were on duty hours. But at the moment, he allowed himself to have what he needed. Leaning in, he rested his head on Aidan's shoulder. His words came out broken. "I am so *sick* of losing people."

Aidan's warm arms wrapped around him. "I know, Kev. I know."

Event File 18
File Tag: Community Buy-In
14:30-09-11-2160

"Alright, everyone," Liza stated, addressing the garment workers' union, "let's go through it one more time. On September seventeenth, we—" she pointed at a woman named Alice, who sat up straight in her chair.

"Don't come in to work, and put the sign in our window."

"Great. And every day, morning and evening, you—" She pointed at a man called Charles, bent with decades of work on a stitching machine.

He gave her a little smile. "Check in with our contact triads on the Common Ground."

"Great, and when you're called by your superiors you—" She pointed at a young woman called Lily, who shrank in her chair as if Liza's finger was a gun.

"Read the statement, ma'am?"

"You've got it!" Liza agreed with a smile for her. "And if they start saying anything about your Corporate Contract, hang up. They're definitely going to send you several rounds of threatening messages, and then they're going to shut off your pay. Everyone's got their stipend portal set up, yeah?"

Heads nodded around the room.

"Thing is," Matthew added in the back of the room, "I want to know how we keep them from tracing this money right back to us?"

"It's an important question, thanks Matthew," Liza replied, "and we wouldn't want anyone to feel that they're doing something dangerous by accepting the stipends. These payments are funded by donations from human-rights programs overseas, but they're also funded by accounts full of money that people high in the Corporations have stolen."

She expected the ripple of unease, and she gave it a beat to happen. "Our technical and financial people have been getting into and doing what amounts to a citizen's audit of the bank accounts for all seven Corporations. We've found thousands of illicit bank accounts where managers and CEOs sock away funds they've gotten illegally. As we speak, reports on all the dirty details are being sent to Corporate offices, with a statement that they will be released on both the Mesh and the Net if attempts are made to reclaim the cash. So if the owners of the money try to come for it, they'll know that it will cost them the publication of where they got it."

"Miss?" An older woman who'd given her name as Clara quavered in the back, "I never stole nothing in my life..." She trailed off, embarrassed, but Liza got the drift.

"I know, Clara. And you're not stealing now," she offered. "They make this money through bribes, through contract falsification, and in some cases straight-up embezzlement. We've found cases where funds for new infrastructure projects went directly into these accounts, and new water projects and roads were never even started.

"You're still drinking rationed water that's gone through corroded pipes, still dealing with brown-outs when the heat waves overload the power grid, still on Calorie Resource Restrictions every time the harvests don't work out, and the money you worked to create for the projects that would have fixed those problems went into someone's pocket instead.

"So, what we're doing is getting that money back to the people who worked hard for it. We still believe that the salaries the Citizen Excellent Standing and Citizen Secure Standing populations are paid are obscene, and that nobody should have over a billion dollars while someone else is struggling to get food—" she paused to let a little cheer pass — "but I can promise you that the only money we take is reclaimed from activities that are unquestionably illegal. It was never their money to begin with: it's yours. We're giving it back."

This time, she let the cheer run for a bit before she clapped her hands. "Alright! Great. So, let's get everyone set with their signs and get going."

She handed out the signs with a smile for everyone, and a little extra pep for the last person in line; the young woman who'd answered her question as if she'd been afraid the words would cost her.

"Are you feeling better about things, Lily?" She asked.

The nervous young woman tried for a smile. "I guess, it's just... we're not going to be alone doing this, right?"

Liza shook her head. Reaching for her tab, she brought up the Common Ground and pulled up the window for unions who'd approved the general strike across the country. "Every one of these dots is people just like you who won't go to work when the strike goes live. You won't be doing this alone. You'll be doing it with so many other people. Millions."

The girl bit her lip, eyes wide. She glanced up at Liza. "You're sure?"

Holding her eyes, Liza nodded. "I'm sure. No one fights alone. Okay?"

The kid nodded, starting to really smile. "Okay."

Liza nodded in the direction of the door. "Looks like your friends are waiting. Better catch up."

The last smile the girl had given her kept her own mood high as she tidied up, folded the chairs and set them back in place in the event they'd advertised as a book club, held in the attic of a little book store on an Independent Operator's License from Zoncom. It had gone pretty well, all things considered, and tomorrow—

"Ma'am, you're requested to stand still and make no sudden movements. You're under arrest for violating the Zoncom Antisocial Behavior Act."

The words froze Liza. She didn't turn, didn't move. Standing still, she heard two sets of boots come into the room.

"Please remain calm and raise your hands. Put them on top of your head."

Of course. That was the first step of an arrest. Hands on top of your head. Liza moved her arms so that she'd appear to be complying. Hands on her head, she moved her pinky finger and tapped one of her special hairpins three times.

She waited until the screaming and the vomiting was done. The two Peacekeepers were on the floor, their earpieces still buzzing with the residual tone that the tiny emitters in Liza's special hairpins were designed to play on the frequencies that the most common Corporate tech used. Pulling one of her throwing knives, she stabbed it carefully through each man's tab, then through the weak point where the plastic casings of their guns met the barrels.

In the vids, this was the point where some crazy protagonist would jump through the window. Of course, that was stupid; for one thing, modern windows were made to be double-glazed, shatter-proof and heat resistant. For two, if you were stuck somewhere where you could break it, the cheap single-paned window that went into Citizen Poor Standing houses would cut you to ribbons before you got through it.

She did what anyone with a brain did: she opened the window, walked onto the fire escape, and stepped down to street level, calmly reversing her coolant-lined jacket to show another set of colors on the other side embedded with a QR code that confused the cameras. She pulled the pins out of her hair, and a neat braid uncoiled to hang down her back. Sliding on a pair of sunglasses, she started walking. Her heart might be going a million miles a second, but she would not run. She knew better.

Damn it. Was someone in the garment-workers' union snitching? Or had it been the bookstore owner?

With a movement this big and diverse, it was so hard to tell. She didn't know who or where the problems were. And she hated that.

Well, at least the union members had gotten out. And now it was her turn.

She did the smart thing and blended with the crowds in the pleasant little Tennyson Street neighborhood, buying a frappuccino, acting like any other consumer for a bit. Then she got on the train and headed back downtown, down into the shanty-towns and warehouses of the Santa Fe Street area. Pulling out her tab, she sent a message.

Message Handle: Queen Of Clubs
Message Authentication: LL3l3echidna
Message: On my way. ETA 15-30 mins.

A moment later, she got a response that made her roll her eyes.

Message Handle: Queen Of Spades
Message Authentication: Dingorr3432
Message: Great, thanks for the

heads up. Would've hated to shoot
the wrong person when they knocked on the door.

She found the little house without too much trouble, and approved. It looked abandoned, with weeds in the yard and a facade that really didn't attract anyone's interest. Perfect.

Walking to the back door, she knocked six times. Tweak pulled the door open.

"Oh. You. Good!"

"Hi Tweak," Liza acknowledged as she stepped in. "How are things here?"

"Amazing! Amazing!" Grinning, Tweak grabbed a box and thrust it at Liza. "My b-b-beans!"

Naomi grinned, leaning against a wall. "Kevin sent us enough coffee beans for the whole stay, in the mail. The delivery kid had to knock on the door to make sure he had the right address. I nearly shot him."

"Thanks for the self-restraint," Liza replied with a smile, looking through the box. "Wow, he did great. If we stretch it, we should have enough for the whole assignment." Pulling the handwritten note tucked inside, she read it. "For standing watch in the evenings. Tweak will have the lion's share; this is her tree, after all. Enjoy, Kevin." She shot Tweak a look. "Just don't bounce off the walls or blare the music; the rest of us want to sleep when we're not on watch."

Tweak ripped off a parody of a salute, grinning at the box, before trotting into the living room where Inyonoi was sprawled out reading something on his tab.

"Hey! Hey hey hey! We got real coffee! Real coffee for standing w-w-watch! Kickass!"

"Well," Naomi offered as she watched Inyoni all but jump off the couch, "they look like they're going to have fun."

Liza nodded her agreement. "Where's the rest?"

Naomi nodded down the hall. "The family already closed their door and went to bed. You and I have a room, and Inyoni and Tweak have one."

"Is that a great idea?" Liza asked, eyeing the man grinning down at Tweak. He seemed alright, but still…

Naomi shrugged. "There are two beds in each room. Inyoni was kind of sweet actually, asked Tweak if she wanted him to sleep on the couch. Weirdly, she was cool with him being in the room."

She turned her head, studying Liza. "You're shook."

Liza nodded, letting a little of the tension drain out of her as she locked the door and turned on the hands-off arc. Electricity fizzed between the two boxes on either side of the door. There. They were safe in the house, for a given value of safe.

"I had to deal with an arrest attempt after the meeting. They were coming for me; there were only two of them, which tells me they weren't after the whole Union. Or they really did think I was the only problem. I need to sit down and get in a report about it. I want to know how they knew where I was."

"Yeah," Naomi agreed, mulling it over. She glanced around the room, studying the ceiling. "Tweak checked earlier; we've got a bunch of masking tech around this house, so if there are any trackers we picked up that we don't know about, they're going to start showing coordinates a long way from here. So, we're okay for now unless somebody specifically tells the Corps where we are."

Liza's brows rose.

Naomi nodded, pressing a finger to her lips. "Later," she murmured. "In the room."

"Right," Liza agreed.

"You eat yet?" Tweak called, and Liza stepped into the little kitchenette. "Not yet, what've we got?"

"Lots!" the kid called back. She sounded happy.

Liza took the time to eat with everyone. After that, she yawned hugely. "Okay, I'm done. Inyoni, Tweak, you've got first watch, yeah?'

"Yep!" Tweak agreed, her fingers playing little percussion beats on a bag of her coffee beans. "Ready!"

Liza eyed the kid, reflecting on the fact that nobody on the planet needed caffeine *less* than her. "Promise to keep it down?"

Tweak rolled her eyes. "Yeeees, *Mom.*"

Liza sighed. "Well, I'm getting some sleep. Night, folks."

"Gonna turn in myself, I think." Naomi agreed. "Maybe finish a drawing I want Aidan to engrave. We're working up something for Abigail's birthday."

"Cool," Tweak agreed, grabbing her tab and starting to type.

"Night."

"I really hope she doesn't overdo the caffeine," Liza sighed as she closed the bedroom door. Naomi chuckled. "Relax, she's settled down pretty well."

"Hope you're right," Liza offered weakly. "You choose a bed?"

Naomi shrugged. "Not yet. Your call. How are the unions?"

"They seem good. I keep checking the Mesh, and things are looking up," Liza offered, taking the bed closest to the wall. "Out of all the meetings, only about ten percent are getting broken up, and only one percent are getting arrested. We've had about one big arrest a quadrant; that's still too many people, but it means we are keeping good security. There were two union chapters arrested during a meeting in the Freshwater Quadrant, one ArgusCo and one Cavanaugh. Get this; in the Argus case, people are rallying around the jail to get them released." She sat up, showing Naomi pictures on her tab.

The blond woman shoved her hair back and leaned in. "Wow. They're not kidding about this."

"I know," Liza agreed. "Here... there's news all over. It's not in the mainstream feeds, but it's blanketing the Mesh. How have the civilians been here?"

"You mean have I seen anything suspicious," Naomi observed. She dropped easily onto the bed nearest the door. "And the truth is, I don't think Inyoni is in on this, but the timing on what the Corps have caught since he came on is fishy. So, something's going on for sure. But right now, I'm going to say, don't assume it's him."

"Think so?" Liza asked.

Naomi nodded. "Think so. But hey, better safe than sorry." She sat up, crossing her legs. "You still worried?"

Liza nodded, staring at the ceiling. "I just... I don't know. It just feels *off* somehow. But maybe I'm just freaking myself out here?"

"Or maybe you're amped up from weeks of vigilance and moving, and everything feels potentially dangerous?" Naomi suggested. Liza nodded. "Yeah, maybe. Maybe I'm being paranoid."

"I wouldn't go that far," Naomi offered. "And while we're on it, we've got another thing to think about. You noticed the way Tweak's acting?"

Liza blew out a long breath. "You caught it too, hunh?"

Naomi nodded. "I'm starting to think she's got a crush going."

"Yeah," Liza agreed. She shook her head. "Tweak, of all people…"

"No kidding," Naomi acknowledged. "Who'd've thought."

"Should we have a talk with her?" Liza asked, glancing at her friend nervously. "I mean, at least about the mechanics?"

Naomi's brows shot up. She snorted a laugh. "We are the absolute *worst* people to have 'the talk', you and me. I don't know half of what we're talking about."

"I know," Liza agreed, trying not to groan. "I mean, two ace women trying to give a Gamma girl 'the talk'. It sounds like the setup for a bad joke."

"We'll be walking into a bar any second," Naomi agreed with a grin. Liza sighed. "Sometimes I wonder how these situations even happen. I think they're still at the crush stage, but…"

"Yeah, but." Naomi nodded. "There's always a 'but'."

"Think we should at least… I don't know, tell her to be careful?" Liza suggested.

Naomi cocked her head. "Want to get called 'mom' again?" Liza flopped back on the bed. "No," she grumbled.

"Then I say we let it ride till we get them home, and then we hand it over to My Big Brother the Relationship Doctor," Naomi offered.

Liza couldn't help but laugh. "Tell me you're going to call him that to his face?"

"Already did," Naomi grinned. "As long as it's not *his* relationships, he's great at that. So yeah, let's just let it ride. They'll figure it out."

In the living room, Tweak opened the bag of coffee beans, took out a handful and held them out to Inyoni, grinning. "These. Off my tree. Beautiful, real big now. My baby."

"Didn't know you grew coffee," Inyoni muttered as he took the beans and held them up to sniff. "I mean… you said the base grew stuff, but not you… how'd you manage real coffee?"

"The guys." Tweak replied with a grin so wide it hurt. She simplified the truth; Liza would be mad if she talked about Coomb Olwen and their seed bank. "Found them. The ag guys bred it with some other c-c-cool seeds we got; I helped with the c-code on the genomes. And we got something that'd live for us. Then I planted it. I watered it. I read about coffee trees. Coffee picking. Everything. I do everything. Kids help me pick. Then I do the rest. Peel, age, roast. My buddies, Janice and Topher. Made me a r-r-r-roaster, on the r-r-roof. Takes time, but it's worth it. K-kevin sent my grinder-p-press too." she added, gesturing at the thing half way between a thermos and a detonator. "Made that. Got big ones on base for b-b-b-breakfast."

"There anything you can't do?" Inyoni asked, carefully handing the beans back. "Makes me feel all useless, hearin' the great things you can do."

Tweak laughed, though the words made her feel like a fake. He was asking if there was anything she couldn't do. The answer was 'so damn much'. Starting with talking right and going on up the line.

"That's just messing, n-no big. Feels good to be away from the screen for a little while, you know?" Grinning, she dropped just the right amount of bean into the lid of her grinder-press and turned the handle. The press ratcheted around for a while. She checked the canister and nodded at the nice pile of grounds that had fallen down into it. She got out a pot, filled it with water and stuck it on the stove. It binged a second later, and she poured boiling water from the pot into the press.

"Goddamn, is it always that loud grinding the beans?" Inyoni grumbled. Tweak glanced at him; he had his hands over the sides of his head. "Oh. Shit. Sorry, yeah. Beans stay fresh longer. N-next time, I'll warn you first."

Inyoni nodded. "Yeah, that'd help. Thanks." He settled in a chair by the beat-up kitchen table and propped his chin on his fist, watching Tweak work.

Tweak moved fast, grabbing cups, checking the press, tapping her foot, then triumphantly setting a steaming mug in front of Inyoni. "We can have four each, tonight. Any more, we r-run out t-too fast."
She propped her elbows on the table. "So, try it! Whatcha think?" She watched with her heart in her mouth as Inyoni carefully lifted the mug and sniffed at it.
He took his first sip, and a happy little moan came out of him. "This's *so* much better than the crap they got for sale most places."

Tweak gave a laugh. "That stuff's not coffee. Stuff's garbage. Never seen a real tree." She clasped her cup to her chest, shooting an irritable glance at the overactive AC panel. Later tonight, she was going to have to take that apart and fix it. She hated being cold.

"Hafta dump it full of sugar to hide the taste," she continued. "Good coffee, real coffee? Don't need it."

Inyoni murmured an agreement, staring into his cup. Another blast of frigid air assaulted the room, and she glared at the unit.

"Hey. You cold?" Inyoni asked. "Got blankets over there. You could sit on the couch."

Tweak shrugged. "I'm fine." Then she glanced at his face, studied it, and gave him a smile. "Okay. Lying. Cold."

"C'mon. We can keep watch over there." Inyoni grinned at her and stood up, taking his mug over to the couch. Unfolding the blanket, he held it out for Tweak.

Tweak balanced her mug and the coffee press in either hand, taking a careful seat on the couch. When he sat beside her, it was like opening the door to a furnace. The feel of him so close radiated along her skin. For a moment, she instinctively pulled away. But the warmth brought her back.

"'Can't really feel if I'm too cold, much," Inyoni muttered after a moment of silence. "Or too hot."

"Lucky bastard." Tweak remarked, wrapping her arms around herself, the blanket up to her chin. Her cup shook in her hands as the temperature in the room continued to drop. It was never this cold on the base. It probably felt nice to the Alphas, but she was made for the heat, literally. This sucked.

Inyoni cleared his throat. "I, uh... know you don't like people touchin' you, but... I... um. Fuck it. Never mind."

Tweak glanced up, eyeing him. "Never mind what? Spit it out."

"I just thought we could... I dunno... I could help you get warm." Inyoni fidgeted with his mug and took a swig of coffee, tacking on, "not anythin' weird or nothin', just... well, heat's gonna stay better if we're closer together."

Tweak stared at him blankly, brows rising. Then she smirked. "Really?"

Inyoni looked at her, smiling just a little. "Well, last time I touched you, you kinda bit my head off. Figured wasn't worth it to just... hug you without askin'."

Tweak nodded, giving him the point. "Yeah. I'm a d-dragon. I bite. Bad habit. Hard to break..." she stared at him for a long moment, considering. "You warn me first, I don't bite. Touch is okay if I know it's coming. Deal?"

Inyoni blinked at her for a moment, before grinning slowly. "Uh, yeah. Deal. So... you still cold?"

Tweak nodded. "Freezing."

"Then lemme warm you up?" Inyoni carefully balanced his mug on the arm of the couch, and spread one arm invitingly.

Nervously, Tweak moved, settling herself a little closer as Inyoni put an arm around her. Her back tingled with the contact, the touch taking over her perceptions for a moment. She drew a long breath. "Want more c-coffee?"

"Yeah. Stuff's great."

The coffee gurgled into the cup. "Yeah." Tweak agreed. "Great... not a lot of c-coffee trees around."

"Yeah? What happened?" Inyoni asked. Tweak pulled out her tab, bringing up her page of coffee inspirations. "Been r-reading. The wild ones, they get too hot, they get this disease. R-r-roya, it's called. They die. So, lots died before they could gene-mod them. But the new ones, they're okay. They're sur-rviving. The gene mods are s-saving them."

"That's cool," Inyoni observed.

Tweak glanced up at him. "Wanna see more?"

"Sure," he agreed. She grinned. "Check this out," she offered. Bringing up her playlist of coffee info vids, she hit play. They went through the history of the trees, the gene modification programs in other countries to rescue the trees, and all the types of coffee tree and preparations there had once been: the amazing variety and creativity of them.

"One day, I wanna bring more of those back." she remarked softly as the night edged towards morning. "Wanna find what got lost."

"Think there're genetic records of 'em anywhere?" Inyoni asked, stifling a yawn and finishing off the last of his lukewarm cup. "Maybe someone could gene-splice or somethin'."

"Somewhere. Sure. Just gotta find it." For a moment, Tweak considered it. Liza wouldn't like her saying this...eh, fuck it. She blurted it out. "We already found one seed bank. Breeding new stuff all the time. We get plenty of stuff for the garden. We get home, you'll love it."

"You found a seed bank?" Inyoni repeated in quiet awe. "Thought they were just stories. Things to make us feel better, y'know?"

Tweak shook her head. "Nope. Real. Found it. Everything grew." She watched the dawning awe on Inyoni's face. Had she looked like that at first?

"Just gotta protect it." she added quietly, thinking of the friends she'd made in the hidden mountain town of Coomb Olwen, built around the seed bank. She almost said something about their amazing work, but that was dangerous. She could tell him later, when they were home and safe.

Inyoni nodded slowly. "Wow… you said you had a garden, but a seed bank… got any idea if there're others?"

"Some day, we'll find out." Tweak murmured, eyes heavy lidded. His warmth had eased all the buzz out of her muscles; she felt like the kitten Blake always called her back home. She glanced back at Inyoni. Then, very gingerly, she laid her head back against his shoulder. "Hey. Thanks."

"For what?" Inyoni asked as he moved to wrap the blanket tighter around them. But Tweak didn't know how to answer.

Event File 19
File Tag: Mission Report
06:30-09-12-2160

The sun was just starting to pierce the blinds when Liza opened her eyes. Stepping into the bathroom with her folded clothes in her hands, she got herself ready for her day. Hair brushed, pinned and in place. Jacket straight. Rank patch…

For a moment, the weirdness of this assignment washed over her. She didn't have her rank patches. She didn't have any of her insignia. She hadn't been without them since she was a kid. She didn't really feel dressed without them.

It'd be *so good* to get home and back into routines. Familiar routines. Routines that made some sense. This civilian training work was incredible, but she was starting to feel the strain of constant unfamiliar situations, new faces and endless vigilance. She felt stretched thin by the wariness, ground down by the relentless questions. Not to mention, the constant noise just waiting to scream at her from every corner of the Grid. At least it was quiet in here.

Dressed and ready, she padded into the kitchen. With any luck, Tweak and Inyoni had left some of the coffee, and she could reheat it.

The coffee press was on the table in front of the couch. On the couch, the two young people lay sprawled, fast asleep. The sight was enough to stop Liza in her tracks.

Tweak was sleeping in her new crush's arms, head pillowed on his chest. She was completely relaxed, breathing deep. For a moment, all Liza could do was marvel. The kid who'd freaked out every time anyone got near her was lying in someone's arms. The girl who'd panicked and attacked like an animal when anyone so much as touched her a couple years ago was making a connection like *this* with somebody. She had come such a long way.

But she was also asleep on duty. So Liza did her own duty and cleared her throat. Tweak sat up as if she'd been electrocuted.

"Next time you're on watch, drink some more of this," Liza suggested, pouring herself a cup of the cold brew. "We really need people to stay awake during the watch, okay? Naomi and Jillian will take the next turn."

Tweak nodded, ducking her head. "S-sorry, L-liza. My bad."

"Just don't fall asleep next time," Liza replied with a smile for the little coder. She really was trying, these days. Liza nodded down the hall. "You guys should probably go sleep in your beds, that's better than the couch."

"Yeah," Tweak agreed, rubbing at her eyes. She bounced to her feet. "In a while. C-coffee, got c-code to check over. Then I'll nap."

"Wha?" Inyoni asked blearily through a yawn. "Fuck, did I zone out?"

"You were asleep when I came in," Liza agreed, and damn if she wasn't giving the guy a smile. She couldn't help it; he was so gangly and out of sorts that he looked like a baby giraffe at the holograph-zoo, tripping over his own feet as he tried to get up.

Maybe Naomi was right. Maybe the kid wasn't so much of a danger after all.

Maybe.

"I'm going to get breakfast started," she offered, "Tweak, you've got the coffee?"

"Yep!"

Liza gave herself a moment to take the sight in, smiling as the girl bustled with her kit. Then she got down to the cooking. Pulling egg concentrate from the fridge, she opened the carton and poured the creamy yellow mix into a pan to fry, then pulled a couple of nutrient muffins from their tight, crackling packaging. She set the brownish wafers on a plate and sprinkled them with a little water from the tap. With quiet little hisses of indrawn air, they started to puff up into muffin shape. They weren't her favorite things in the world, but they did have a long shelf life, and they were a whole lot better than calorie bars. She'd count her blessings; someone had even added a little bit of fresh fruit and veggies to the fridge. By the dirt on them, Liza guessed someone from the Grapevine had snuck stuff out of a field processing area. Nice of them. She scrubbed down a couple of apples with washing powder, rinsed them quickly, and cut them up to go with the muffins. The eggs were nearly ready, and she stirred them now and again as she worked. In the other room, she could hear the rest of the household coming awake: Cameron's rumbly voice was interspersed with Tweak's squeak. The baby made lots of little noises here and there.

"You look happy." Naomi remarked, leaning against the countertop. "Good news?"

"Tweak and Inyoni fell asleep on each other," Liza murmured, her voice low. "She actually let him *touch* her."

"Seriously?!" Naomi exclaimed. A couple heads rose in the living room. Stepping into the kitchen, the munitions officer dropped her voice.

"You mean... okay seriously? She doesn't even let the gang at home touch her, most of the time."

"She doesn't even let Billie touch her very much," Liza agreed, "and those two are practically blood."

Naomi nodded. "I thought the kids might bond a little on watch but...wow…"

"Is there food yet?" Tweak called from the living room. "The b-baby's trying to eat the c-c-couch!"

The conversation was still on Naomi's mind when she shut the door of the room she was sharing with Liza and pulled out her tab. Methodically, she got her two pistols, fighting staff, knife and rifle out, spreading a cloth on the bed and laying them across it. Setting up her tab, she brought up a screen and put in her brother's callsign. A beat later, his face came up on the other end. She breathed a little easier when he gave her a little wave. "Hey Omi. You okay?"

"Hey Aidan," she gave him a smile as she started sharpening her knife. It was in good shape, didn't really need much. But she needed the work.

"I'm good. Getting settled in with the civvies. Keep me company while I get my weapons up to scratch?"

"Sure," her big brother agreed, "how's the situation?"

"Not awful," Naomi offered as she pulled the magazine from her handgun, emptied the chamber and started disassembling it. "The new folks are still skittish as hell, but they're starting to settle. They're better than Tweak so far."

Aidan chuckled. "Well that's good news. Kind of a low bar though."

"Don't let her hear you say that," Naomi replied with a grin as she laid out the weapon's parts. Aidan laughed a little. "Yeah, well. You didn't see her when she first got signed up. She's a hell of a lot better than she was."

"I didn't see her, but I heard some stories," Naomi agreed as she ran a brush through the barrel, following it up with a cleaning rag. She glanced up at her brother's face. "How about you guys? How's the base?"

"Mostly good," Aidan offered, but the words came out in a sigh.

Naomi cocked her head as she applied CLP oil. "What's the mostly?"

"Jim's gone out on recuperative leave," her brother admitted. "And I kind of get the feeling that he's going to decommission from there."

Naomi studied her brother as she set down her service piece and picked up her rifle. Her fingers went over the weapon's body, taking it apart in an easy rhythm. "And how's that hitting for you?" she asked quietly, watching his eyes, the set of his shoulders. Aidan's signs of going downhill were subtle, but she knew them. At least this time, the circles under his eyes weren't so dark, so he was sleeping. That was good. "You think that's on you?"

Aidan shrugged, giving her a sad little smile. "I think it's life. And I like writing his decommission paperwork a lot better than I'd like writing a death certificate for a good guy. But yeah. I'm going to miss him."

Inside, the little part of her that'd sat up on high alert relaxed. Her brother wasn't deflecting or turning inward. Okay.

Aidan must have caught onto where she was going; he leaned back and gave her a little shake of the head as she went through the steps on her rifle, the soft smile she only saw when they were alone on his lips. "Relax, Omi. I'm good."

"Yeah," she acknowledged easily, "you are. If you've got the bandwidth, we can worry about something else together."

"Yeah?" Aidan asked, sitting up a little straighter. "What's going on?"

"Chill, big brother," Naomi chuckled, checking her rifle's barrel one last time, "nobody's bleeding. But I think Tweak's falling in love." She chambered a round.

On the other side of the screen, her brother blinked like a man smacked between the eyes. "Wait... what?"

"Falling in love? Twitterpated? I bet your husband has fifty words for it?" Naomi suggested.

"Tweak? Tweak's in... I mean, what does Tweak in love even..." The man waved his hands vaguely, "I dunno, look like?"

Naomi tapped her bottom lip with one finger, rolling her eyes and playing up the look. "Weelllll big A, she's about four foot nothing, black hair, and—"

"Omi!" Aidan groaned. Naomi gave him a patient look. For a guy as perceptive as she knew he was, he sure could be slow to get a clue sometimes.

"I'm ace, man, I'm not dense."

"I didn't mean.... oh come on Omi, I mean I would've missed it." Aidan backpedaled weakly.

Naomi smirked. "Big brother, you're kinda saying something about yourself here."

Aidan sighed. "Dammit, Omi..."

She couldn't help but smile when he got that way. "Okay, okay. She's cutting this guy Inyoni all kinds of slack. Offering to keep him company when he's bored, reassuring him, stuff like that. And get this: she fell asleep snuggled up against him last night. Can you believe that?"

"Wait, *Tweak* fell asleep *on another person?*" Aidan exclaimed, eyes gone wide. "Are you shitting me?"

"I know, right?" Naomi agreed, grinning as her hands worked their way over her weapons.

Aidan tapped the side of his head. "I think I need a software update before I can parse that..."

"Crazy, hunh?"

"Crazy is right," he chuckled. For a few seconds, they just smiled at each other. "Wait, did she fall asleep on duty?" Aidan asked, as if that had just hit him.

"Mas o menos," Naomi waved a hand. "It was like, four in the morning when she crashed, so Liza talked to her, but it's not a big thing." She lifted her folding staff, popping it out to its full length and adding a little lubricant to the joints.

"Still," Aidan began, and Naomi shrugged.

"Liza talked to them. So, how many other Gammas have signed up?"

Aidan's smile faltered. "Um... honestly, Omi? None."

"None? At all?" Naomi blinked. "How many other operatives are recruiting Gammas?"

"About twenty," Aidan sighed. "And yeah, none of them have had the kind of luck Tweak has. A couple people confronted Gammas and got beat to hell. One guy got shot, and a lady got stabbed."

Naomi blew out a breath. "Well shit." She glanced up at her brother. "Think we should tell Tweak?"

Aidan sighed. "Well, I think if you don't and she finds out we knew, she'll rip us a new asshole."

"So that's a yes," Naomi suggested. Aidan nodded. "I'd say so."

"At least tell me things are going as good for the other teachers as they are for Liza?"

"Yeah, actually," Aidan agreed. "That news is coming in good. The sign-up number for the Unions is up to six million people. Probably between four and five million will get in on the big stay-home protest, more if we're lucky. The Meshnet just hit fifty million users. In some of the looser-regulation spots, folks are putting on some pretty cool demonstrations. Oh, and did you see the wack-a-mole picture?"

"The what? No," Naomi checked the rail of her backup piece, wiping away the tiny bit of grime that had built up since its last weekly cleaning. She glanced up when she heard her brother start to chuckle. "That good?"

"Take a look," he offered, and tapped his desk.

A secondary window popped up for Naomi. For a second, she stared. Then she burst out laughing. "Oh...man...oh wow." she wheezed. "Was this our guys?"

"Nah, but they're in love with it and they can't wait to do it," Aidan laughed.

In the window, a ferrety man was tied to a lampost. A black gimmie cap with googly eyes and a pink nose had been shoved onto his head, and a placard hung around his neck read 'hello, I am a mole'.

"People are getting serious about the reputation damage without physical injury," Aidan added with a grin. "This dickhead will never get into another organization, not with this picture all over the Mesh. Commander Hall sent this to me with a note saying this would be a great approach, and the whole base started asking when they get to do it. Alice is knitting mole caps."

"Hope she doesn't have to knit too many, but man, I'm loving this," Naomi agreed. "Way more fun than a bullet in the brain."

"Kind of good, to be moving away from bullets," her brother agreed.

The words hit her a little funny, but she nodded. "Yeah." She studied him for a moment. "You're okay, yeah?"

Aidan sighed, rubbing the back of his neck. "I mean, I'm tired, I'm worried about Logistics losing somebody and the weight that puts on the rest of the division. And Kevin's being a workaholic again, trying to get you guys an extraction. But honestly... I feel like things are gonna change, Omi. And yeah. That feels good. So I'm good. I'm okay. I don't know how we're getting there, but I see us headed somewhere new. And that feels good."

"It does, doesn't it?" Naomi asked, smiling at her big brother. "Okay big A, I'm not going to eat up your day, and my guns are clean. Go ahead and get back to it."

"Roger," Aidan agreed with a nod. "Hey, Omi? Love you."

Naomi had to smile. Her brother, the sap. "Love you too, big brother. Hang in there."

"You too, Omi. Talk in a while."

His screen flicked to the default Mesh window. Naomi let out the breath she'd been holding, staring at her weapons. Prepped and ready, their matte finishes all retouched. They were beautiful, in their own way. And pretty soon, they might not be necessary at all.

Kind of good to be moving away from bullets, her brother had said. Naomi's whole life had been bullets. Bullets and bombs, the fight and the grind. Who would she be without that?

She really didn't know.

Event File 20
File Tag: Strategic Approach
12:30·09·18·2160

"Still nobody, hunh?"

Tweak glanced up from her check of the Gamma recruitment paperwork for the millionth time, giving Inyoni a weak smile. "Nah. No dice."

That was the worst thing about this situation: there was so much time, and so little to do with it. It was too easy to start going in circles like a stupid fish in a bowl. Sure, she had plenty of bug-hunting and hole-patching to help with on the Mesh, and she had her usual work on the Net, but none of that could hold onto her mind. It was busy work, and that left too much time for thinking.

Inyoni nodded at the bed. "Can I sit?"

"Sure," Tweak agreed, scrolling. Was talking and getting people signed up really that hard? For everyone?

The mattress let out a little sigh of air.

"Hey, uh, Tweak?"

"Yeah?"

"Uh…" Inyoni shifted in his seat. "You wanna hear something stupid?"

"Shoot," Tweak offered, rolling onto her back and projecting her screen over her head.

Inyoni cleared his throat. "Uh... I was thinking. I... when you said you were the Golden Dragon, I... I mean I about got on my knees. You're a legend. You're like some kind of saint of the Net, the way they tell the stories."

Tweak looked up. Then she cracked up. "Me? Saint? As if!"

"Okay, god of the Net, then," Inyoni tried.

"Goddess!" Tweak corrected, sitting up and crossing her legs. "I'll be a Net Goddess, sure. So?"

"So..." Inyoni did that funny thing she'd started to notice him do when he was nervous, reaching up and fiddling with the tip of one of his ears. It looked weird, because his hand disappeared into the holo and made the whole thing flicker, but it was nice when people had tells like that; it made them easier to read. "I mean..." Inyoni stopped, took a breath, and started again. "So...if the Dragon had talked to me online...you're one of those people that anybody would listen to. If I was sure it was the real Golden Dragon talking to me... I mean, I woulda jumped off a bridge if the real Golden Dragon showed up in my feed and told me I'd fly. That was before I knew the real you, but... yeah?"

"Before you knew me, hunh?" Tweak asked, resting her chin in her hand. "How about now?"

Inyoni gave her a funny little smile. "I guess now, I'd still do it, but maybe I'd jump with you beside me and ask what kinda code we were using to power the wings. I mean, I did tell you I'm a jackass. I'd totally do it."

Something funny and fizzy happened in Tweak's chest and ran all up and down her insides. She grinned. "Yeah?"

"Yeah," Inyoni agreed. Straightening, he cleared his throat. "But what I was thinking was... uh... what if you figured out how to send a message to Gammas? A safe message, something validated? And you gave Gammas a time and place to show up and be picked up, and the Dusters promised to go get them? I mean... yeah. People dream about getting you to help them. They talk about you like an angel who'll come an' save people like us."

Tweak blinked. "Wow... uh... y-yeah?"

"Yeah," Inyoni agreed. "Yeah. So... whatcha think?"

Tweak tipped her head to one side, then the other, letting the thought roll around like a marble inside her brain. Her fingers fiddled with the bandage around her hand.

"Hunh. I mean...cool, but...hunh."

The idea that she'd somehow become a hero—no, more than that, some kind of savior story — didn't really fit in her brain. People thought she could save them?!

But maybe... just maybe, she kind of could. Inyoni's words rolled around and around, setting off thoughts. Proving who she was would be a trick. Proving it safely could be done, but what could she do in a message or a vid to make it sink in with the people watching? So much stuff could be faked. So much noise was out there, drowning out the signals.

And that was only if Aidan said yes. She'd have to get this approved. Then she could figure out how to make it work.

"Uh... you okay?"

"Hunh?" Tweak raised her head. "Oh. Yeah. Thinking. Ideas. Lots." She bounced off the bed, trotting out of the room. "Liza!"

"What, Tweak?" Liza asked, sounding a little freaked. "I'm trying to get this big AgCo speech ready to go. What's going on?"

Tweak crossed to the table where she was sitting, grabbed a seat and dropped into it. "Bird. Has. An idea. Help me with it?"

Liza set the half-written speech she was working on aside. "What's the idea?"

So Tweak told her. Liza let out a little groan, and closed her eyes.

"Liza?" Tweak asked, a little weirded out. "You okay?"

"No, Tweak," Liza muttered. "No, I'm not okay. I just got handed one of the most dangerous, insane plans I've ever heard. I'm not okay."

Tweak rolled her eyes. "Drama queen. So, c-can we c-c-call Aidan? See if he likes it?"

"You want to... what?" Aidan didn't sound a lot happier about it than Liza had. "Tweak... um, okay, I really don't like the idea of you being on camera."

"Yeah, but n-nobody's gonna buy a written statement! It's gotta be a vid! I can make it s-s-safe!" Tweak explained. "Lookit: we do the vid, I encode the p-pixels with an erasing algorithm. Screenshots, facial recon-nition, all of it, it w-won't be able to r-record the image. It'll just erase itself. Easy."

"How about people's memories?" Liza put in, razors in her voice. "If we plaster the Net with your face, you'll never be able to go on the Grid again! And doing it before we get out of here—"

"Means I w-wear a holo mask from now on, l-Liza. Jeez," Tweak sighed. "I thought about it. Sure, new risks. But shit, we g-gotta play if we wanna win! I already know they want me. When I took down the Grid, I knew it. Not scared."

"If this doesn't scare you then you're nuts," Liza muttered. Tweak barely held herself back from flipping the taller woman off. She ignored her instead. "Aidan. Whatcha say?"

Aidan stared into the middle distance for a couple seconds.

Tweak waved a hand. "Boss?"

The blond man started. "Yeah. Okay, I'm going to say I need to send this up the chain of command. I can't give you an answer right now, Tweak. But I can start the conversation. How's that?"

Tweak shrugged. "Sounds good. Thanks, boss."

"Don't thank me yet," Aidan sighed, signing off.

That night, Tweak watched as the doors to the other rooms closed. She glanced at Inyoni, smiling. "So. C-can't fall asleep this time. What do we do to stay up?"

"I was thinking about that," Inyoni replied, flopping onto the couch. Against the far wall, the hologram showing their full security setup glowed. "I figure, there's a lot of vids I didn't see when my score was too low to get into theaters. So I say we do a movie binge till we get bored, then... well, I suck at cards, but I can play chess. You any good?"

"You play chess?" Tweak asked, surprised.

Inyoni ducked his head. "Yeah, I learned. Old guys used to play me in the park when I was little. So, you wanna?"

"Sure," Tweak agreed with a smile. "Sounds fun. What vids?" Tweak made sure to position the vid screen so the security feed was always in the line of sight, bringing up the smaller screen beside it for them to watch on.

It turned out Inyoni had the same thing for car-chase vids that she did, and that was great. They geeked out on a couple drag racing and car chase flicks, bouncing between laughing at the action and critiquing the CGI, but it got old by the third flick. The security feed buzzed along easy beside the vids, not a speck of trouble on it.

"Okay, game!" Tweak declared, turning off the vid screen. Pulling out his tab, Inyoni unfolded the hologram of a chess board.

"I read the rules," she remarked as his fingers set pieces made from light in the air. "Sounds fun."

Inyoni grinned at her across the game board of light. "Maybe this's a game where I'll actually have an advantage over you for once."

Tweak gave him the grin she used to freak guards out with. "Bet you anything you lose."

"What're we bettin'?" Inyoni asked mildly, making his first move. "Ain't got cash or nothin' to put up."

"Doing dishes." Tweak judged, poking a pawn forward. "Loser loads the dishwasher."

Twenty minutes later, she set her bishop down and grinned. "Checkmate."

"Fuck," Inyoni muttered under his breath, scowling at the board. "Fine. I got dishes. 'Nother try."

Tweak nodded sharply. "Best four outta five."

"We still bettin' dishes?" Inyoni asked as he reset his pieces. "We bettin' somethin' else? You just got lucky first time out."

"Four outta five. Dishes. Play." Tweak chirped. "C'mon."

Four games later, Tweak sat back, crossing her arms and grinning. "Okay. What are we betting on n-now?"

Inyoni held his head in his hands, glowering at the board. His fingers disappeared into his holo, fiddling with the ends of his ears. "I used to be good at this! I'm gonna win this time. So. Loser's gotta deal with the baby next time we're on babysittin' duty."

"You poor b-bastard. You got it." Tweak declared, swigging her third cup of coffee.

Inyoni gave her a wild grin, drained his cup, and reset the pieces again.

Three games later, Tweak set her queen down and cheerfully knocked over his king. "Better bet something you don't care about next." she remarked smugly, then glanced at the clock. "Wow. This game's good for time. Lookit, four."

If she was right, Inyoni was grinding his teeth. "Still got time," he grumbled. "One more?"

"Sure." Tweak agreed amicably. "Whatcha betting?"

Inyoni was still for a beat. Then the absolute dumbest grin spread over his face. "I win, you gimme a kiss. You win, I keep my holo off all day."

Tweak blinked, a bewildered grin crossing her lips. "Seriously? What are you, fifteen?"

"What are you, scared?" Inyoni teased, resetting the pieces again. "Got somethin' better?"

Tweak's eyes narrowed. "You're gonna lose so bad you c-cry."

"Bring it." Inyoni made the first move again. Tweak brushed her black hair back from her eyes, and got to work.

This time, the game lasted longer than half an hour, a lot longer. An hour and a half later, Tweak stared at the board in shock. "Bull. Shit."

"Check-fuckin'-mate," Inyoni crowed.

Tweak rolled her eyes. "One time. Got lucky. Get over yourself."

Inyoni grinned at her like an idiot. "But I still won. Means I get a kiss. Makes up for dish duty and baby shit."

Tweak gave him a patient look. "One. Kiss."

Inyoni just grinned back at her. "Yep."

With an irritable little grunt, Tweak leaned forward. "Okay winner, get it over wi—"

And then his lips were on hers.

The heat was intense. The sensation burned through her. She hadn't realized just how much sensation was in her lips. She hadn't realized how nice it would feel, either. Inyoni lifted one hand to cradle Tweak's head. She jerked when he touched her hair, but she didn't pull away. This heat was too good, and her body was singing. Her skin burned, but for once in her life that wasn't a bad thing.

Inyoni's hand slid lower, cupping one shoulder, pressing them together. The kiss went on for the rest of time.

It was Inyoni who broke it. He smiled sheepishly. Tweak stared at him, breathing hard, feeling cross eyed. "Some... k-k-kiss," she managed, finally.

"Yeah," Inyoni breathed, his hand still resting gently in the curve of her shoulder. He swallowed hard. "We could... uh. Try again. If you want."

Tweak gave him a small, sharp smile. "The bet was for one."

"No harm in tryin'," Inyoni replied with a soft chuckle. He let his hand drop away. "Guess... guess we oughta clean up, 'fore the others get up."

"Screw that," Tweak snorted. Leaning forward, she kissed him again. Inyoni sighed happily. Tweak shivered a little every time Inyoni's hands touched somewhere new; her neck, her cheek, her back. Then a hand trailed down her arm.

She jerked away, breaking the kiss, scrambling backwards. He'd touched her arm. Had he felt her scales under the bandage?

"What?" Inyoni asked, eyes wide. "What'd I do?"

Tweak shook her head. "N-nothing. You're g-good. N-nothing wrong." Hugging herself, she tried to smile for him. It wasn't his fault. But he'd touched her arm. And if he got any closer...

"Cups. Gonna n-n-need to be s-s-scrubbed. C-c-coffee s-stains." Then she was up and moving.

Behind her, Inyoni rolled off the couch and followed her into the kitchen. "I got dish duty, remember? I got it."

"Fine." Tweak agreed, and darted out of the kitchen. She needed space. She needed *air*, dammit. And there wasn't any in this place.

Heading for the room, she closed the door. Leaning against it, she panted as the terror rolled through her.

Event File 21
File Tag: Strategic Withdrawal
10:30·09·22·2160 / 12:30·09·23·2160

Tweak spent most of the next two days on her tab, headphones jacked in. It was a good way to be left alone. Most of the time, she would sit in the bedroom, though sometimes she wandered out into the living room to flop on the couch. She felt like a bitch doing it.

Admit it, she told herself. *You're too chickenshit to try with him.* The thought taunted her. *You're chickenshit, and you're hiding.*

She didn't even have a really neat code to hide in. Her fingers and feet tapped constantly as she worked.

If anything, Jillian and Cameron were starting to relax, and of course they had a baby to distract them. They watched vids on the couch, snuggling, or Jillian read storybooks to Cameron and little Jenny. Father and daughter both closed their eyes and relaxed when she did that; it was kind of cute. Liza was still freaking out prepping for her next big talk, and Naomi was doing a total reorganization of her media collection when she wasn't doing some kind of workout routine. They were all figuring out ways to kill the time, but nothing seemed to settle Tweak. She missed her coding rig so bad. She missed working in the garden. She missed doing *something*, damn it. Worse, she missed home. She missed hanging around and shooting the shit with the guys, all goofing around and no pressure. Right now, the only person she really wanted to talk to in the house was pressure to the max.

She settled for messing around on the Net, coding in new backdoors to EagleCorp and NatBank systems that could be used later. It wasn't much, but it was better than nothing. And she paced.

The afternoon of the fourth day felt like it'd never end. In their room, Jillian's family slept. On the couch in the living room, Liza and Naomi played cards. Inyoni was out buying everyone food. On the guest bed, Tweak fidgeted. Finally, she got so bored that she decided to do a bandage change. The ones she was wearing were getting messed up anyway. Pulling the door closed, she grabbed two clean white rolls from her knapsack, undid the clips that held her Ace bandages in place, and began to unwind them.

Her arms came to light, the scales gleaming. Just for a moment, she stared at them, turning them this way and that. They shimmered in the light.

Dragon skin, that's what her dad had called it. He'd tried to make it a good thing, with his crazy Chinese dragon spirits and their blessings. *My lucky dragon girl*, he'd called her. She could still remember the tone of his voice when he'd say that. 'You are my lucky dragon girl.'

Tweak sighed, and opened the new bandages. "Lucky dragon girl. My ass." she whispered to herself as she wound the white bandage, covering the scales. If she'd *been* lucky, all the shit that had gotten dumped on her would have hit somebody else. But it hadn't.

The tab buzzed with a vid call request just as she was finishing, and she jumped as if someone had caught her murdering a puppy. "Shit!"

The door of her room opened, and Naomi stuck her head in. "You okay, kid?"

Tweak swallowed, catching her breath. "Y-yeah. S-s-surprised. S-s-sorry." Grabbing up her tab in both hands, she accepted the call.

The screen shot up from the device's surface and broke itself into three sections. In one box was Aidan's smiling face, but the other two showed Hall and Hernandez. Tweak's heart rate kicked up. *Regional Commander* Hall and *Quadrant Councilor* Hernandez, she reminded herself. Titles. She had to remember to use titles. She tried for a salute. "S-sorry. Tab was out of r-r-reach. Sirs. Ma'am." That was what Aidan was always telling her to say: it was always sir and ma'am and titles and naming their rank for the brass. She still kind of hated it, but right now it gave her something to say that wasn't 'what the hell?'

Hernandez gave her a nod. "Officer T. It's good to see you again. We've been discussing your proposal, and at this point we'd like to get your feedback."

"Yeah?" Tweak asked, not sure where this was going.

Hernandez steepled his fingers. "We've run the situation through our modeling algorithms, and a couple public-relations people double checked it. We think we have a good approach for you to reach your demographic during this absolutely vital window, but it is a lot to ask of you."

"We think that if you were to go on camera with your biological divergence in view, speaking directly to Gammas as a Gamma, you'll win hearts and minds," Hall finished. "What do you think, Officer?"

Tweak blinked. *Biological divergence?*

Then it clicked, and her heart went into overdrive. "You m-m-m-mean…" She swallowed, massaging her throat. "Go on c-c-camera. N-no b-b-bandages? Show m-m-my arms?"

"Yeah, Tweak," Aidan agreed. "That's what they're asking. But it's not an order. Isn't that right, ma'am?" he asked, and Tweak heard that note in his voice he usually had when he was telling her not to be a shit.

Hall gave him a slow nod. "Base Commander Headly-McIllian's right; this isn't an order. The National Council is debating the idea. Since you are one of our most valuable tech people, there's not a lot of appetite for putting you at such serious risk. Many believe that asking you to make yourself as visible as this is putting one of our most valuable people unnecessarily on the line. The fact that you're currently in enemy territory only exacerbates the risk. On the other hand, this is the time to strike while the iron's hot, and this amount of activity gives us the best possible window for allowing people who are usually under intense scrutiny to move freely and make their escapes. Waiting the remaining weeks until you're back on secure ground to film might lose us the advantage. There's quite a discussion happening."

"It's more of an argument, really," Aidan added. Hall cleared her throat in that 'you're on thin ice' way some Alphas did, but Aidan just smiled at her.

"Which is why we wanted to hear your thoughts," Hernandez added. "Given the situation and your own experiences, is this tactic something you'd be comfortable executing?"

Comfortable?! The word was a hysterical scream in Tweak's head, though she didn't make a sound. *Did he really just ask me if I was comfortable showing everyone how messed up I am?!*

"Officer T.?"

"C-c-c..."

"Deep breath, Tweak," Aidan suggested quietly. She nodded, massaging her throat. Popping out one of her anxiety pills, she slipped it under her tongue.

"Personally, I'm against this move," Hall stated crisply. "If you'll excuse my bluntness, you're not just some Gamma who can reach other Gammas, Officer. You're one of the best coders we have. I don't have much interest in making someone like you a target for every security contractor, Corporate man, and frankly idiot in our ranks who might take issue with your genetics."

Tweak blinked. Shit, she hadn't thought about that. But yeah, of course there were assholes in the Force. Hadn't Aidan's own dad beat him up for being trans? Hadn't officers come down on Sarah and Yvonne, and Kevin and Blake about being gay?

Shit. As if this problem wasn't sucktastic enough.

"I'll lay out the case in favor, then," Hernandez put in. "Officer T., you are the ace up our sleeves in this situation. Your social capital under the name of Golden Dragon gives you incredible clout with the parts of society we're trying to reach. And we think we know how to make it really worth our while." Leaning in, he gave the camera a smile that was almost a grin.

"Do you remember the work you did recently on inserting broadcasts directly into the vid feeds of the Corporate news channels?"

"Y-yeah?" Tweak asked, feeling her scales standing on end under the bandages.

"What would you think about, in future, creating a promotional video to be placed in the Corporate feeds?" Hernandez's eyes were intense enough that Tweak looked down at her hands, listening to his voice. "If we could create short clips directing people to get on the Mesh and watch for you there..."

"Then we'd have an even bigger target painted on the girl, sir," Hall sighed. "Not to mention, poking seven sleeping bears in the eye. With all due respect, I don't approve of that approach."

"Councilor? Commander?" Aidan put in. "The point of this call is to ask my officer what she's comfortable doing. Respectfully, I'd like to get back to the focus of the call."

The two big brass folks blinked in their boxes like surprised pigeons in cages.

"Of course, Base Commander," Hall said eventually. Aidan gave her a nod, then focused on Tweak again.

"Tweak? Is this idea okay with you?"

Tweak swallowed hard. "C-c-can I have t-t-time to t-t-think ab-b... ab-bout it?"

"Of course," Hernandez agreed. "We can begin arranging the basics for a video on the Meshnet, while you're considering. Can you give us an answer by the end of this week? Since that will coincide with the first General Strike and your extraction, it should time out well." Not trusting herself to speak, Tweak nodded.

"Okay," Aidan cut in, "my officer's giving provisional consent, so I'm comfortable continuing the discussion. May I dismiss my officer, Councilor?"

"Dismissed, Officer T.," Hernandez agreed with a nod. Tweak nodded, and flipped the screen out of existence with shaking fingers.

Curling over on herself, she whimpered as the sick fear washed through her.

They wanted her to out herself to the whole world. To everyone. And not just the Mesh. The Corporate news. They wanted her to be naked in front of a world that *hated* what she was.

The weight of the thought crushed her into the bed. Tears soaked the sheet.

In the kitchen, the refrigerator hummed in the drowsy quiet. Liza ran over her speech one more time.

The TV's sudden noise made her catch her breath.

"Today, masked provocateurs have briefly disrupted work across the nation. Chanting 'not enough hours in the day, give us a break or give us more pay!', they marched through insecure offices and production centers. Jack Hamilton, CEO of EagleCorp, made a public statement on his steps to increase security in—"

"Can you watch that with 'buds?" Liza asked, trying to keep the irritation out of her tone. "I need to get this speech memorized."

"Sure, but did you see this?" Naomi called over.

Liza nodded. "The Unions voted on it as a warmup to the big stay-home. All of them are taking turns marching at other people's workplaces, where it's safe. They called it the Make My Day action, because they'll be making other workers' days. It's enough to annoy the management, but it's not the fault of the workers at any one spot; they don't even know when the other unions will show up. So there's nothing direct the management can do to punish them."

"Hunh. Smart!" Naomi approved, putting in her 'buds. "I'll let you know how the news tries to twist it up."

"Thanks, Naomi," Liza agreed distractedly, running over the words. This had to be perfect. She had to get this right.

Quiet came down over them again. Liza re-read the words of her speech, whispering them under her breath to make sure they came off her tongue without a hitch.

"Excuse me, miss?"

Oh what now? Liza raised her head and erased the thought from her face, pulling herself out of her focus.

Jillian nodded at the table. "Do you have a minute?"

"A minute, sure," Liza agreed, glancing at her tab. "I have to give an important talk over in the Highlands at sixteen-hundred, but I can spare time until then. What's going on? Do you need something?"

"No, it's just..." Jillian took a seat, carefully crossing her ankles and arms. She glanced up, and Liza got that funny jolt again. Jillian was saving her last set of contacts for the trip off the grid, so Liza had started learning to handle inhuman eyes in a human face. She would have thought living with Damian would get her ready for that, but this wasn't the same. Damian's eyes were obviously technological. Jillian's eyes were an animal's, yellow and wild in a carefully neutral human face. It still messed with Liza's head.

"I wanted to talk about Tweak and Inyoni," Jillian began. "Do you think they had a fight?"

Liza blinked. "Um... well, probably. I hope they work it out, but I'm really not the one to get involved. I don't even like this kind of situation in books. Knowing Tweak, it's probably best if we just let her sort it all out."

Jillian nodded carefully. "Yeah... I guess... only... sometimes when couples fight, one person rats the other out. I... I just don't want to get caught in the middle of that. I don't want to get my family caught in that."

Now Jillian really had her attention. Liza sat up, her stomach tying itself in a knot. "Have you seen any signs that Inyoni's planning on that?"

The woman shook her head, looking like she'd bolt any second. "No, but... if he goes to turn her in, or if she calls the Peacekeepers on him..." She shrugged helplessly. "They won't care who called, they'll take us all."

For just a moment, the thought twanged Liza's nerves. But she knew better. She shook her head. "I don't know Inyoni, but you don't have to worry about Tweak. She'd never do that."

Jillian's strange eyes fixed on her. "How do you know?"

"Because I know Tweak," Liza stated. "If you crossed her, she'd be happy to take you apart. But if you're one of her people, if you're there for her, there's nobody more loyal on this planet than her. I've seen her in action. She'd tear down the world if it saved somebody who cares about her."

Slowly, Jillian nodded. "Okay. And how about him?"

Now Liza's nerves really twanged, fast and hard. "I can't speak for him. I don't know him. But..." She let out a breath. "Tweak didn't trust me for three years. And she's trusting him right off the bat. So I'm going to trust her. Because I know I can."

I never thought I'd say that, but I'm not lying, she realized. *I can trust the girl here. She might be a little wild sometimes, but there's nobody I'd trust more for this. Man, is that ever weird to realize...*

Slowly, Jillian nodded. "If you're sure about that, I guess I'll try to be, too."

"I'm sure," Liza agreed. "So, is there anything else? I don't want to be rude, but I give my first talk to the Denver chapter of the Ag Workers' Union in two hours, and I'd like to be ready for it."

Jillian shook her head. "Only thing I want is to hear that my family's safe. And you can't tell me that."

"I can tell you that we'll do everything we can to protect them," Liza offered quietly. "And these days, that's a lot."

Jillian nodded without a word. She stood, carefully tucked in the kitchen chair, and went back into the living room. Liza watched as she snuggled up with her husband, taking their child in her arms.

Event File 22
File Tag: Mission Compromised
15:30-09-23-2160/17:30-09-23-2160

The time snuck up on all of them. Sooner than Naomi would have liked, she was closing the door of the safehouse at Liza's back and heading out with her. The first AgCo meeting Liza was supposed to address was being held in a CSS AgCo manager's house. The Folder had really done a hell of a number on AgCo loyalty; even some of the middle management were coming over to their side now. They weren't exactly friendly about it, Naomi reflected as Liza rang the bell. But they were decent. And they were furious at upper management for the ways they'd gone against all the Christian teaching that American AgCo worked so hard to indoctrinate in their kids. That anger was useful.

She gave Liza a glance. The woman was brittle as a block of ice, breathing too fast. Not good signs.

"Hey Liza?" The taller woman shot her a glance. Naomi smiled. "Deep breath. You're doing good."

Liza's body language relaxed a little. She even managed a tiny smile. "Thanks, Naomi."

Three locks clicked, and the door opened. The chapter president gestured them in. Closing the door and locking it, the old man turned and shook Liza's hand. "Good to see you," he offered, but his eyes were wary.

The home was beautifully appointed inside, all white adobe and natural wood. In a living room as big as a base canteen, the union sat carefully on folded chairs, avoiding one another's eyes. Naomi took a spot at parade rest behind Liza, double checking the 'bud in her ear and the holo-contacts she had connected to the alerts and security system on her tab. Thin green readouts came up, noting every person who walked by the house in her right eye. Her left eye was giving her readouts of the area for a four-block radius. A little distracting, but a lot better than getting approached unawares.

Running her eyes over the assembly, she realized with a jolt that they'd chosen seats by Purity State. She figured it out partly by the little Purity Badges some of them wore, and partly by skin color. The further back in the room people were, the darker their skin. She'd never seen the Purity State system in action. The sight sent a little wriggle of revulsion through her guts.

"Alright everyone," the union president began, "This's Miss Liza, who's come from the Democratic State Force to have a talk with us."

"Hello, Miss Liza," the gathering chorused in unison. Liza's back went even more stiff; Naomi hadn't realized that was possible.

"Good afternoon, everyone," Liza began. "I was told by your chapter president that you'd like to have a discussion period before we go into the body of what I've come to teach."

"Miss Liza's gonna get all your questions answered," the chapter president interceded. "Jus' remember, I expect good manners. Remember Galatians 5:23: meekness, self-control; against such things there is no law."

It was a little bit of a shock when the whole room repeated the words. Man, was that creepy. Liza shared a look with Naomi. Naomi did her best to say 'well, we're here now. I hate it too. Get it over with,' with her eyes.

Straightening her spine, Liza turned her attention to the crowd.

"If everyone with questions will raise their hands, we can get started."

A forest of hands shot up. Liza pointed. "I think the gentleman in the back was first. Red shirt."

A Black man tentatively stood, his ballcap crushed in his hands. "Uh, yes ma'am. So... if we sign up, I'm worried about what'll happen to my family. If they see me in this..." he shrugged helplessly.

"You're right," Liza agreed. "If you were doing this alone, you'd be in real trouble. Which is why you're not. The goal of this movement is to get at least four percent of the entire American population to stand together. So, in a very real way, what keeps all of you safe is one another. Everyone working together, across the country, will make it less and less likely that any single person is picked out. But we do have protective measures for you. Please know that the Force has created a stipend system to support the families of our people. You'll be able to log into the Common Ground app and find the portal. This stipend is guaranteed, no questions asked. That's a promise the Force will stand by."

"What Purity State's it for?" Someone called. Liza smiled. "All of them. We don't care what class the Corps tells you that you are. It doesn't matter to us. You're the people who we're standing beside."

"Are we paying for this?" somebody in the first row demanded. "I'm not paying for someone who doesn't do his share to have an easy ride."

"This money isn't coming out of the pockets of individual citizens," Liza explained, "Though, in a way, it's come out of all your pockets via corporate extraction. What we want to do is put it back."

In the front rows, people shifted uncomfortably. People in the back rows sat up straight, eyes bright.

Liza must have caught on to that. She drew a breath. "Let's get something cleared up right now. It's not going to be comfortable. But first, I need you to do something. Raise your hand if you want to make sure babies don't get turned into dog food and poor people don't get turned into bio-diesel again."

Every hand in the room shot up. *Big surprise,* Naomi thought, watching the readings on her contacts.

Registered: Group, 4 individuals, 4 blocks away.
Registered: Individual, 50 feet away.
Registered: Group, 6 individuals, 2 blocks away.

Of course nobody wants to admit that they're the one who thinks it's okay to murder babies. The poor, maybe, that they can justify. But nobody wants to look in the mirror and say 'I think killing babies is okay'. Too bad they don't hold onto that when babies grow up.

She sighed quietly. *Holy shit, I'm getting cynical these days...*

"Okay," Liza continued. "With that in mind, I'm going to take the first steps on a discussion that will get us to a place where that won't happen again. But this is what I need to ask: everyone in this room needs to listen with your ears, and your heart. What you're going to hear won't be easy. But it will be true. Raise your hand if you want to hear what I've got to say."

The reaction was a little more tentative this time, but eventually, the hands all went up.

"Okay." Liza fell into parade rest. "This is the thing. All your lives, you've been told that your Purity State and your Citizen Standing Score told you what you're worth. To God. To other people. To society. Maybe even to yourself." Standing like that old statue in New York, Liza looked out over the gathering with calm eyes. "But what they told you wasn't meant to help you become a better person. It was meant to give the Corporate owners control."

Liza was magnetic, but Naomi wasn't here for the speech. She was here to watch their backs. Carefully, she checked the scrolling readings.

Registered: Group, 3 individuals, 4 blocks away.
Registered: Group, 2 individuals, 150 feet away.
Registered: Group, 9 individuals, 3 blocks away.

Liza's words washed through the room, underlaid by an eddy of nervous grumbles from the AgCo members.

"We've all been tricked. And we've been tricked for a very long time. If you look way, way back into our history, back when this country was founded, you'll find laws from the original thirteen colonies that outlawed African-Americans and European-Americans—whites and blacks—from working together. You find laws saying that if two people from different races ran away from their owners together, there were extra punishments. One person was running away from maybe ten years of indenture, and the other one from a lifetime of slavery. But they *were* running away together. You don't make laws against things that don't actually happen." Liza paced the room. It was hard not to watch her when she got in this mode.

The front of the crowd was starting to look ugly. Naomi ran a finger over her guns, concealed in their holo-holsters on her belt, and her collapsible fighting stick. She was starting to love that thing. Up in Coomb Olwen, they did a kind of fighting that used a walking stick with a knob on the end. Up there, they called it something that sounded like 'batarakt'. She just called it good fighting. She'd picked up a lot of tricks from friends up there and adapted the style to a foldable staff with a weight on one end and a spike on the other. She just hoped she wouldn't have to pull it on the people they were supposed to be winning over here.

The readings scrolled by in her contacts.

Registered: Individual, 4 blocks away.
Registered: Group, 2 individuals, 375 feet away.
Registered: Group, 6 individuals, 2 blocks away.

"So, why did they do it?" Liza asked the room. There were some grumbles, but no answers.

"Because," Liza answered, "If indentured servants and enslaved people had worked together for economic justice, *they could have made the landholders change the system.* And the landholders knew it. 'Woah,' they said, 'If everyone below us ever stands up together, we're toast. What are we going to do? I know. We'll make the European servants feel superior to African slaves. We'll talk the poor Europeans into believing that any gains by Blacks came at their expense. We'll teach them that all of this is a zero-sum game, and that what one person wins, the other person loses.' And that's the system that the Citizen Standing Scores and the Purity Standing are still perpetuating today. They're not about how worthy you are. They're designed to keep you fighting one another."

"Bull!" somebody shouted.

"Really?" Liza called back. "Because this happened." She tapped her screen, and a page shot up. "Bacon's Rebellion. 1676. Indentured European servants and African slaves rebelled against the government together. It's a long story and it isn't pretty. There aren't any good guys in this story, and there aren't any heroes. I'm happy to discuss it later in our talk in detail. But I want you to know about it, because after Bacon's Rebellion, they put in more and more laws to separate whites from blacks, take away rights from African Americans and give more to European Americans. They gave extra crumbs to one set of poor people instead of another, and told them that God wanted it that way. *And they kept the cake.* This was how they made sure the people who didn't have a voice and didn't have a vote *never* got together again. The people in power tricked our ancestors into seeing each other as different kinds of people. And it *worked.* For way too long, it worked. But that isn't what the Bible teaches any of us, is it? Remember Hebrews 2:11-12: for indeed he who makes holy and those being made holy all have the same origin, and so he is not ashamed to call them brothers and sisters."

Naomi blinked. Since when did Liza know the Bible?

Well, probably since she started prepping for this speech, because she was smart. She knew her audience. If she thought about it, Naomi could lay a good bet that Kevin had coached her on the biblical stuff.

In her ear, the warning system blipped. She checked the readouts. Nothing to worry about.

"But it's going to stop working now. Stand up, everybody. Pick up your chairs."

Hypnotized, the group moved. "Make a circle, everyone," Liza continued. "Sit beside each other. You're all brothers. You're all sisters. You're all Americans and—"

Naomi's contact screens flared red.

Registered: Group, 23 individuals, 150 feet away.
Registered: Group, 30 individuals, 750 feet away.
Registered: Group, 32 individuals, 3 blocks away.

"Liza. Trouble," she called.

The room froze.

"Alright, everyone," Liza began. "It looks like we're going to need to evacuate. So I'd like everyone to—"

Her words were lost when a chunk of concrete came sailing through the nearest window. The door shuddered, splintered, and gave.

Yelling, a crowd of men poured into the house. Naomi felt herself step into the cold distance of a fighter as she took in the weaponry. Bats and pieces of rebar, chains and pieces of lumber, fists and heavy boots. Plenty of rifles in holsters on backs, but not very many in hands. These people didn't want to kill right away. No, they wanted to maim and beat. They wanted blood on their knuckles.

The room was full of shouting. The Union was going down. Get to Liza, that was her job. Get to Liza, and get her out.

This wasn't the kind of room for gunplay. Nope. This was time for the stick.

It slid into her hand easy, shaking out into a staff.

Some asshole came snarling at her, yelling something about heathen whores. She snapped her stick out in a fast jab, caught him in the diaphragm, and watched him fold over in a wheezing heap, just the right height for her knee to slam into his face. That took him down for keeps.

Another guy roared and came at her. Switching hands, she snapped the stick out to the side, catching him in the throat with the knob and dropping him like a stone. Some son of a bitch tried grabbing her hair. Bad move. She swung her stick back and around, and felt the spike in the end sink down. She wrenched it back, heard the blade cut and the bastard yowl, and she was loose.

Somewhere, a woman was screaming. What a shit show. Where the fuck had all this come from?!

She slammed her off-arm into a guy's gut, and that got him out of the way. Swings of her stick moved the bastards and cleared her path. And there was Liza, both knives out and swaying like a rattlesnake about to strike, standing over a woman with blood running from her head. Naomi came up on her left, caught her eye, and got her back.

"We need out," she called, back to back with the taller woman. "Let's head for one of the windows, get out along the side of the house."

"We have to do something for these people!" Liza called back, slashing a knife across an arm that came within reach of her blades. Blood fountained.

"We'll do more good if we get out and hit the panic button," Naomi replied, snapping her stick out and clocking a bastard going after some kid not even half his size. "We need backup! We need—"

A gun went off, and then another and another.

"By order of EagleCorp's Peace And Prosperity compact with American AgCo, this Peacekeeping unit will reinstate order and arrest the culprits! Resistance will be met with deadly force!" A voice bawled through a bullhorn.

Naomi hissed in a breath. "Liza. Out. Now!"

Liza gave a long groan of frustration, but she didn't resist when Naomi tugged her arm. Together, they fought their way to a window, shoved it open, and rolled out. The Peacekeepers were still focused on the front door. Good. They had a little time.

"Put away your knives, fast," Naomi whispered. "We gotta move."

Carefully, she unfolded a slick poncho, passing it to Liza. Really what they needed were suits, but those would take too long to put on. They'd have to settle for ponchos with the hoods up, the visors down, and hope it'd be enough.

"Where?" Liza whispered as they both activated their slick ponchos.

"Storm drains," Naomi whispered. "Best place. Look for a drain cover."

As they looked, Naomi mentally kicked herself. All those little groups of civilians. Those had been the thugs getting together in twos and threes, hadn't it? They'd known enough not to show up in an easily spotted mob until it was go time. She'd have to remember that and pass it on. Figuring out how to plan for that was going to suck; they couldn't wire the systems to tag every single passerby as a threat.

The drain cover was locked down, of course, but a quick bit of work with a code scrambler popped it. And they were down and in, sliding the drain cover over their heads.

"Sensors down here aren't as good," Naomi muttered. "Okay, let me get the schematic up on…"

She blinked at her tab. Four calls from her brother. She brought up his mesh connection and pressed Voice Call.

"Hey," she murmured into the tab, waving Liza to follow along the walkway.

"Hey Omi," her brother's words were a long sigh of relief. "How are you guys?"

"Both in one piece," Naomi offered as they navigated, using the schematic on Liza's tab. "How'd you know we were in trouble so fast?"

"You're on the news, Omi," Aidan explained. "Shit-Eating Steve is up on his AgCo podium ranting about… well, watch it when you're at the safe house. Upshot is, he's got all kinds of pictures of the teachers in the Western Quadrant, the Tidewater Quadrant, the Appalachia Quadrant, Gulf Quadrant and El Norte Quadrant too. You're all on AgCo's Moral Deplorables lists now, and you're on the EagleCorp Most Wanted list too."

"Well fuck," Naomi sighed. "This night just gets better."

"No shit," Aidan agreed grimly. "So, where are you? Do you need backup?"

"We're in the stormwater system," she explained. "I think we're okay. We can follow it down to the safe house; it's a couple miles, but the schematic says we're clear. If we could get backup here now—and I mean right now—I think we could help the poor bastards who came for Liza's talk, but in fifteen, twenty minutes, it's gonna be all over."

She heard Aidan sigh. "I'll get with their chapter president and—"

"They probably got him too," Naomi put in.

Her brother groaned. "Fuck. Okay, I'll reach out to the Grapevine. They'll know what to do. Be safe, Omi."

"You too, big brother." Naomi agreed quietly. Sticking her tab back in her pocket, she jogged to catch up with Liza.

The muzzle of a gun met them at the door to the safe house. Naomi gave Cameron a look that she really hoped he read as 'I have no more fucks to give.'

"First off, that's not how you hold a gun, man. And it's shaking. You'll shoot your own foot in a second. Second off, get out of the way. I am so done right now."

"The tab says her voice print matches, Cam," Jillian's voice called inside. "Let her in."

Looking dazed, the big man stepped back. Naomi and Liza slid inside, shucking their slick ponchos.

"Are you okay?" Jillian asked, rocking her baby anxiously. Naomi blew out a breath. "Well, we're not dead. But we heard we're on the news." She glanced around. "Where's Tweak?"

Jillian nodded at the hall. "In her room. She saw the TV, and she ran in there and slammed the door."

"Inyoni?" Liza asked, voice tense. Jillian glanced at her. "Sitting on the floor outside the room. Trying to talk to Tweak through the door. I think she might be crying."

"That bad?" Naomi asked, stepping into the bathroom for some toilet paper. Carefully, she cleaned the blood from the knob of her stick, then the spike. She needed a second handful to get it really clean. A little noise made her glance at the baby, but she realized it was Cameron whimpering. The big man was curled up on himself, arms around his knees, rocking.

"That bad," Jillian agreed as Naomi worked. "You should watch it. We're going to go into our room, Cam and Jen and I. We...don't need any more tonight."

"Yeah, I get that," Naomi agreed, feeling the lead in her muscles now that the fighter's high was wearing off. "Okay, go ahead. We'll take care of all this."

After all, that was what she did. She took care of things. Even when the things exploded in her face. Especially then, maybe.

"What channel should we turn to, the Grower's News?" Liza asked. Jillian stared at her with blank yellow eyes.

"All four Conservative Corporations are airing it. You'll find it."

That couldn't be good.

Naomi flicked on the TV and flipped the channels. Sure enough, Steven Evers' face came up on the screen. Flanking him were his best buddies; Jack Hamilton of EagleCorp, and Bob Walton of ArgusCo. In the center, good old Shit-eating Steve stood with his hands on the podium. Incredibly fit, tan and topped with a neat thatch of gleaming white hair, the guy loved playing up his image of a clean-living farm preacher. Usually he was giving the camera that ridiculous grin that had earned him the nickname, but today there wasn't a smile in sight. The old bastard looked furious.

"Good evening," the agricultural CEO began. "It has come to our attention that there are seditionists entering your communities, speaking to gatherings of our citizens. We have captured images and recordings of dozens of these *sinners* in their acts."

He waved a hand, and the screens around him lit up with faces and video clips. Naomi spotted herself showing someone how to handle a wrist lock, and Liza speaking. She saw a couple nodding acquaintances here and there; all great Dusters, all trying to help people. Cold tension settled in her muscles as the Corporate head folded his hands around the lectern, the images of everything they were trying to do showing behind him.

"It is seldom I reply to the actions of vermin such as these, but this time, this time I just feel I must." He raised his hands and his eyes, gesturing at the ceiling. "My sainted great-grandfather's voice spoke to me from Heaven, and whispered 'boy, I started this Corporation to protect these people. Now it's your turn." Lowering his eyes, he leaned forward on his podium. "First, let me speak directly to my citizens. People. You were signed into covenant with God and American AgCo the day you were born. You're God's chosen, those who till the soil. And yet, and yet you have *sinned*. You've let these fork-tongued vipers whisper to you about what *they* call freedom and equality? You should be ashamed, folks, listening to that ridiculous mishmash of words I'm sure you called speeches. We have recordings of what these sneaking seditionists whisper and rant. And I say to you now, that it is utter trash. It is vile, self-serving and, no doubt, the criminals who speak it sought to sway you by being the trigger-word proclaimers, the *abomination* lovers, the offerers of false promises to forgive your sins or tell you they were never sins at all, the race-baiters proclaiming they cannot be racist because they are only being racist against white heterosexuals.

"And by that I mean *you*, people! They hate *you*! Ignore what the lying serpents told you. They want to overthrow a decent way of life ordained by your Corporation and God Himself! And sin comes with judgment." The screens flicked to images of Peacekeepers beating the Force soldiers and union members. Gas. Bloody faces and arrests filled every screen. In front of that quilt of carnage, Evers spread his hands. "Don't suffer with the sinners, folks! Turn away from them and repent! For those who repent, they shall be spared."

He clutched the sides of the lectern. "Now, let me speak directly to the criminals." He jabbed a finger at the screen, little flecks of spittle in the corners of his lips. "I'm speaking to you, sinners. I'm speaking to you, terrorists, genetic abominations and miscegenators, sodomites and perverts, you slithering creatures who have the gall to come into the homes and businesses of good people, upstanding people, and lead them astray. You're pathetic, really. The shame of it is, you will never understand it, not until the fires of Hell scorch you.

"And believe me you *will* feel the fire. But by then, it will be too late to repent. I will root your poison out of the breasts of the people I've been entrusted to protect, and standing here, I entreat everyone I know to do the same."

His lips twisted in a sneering little smile. "I know, I know; you'll tell yourselves you couldn't care less what I say, but you should. You really should. Because me, and my good friends Jack and Bob are coming for you. And we're bringing every upstanding citizen with us. And when we're done with your morality executions, there won't be anything left of you on God's green earth but a red stain on the sand in the Hall of Repentance. We will expunge you. So you'd better care. Because we're coming."

The audience exploded with thunderous applause. The sound made Naomi want to hurl.

Liza snapped the screen out of existence. Nobody moved. In the silence, muffled weeping whispered from the next room.

Event File 23
File Tag: Actions On Contact
22:30-09-23-2160

In the dark, Tweak held herself together, trying to keep from breaking. She could feel the edges of her scales cutting their way through the bandages. She could never hide. She'd never be able to hide well enough. They were coming for her. They were coming for her, and they were going to dissect her. She was going to end up cut to bits. She was never going to get out of here.

Someone was calling her name. She didn't know who it was, but she couldn't answer. She could barely breathe. Her throat was a cinched noose of muscle. The shakes just wouldn't stop. The terror was a breaking storm, and she was a tiny animal battered by it. Helpless. Exposed. She was going to die. They were going to see her, and she was going to die.

The door creaked. The floorboards squeaked.

They were coming. They were *coming.*

She balled herself down against the bed, whimpers choking in her throat.

"Tweak? I'm gonna take a seat, kay? I won't touch you or nothin'. Swear. Jus' gonna sit."

The bed compressed. It was Inyoni's voice. Inyoni's words.

The storm rolled through her, tearing at her. Lightning flashed inside her head. The tears poured down.

She couldn't tell when it eased up, but at some point the tears slowed. The lightning eased up.

She wiped snot on her bandaged arm, raising her eyes. Inyoni had turned his holo off, and he looked sweet and cockeyed and worried, one ear stuck out to the side and the other down. He looked like a messed up windmill.

Messed up. An abomination. Just like her.

The tears came again. She lowered her head against her arms, and the scales there scraped their sharp edges through the fabric of her bandages.

Quiet filtered down between them; a soft quiet. A quiet that had air in it for Tweak to breathe.

"Scary stuff, hunh?" Inyoni's voice was like his touch, safe and easy. Tweak swallowed hard, nodding. She didn't trust herself to speak, not yet. "Yeah," Inyoni murmured. "I about pissed myself, he started pointing at the screen."

"It's always the s-same," she whispered. "People s-start to w-w-win, and the b-bastards come in and wreck it all. It always happens. Always. And n-now it's happening again."

"Not always," Inyoni suggested.

Tweak shook her head. "Always. All over t-time. Every time people make something g-good, every time they even s-start, some b-bastards c-come in and b-break it. Every time." Tears left wet patches in her shirt and trailed down her throat as she choked the words out. "History. You get something good, build a farm, build a house, build a town. Real soon you get some b-bastards coming to t-take it away. Make it theirs. Or break it." She swiped an arm across her face. "And every p-p-plan we m-m-make gets wrecked. Even l-Liza's speech. They didn't even let her finish. It was b-beautiful, and they didn't even...and then that b-bastard gets to spit shade and c-call people ab-b-b...call us that, and n-n-nobody shuts him up, and he shits on everything. It just keeps g-g-going that way. And I d-d-d... I c-c-c.... I hate it. I hate it."

"Hey, uh, Tweak?" Inyoni asked. She glanced up, not sure if she could take his eyes.

His ears had gone up a little, and he was smiling, knees drawn up and arms gangled out to let him lean back. His white angel wings gleamed softly.

"I'm not disagreeing. I just wanna say, you know what? Fuck that guy."

She couldn't help it; she laughed. Inyoni's smile widened. "I'm serious. If he can't see that a girl like Liza's got a point and a girl like you's beautiful, then fuck him."

Tweak's breath choked in her throat. When she got the word out, it sounded like a croak. "B-beautiful?"

"Yeah," Inyoni agreed, nodding. "You're beautiful."

Glancing down, Tweak shook her head. "You c-c-can't say that."

"Why not? I'm lookin' at you. And I think you're beautiful."

"You c-c-can't see all of me," Tweak parried.

Inyoni glanced at her arm. "I bet I still call you beautiful when I see your arms. Wanna check me?"

Tweak's throat felt like sandpaper. Her hands shook when she wrapped them around herself. She couldn't find the words; she only shook her head. "Y-y-you'll hate it."

"Bet I won't," Inyoni offered. Softly, he let his fingers touch hers. "Lemme see?"

Tweak dropped her eyes. "You see...you see, you'll be gone." she whispered, her voice strange in her own ears.

"You're sittin' on my backpack, and it's got my spare clothes," Inyoni pointed out mildly. "Lemme see. Come on. I can't run when you're sittin' on my only good pair of pants."

Tweak mopped at her face. "S-s-scared." she whispered. "So s-s-scared...."

"Won't go nowhere," Inyoni promised quietly.

"Promise?" Tweak asked, hearing the breaks in her own voice.

Inyoni nodded. "Swear."

Tweak drew a shuddering breath. The world wanted her dead, sure. But this guy with his soft llama ears thought she was beautiful. And he was a Gamma. He knew what seeing weird in the mirror was like. Maybe he really could see her without wanting to run. And maybe if he saw, and he didn't run... maybe...

And maybe she'd die without finding out, if she didn't try it tonight. She didn't want to die without knowing.

She closed her eyes. "Okay."

The first clasp clicked as it opened. Her fingers peeled away a layer of white cloth. "You never asked. Why I'm the g-Golden d-Dragon."

"Figured you'd tell me," Inyoni's voice replied. Tweak nodded, eyes closed. Her hands shook as she unwound the loop of fabric. She sucked in a breath, desperate to fill the silence. Folds of bandage slithered down, sloughing away. She didn't dare look at Inyoni's face. "My d-dad used to have this joke. My name. My real n-name. It's Lung Tung-Mei," she whispered as she worked. "They called me Tammy Lung, over here." She swallowed hard. "Lung means dragon. My d-dad said we had d-dragon blood." And now she was bare to his eyes. "My dad. Said me. Being born. Was p-proof. About the dragon blood. Lucky Dragon Girl. That's what Mom and Dad called me. My brother. Bao Li. His n-name meant 't-t-treasure'." She stared at her shimmering, scaled arms, words whispering out. "He was their treasure. I was their dragon girl. I was supposed to p-p-protect him." She drew a shuddering breath. "So, yeah. You're Bird? I'm Dragon."

Silence. Tweak opened her eyes, gut twisted up with fear. "Say something? Please?"

"You really are a dragon," Inyoni whispered, eyes wide. Moving slow and easy, he took one of Tweak's hands up and kissed her wrist, where the scales were the deepest gleaming caramel. "I don't know how, but I think I walked into a fairytale."

Tweak gave a weak, shivering parody of a laugh. "Bullshit."

"Nah, I'm serious," Inyoni replied quietly, dropping another kiss a little higher up her arm. His lips were warm, soft against the tough dragon scales. The sight of him kissing her arm made Tweak feel like she was about to cry all over again. When he looked up and smiled, goddamn if she didn't actually feel tears prickling up behind her eyes.

"You look like magic, Tweak. The light on these scales...wow."

Tweak smiled weakly, feeling like she might start shaking from relief. She swallowed. "Um... on my legs too."

"Yeah? Can I see?" Inyoni grinned. "I mean, if you ever wanna take your pants off, I'm in. You wanna?"

"You're serious." she whispered, awestruck. "You're serious. You're not freaked."

Inyoni cocked his head, ears out at ninety-degree angles "'Wha? Course I'm not. Why would I be?" He reached out, one finger tracing the outline of the nearest scale. "Tweak, babe, I got fuckin' donkey ears. So, if you wanna hang around with a jackass, I'm real proud to hang with a dragon. And yeah, *you are beautiful*. Anybody says different? Fuck 'em."

Tweak stared at him for a handful of heartbeats. Then she leaned in and kissed him hard enough to drive the air out of both of them.

Tweak's tab buzzed with an incoming vid call. She jumped into the stratosphere. One hand scrabbled for her tab, while the other yanked on her jacket. That'd work to hide her scales for now. She blinked at the Meshnet vid request.

"T-tamira?" What was the head of one of the Zoncom entertainment union chapters calling for, this late at night? "Weird..." She muttered, accepting the call.

The image fizzed up, the Black woman with curls done in a tight, traffic-cone orange fade front and center. Around her was a crowd of nervously grinning folks. She flashed Tweak a smile. "Hey Miss Tweak. It's Tamira from the Media Communications Union. You told us to call you up if we had some ideas?"

"Y-y-yeah?" Tweak asked, angling her tab so that the camera wouldn't pick up Inyoni.

"Well," Tamira began, "AgCo just had us do a rush after-hours job. They sent their material to us, and we had to master it, prep it, and get it out to all the streams AgCo is paying for. So yeah, we just had to help get Shit-Eating Steve's speech out there. And since we're all sick to death of that trash—" around her, her union-mates whistled and clapped—"we took a vote on it. We think we can do something."

"Yeah?" Tweak asked, double checking the hang of her jacket out of the corner of her eye.

"Well," Tamira explained, "this chapter here is the team that does the technical side of mastering, sound-modulating and releasing for big news and entertainment broadcasts. Football games, speeches from all the execs, all that kind of stuff. We have buddies in the Union who specialize in media optimization and creating watcher engagement. So, we called up our union head."

Tweak nodded along, wondering where all this was going.

Tamira grinned. "The upshot is, if you can record us a speech that claps back at Shit-eating Steve's garbage? We'll air it on all seven news streams. We want to do it back to back with Steve's speech. Every time it airs, yours does. And once it's aired, the media op folks are talking. They're going to take what you say, find the salient lines, and create a media blast to go out across the Net and the Mesh. They're gonna call for a national day-long event in support. If you can make sure the drones stay off us, we can get a whole nation of people out and dancing in the street."

"We're thinking of doing something with masks," a woman with the lime-green eyes of people gene-modded for administrative assistance added. Tweak wished she could remember the lady's name. "That will make people feel more secure, and it'll emphasize a carnival element to the whole thing. We can send out a diagram for a mask to wear as part of the media blast; people can print them on consumer rigs."

"That'll let all your teachers have the cover they need to get out safe, yeah?" Tamira asked.

Tweak stared at the woman through the screen.

"You... seriously?"

"Well yeah," Tamira grinned.

"We had a vote!" A wispy little guy with ear gauges that made his earlobes huge—Tim? Ted? Something like that—added. "So, when can you get it to us?"

Tweak sat up in bed. "I g-gotta get it approved. C-can I c-c-call you tomorrow at lunch?"

"Sure," Tamira agreed. "That works, we've still got to do a lot of organizing on this. See you then."

"Wait..." Tweak swallowed. "What if you g-guys get in t-t-trouble?"

Tamira grinned. "Oh, we'll just say the terrible Golden Dragon hacked us. We're all so scared and horrified." She made a fake-scared face.

Tweak grinned. "Awesome. Awes-s-some! Thanks!"

Tamira shrugged. "Yeah well. See you!" She turned her screen off, shutting out the sight of the media team waving.

Grinning, Tweak bounced off the bed, snagged one more kiss from Inyoni, and took off running. "Guys! Guys guys guys!"

"What?" Liza demanded, on her feet when Tweak skidded into the living room. Naomi was grabbing her gun.

"C-call Aidan! Get Hall! On the tab!" Tweak demanded.

"What the hell, Tweak?" Naomi asked, blinking.

Grinning, Tweak planted her fists on her hips. "Liza. You're g-gonna finish your s-speech And *everybody* is g-gonna see it!"

Event File 24
File Tag: National Strategy
13:30·09·24·2160/16:30·09·24·2160

"Anything yet?" Tweak asked, pacing to burn off the energy fizzing under her skin. Naomi gave her a patient look. "Not since five minutes ago, when you asked."

Tweak cringed. "Sorry. Just... shit. I hate this!"

"Yeah," Naomi agreed, stretching through some kind of muscle routine. "This is why I liked being a grid operative. No waiting around for somebody to vote."

"They're actually moving incredibly fast, for National Command," Liza offered from the couch. "They've already convened, heard the proposal from the Media Union and us, and they're voting. That's lightning-fast."

Tweak sighed. Not fast enough, seeing as they were still standing around waiting. She flopped onto the couch beside Inyoni. He put an arm around her. The touch grounded her, making her feel less off the wall.

"Any word on how—" Inyoni had begun to say, when the tabs buzzed. Tweak, Liza and Naomi all snatched for theirs.

"Let's just put one on the table," Liza suggested. "That will make a group call easier."

She brought up the call, enlarged the window, and hung it at head height for everyone sitting on the couches. Tweak's heart was in her throat as Liza accepted the call.

On the other end, Aidan, Yvonne and Kevin grinned at them.

"Top of the morning, everyone!" Kevin was doing some sort of showing off actor-type thing again; she could tell because he always did some dumb thing with words. That either meant he was really happy, or faking it because he was freaked and covering. But if Aidan and Yvonne were smiling too, that had to be good. Right?

"Okay," Aidan added, "we've got an itinerary to walk through. But the short story is: day after tomorrow, all of America throws a party. Today, you guys have a speech to give."

There was more to it, of course. There was always more to it: details, planning, all the stuff the National Council had given orders about and all the details that would make things work. But soon enough, Liza and Tweak were in the back bedroom where the light was brightest, and the blue walls made it look like a studio. Max from the media union had come over to help them do some makeup—that had sucked balls—and get the room just right. He was standing with his high-quality vid kit, waiting. They'd already walked through the speech that Liza had submitted twice, and Tweak had already taken her anti-anxiety meds. She could do this. She was ready for this. Liza would do most of the talking; Tweak would finish it.

She ran a hand nervously over one arm. It still felt weird to have air running over her scales. But showing what she really was, that was key to this whole thing. And she was fucking done with letting the Corps make her feel the way she had last night. So she was in a black tank top that showed off every inch of her arms, and she wasn't hiding a thing.

"Okay, are we ready?" Max asked, glancing between Liza and her. Tweak nodded.

"I've got the speech on the prompter here," he pointed at the holo hanging over his left shoulder. "So we're all set. I'll count down from three."

Liza drew a deep breath. "Okay. Okay. We're ready."

Max nodded. He counted his fingers down: three, two, one.

The recording light went green.

"Fellow citizens," Liza began, "Last night, the CEO of American AgCo addressed the nation. Today, please give me a little time to offer a response.

"Some of you may know me, or know of me. I go by the code-name of the Queen of Clubs, a member of a Democratic State Force unit known as the Wildcards. That's right; I am a member of the Democratic State Force.

You don't need to turn off your TV when you hear that. Listening to me won't put you in danger." She smiled a little, a sad sort of look.

"Last night, the gentleman in ownership of American AgCo said that we should care. I'd like to reply to that. We *do* care. We care about the life, the rights, and the wellbeing of our fellow citizens. We care about whether people are afforded dignity: not according to their Citizen Standing Score. Not according to what they can provide their Corporation. We care, because you are *human beings.* Every one of you deserves to be treated as a human being, with a human soul, human potential and human rights. Every one of you has the *right* to a voice in your own society and *your own life.* The corporations have told you that you have to earn the right to decent treatment. They told you there was a number on your worth to society. But I need you to hear this: *they lied.*

"Your corporation has *lied* to you. All of you. Whether you're Zoncom or AgCo, Argus or Eagle, every one of you has been told a lie. They have told you that you have to work hard enough to earn the good life, but they've put all the systems in place to make sure it's always just out of reach. They have told you that all of this is a zero-sum game, and that what one person wins, the other person loses. That's kept you fighting with the guy next to you because he's the wrong color or loves the wrong person, *so neither of you ever look up at who's on top and ask them why they have so much.* Those numbers on your cards? They're not about how worthy you are. They're designed to keep you fighting one another."

Liza spread her hands. "All your lives, you've been told that your Purity State and your Citizen Standing Score represent what you're worth. To God. To other people. To society. Maybe even to yourself." Liza looked into the camera with calm eyes, and Tweak's heart soared. "But what they told you wasn't meant to help you become a better person. It was meant to give the Corporate owners control. And what have the people in the top positions done with that control? They have broken every rule they told you to follow. They have told you that you have to be moral and upstanding, and when you're not looking they make deals that sell babies for dog meat. They have told you that if you are honest and good, you get ahead. But they drop the Citizen Standing Scores and ruin the lives of anyone who reports the dishonest behavior of a superior. They have put low-Standing citizens on calorie restrictions, while high-Standing citizens get fat.

"And they took your agency away. They tell you that you shouldn't do certain things with your body depending on your Corporation. They all tell you it's for your own good. It's your body, but they think they have a right to dictate how you live in it. If you complain, they tell you that you have a contract with them. *But someone else held the pen and signed that contract for you.*

"What they are doing is *lying to you.*" Liza's fist smacked into the palm of her hand in time with her words. *"They do not have a contract on your soul. They do not own your body.* Every one of us is *born* with human rights. You and I were *born* with human dignity. *You do not need to earn these things.* Every one of us *is born with them.*"

Liza drew a deep breath. "Last night, Mr. Evers said he and his people were coming for me, and people like me. He could come for me any day. And he could come for you tomorrow. He thinks he gets to decide who is moral, and who is punished. It doesn't matter how good of a person you are; if you annoy those in power, they come for you. You may not want to admit it. But you know it's true, every time someone misbehaves and the terror of what happens next rises up in you."

Liza's voice dropped, soft again now. "It wasn't always like this. And it doesn't have to be. In this country, we used to have two documents that told us who we were as citizens; not of a Corporation, but of a *nation.* 'We hold these truths to be self-evident, that all people are created equal, that they are endowed by their Creator with certain unalienable Rights, that among these are Life, Liberty and the pursuit of Happiness.' That's what one of them said. 'We the People of the United States, in Order to form a more perfect Union, establish Justice, insure domestic Tranquility, provide for the common defense, promote the general Welfare, and secure the Blessings of Liberty to ourselves and our Posterity' said the other.

"*That's* what they wanted for you, and me, and all of us. If you look around and you feel like you're treated as equals, that you have the right to life, liberty and the pursuit of happiness *no matter what the number on your citizen card is,* then things are fine."

Liza spread her hands. "But if you look around and you say 'wait, I don't have the right to walk into some stores because of the number on a card. I get told that I don't eat today because there's a calorie restriction on my Citizen Standing. My boss just kicked my neighbor out of his house because he got sick. My friend's baby got taken away because her genes weren't perfect. And I don't get to say anything about it, because if I do they'll call EagleCorp on me?' Then this is *not* the America your ancestors wanted for you. This is *not* liberty. If that's what you see, then do this with me.

"Start standing up. The Corporations tell us that we will be punished if we take a stand. They tell us they're coming for us. But if *every one of us* stood up *together*, they couldn't take any one of us. If they come for one of you, they need to know that they'll have to deal with *all of us*. And they need your work. They need you to show up and do what you're told. They tell you that you need them, but they *are lying.* They need you. So what happens when you say no?"

Liza waited just a beat, drew a breath. "It's time we all stood up and stood beside each other. Every kind of person. From every Corporation. It's time we stood as equals in the Creator's eyes, look the CEOs in the eye and said, 'no. That's enough. You don't own us.'"

That was her cue. Tweak stepped in beside Liza. "She means it. We mean it. Every kind of p-person. Is part. Of this." She planted her fists on her hips, giving the camera a grin and a perfect view of her arms. "They call me the Golden Dragon. I'm an officer in the Force. I have a family there. Black, white, Asian, Lebanese, Mexican. Alpha. Gene mod. Gamma. We're all family. We all take c-care of each other. Because we're all p-people. We're all g-good at something. And we all matter."

She spread her arms. "I'm the Golden Dragon. I took down the Citizen Ratings. I took down the CO-WY G-grid. I took down the drones, and I'm g-gonna keep taking them d-down. And I'm standing beside you. Every one of you. Whoever you are. Whatever you are. If you're a g-Gamma and you're out there watching this, find me on the Common Ground. You are part of this family too. Everybody. Come to the Common Ground. There's a place for you here."

She drew a breath, and grinned. "I'm the Golden Dragon. And I'm telling you. First, we're gonna stand together. And then, we're gonna fly together. It's t-time for everything to change."

Event File 25
File Tag: Nested Concept
18:30-09-24-2160/20:15-09-24-2160

"Holy crap," Aidan murmured as the Force logo replaced Tweak's face on the screen.

And then everyone in the rec-room was cheering, the whole crew laughing and slapping each other on the back, hugging and kissing.

"Lord almighty, those girls!" Janice crowed. "You show Shiteater an' all them fuckers, Liza!"

"I mean... I read the speech, I knew what she was going to say, but... holy crap," Aidan repeated, shaking his head in awe.

"I always told Liza that her oration was stellar," Kevin agreed, his elation unbound. "And did you see Tweak! Good God in Heaven!"

"I know, right?" Sarah agreed, turning to grin at him. "Holy shit, she absolutely nailed it! She was badass!"

"Of course she was! She's a dragon!" Yvonne laughed, hanging on her wife. "And she's gonna barbecue the Corps!" Laughing, Kevin let the girls tug him into a three-way hug. He got loose eventually, grinning. "Well, now that they're on the news, I'm going to need to rework a few plans. Aidan, my love, we've got work to do!"

In Aidan's office, Kevin pulled him close for one exuberant kiss. "They did it!"

"Hell yeah they did," Aidan agreed, grinning. "Now we just have to do our bit."

"I'll have to join them at that safehouse rather than dropping off credentials; they'll need me if they're going to perfect the details of the disguises they need to exit the Grid safely," Kevin acknowledged, nodding to himself as he pulled out Aidan's spare chair. "I'll need to reconfigure some Synth and paperwork for Tweak, Naomi and Liza, and I'll take pictures of them in situ once we've got them in the costumes to complete the charade. I'm a bit worried about being tracked, given the current situation, but be that as it may. We're still waiting on the word from the Media Union on what type of cover they can give us, and... wait." He froze. Then he smacked his forehead. "Lord, I'm an ass! We can't do this the way I was thinking at all!"

"Wait, what?" Aidan blinked. Kevin turned to him with a knot in his gut. "We need Tweak on her rig and heading the techs to protect the protestors, don't you see? If they're protesting and the drones arrive…"

"Fuck, you're right," Aidan groaned. "They said local extraction was in the hands of local talent during the big meet, but there was so much going on... fuck. Okay."

Dropping into his seat, he brought up his work screens. "Okay, so, we need to extract Tweak the night before everything goes wild. Which means getting her the credentials pretty much today. I don't want you making two grid runs, not as hot as you are on the grid right now."

"I'll get Yvonne," Kevin agreed, turning and jogging out of the office. Yvonne was still partying it up in the rec room, so at least she wasn't hard to find. Grabbing her hand, Kevin towed her back to Aidan's office.

"Alright, here's what works," he offered, bringing up another set of screens and moving tasks around their itinerary as all the pieces slid and clicked together in his head. "Yvonne, I'll trade places with you and take care of this Fringe trading run, this exchange and this pickup. I've shown you all the theatrical tricks I've been learning; do you feel confident about getting Tweak ready?"

"I guess?" Yvonne's answer sounded more like a question.

Kevin glanced at her. "You guess, or you're sure?"

Yvonne raised a hand and started chewing on her cuticles. She sighed. "I... Kev, with her as hot as this, I don't trust my skills here."

"Appreciate the assessment; we'll call Umberto," Kevin agreed with a nod, tapping in the call sign. He smiled when his godfather picked up. "Evening, Tio Berto."

"I'm starting to like this Mesh thing; it means I get to see you every month," his godfather observed, smile-lines creasing his rich brown skin. Kevin smiled at the old man, but he didn't have time for too many pleasantries. "Afraid it's not a social call, tio."

"I wouldn't say so, not with your girls all over the news," Umberto agreed quietly. "What do you need?"

"An extraction for one member of the group," Kevin explained, "but it has to be tonight."

Umberto nodded. "Let me make some calls. I'll see what I can do."

"Gracias, tio. Vaya con Dios."

"Vaya con Dios, mijo," his godfather agreed, flicking off the screen. And then the waiting began.

Waiting was hell. While Yvonne and Aidan talked, Kevin flicked through possible approaches to the problems, bringing up screens and dismissing them. Yvonne drifted off after a bit, and Aidan worked quietly at his side. Kevin was glad of the company.

"Hey Kev?" Aidan murmured eventually. Kevin raised his head. Aidan turned, grinning at him. "We just got the media blast from the union. Tweak's gonna flip."

He turned his screen, and Kevin had to laugh.

Let's Fly For Change: Dragon Days! The media read in gigantic block print, interwoven with a roaring golden dragon. **National Block Party. September 25-September 28. All Citizen Standings, All Corporate Citizenships! Get Out And Dance For Social Change In The Street! Wear Yellow Clothes And Dragon Masks. Print Schematics Attached. Tell The Corporate Heads: First We're Going To Stand Together. Then We're Going To Fly Together. It's Time For Everything To Change!**

"Well, it's official. Tweak's a legend," Kevin chuckled. "And I wager she'll never let us forget it, either." Leaning over, he pecked Aidan's cheek. "Let's just hope the dragon really is lucky."

"Okay, thanks Kev," Liza gave the man on the other side of the screen a quick smile, switching it off.

"Alright, Tweak, you better pack. You're out of here at oh-two thirty. They're getting you out on a shipment of lettuce. It's probably a good idea if you go to bed early, grab a couple hours' sleep, and get up at oh-one hundred. Do you want a hand packing?"

"I got it," Tweak replied numbly. Her eyes were still riveted on the poster that had been sent out, and the mask that had come with it.

Dragon Days. Everyone was going to dress up as a golden dragon. They were dressing up for her.

This couldn't be real.

"Tweak?" Liza asked.

She blinked. "Yeah. Y-yeah. S-s-sorry. Bed. Yeah."

She did go to bed. But sleep was the last thing on her mind. She spent an hour double-checking the coding of a button labeled 'Gamma aid and protection' on the landing page for the Meshnet, and hooking that up to couriers who'd agreed to get the Gammas to the safe coordinates that everyone had planned across the country. Now that people were sure to start clicking it, it had to work. She made sure it did.

But even that project didn't last forever. Eventually, she was lying in bed, staring at the ceiling. Her brain was spinning. She didn't bother to get undressed; she'd just have to put the clothes on again in a couple hours. So she just lay there, and thought. Way too much.

If the Media Union was right, people wanted to throw a party across the country because of what she'd said.

If they were wrong, every one of the Union teachers was in deep shit. Anyone under this roof could be dead tomorrow.

Tomorrow, she'd either be a legend who saved so many lives, or a dead shithead who fucked it all up.

And she had no way to know which it would be.

The door creaked a few hours later.

"You asleep?" Inyoni's voice whispered.

Should she answer? Should she let him think she was asleep?

Would that really do any good? Or would it be another way she chickened out?

And if she never saw him again after tonight...

"No," Tweak answered. She rolled over and sat up, watching him.

Inyoni stood very still for a moment. Then he crossed the room and dropped to sit beside her. His fingers brushed hers. "You okay, Tweak?'

Tweak shrugged. "No. I'm a c-ch-chickenshit."

"'Cause you're scared 'bout tomorrow?" Inyoni asked. "That ain't bein' chickenshit."

Tweak shook her head. "Not that. Hedgehog. Ever seen one? That's me. But I need to stop. Gotta stop. For.... for y-you. If I d-don't, and you..." she swallowed hard. "I'm scared. Shit scared." her eyes met his in the dark. "I'm shit scared. But I'm trying. And I want to be with you."

Inyoni studied her face for a long time. "I ain't gonna die tomorrow, you know. I done lots harder than gettin' through some paperwork checks. It's you who they're lookin' for."

Tweak shook her head. "Not just that. Not..." Tweak swallowed. "Not just s-s-s-scared of t-that."

"I know you got trouble talkin', but... we gonna be tight, you gotta talk to me," Inyoni murmured. "I get it. I do. It sucks, all this stuff. But I ain't goin' nowhere, you know. You're bringin' me to your base so I can stay... and I like you. A lot. Even when you're bein' all weird and not talkin' to me."

Tweak stared at her fidgeting hands, smiling weakly. "Easy to say that right now."

"Yeah, well, who else'm I gonna trust to make sure I'm not bleedin'?" Inyoni tried to smile.

Tweak gave a weak chuff of a laugh. Then she raised her head. "Just k-k-kiss me? Please?"

Inyoni smiled. "Yeah." Leaning in, he pressed his lips over hers.

Tweak pushed her whole body into the kiss, moving until she was sitting in Inyoni's lap, her hands on his thighs. When his hands touched her, she let the sensation fill her mind. She reached up to flick off his holo and stroke one of his ears. Inyoni swallowed hard. He carefully ran his hands up under her shirt. "You want... uh... more than kissin'?"

"Want you." Tweak stated, hoping that he heard everything she was trying to say in that. She wanted him with her. She wanted him alive, and safe. And she wanted him the way her body told her it wanted air and food.

Inyoni murmured his agreement as he kissed her again. His fingers fumbled with the clasp of her bra under her shirt. Tweak helped him out, leaning back and shucking shirt and bra in one quick move, before helping him out of his shirt. Her body fizzed with the touch of his skin against hers. She felt as if she were filled with bubbly wine. One of his ears held gently in either hand, she kissed him again, deep. Inyoni's ears twitched in Tweak's fingers as he kissed her back. One hand slid gently up her arm, caressing her scales. He wanted to touch her scales. He really did. She kissed him harder, trying to hold onto that thought. Her hand traced down his pants, fumbling open the fly. Getting a guy out of his pants was a lot less sexy than it looked in the vids, but she got back in his lap eventually. His hand slid up her sides, exploring her skin. Tweak's head dropped back, a little squeak of pleasure escaping her. She'd never realized this would feel so nice. Fumbling, she reached in her back pocket. "Condoms. Got them here. Show me how."

"You never done this before?" Inyoni asked, surprise in his voice.

Tweak gave a breathless gasp of laughter. "N-nobody touches me, r-r-remember? You're the f-first."

He stared up at her, wide-eyed. Man he was gorgeous, with his tattoos glowing gently, making him look like a dark angel.

She traced his ink with one finger. "Could fly away. Any time. With these."

"Yeah, I wish," Inyoni muttered, pulling her into a kiss again. Very gently, he pressed her down on the bed and stretched out over her. He still had his boxers on, the open condom in one hand. For a moment, Tweak froze, heart hammering. There was nowhere to go, no air to breathe, and her whole body twanged with fear. She almost jumped out of the bed. But she drew a deep, shaking breath. "N-n-not like this. N-n-need t-t-t-to b-b-breathe. C-c-can I r-r-ride?"

Inyoni pulled back. "Yeah… sorry. Here. Just lemme…" He rolled over and pulled her on top of him. "Better?"

"Yeah." Tweak agreed, breathing easier. She grinned, feeling his body beneath hers. Every touch was a new thrill. "Want the b-b-boxers off?"

Inyoni swallowed hard and nodded against the sheets, holding up the condom. "Yeah… gotta put this on. Gotta get you naked, too."

Tweak laughed weakly. "Yeah. Guess so."

"So, those scales on your legs?" Inyoni asked. Tweak froze.

"Y-yeah?"

"You got bandages on over them?"

"Y-yeah?"

"Awesome," Inyoni grinned, his ears shot up like a hare's. "Means

I get to unwrap you. Can I?"

She laughed. "Y-y-yeah. Sure. Just lemme g-get the pants off."

Quickly, she shucked her cargo pants and stepped to the side of the bed. Inyoni grinned. "Think I'll start with these," he suggested, tracing her underwear. "Can I?"

"Yeah," Tweak agreed, barely finding the air to get the word out.

Tweak drew a few shuddering breaths as he moved, sliding down the fabric. For a second, he raised his head and grinned at her. Then he lowered his head, and his tongue slid down across her clit as his fingers got to work undoing her bandages. Tweak whimpered. She couldn't hold it back. No one had *ever* made her feel like *this*.

His tongue sped up as the last of the bandages fell away, and he stroked her bare legs. His fingers pressed the condom into her hand.

"Hell yeah." Tweak whispered, dropping down on the bed beside him before her shivery knees gave out. She fumbled with the thin rubber and slid it on.

Inyoni kissed her again and again, his hands running up her scaled legs and over her hips. One hand dipped between them to tease her clit, and Tweak groaned. She couldn't help it. "Bird?" she panted. "How... next?"

"You lemme know if I hurt you, 'kay?" Inyoni breathed, teasing her as his hard dick pressed against her leg. Moving slow and soft, he slid two fingers inside her.

Tweak couldn't get out much beside another small moan and an arching of her back. Words were hard enough at the best of times. Right now, there was no way they were going to happen.

Inyoni took it just the right way. Gently, he shifted under her, and his hands guided her onto him. Tweak squeaked as he entered her, squirmed as the new sensation arched and burned inside her. Then he moved, and the sensation changed, and she bit her tongue to stop from yelling. This was a complete overload. It was pain, but it was joy too, and it swamped her, fried out her senses, panicking her and exciting her all at once. His fingers touched her, and she arched, tensed, and heard him groan.

Inyoni grabbed her hand and twined their fingers together, his other hand on her hip as she struggled to get enough air. He pushed inside her again and again, and again, and... and then Tweak's body exploded like a firework. That was where he held her, keeping her in a rhythm, guiding her and rocking her. She'd never felt anything so powerful as the moment when they both came. It was... she didn't have a single word for it. It was too big for words.

She flopped down against his chest, breath and tiny sounds of joy panting against his ear.

"Fuck," Inyoni whispered, his arms tight around her. "Holy fuck."

"Got that right." Tweak mumbled, still catching her breath.

They lay together for a long time before Inyoni moved. He kissed her gently and whispered, "still scared?"

"Less," Tweak whispered. "Long as you don't get k-killed tomorrow, we're good."

"Not plannin' on it," Inyoni muttered in reply, his fingers running lightly across her shoulder. The touch left little trails of sweet feels behind.

"Still scared for you." Tweak whispered. "Wish I was running it w-with you."

Inyoni shifted to kiss the top of her head. "Ain't nothin' gonna happen. Corps don't know I'm even alive. Won't be lookin' for me."

"Still scared," Tweak whispered. "Always scared. Be careful."

"I will," Inyoni promised quietly.

Hours later, there was the quiet knock on the door. "Tweak? Time."

For a moment, Tweak held onto Inyoni in the dark.

"I'll watch the Net. Watch your back," she whispered.

"Yeah," Inyoni muttered into her hair. "I know you will."

Tweak smiled, listening to his heartbeat in the dark. Then she forced herself up. "Gotta go. Gotta g-get dressed."

Inyoni yanked on his clothes along with her, and walked her to the door.

Liza gave her a smile. "Your ride's waiting in the front room. We've got a pack of food for you; you can eat once you're under cover."

"Awesome, L-liza. Thanks," Tweak offered.

In the living room, a trucker got to his feet and smiled. "Ready to go?"

"Yeah," Tweak agreed, pocketing the packet Liza held out for her. Turning, she looked up at Inyoni. He smiled, and her heart ached.

Stepping close, she wrapped her arms around him and squeezed him tight.

"D-d-don't die. Kay?"

His arms were warm around her.

"Kay."

"P-promise?"

"Promise."

He held her tight. Safe. For just one more moment, they were safe.

Her ride cleared his throat. "Folks? We got a schedule."

Tweak forced herself to let go. She gave Inyoni a last squeeze of the hand, a last smile. "You promised. R-remember." Then she followed the contact out the door, and out into the dark. She wouldn't let herself look back.

"And that's the last of it," Kevin announced, stepping back. "Take a look."

Naomi looked in the mirror, and had to fight not to bust out laughing.

"Seriously, man? You made me into a synth bro?"

In the bathroom mirror stood a bulked up dude with the kind of synthetic bling that always made Naomi roll her eyes. Kevin had really had fun with this; he'd brought sleeves with padding, a voice modulator, a holo, the works. He'd balled her hair up under a skin-shaded cap, and covered her with the chrome-plated inserts that swaggering Zoncom and Techo douchebags got done. He'd even sprayed her nice, serviceable arm with flashy chrome plating and—worst of all—stuck color-changing flash strips along it. She looked like a chrome-plated douche canoe.

Naomi gave Kevin a smirk. "Aidan's gonna have your balls for this, y'know."

Kevin gave her a cockeyed grin right back. "Well that sounds fun."

Naomi snorted. "I liked it better when you were still easy to embarrass. You made me look bigger and tougher than he does."

Kevin shrugged. "You've got the build for it. And besides, my dear girl, you look like a walking Fragile Male Ego. I don't think your brother will be impressed."

"At least you got to be your own age," Liza adds, her own voice cracked and shrilled out of all recognition. Naomi turned, and busted a gut laughing.

"Holy shit, you made her into your granny!"

"Hardly," Kevin demurred. "My grandmother wasn't nearly so stereotypical."

Liza's holo-mask and her disguise was your classic Bitchy Granny Who Will Call The Manager, from the slightly blue-tinted hair and the tattooed eyebrows that went out of date twenty years ago, right down to the opalescent nail polish and the frumpy dress with a neat little interlocking set of EagleCorp birdies on the hem.

"I swear you picked these disguises on purpose," Liza grumbled, and even her voice was old and thin.

Kevin grinned. "Oh, anything is possible. Come on, into the living room, council of war."

Cameron and Jillian stared like Naomi had grown another head when they all took seats in the living room. Kevin didn't waste any time on their shock. Pulling up a map, he waved his fingers in the air, pulling and grabbing to zoom in and outlining three routes. Blue, yellow and red lines followed his fingers. "Now, here's the plan. Liza, your route is blue. You'll take little Jenny and go with Jillian. Nobody's looking for a mother and granny with a baby on a little train jaunt. But you need to act the part, remember. Complain to a Peacekeeper here or there about all these awful hooligans in the dreadful costumes."

"Alright," Liza agreed.

Kevin turned to Naomi. "And you're on the red route; you're going with Cameron, just boys out on a boy's day to see the sights and have a few beers."

Naomi glanced at Cameron, who'd been done up as another synth bro, big metal hands with color-shifting flashing across the knuckles and all. The animatronic gloves hid the way his hands actually looked, and the synth mods fit him. Now he just had to look tougher and less like a kicked dog.

"And that just leaves Inyoni and me, who are going to take the scenic route," Kevin finished. "We're going to be Dragons in the dance outside."

Naomi cocked a brow. "Y'know Peacekeepers aren't going to feel real friendly towards anybody in a Dragon mask."

"True, but there are about five hundred thousand people dragon-dancing out in those streets," Kevin offered, jerking a thumb over his shoulder. "I doubt we'll be noticed."

Naomi blinked. Liza made a little 'erk' sound. Cameron's jaw dropped   open.
"Five... five *hundred thousand*?" Jillian whispered.

Kevin grinned. "Five hundred thousand and counting in Denver alone. They're estimating that it's four million across the country."

Now, Naomi was floored. "Holy... shit."

"Holy *fuck*," Inyoni whispered.

"Indeed!" Kevin crowed. "It's like I've been saying for years! People want to stand up. Now we've given them the means, and *they are*! Doesn't this rock?"

"Uh...is that good or bad?" Inyoni asked.

That pulled Naomi back around with a laugh. "So, when do we go?" She asked.

"As soon as possible, and with all haste," her brother-in-law suggested, grey eyes bright. Naomi recognized the gleam there; it was just like hers.

Liza and Jillian were the first to leave, baby Jen swaddled in Jillian's arms.

"You're up next, folks," Kevin stated an hour later. Naomi nodded, giving her weapons one last check in all their hidden corners of the disguise.

"Roger," she agreed, still weirded out by the voice modulator messing up her tone. She stood, eyeing Kevin up and down. Reaching out, she gave his shoulder a squeeze. "Hey. You come home soon, okay? Don't make my big brother worry about you."

"Roger that," Kevin agreed. "See you back home."

"See you soon," Naomi agreed. She nodded at Cameron. "Come on, big guy, show time."

Terror in his eyes, the big Gamma stood and followed her.

Tweak dropped into her coding chair and brought up every surveillance program she had. The grid was at her fingertips. Now she just had to be good enough to handle it. At her side, she brought up the group call for the Code

Monkeys for the second day in a row. Technically they were the Inter-Quadrant Technical Solutions Committee: ten of the best coders in the nation, each with ten teams of coders reporting to them, and Tweak in the center acting as the coordinator. But they all knew they were code monkeys, and they stuck with what they knew.

"Hey everybody," Tweak offered. A chorus of ten 'hey's and smiles ran through the circle of faces on the screen. Tweak gave them a grin. "Everybody g-good to go? Where are we r-right now?"

"Drones are disabled in all eleven Quadrants," Fatima offered, typing away already. "We're all good there, now that we're in the source code."

"The Eagle-scrambling is going great," Nathan chipped in. "We've pretty much jammed all their signals. They're starting to call each other on their personal tabs, but it's a hell of a lot slower."

"What're we using for j-jamming? The d-declaration, yeah?" Tweak asked.

"Yep," Nathan agreed. "Playing lines from the Declaration of Independence on a loop, so they can't talk to each other through it. It's driving them up the goddamn wall."

Tweak nodded. "So, we r-ready for today?"

Deniki cracked his knuckles, grinning. "Hell yeah."

"This is gonna kick ass," enthused Ethan in his dumb 'coders do it with frequency' hat. Darnisha grinned, giving the screen two thumbs up.

Tweak nodded, fingers on the keyboard. "Okay. Whatcha got?"

Kevin closed and locked the door of the safehouse. The streets outside were ablaze in yellow. In every direction, people were moving. People were dancing. Someone had set up a makeshift amp system, and they were blaring the music.

"Woah," Inyoni muttered under his yellow dragon mask. "Even down in neighborhoods like *this* folks are at it?"

"There's a fire of hope even in the most insalubrious surroundings," Kevin offered quietly as they moved into the crowd. He wished he had more peripheral vision through the slits of his mask.

"Inso-what now?" Inyoni asked behind him.

Kevin smiled behind his disguise, and waved a yellow glove.

"Never mind. You can join the others making jokes at my expense when we're on base."

All around them, people were dressed as dragons. The costumes only got more elaborate as they moved into better-Standing neighborhoods. One group had put together a Chinese dragon with a sculpted head and many people under cloth making up the body. The dragon had holo-projected wings that read 'take the chains off, let us fly!'

All around him, the words of Liza's speech shone in holos, blazed on printed signs, and shouted from handmade placards. 'They Come For One, They Deal With All!' shone on t-shirts. 'Throw Out Your Citizen Card!' shone on a banner. 'They Don't Own Us!' was written using every medium imaginable. He looked up as a set of consumer drones flew overhead, forming the shape of a dragon, and marveled.

Working to hold his focus, he led his charge through the golden day spiced with music and the scent of far-off wildfires. It would have been easy to become giddy on the sheer excitement of this day. But he knew his job. If he wanted to survive this, he had to keep his head.

"Stay close and stay ready," he called to Inyoni as they slipped into a quieter side street. "You never know what—" That was when the first dart shot down. With a swallowed gasp, he sidestepped. "Oh God damn it all!"

The atrium smelled like antiseptic and electricity as they stepped up to the gate. Liza's mouth was dry.

Jillian fidgeted as they waited for the train to show up. Liza did her best to relax, standing easy. Their Citizen Cards and synth would get checked when the train pulled up. That would be the moment of truth. Right now, she just had to hold the baby, stay calm, and wait.

A small hand slipped around her finger, and squeezed. She glanced down at baby Jen with a grin. The holo over the baby's face made her appear to have big green eyes, like her mom.

"Who's a cutie?" Liza murmured, smiling down. The baby cooed.

The train hushed into the station and people piled off. Peacekeepers stood at every door, ident readers and DNA scanners in hand.

Schooling her face, Liza handed over her Citizen Card. Her stomach lurched as the agent's hand closed over it. The badly-shaven man scanned the card without really looking at her, and handed it back when the reader beeped its positive note. "Seat on the left, ma'am."

"Thank you, Officer."

And then it was Jillian's turn. Liza held her breath as the woman handed her card and Jenny's over. Liza watched as if the world had slowed down. *Please*, she thought. *Please, please, please...*

The reader glitched for a second as little Jenny's card swept through. Liza could have sworn her heart stopped.

"Stupid thing," the Peacekeeper muttered under his breath, swiping the card again. It beeped this time, and he waved Jillian through.

Liza's heart fluttered like a bird's as the door of the train shushed closed behind them. She fixed her eyes on the baby in her lap and grinned. *They'd done it.*

From his belt, Kevin drew his own pistol, aimed and fired. One bounty hunter fell as he turned to Inyoni. "There'll be others. I'm a bit of a hot commodity, unfortunately. It looks like I've been tracked somehow. We have to get to the garage where the bike is." Pulling up a navigation panel, he put in his destination and let the tab calculate the clearest path while he glanced up at Inyoni. "We're going to need to run. Can you keep up?"

The taller man pushed his mask up, and gave Kevin a mile-wide grin. "Man, I'm a fuckin' Gamma. Try me."

Kevin grinned. He was going to like this fellow. "Alright then. Three, two... go."

Side by side, they took off.

"Just relax," Naomi repeated for what felt like the millionth time. Cameron was jumpy as hell, and keeping him calm had been the hardest part about this so far. He'd been a mess out on the streets full of protestors, flinching at every noise. Which was a shame, because the sight up there had been incredible. So many people. So many dragon masks. So many voices saying they'd had enough of the bullshit. Naomi was still high on it. She couldn't wait to tell Aidan.

The musty smell of the basement rolled up to meet them as they descended, reaching the cache in a wall where two slick suits were stashed. She flicked off the voice-modulation box on her throat. Finally, she sounded like herself again. "Get this on. Tunnel. Through here."

"Only two suits," Cameron muttered as they tugged them on. "What 'bout everyone else?"

"Relax big guy; they're taking other exits. They're good," Naomi explained softly.

Cameron didn't really look like he trusted her, but he nodded and pulled the hood of the slick suit up. And then they were into the tunnel dark.

The walk went on forever. Seeing the sun on the other side felt like a blessing. Climbing up and out, Naomi hunted around and brushed off kochia, pulling the slick tarp away from the bike she knew was there. She gave Cameron a grin as he straddled the machine behind her. "Okay, hang on."

Turning on the engine, she took off.

They pulled up in a cloud of gritty dust miles and hours later. Cameron glanced around. "What're we stopping for?"

Stepping off her bike, Naomi smiled, took a few steps, and lifted aside the slick tarp. She pulled her tab, tapping in the call handle: AceOfSpades.

"Hey big brother."

"Hey," Aidan replied tightly. "Where are you?" Naomi grinned. "Home."

"Numbers are ticking up," Nathan offered, his face blue-lit by his screens just as Tweak's was. "Two hundred twenty-four of the five hundred teaching teams are home now."

"Twenty-five," Tweak corrected, seeing Naomi's note out of the corner of her eye, and Liza's note right under it. "Another of mine just g-got in. Two people still out. Coming."

"How many captures?" Ethan asked.

"Eight so far," Daniel replied. "Looks like the training's working. Every time the Peacekeepers grab somebody, the Dragons swarm in and pull the person away."

"Awesome!" Tweak grinned. "Okay, so... uh-oh. C-c-common Ground. Panic button. L-looks like the third island of the Seattle Archipelago."

"On it," Ethan agreed. "Getting a team on this... yeah, it's

Peacekeepers kettling a bunch of Dragons down an alley. Okay. I got a team on it."

"Another one over here," Darnisha called. "New Netherland Quadrant, looks like Columbia, wall of Peacekeepers... okay. One of my teams is on it. Approach is to play the Declaration of Independence in their ear-pieces, followed by the Young Professional's Union statements about what they want the world to look like. Morale should drop, and it'll make it impossible for them to communicate and regroup without taking off their helmets. Sound good?"

"Yeah," Tweak agreed, then flinched as a new window popped up "Fuck. Alert out on one of my guys! B-bounty hunters!"

"Do you have ISP's on the hunters' gear?" Deniki asked. "When you do, we'll take them down."

"Gimme two s-s-seconds," Tweak agreed.

Skidding into the garage, Kevin leaped onto the bike coded to his DNA, snatching up his helmet and shoving the extra back at Inyoni. Damn it, how had they found him so quickly?! He'd taken every security measure. God damn it all to the ninth circle of Hell!

"Get on!" he shouted over his shoulder, barely hearing the words over the roar of his own pulse in his ears. "And hang on!"

He didn't know how many bounty hunters there were, but it didn't matter. If he could drive fast enough, they'd be fine.

A dart gun hissed behind him. Darts. That meant someone wanted him alive. Not good.

"Can you shoot?!" Kevin demanded into his helmet mic as they snarled out of the alley. He smacked his service pistol back into Inyoni's hand. "At least keep their heads down!"

The bike skidded around a corner, brushing its riders up against a wall, then hissed up the road. But that road had a panel van blocking it, and Kevin cursed. "Hang on tight!" he added, and the bike snapped sideways, darting down another alley. Inyoni's voice yelped a curse in his ear. Kevin could only hope the boy was keeping his seat well enough.

"Where the fuck are you going?" His passenger gasped.

"Out of line of fire preferably!" Kevin muttered into the mic, frustration tight in his voice. "Oh, by the way, this bike makes nice sharp turns, so do keep a good grip. And watch the rooftops! I'll lay odds that's where we'll get hit from!"

"You think they're followin' us?"

"Sure of it," Kevin agreed tightly. "They like to keep up with prime targets!"

The engine sizzled and spat as the bike took another hair-pin turn, the balconies overhead blocking out the light.

There was an explosion above their heads, a sound like a bottle rocket going off beside you. Kevin let out a jubilant laugh. "Sounds like Tweak's gotten in on the game! I pity the poor bastards!"

There were several more small explosions above, and a few screams. Behind them, a body fell from a roof, just a silhouette blurred by the bike's speed as it zipped down a new set of alleys.

"Think that's all of 'em?" Inyoni asked. "Don't see anyone else."

"First rule of the game," Kevin threw out, eyes narrowed as he navigated the bike at its breakneck speed, "never make assumpt-oh dear God HANG ON!"

The weighted net slammed down on them. It didn't hurt so much as knock the breath out of his lungs, but it was enough to loosen his grip on the handlebars. As the weight settled, the bike skidded and toppled, slamming its riders to the ground. Kevin had the good sense to tuck his knees against his chest and try to roll, but it wasn't incredibly helpful. For a moment, he lay still, panting and cataloging bruises. If he survived this, he was going to ache like the devil tomorrow.

With a sharp intake of breath, he tried to push against the mesh. No good. Gravimetric filaments kept several hundred pounds of pressure on every inch. Instead, he crawled under it to the bike, where his companion was lying trapped. Wedging his shoulder under the bike, he pushed with every genetically-perfected muscle fiber he possessed. His arms burned with the effort. "I'd get out if I were you," he grunted. "I can't hold this long."

Inyoni scrambled out from under the bike as best he could, the micro-steel net scraping against his skin. Kevin released the bike with relief, and let the net pin him back down.

"Just breathe," Kevin advised, panting for air. "Save your strength. Stay calm."

There was a slither, a thump, and then there were six faces grinning down at them.

"Hey, boys." the lead hunter nudged Inyoni in the ribs. "It's payday."

Kevin rolled his eyes. You'd think these people would learn some decent lines.

Tweak desperately flicked screens. Under her breath, she cursed, her fingers dancing.

"Stay calm," Deniki suggested.

Tweak bobbed her head. "T-trying."

"Stay calm." Kevin murmured under the wire mesh, then grunted as a boot caught him in the gut.

"Who said you could talk, Duster?"

"Hey now, be nice, we want them pretty to turn in!"

Kevin breathed against the pain in his gut, his knee, his side, and counted. *Twenty seconds,* he thought. *I've timed her with a stopwatch. She already had a lock on my coordinates. So, twenty...*

Tweak's fingers danced. She'd followed the hunter chatter from the streams she'd flagged and written algorithms to watch. She'd followed their report of a surveillance photo of a known Duster. "Stupid, s-s-*stupid*!" she growled as she typed. "K-Kevin should have watched his b-back! M-moron!"

"Got their nav and communication gear," Fatima exclaimed.

"Great," Tweak acknowledged. An image flashed across the screen. Inyoni and Kevin, stuck under a gravimetric net. "Shit! S-s-*Shit!*" Tweak hissed.

On her feed, the hunter crowed. 'One terrorist and one suspect bagged!"

"Like. Hell," Tweak snarled, and pulled up a bot, instructing it to find and get into the command structures of every registered Corporate comm unit in the alley.

"Gotcha." Tweak hit a button, and grinned. "Take that."

Five, Kevin thought. An ear-splitting noise rent the air. With screams, every one of the bounty hunters dropped.

"Hmm. She's improved her own time." Kevin remarked, smiling as relief welled in his chest. "I imagine she's shut off the grav on this net too. Help me push it off."

Without the gravimetric pressure in the microsteel filaments engaged, the thing was as light as a sheet; the two men shrugged it off easily. Kevin dusted off the riding gear under his mutilated costume as best he could, glad it had taken the beating rather than his skin. He glanced at his contact, who hadn't been so lucky, and frowned. The boy was still sitting on the concrete, looking himself over dazedly.

"Oh dear. You alright?"

Inyoni glanced down at his torn costume. He frowned at the scrapes and cuts on his arm, sighed, and reached a couple fingers into torn flesh to pick gravel out of the long gash near his shoulder. "Had worse."

Kevin blinked. He'd been told that the boy couldn't feel pain, but watching what that meant in the field was a little unnerving. "Er, yes. Now..." stooping, he knelt beside one of his attackers and shook his head. "Looks like she blew out their ear drums when she overloaded their comms. Nasty. Very effective, but very nasty." He glanced up, considering. Perhaps Naomi was right about this; maybe Tweak did have a crush on this boy. Everyone had been debating it at home. He'd laid his odds that Tweak would fall in love if she was ever given a chance she felt safe in taking. Yvonne and Sarah had called him a romantic for that. But perhaps he wasn't so mistaken after all.

"I take it you've made friends with our Tweak?" He asked lightly. "She only gets this vindictive towards the enemy when she likes you."

The boy ducked his head. If he got any more sheepish, he'd say 'baa'.

"Uh. Yeah. Friends," he muttered.

Kevin grinned. Bingo! For once, *for once,* he'd won the betting pool. Yvonne and Sarah both owed him twenty dollars. Finishing his check, he straightened. "Well then! Let's get out of here. Up you get."

Kevin offered a hand, and the young man took it. With a smile, Kevin tugged him to his feet. But the smile faltered when Inyoni toppled back down to the concrete.

"What's the matter?" Kevin asked, kneeling beside him. Eyes frightened, Inyoni shrugged. "Dunno. Leg's not bendin'. Don't see no bone stickin' out, do you? Oh, crap... this one's not all funny, is it?" He scowled down at his left leg, stuck straight out in front of him.

Kevin's brows drew together. "Er... try and bend it?"

Inyoni shook his head, his eyes panicked. "Can't. Won't work."

"Oh dear. Sorry about this, but needs must..." Pulling out his pocket knife, Kevin carefully slit open the fabric of Inyoni's pants. And, yes, there it was. An ugly, crooked protrusion showed where the man's patella had displaced; the area was already beginning to swell. He'd been afraid of that.

"Well. That explains it." He glanced up. "You've dislocated your kneecap."

"Shit, yeah, guess so," Inyoni muttered. With nervous fingers, he felt along his leg, twisting his shin from side to side with both hands. "You any good at getting knees to go back in?" The young man asked, raising his eyes. The sight of him treating such an injury so calmly made Kevin a bit sick.

"Er... yes, I've some experience. The patella—excuse me, the kneecap—lifts up and slides to the left to go back in. Do you want a hand?"

Inyoni nodded. "Can you? Don't want to make it worse..."

Kevin nodded grimly. "I'll give it my best shot, though our medical officer will have my hide for this if I make a hash of it. Here goes..." He put his hands in all the right places, and pushed. There was a squelching, squeaking pop.

"It done?" Inyoni asked.

Kevin swallowed. "I think so. Try bending it, carefully."

Inyoni moved his leg, and gave a relieved grin as the joint bent. "Thanks."

Kevin nodded, feeling a little green around the gills and hoping that it wasn't showing too much. "No trouble at all. Come on, lean on me as you get up and let's go. We've got a long ride ahead."

It was late when they finally rode up to the base, but the inner door was flung open as Kevin pulled the bike in. He looked up, expecting Aidan. But it was Tweak who stood in the doorway, staring at him, her chest moving too fast.

No, he realized, not at *him*; at the boy riding behind him.

Carefully, Inyoni stepped off the bike, wobbling on his good leg and staring around the garage. "So... this's your base?"

"Yeah," Tweak agreed quietly, stepping over to stand beside him. To Kevin's surprise, she reached out and took Inyoni's hands. "Look like shit." she whispered.

Inyoni grinned at her. "Yeah, but I got here. And I didn't die. Like I said."

Tweak nodded, staring at her hands, intertwined in the young man's. Then she reached out, tugged him inside and hugged him in one movement. Kevin considered saying something about the leg, but you didn't interrupt a miracle like this. He stood quiet instead, ready to render aid as needed. Inyoni lurched back against the wall to keep from falling over as his weight hit the injured leg, but he hugged Tweak back all the same, burying his face in her hair. "You smell good."

Tweak snorted a laugh. "You smell like blood and c-c-c-concrete."

Kevin chuckled. "All right, you hugged the hero, now let's get him cleaned up."

He served his escort duty as a gentleman should, acting as Inyoni's crutch to get him down the hall and leaving the couple in Damian's capable hands. That done, he turned and headed for the dormitory. Opening the door of his quarters, he leaned against the frame.

"Hello handsome. Doing anything tonight?

Aidan looked up from a carving project, grinning as he set his work down and stepped across the room. He pulled Kevin into a kiss that crushed the breath out of him and made his heart leap.

"I'm planning on holding on to you all night, now I've got you back," Aidan murmured, leaning his head against Kevin's shoulder. Kevin laid a kiss on the top of his head.

Event File 27
File Tag: Unit Integration
19:30-09-25-2160

"So." Bits of concrete clinked into a bowl that Alice had brought Damian."You can't feel pain," the doctor observed, tweezing another pebble out of Inyoni's shoulder. "At all."

"Never could," Inyoni agreed patiently. Water slopped as Alice sponged away the caked blood. The liquid in the bowl was already pink. Tweak watched, feeling fidgety. She wished she could do something for Inyoni right now. When he'd been in danger, she could do something. She'd blown drones out of the sky to protect him, hacked everything in sight. But now, all she could do was watch him get doctored and smile at him whenever he looked her way. He was a mess; there were bloody scrapes all down one side of him, and his knee was in a brace. An autopad was being smoothed over his shoulder.

"I think that's everything," Damian said eventually. "Nanoids have started work on the knee, the temporary ligament scaffolds are in place, and it's stabilized."

"So, can I sit up?" Inyoni asked. Damian nodded. "Carefully, yes."

"Great." Inyoni sat up, smiling at Tweak. "See? It ain't bad."

"I have to disagree on a professional basis," Damian put in dryly. "Be careful with that knee for the rest of the month, all right? I'm strongly suggesting that you don't walk for the next three days."

"Don't hurt," Inyoni replied with a shrug. "And it ain't like I can check this place without walkin'."

Damian frowned, crossing his arms. "How smart do you think it is to ignore a medical suggestion?"

"D-Damian," Tweak interjected, "Shut up." Moving from her perch, she draped Inyoni's arm over her shoulders. "He can l-lean on me. He's good. We're good."

"So," Alice put in as she started cleaning up, "should we tell Liza to get a room for you, or has Tweak got that covered?"

Inyoni hesitated, looking at Tweak. "Uh... dunno."

Damian glanced at Tweak. Over his flat black eye implants, his eyebrows quirked. For a second, he even smiled. "I figure you two will do better together. On her own, Tweak tends to punch people."

"Hey!" Tweak exclaimed.

Alice smiled as she disinfected the diagnostic chair. "Sorry, sweetie, but you do. Inyoni, you can hobble around tonight, but don't go far. Topher will have crutches for you tomorrow, so you can stop leaning on Tweak."

Inyoni gave a quiet chuckle. "'S'all good. Think we make a good team."

"Yeah," Tweak agreed quietly, giving him a smile. "Good team."

Together, they walked down the hall. "Wanna c-come m-meet the crew? Some people up. In the rec." Tweak offered.

Inyoni glanced down at her with a crooked sort of smile. "Think we can get away with just sacking out? It's been a fuckin' hell of a day."

"Sure," Tweak agreed. "We can p-party t-tomorrow. Um... bed?"

"Yeah," Inyoni agreed quietly. "Uh... you really don't mind me stayin' in your room? I mean... we ain't exactly... are we?"

Tweak gave a shrug with the shoulder he wasn't leaning on, her eyes on his. "Don't know. Are we?"

"You wanna?" Inyoni asked.

Tweak bit her lip. Finally, she pulled herself together and gave a nervous jerk of a nod. "I wanna. Too fast?" she asked, her voice small.

Inyoni shook his head. "Nah. Don't think so. I mean... no tellin' how long we got, right? Might as well make it good."

"Way to look on bright side." Tweak retorted with a little shade, but her fingers twined in his.

"Ain't lyin'," Inyoni replied, squeezing her hand gently. He smiled again. "C'mon. Let's go to bed."

Tweak smiled, nodding slightly. "Yeah. But I got something b-before bed. Wanna show you."

"'Kay," Inyoni agreed with a smile that made her heart jump.

Tweak helped him down the hall to the outer door, and into the garden. Beneath the slick tarp, under the moon, it glowed silver.

Quietly, Tweak got Inyoni to the little tree and stopped beside its pot, smiling up into its waxy green leaves. She helped him lean up against the side of the nearest garden bed, keeping hold of just his hand now that he had something else to lean his weight against. "Okay?"

"Woah," Inyoni breathed, eyes wide. He barely managed to steady himself, he was so busy looking around. "This is… wow."

"Think so too." Tweak agreed softly. Reaching behind her, she patted the tree trunk. "Iny-y-y-yoni? Meet C-Coffee."

"Woah," Inyoni repeated breathlessly, leaning back to look up at the branches. "Never thought I'd see this…"

"Welcome to the W-wildc-cards," Tweak murmured. "You see a lot of stuff here."

Lowering his eyes, Inyoni grinned. "Amazin'. Just… *man.*"

"Yeah," Tweak agreed quietly. He was right. It was amazing. All of it; this night, the way his hand felt in hers. The protest. The way it was all falling together. The way he'd fallen into her life. Amazing was the only word for it.

In silence, they sat listening to the night. Then Tweak stepped in and, softly, kissed Inyoni. He kissed her right back. They necked until Tweak's skin was on fire with excitement.

"B-bed," she whispered. "Now."

"Where's it?" Inyoni whispered.

Tweak's hands grabbed his. "C'mon."

Her room was the way she'd been keeping it since Billie moved her stuff out; a nest of work tables full of projects, with her bed stuck in a corner out of the way. Her space. Her nice, safe nest full of neat things. And now there was a bird in it.

She got him sat down and got his weight off the bad knee, that was important. Her fingers traced his throat as they kissed, and switched his holo off.

Inyoni grumbled and pulled away to whisper against her lips, "I got mine off, you gotta take yours off, too." His hand trailed down her arm, unclasping one bandage.

Tweak gave a weak laugh. "You want 'em off, you take 'em off." She managed to keep the nervousness out of her voice, just.

Inyoni chuckled and did as he was told, making a sexy striptease of unwrapping the bandages. His fingers trailed along the scales on her arm. "Better."

"Best." Tweak agreed, pushing his shirt up until it caught on his arms. "Off."

Inyoni agreed with a grunt and pulled away to take the shirt off completely, tossing it away. Then he turned to Tweak with a grin, pulling her shirt up and off, too, and teasing her as he was taking her bra off.

"You wanna fuck?" He breathed. "Just checkin'."

"You okay to fuck?" Tweak asked, her system just about overloading with what he was doing. "Your knee…"

"If you ride, my knee ain't involved," Inyoni suggested in a whisper. His tongue flicked her nipple, and she squeaked. She only managed three more words that night.

"Okay. Cool. Yeah."

Tweak woke slowly in the morning, her fingers running up and down Inyoni's arm in the light coming through her slit window. She frowned and opened an eye as her fingers encountered something gritty. For a moment, she stared at her hands, trying to figure it out.

Then she sat up with a jolt. "B-b-blood!"

"Huh?" Inyoni woke slower, blinking sleepily at her. "What? What's—oh. I'm bleedin'?"

"You're b-b-b-b-bleeding!" Tweak repeated in a choked groan. "Why d-d-d-didn't you *say*?!"

Inyoni gave her a patient look. "I can't feel it, remember? Where is it?"

She stared down at him, and at herself, daubed all over with dried blood. A sound like a cat in pain came out of her throat. She'd made him bleed. She'd done this. "Ev-v-v-verywhere. F-f-fuck…." then she raised her eyes, and frantically started checking him over.

"Hey. Tweak. Breathe." His hands caught hers. She looked up into his eyes, terror cinching her throat. He smiled a little. "C'mon, Dragon. Breathe. This happens. I'm good. I ain't woozy, an' I don't feel lightheaded. It's all the little scrapes from last night. We knocked them open. It's no big. Breathe for me?"

Slowly, her breathing evened out. She sat back, wiping her hands. "Y-yeah. N-not that b-bad. Don't do that. Scared me shitless!" she added, half laughing.

"Sorry," Inyoni muttered, his ears dropping sheepishly. "Forgot I'm all beat up."

Tweak shook her head, at herself as much as him. "Gotta watch that." Standing, she kicked her shirt up and caught it in the air. "Before breakfast. Damian. Fix you up. All the b-bleeding. Check the knee. Then breakfast. Then talk to Aidan, maybe. You ready? Get you s-set up?"

Inyoni finished pulling his shirt on over his head and looked at Tweak. "You gonna leave the bandages off, Dragon?"

Tweak froze. Leave her bandages off. In front of all her friends. Sure, she'd done it in front of the country. But these were her friends. This was her *crew*. If they didn't like it…

She stared at him, swallowing hard as she felt her heart begin to race. "I n-never..." she shook her head, arms wrapping around her torso.

Inyoni's long, bright glowing arms wrapped around her. His lips brushed the top of her head. "Don't have to. I just like lookin' at 'em. Think they would, too."

Tweak snorted. "Freaky." But she looked up at Inyoni, and smiled weakly. "You're not s-scared?"

"'Course I'm not," Inyoni replied with a grin. "I got donkey ears. Scales ain't scary. Dragon arms're way cooler'n jackass ears."

"Asshat." Tweak laughed. "Meant you're not scared of... s-showing. With my people?"

Inyoni's ears lowered at that. "For real, Dragon? I'm scared shitless."

Tweak stared at him, brows knit. Then, carefully, she nodded. "Me, too." She drew a breath. "No holo for y-you, no c-cover for m-me. Deal."

Inyoni took a deep breath and nodded. "Deal. No holo, no cover. Sides, they'll probably be laughin' at us doin' the Three Legged Walk down to chow too much to notice, anyway."

Tweak tried for a smile, her hands shaking in his. "Deal."

With Tweak supporting Inyoni's weight, they hobbled out and down the hall together.

Event File 28
File Tag: Measure of Effectiveness
09:30-09-26-2160/18:30-09-30-2160

Aidan sat in the best place on the planet; one shoulder pressed against his sister's, and his free hand on his husband's knee under the table. The two people he loved best were home. For today, life was pretty damn good.

He glanced over as his husband gave a little cough. Kevin blinked at him, nodding at the canteen door. "Aidan? Do I need my eyes checked again, or am I actually seeing this?"

Aidan glanced over, and nearly choked on his coffee. Tweak was in the doorway, helping to support one of the new Gammas; the one Kevin had been talking about. Inyoni, that was his name. Now he saw what made the guy a Gamma; he had cow ears. But it was Tweak that put his brain on standby. She wasn't wearing her bandages. Her scales gleamed like jewels in the canteen lights.

The room had gone silent around him. Tweak glanced around at her friends, and Aidan followed her gaze. Jaws hung open. The silence thickened. Shit, he needed to do something before she felt rejected and—

And then Janice stood. Sauntering over, she shook Inyoni's hand.

"About donkey-fuckin' time somebody got this girl to take those damn rags off. Nice to meetcha, m'name's Janice. Don' mind these pissants." She glanced around, and crossed her arms. "What, you guys never seen a Gamma before? Close your mouths 'fore you all catch flies an' end up with maggots for brains."

Her words broke the silence into shards of laughter.

"I can't believe it." Kevin muttered. "I absolutely can't believe it."

"I hear that," Aidan agreed weakly. "But hey, I call this a serious win."

Around him, there was a rush and clatter as Tweak sat down beside Billie, introducing her new squeeze to her oldest friend. Topher leaned over, grinning. "From what I hear, you did good!"

"Good? I did kickass." Tweak retorted, grinning. "And I want b-breakfast!"

Billie laughed. "Yeah, I figured. I made your favorite."

"S-sausage! Smelled it!" Tweak crowed, grabbing the plate of biscuits and plant-based sausage Billie held out. "Donkey-fucking?" she added as she did. "Janice! Seriously?! Come *on*."

Janice just grinned.

"Man, this shit's *good*," Inyoni muttered after his first bite. He grinned at the people around him. "Could get used to this!"

"Told you," Tweak agreed, smiling wider than Aidan had ever seen.

The crew was really in the mood to talk. It took a long time for Inyoni to get introduced to everyone, given that people kept popping in and out, interrupting each other, congratulating Liza and Tweak on their speech for the umpteenth time, asking Inyoni questions, and generally making a racket.

While the crew got their excitement out of their system, Aidan studied the couple with the baby. They'd been introduced the night they came in, but so far, they were keeping to themselves. That was his job to take care of.

He gave Kevin a quick squeeze of the hand. "I'm going to go sit with the new folks and start working on them."

Kevin lowered his head and nuzzled Aidan's neck for a beat. "Say something if you need backup."

"Roger," Aidan murmured, letting himself bask in the touch for a bit. Eventually he stood, picked up his tray, and moved on down the table.

"Hey folks," he offered. The wife—Jillian, he reminded himself—looked at him with frightened yellow eyes. The husband—right, Cameron—dropped his gaze, his body language screaming 'I'm in submission mode.'

"Sir," Cameron grunted.

Well that wasn't going to work. "First things first: I'm not 'sir.' I'm Aidan. I might be the commander here, but this base is a home and a family, first, and Duster outpost second. If you need anything, you come to me or my husband Kevin, or Liza, and we'll do our best to get it for you." He took a sip of his coffee. Man, he'd never get over how much better this stuff was. "So, once you're settled, I would like to see you in my office within a week to discuss what you want to do going forward. Will that be enough time to feel like you're settling in?"

Jillian glanced at Cameron with those slotted goat-pupil eyes, gently bouncing baby Jenny in her arms. Cameron stared nervously at his breakfast, nodding mechanically.

"And by the way," Aidan added with a quiet smile, "you're all welcome here."

He glanced up at a loud squeak, and realized that Tweak had scooted herself and her tray right down the table, Inyoni trailing her. Tipping her head, she grinned at the other Gammas. "Hey. Guys. C'mon. It's ok. This? This's home. Serious. It's cool." She jerked her thumb over her shoulder. "C'mon. Nothing to be s-scared of. Everybody here's cool."

"It's just… we're not fighters," Jillian muttered quietly, shifting her hold on the baby and refusing to meet Tweak's gaze. "Only useful skill we had between us was my factory work. What in the world are we supposed to do here?"

Aidan glanced between them. "Lot of people arrive here clueless," he offered. "Some of us were just kids when we got here. My husband was. Now he's the logistics officer. My hydroelectrics officer arrived at seventeen, and all she knew was picking vegetables. My motor pool guy got here at fourteen, and now his work's asked for around the state." He shrugged. "People find something they like, and the crew teaches them."

"People teach," Tweak reinforced. "People help. Each other. Here. It's what we do."

For a moment, Aidan couldn't help but look at the brave young woman sitting beside him, and think back to the terrified street girl he'd met five years ago. Man, had she come a long way.

"We don't want to be bullet-catchers." Cameron muttered, staring at his plate. "I don't want to fight."

Tweak's fingers began to tap on the table. Uh-oh. Any second now she'd—

"Pull your head out of your ass!" Tweak spat. Yep. There it was. Tweak, losing her patience. "No m-more bullshit," the little woman continued. "Sit here. Eat real food. Meet people. Make friends. Don't get your head. Up your ass. Again. Got it?"

Jillian stared at her for a long moment. She swallowed hard, moved Jen to one arm, and placed the other on Cameron's shoulders. "We signed up for this, Cam…."

Cameron was still staring at Tweak in shock.

Tweak was still tapping her fingers on the table. "These. People. Are. Okay. Got it?"

"I got it?" The big man finally managed. Tweak nodded sharply. "Good. Dozer. Needs help. His back. Is. M-messed up. Needs help l-l-lifting. Wanna help. With that?"

"Did I just get called old an' busted?" Dozer grumbled to Milo further up the table.

"Fraid so, man," Milo agreed. "Us old guys get the shaft, don't we?"

"Don't we *ever*," Blake agreed with exaggerated bitterness.

Aidan let his people do their thing; he kept his attention on the new folks. "I don't want you to feel like Tweak's giving you orders here. She's trying to give you some good ideas."

Tweak nodded. "Yep."

"Speaking of ideas," Kevin added, stepping over to stand with his hands resting on Aidan's shoulders, "I'd be glad to have your talents in the logistics division once that knee is functional, Inyoni. We need people who can run and think at the same time. And you met the first qualification of the position already."

"Yeah?" Inyoni asked.

Aidan heard the warmth in his husband's voice. "Yes, you didn't fall off the bike or scream about my driving skills."

Inyoni's ears perked up. He gave a nervous little smile. "Um… yeah. Okay."

"And Janice," Tweak added. "You need help. You work. Too hard. J-j-jillian. Factory. You know gear. Wanna help with w-water?"

"While I'd prefer it if some folks *asked* me if I want help first, I like the sound of that," Janice agreed, giving Tweak just a bit of a look.

Eventually, Jillian managed a little smile. "I guess I can give it a try."

Aidan nodded. "Think about it this week. Everybody's welcome in my office whenever; we'll have a longer talk and get you set up."

It took Inyoni two days, and he showed up with a bit of a limp and a sheepish "Tweak says I gotta talk to you." But he did sign on for logistics and requisitions. Kevin and Yvonne took him under their wings after that and started taking him around on all the local runs, getting him introduced. Aidan filled out the guy's paperwork and counted his blessings; now he didn't have to decide whether to give up on Jim and start a base recruitment search or not.

In the back of his mind, all the time, the thought of the big stay-home protest sat like a boulder. It was coming up. Everything was prepped. Now they just had to wait and see. And that waiting was the hardest thing in the world.

It took another two days for Jillian to creep into his office and treat his guest chair like a set trap, sitting as if it might go off at any second. Aidan gave her a smile.

"Jillian, it's good to—"

And because life never got boring around here, that was when a call came in.

"Sorry Jillian, one second." Aidan grabbed his tab, and checked the call sign. Sure enough, there was a request for a vid call, from Sanctuary Station. Hunh. Hoping the friendly Fringe camp wasn't in trouble, he accepted it. Big Tony's face came up on his screen.

"Hey Tony," Aidan started. "You guys okay out there?"

The Fringer on the other end of the line grinned. "Well hey there, Aidan. About that deal we made, giving people the coordinates at our bus stop to meet you folks?"

"Sure," Aidan acknowledged, nodding. Tony held up his tab. "Well, I got your first bus." On the screen, a battered pickup packed with people idled outside the pre-dissolution bus terminal that had once served a dead community out near Sanctuary Station's plot of land. Not only was the cab and the truck bed full; three people were sitting on the roof.

"Alright," Tony called, "who wants to talk?"

There was a beat of stillness. Aidan looked a little closer at the crowd. Everyone in the packed truck seemed to have a hoodie on, or a hat pulled low over their face. Everyone was hiding. That probably wasn't surprising, if they just ran the Grid, but still, it was a little weird.

The driver cut the engine and, very carefully, stepped over to help someone out of the back of the truck. There was something a little weird about the lady's gait, but Aidan couldn't place it.

Stepping over, the woman lowered her hood. Aidan blinked. The woman didn't have any eyes. There were just sunken spots in her face, covered with tiny, tight-shut eyelids.

"They said this is where we come to meet the Golden Dragon?" the lady asked. And it hit him like a ton of bricks. Gammas. A whole truck full of Gammas, coming to meet Tweak. Coming to join up. Holy shit.

Aidan grinned. "Stay on the line, ma'am. I'll go get her, and we'll get you folks picked up."

Hanging up, he grinned at Jillian. "Let's reschedule our talk for tomorrow, okay? I'm going to need to scramble for a bit. I've gotta get somebody to fill in for Tweak on her stuff and get her out there."

Three hours later, his tab pinged with a message from Kevin. A picture attachment blipped up to hang in the air. In it, Inyoni was sitting on the truck's hood, long ears stuck straight up and Tweak in his lap, grinning like a little kid. Around them, about twenty Gammas stood smiling.

"I think the plan worked!" Kevin's note read, in the understatement of the century. Laughing, Aidan shook his head and read the rest. **"Getting everyone settled. Be home in time to watch the news with you. -Kevin"**

That deflated Aidan a little. The news. Right. Moment of truth. That was when they'd all know if this worked out.

Tweak came back to base on an emotional high, practically bouncing off the walls and talking a mile a minute. "S-so awesome. C-can't b-believe it! This is gonna be s-s-so awesome!" Aidan poked his head into the hall at the sound of her voice, and she gave him a wave, grinning like a pumpkin.

"Hey boss!"

"Everything go okay?" He asked. She laughed, spinning in a circle and hugging Inyoni. "Awesome!"

"Good to hear," Aidan agreed, one eye on the clock. "Grab some food and head to the rec room; we're going to watch the news together. See what's going down with the stay-home."

"Kay," Tweak agreed, turning and trotting back down the hall with her boy in tow.

It was funny how time raced when you wanted it to slow down. Stomach doing flip-flops, Aidan shut his work screen down and headed down the hall to the rec room. Everyone had taken seats on the couch or the floor in front of the vid screen.

Kevin gestured him over to the seat he'd saved, smiling that tight smile of someone getting ready for trouble. "Moment of truth, love," he murmured, squeezing Aidan's hand.

"Yeah," Aidan agreed quietly.

On-screen, a perfectly coiffed woman with dazzlingly purple hair sat in front of the Zoncom logo.

"Shops, businesses and banks shuttered their doors today," the woman stated, "as seven million corporate contractors across the nation refuse to perform their essential duties. The inter-corporate trade rates have plummeted, threatening an economic crisis."

The moment froze like a vid clip in Aidan's head. The air caught in her chest.

"Did they just say…"

Tweak flipped the channel. Now it was a man in a taupe suit with lacquered blond hair and a NatBank pin on his lapel.

"—seven million workers, all of whom stayed home today. In a breach of their Corporate Citizen Contracts that they've called the Send Them The Bill movement, workers are breaking their contract obligations by refusing to perform labor until an extensive set of demands are met, and—"

The room exploded in cheers. Kevin grabbed Aidan in a hug, kissing him until he was breathless. He held onto his guy and laughed, dizzy with the thrill. He'd never believed it could go like this. But there it was, proof on the news. America really was standing up. All of America. All together.

"So, that's the end of all the work you guys were doing?" Inyoni asked, when some of the noise let up.

With a smile, Tweak leaned into his arms, her scales gleaming gold. "Nope. That? That's the start."

Turn the page for a sneak peek at the Wildcard's next adventur

Event file 5
Time Stamp: 6-12-2161/ 6-13-2161

"Okay everybody!" Yvonne grinned at the room full of teens. She had officially landed the best assignment of all time. "Today we kick off our action." She clicked the tiny media projector in her fingers. The little player blared the first bars of a song and an ecstatic handful of words: "We built this city!" She tapped it to switch tracks, and the spoken message began. "It's the workers of this country who create real wealth. We have earned the right to access the capital and resources that wealth has created. We demand a new deal. We insist on a new contract between workers and employers. Meet us at the table, and pick up the pen."

She clicked to its last playlist, and grinned as the anthem of 'We're Not Gonna Take It' came singing out at a volume that was all out of proportion to the tiny device. The kids watched her, eyes dancing. They were some crew: a bunch of Natbank, Zoncom and TechoCo kids everywhere from eleven to eighteen and every rung of the Citizen Standing ladder, all brought together through the kid's clubs some of the Unions were running. The Unions had started the clubs to give kids from lower Standings a chance to get breakfast and dinner, and they offered all the kids somewhere to hang out, relax and get a better education. They had paired kids who asked for help with peers who'd volunteered to do tutoring, so now you had friendships forming all up and down the Citizen Standing hierarchy, and the kids were pretty happy to forget they had Citizen Standing Scores at all if you gave them the chance. But tutoring and hanging out together hadn't been enough for these teens; they wanted in on the action. They'd pestered the adults in the Unions until they'd caved, and asked their Duster advisors for some safer actions that the kids could take. Once she'd heard, Yvonne had done a little begging and pleading with Aidan, and he'd handed over the assignment. Officially, she was now a Civil Disobedience Action Advisor along with her wife. But she was going with 'Official Head Prankster' herself.

One last click turned the little player off as Yvonne held it up. "I'm handing out bags of twenty to everybody. You want to plant these in all the grossest places you can find. What kind of spots are you looking for?"

"Dog shit!" gawky Darnell blurted out, making the other kids whoop and laugh. "Dead pigeons!' Saoirse suggested with a grin a mile wide,"And rats too!" The other teens obliged her with long, drawn out groans of 'eeeewwwww!'

"Dumpsters!" Cloe called out, standing on her tiptoes to see over her friends' shoulders.

"Awesome! Try the output flows for grease traps around the backs of cheap restaurants too," Sarah suggested with a huge grin. "Don't worry about whether it's too hot to place these things, they're tough little doodads."

"And don't forget spots out of reach," Yvonne encouraged, nodding. "Go for places that lardassed Peacekeepers will have trouble getting to. Where do you guys think that'd be?"

"Up fire escapes?" skinny Jared suggested. Yvonne bobbed her head. "Yep, that's good. Where else?"

"On top of lampposts!" A kid with a red mohawk who called zirself Crash threw out.

"And flagpoles too, I can climb a flagpole near my place," Bree added enthusiastically. The teens loved that idea.

"That's great, everybody," Yvonne agreed, grinning. "Just remember to think about the wind when you're up high. It's crazy strong today, and a good gust at the wrong moment--" she mimed a body splatting into the ground, with sound effects. The kids made faces.

"Anywhere you can get that some big guy in body armor can't go, that's where you leave a player." She put up four fingers. "We voted on four rules about placement. What's the deal?"

"Nowhere that it'll mess with mental health, like stopping people from sleeping," Saoirse piped up, red curls bobbing. Yvonne lowered one finger.

"No violence!" Bree called, followed by Crash with "Don't put ourselves in danger to drop a player," and Tim right on zir heels with "Nobody goes placing alone, everybody checks in before we go home."

"And if you get caught, you--" Yvonne prompted.

"Tell them we're part of a geo-caching club placing geo-caching clues!" Jared came back with a satisfied nod of the head.

"Nice, guys!" Sarah enthused. "So, that's the plan. We get all the players planted around the inter-corporate shopping areas, and around every main Natbank, Techoco and Zoncom office we can reach by the end of the day. These things are going to play twenty-four-seven for two weeks. Of course the office staff are going to climb the walls, and then they're going to call Peacekeepers in to get rid of the players. And then--" She pointed at Cloe, whose grin bordered on evil. "Then we activate the Mesh-connected cameras we've got stuck around, and we post clips of Peacekeepers going crazy trying to stop a song."

"And getting covered in dog shit," Darnell guffawed. The kids whooped it up for that, laughing like anything. Yvonne could see in their eyes that they were starting to get the buzz of a good prank going.

"Alright!" Yvonne grinned at the kids, and raised a fist. "Let's drive the Corps batshit!"

The kids hollered their agreement, scattering to their pre-assigned exits from the old warehouse four Union chapters had retrofitted for a community supply center. Yvonne turned with a laugh and grabbed her wife, kissing her good and hard.

"Ready to get out there, Civil Disobedience Action Advisor Flesher?" Sarah asked, grinning up at her.

Yvonne grinned."Hell yes, Civil Disobedience Action Advisor Flesher," She stole another kiss, giving her wife a quick squeeze. "Come on."

There was an art to placing the sound broadcasters for maximum impact with minimum threat. Now that they were out in the field together again, Sarah and Yvonne were all over teaching these kids the skills. Step one was acting casual. Step two was using your imagination. Step three was keeping a huge grin off everyone's faces. Everything else came pretty easy after that. Up and down fire-escapes, across roofs, through alleys they went with their kids, Yvonne keeping an eye on the map. Each time the teens placed a player, they activated it. Its playback loop was delayed by an hour after activation, but its locate beacon turned on immediately. Across the map of the area, yellow location dots were flicking to life.

"Here's a good spot!" Yvonne whispered, pointing out a nest that a pigeon had made in a thicket of bird spikes on a parapet to Crash. Ze nodded. "Spot me?"

"You got it," Yvonne agreed. With a nod, the kid handed her zir bag and did one hell of a parkour run, launching zirself off one wall to kick up off a windowsill, landing neatly a ways over Yvonne's head. She flashed ze two thumbs up in admiration. Man, she wished she could move like that anymore. Not that she was losing all that much speed at thirty-five, but every once in a while she got a wakeup call about what her muscles could and couldn't do. And they probably couldn't do parkour.

Crash got the player settled. "On?" Ze called down. She glanced at her tab, where a new reader winked. "Yep!" She called up. "C'mon, let's--"

"Hey!" a voice hollered down the alley, "What the fuck are you doing?!"

"Book it!" Crash yelped. Yvonne didn't need telling twice. She took off.

"Peacekeepers!" the angry male voice bawled behind them, "Peacekeepers, I need Peacekeepers!"

Yvonne grinned. *Yeah, you just stand there and keep yelling. I'm already gone.*

For all the noise that guy put up, it only took running through a handful of alleys to throw the trouble off. Once she was back in the advert-wrapped shopping streets, she shot Crash a message on the Common Ground. She blinked, wiping her face as a sudden gust of wind blew powdery ash and grit into her face. Clearing her eyes, she typed.

You good?

The response came back from the teen a beat later.

I'm great. Put down another. See you!

Yvonne grinned as she pocketed her tab, sidestepping an obnoxious ad trying to interest her in the ugliest dress she'd ever seen. The weird, ashy yellow of the sky made the holo look even worse. All the advertising holos looked a little drab against the smoky yellow backdrop that wildfire smoke had turned the sky into.

She was riding high by the time she met the kids for their check-in at a different community center. This was the part of the work that always freaked her; holding her breath, crossing her fingers that all the kids she'd encouraged would come back in the door. She knew that one day, someone probably wouldn't.

But today wasn't that day. All sixteen kids came back in, hyped like anything on their prank.

"You guys kicked ass," Yvonne cheered, hugging a couple of the kids who were okay with hugs. "Anybody get hot?"

"I got chased by some guy who works at a shop," Cloe put on her probably-illegal-grin. "He tripped over a trash can."

"We got yelled at by some lardass," Crash shrugged. "He didn't even try to chase us. Lame."

Yvonne glanced over at her wife when a gentle elbow nudged her ribs. "Time, baby," Sarah suggested under her breath. Yvonne nodded.

"Okay, everybody, you did incredible!" She called to the kids. "We need to wrap up now, before anybody's unallotted time puts up a red flag. When the footage comes in, we'll have a watch party on the Common Ground, okay?"

Still babbling, the kids headed for their exits. Yvonne took Sarah's hand and squeezed it. "Yeah, I guess it is. So what's up next?"

Sarah pulled a face. "People's Assembly. We promised we'd go and represent. But tomorrow's that EagleCorp prank," she added, offering a little sugar to get the pill down.

Yvonne nodded, grimacing. "Alright, let's go get the Assembly over with."

Sitting around with a bunch of civvie organizers as they reminded each other of the obvious was a drag. Obvious Point One: the point of all the actions in the Pick Up The Pen campaign was to push the Corporations to negotiate with their workers. Obvious Point Two: everybody needed to push their people to stop using Corps-controlled net and switch over to the Mesh. They were going with the snappier name of Cut the Cord for that push, which definitely sounded better than 'pester people to get off TechoCo's Net.' Obvious Point Three: everything this year was building to a big march and a bunch of rallies to get people to vote next spring. On and on they went with organizational details and reminders and lots of talk about how many good things they were doing. *Yawn.* At least there was some energy this time; everyone was thrilled about the news that they'd be voting for a real government soon. Even with these slow and solid citizen types, there was a lot of clapping and cheers when they talked that over. Yvonne did her best to stay involved and offer lots of smiles; seeing Dusters encouraging them gave the civvies confidence. Liza and Kevin and even Aidan had been telling her it was this boring stuff that'd make the really big changes long term, and Yvonne didn't doubt it. These were definitely the kind of people who'd be in charge of local governments when they got democracy up and running again. But it was so not her scene. She was more of a run around and do things type.

"I thought I was going to fall asleep in my chair," she groaned when they finally got back to their hotel room and set up their security. "What a *drag*!"

"Yeah, but that's democracy." Sarah said, though she was yawning as she said it. They smiled sleepily at one another.

"Tomorrow's gonna be more our thing," Yvonne offered. "We're all set. I double checked all the prep and details with everybody."

"Great." Sarah leaned in, kissing her. "Sack out?"

"Sounds good," Yvonne agreed. "We gotta move early."

They were out the door before dawn in the morning, sneaking through the stillness of the waking city.

"Stop here," Yvonne murmured in the gloom of an alley. Pulling a blue rag from her pocket, she waved it.

Out of the alleyways and corners all around, people came walking. Everything from masks to scarves to streaks of paint had been used to disguise their faces.

"We ready?" Yvonne asked.

"Yep," a voice whispered back. "Everything's where it's supposed to be."

Yvonne's blood fizzed. "Okay, then everybody knows what to do. The fence is disabled. We've got the cameras looped. Flash mob in twenty minutes. Flash crews in place?"

"Yeah," came the quiet reply.

"Anything comes up, hit the panic button," Sarah reminded. "Install crew, you got the tools?"

All sorts of hand tools were held up. Yvonne flashed them a grin. "Awesome."

Turning, she looked out at the EagleCorp headquarters building squatting across Sixteenth Street from her. She grinned. "Let's do this."

Twenty minutes later, every streetlight flared incredibly bright. From every corner of Sixteenth Street, dancers in brightly colored costumes came flowing. The wind whipped scarves and shawls, spattering gorgeous masks with blowing flecks of ash. A marching band made up of drums and a couple trumpets came through the center, keeping the whole flash mob on time as they sang.

Surprised Peacekeepers stepped out to see what the noise was, several still holding coffee cups. At every door, they confronted a corridor of full-length mirrors set in quick-set concrete frames clamped to the sidewalks. Across the top, every mirror carried a motto: Is This Who You Want To Be? Who Are You Protecting? Can You Look Yourself In The Eye?

"We're not gonna take it!" the crowd bawled, the drums pounding out the rhythm. And then the song was over, and the crowd melted away, and the Peacekeepers were left staring at themselves in the mirror.

"Oh my god oh my god oh my god that was *the best!*" Yvonne enthused, arms tight around her wife as they spun in a giddy circle. "It went just right! The best ever!"

"Did you see their faces?" Sarah laughed giddily. "Oh my god, that guy who dropped his coffee!"

"I know, I know, it was *perfect!*" Yvonne crowed, kissing Sarah. "Oh my god I can't wait to see the clips go around the Mesh!"

"Some of it's up already, I bet! And we can see how the action went in other parts of the country ! That was the best!" Sarah squeed.

They bounced around for a couple seconds more, until they'd worn themselves out and just stood, grinning at each other."Time for us to head home, hunh?" Yvonne suggested.

"Yep," Sarah leaned up to sneak a kiss. "Tom will start worrying if we're gone too long."

"Yeah, right, he practically shoved us out the door." Yvonne laughed as they headed out the side door and into the alley. 'I'm seventeen and I can take care of myself, you guys love doing runs together, go on,'" she repeated her son's words with a grinning roll of the eyes. "He's getting so *pushy* these days."

"He probably wanted us out of the way so he could have fun times with Abigail," Sarah teased. Yvonne snorted. "If that's what he wants, it's not us he has to get out of the way; it's Milo."

"Point." Sarah paused for a moment. "We did get him his birth-control implant already, right? And Abbie's got one, yeah?"

"When they turned sixteen," Yvonne reassured, squeezing her wife's hand. "You are such a mom these days."

"Yeah, and I make it look good," Sarah parried, her dark eyes full of laughter. Yvonne shrugged, smiling. "Point. Anyway, which out are we taking?"

"The easy one," Sarah replied, "CAS tickets for the train out to the outskirts, through the Sweetwater Station tunnel and thirty miles home on the bikes."

"Awesome," Yvonne agreed. "We might even make it home for dinner."

The sky was the yellow of a healing bruise by the time they pulled the rabbitbrush and tumbleweeds off the slicktarp that covered their bikes. The wind whipped the crackling weeds out of their fingers, trying to take the tarp away with them. It took Yvonne and Sarah both to fold the thing and stow it in the back-box on Sarah's bike. Yvonne was glad for once to pull on her riding helmet and breathe the recirculated air pumped through its filter; it shut out the smell of smoke, at least.

"Hey Sarah hon, did you check the fire alerts before we got out?"

Sarah glanced up. "Yeah, it looked good on the maps, why?"

"Just checking," Yvonne reassured. She shrugged to herself as she climbed onto her bike. Sure, the sky looked bad. But they'd be okay.

"Ready?" Sarah asked over the comm. "Let's go," Yvonne agreed into her mic, kicking her bike into life.

They tore off across the Dust, the wind slamming them in gusts that came out of nowhere.

"Man, riding sucks today," Sarah's voice grumbled in Yvonne's ear. She made a little sound of agreement into her mic, concentrating on her grip on the handlebars.

Something whipped by her, and Yvonne barely resisted the instinct to duck. A tumbleweed, one of the really big ones. And…she hadn't gotten a good look at it, the wind had whipped it by so fast. Had it been on fire?

"Oh shit!" Sarah gasped ahead of her. Yvonne topped the rise just behind her, and flames speared up to meet them.

"East!" Yvonne yelped into her mic, turning her bike. "We'll go around!"

Another gust sent a plume of smoke racing at them, laying a heavy curtain across the terrain ahead.

"Fuck fuck fuck this is not good!" Yvonne muttered. Sarah's voice laughed nervously in her ear. "You think? The wind's blowing it ahead of us!"

On their flank, the fire roared as it ate up the scrubby prairie, sending plumes of smoke boiling into the air. Rolling balls of kochia raced ahead of the grassfire, spreading it as they tumbled. The wind howled, and the flames raced under its pressure.

"Floor it!" Yvonne rapped out, pushing down the Go pedal for all it was worth. Sarah matched her pace. Together, they pushed their bikes past eighty, past ninety. Still the fire crackled at their heels. The heat felt like it might bake them in their riding clothes like potatoes in their skins. The only part of her that wasn't overheating was her torso under its chill vest. She could feel sweat running down the tip of her nose, dripping into her helmet. *Hot. Too hot. Have to get out of this heat.*

"Fuck!" Sarah yelped as they topped a new hill. "It's ahead of us!"

"Keep going!" Yvonne demanded into her mic. Sweat trickled down her back.

"Baby, I don't know about--" Sarah began, but Yvonne cut her off, her heart in her mouth. "The wheels can take the heat for a little bit. If we drive through the burn, we won't have as much fire coming at us. We just have to move fast!" Matching words with action, she took off.

A stand of Russian Olive trees was belching flame into the sky, crackling as they burned. In another dip in the landscape, an old Black Locust groaned as it fell, smothered in fire. It was like driving into Hell.

"Stay away from the trees!" Yvonne called. She heard her wife snort. "Ya think?!"

Swerving out of the way of a falling branch, she gunned the engine, eyes scanning the horizon. There, a break in the smoke. "Come on!" Yvonne raced for it, the wind howling like a beast hunting prey.

Me. I'm the prey.

A gust of scorching air nearly shoved the bike into a flaming manzanita, but she leaned into it and pushed the bike to ninety-five.

Almost there, she whispered in her head. *Almost there. Almost there.*

The wind turned, and now the smoke rolled over them. Yvonne could barely see for it. "Sarah, talk to me."

"On your left baby."

"Kay. Don't stop!"

"Don't need to tell me!"

And then they were up and out of the low valley, and the air was clear, and they were racing across a gloriously normal section of the Dust with only the yellow sky overhead to tell anyone there was trouble.

They didn't let up until they were within a mile of home.

"Sarah, hon, let's pull up and decompress," Yvonne suggested into her mic. "We don't want to walk in freaking out."

They pulled up beside a convenient rock outcrop and killed the bikes. Yvonne pulled her helmet off with fingers that felt numb. Sarah's face, when her helmet revealed it, looked as shook as Yvonne felt. Her gorgeous eyes were huge, and she was white as a sheet.

For a second, all Yvonne could do was stare at her girl and breathe.

Sarah drew a trembling breath. "That was close."

"Too close," Yvonne agreed. Her voice sounded funny in her own ears. She set the bike on its kickstand and slid down, back against the rocks. Sarah joined her.

Yvonne let herself just sit for a second. Then she looked over at Sarah, giving her a shaky smile. "You know what?"

"What?"

"It was kind of awesome, wasn't it?"

Sarah cracked a wobbly grin, a weak chuckle eked out of her. "Yeah. Yeah, it was." She leaned in and kissed Yvonne quick, standing and pulling her to her feet for a hug.

"C'mon baby girl. Let's go home."

Join the Wildcards' next adventure wherever books are sold!

Acknowledgements

A couple words: thanks to Jessie, who gave me all kinds of tips on writing unions. Jess and Martha, your listening ears and sharp eyes are always invaluable. Alex, your perspective on social issues is always a huge help. Michael and Heather, your enthusiasm and devious minds are a joy to work alongside. Thanks everybody. You keep this whole thing rocking on.

A Note From The Munitions Officer: if you need resources to help improve the world or your life, there's help. Reach out.

Hey. Naomi here. If you're like us, you're probably feeling like a lot of things need to change. But none of us are fighting alone. Here's some resources to help you get where you want to go.

Hang in there. We're fighting beside you.

-Naomi

The Workplace Bill Of Rights

The real-world work we based our workplace demands on is written by the Workplace Fairness organization. Workplace Fairness believes that fair treatment of workers is sound public policy and good business practice, and that free access to comprehensive, unbiased information about workers' rights - without legal jargon - is an essential ingredient in any fair workplace.

That's why Workplace Fairness creates and maintains the most comprehensive, online one-stop-shop for free information about workers' rights. They capture the power of technology to:
- educate workers, employers, and legal services and community organizations;
- foster a community of advocates who believe that fairness works; and
- promote the fair treatment of workers through public policy.

Working together, professionals and citizens concerned with issues of workplace fairness more effectively build community awareness of workplace issues and promote progressive changes in employment law, policies, and practices.

Find it at https://www.workplacefairness.org/workplace-bill-of-rights
Erica Chenoweth And The Nonviolent Action Lab

The work referenced that supports the four per cent nonviolent resistance number is by Erica Chenoweth, "The '3.5% Rule': How a Small Minority Can Change the World," Carr Center for Human Rights Policy, May 14th, 2019

She has expanded this paper into a book: Civil Resistance: What Everyone Needs to Know. New York: Oxford University Press, 2021. She now helps out with the Nonviolent Action Lab. Existing research shows that nonviolent resistance can be a highly effective pathway to defend democratic values and institutions, while also creating transformative change in many domains. Yet many people remain skeptical about the power of nonviolent resistance to effect change. Part of the reason for this skepticism is that information about the power of nonviolent resistance—and up-to-date data demonstrating its power—is inaccessible to many people in the world. By systematically studying and amplifying nonviolent resistance, and synthesizing lessons learned from global movements worldwide, the lab will make it easier for the public and practitioners to embrace nonviolent action as a means of transforming injustice.

Check it out at https://carrcenter.hks.harvard.edu/non-violent-social-movements

Idealist. Org: Mutual Aid Societies

Mutual aid groups offer communities the opportunity to connect, both virtually and in person, in order to share support and resources during times of crisis and beyond. Check a few out at https://www.idealist.org/en/mutualaid

Thunderbird Strike!

The real-world game that Raven's Revenge is based on is called Thunderbird Strike!

In the 2D sidescroller Thunderbird Strike, fly from the Tar Sands to the Great Lakes as a thunderbird protecting Turtle Island with searing lightning against the snake that threatens to swallow the lands and waters whole.

Check it out, play and get involved at https: www.thunderbirdstrike.com/

Fresh Food Connect

Fresh Food Connect utilizes technology to solve two problems—excess garden produce and food insecurity. If you have extra produce, you can schedule pickups via the Fresh Food Connect app. Then their courier team will pick up the produce on bicycles and distribute it in local neighborhoods facing food insecurity.

If you are a home or community gardener in 80203, 80204, 80205, 80206, 80207, 80209, 80210, 80220 DFR will come right to your doorstep to pick up your garden grown produce and share it with community-based organizations addressing food access in their neighborhoods!
https://denverfoodrescue.org/fresh-food-connect/

Beautiful Trouble

The book 'Beautiful Trouble' that Liza mentions is an actual book, and it's linked to a wonderful organization. Recent years have seen an unprecedented surge of social movements and grassroots organizing. From Paris to Harare, Los Angeles to São Paulo, Beautiful Trouble is inspiring and up-skilling local organizers with trainings in nonviolent direct action, strategic campaigning and creative tactics. In a moment of change, there is no shortage of zeal, but sometimes there's a shortage of know-how and strategy. Beautiful Trouble is filling that gap by directly supporting activists in the field with hands-on campaign strategy, direct action planning, and one-to-one mentoring.

Reach out to them at https://www.beautifultrouble.org/, and check out their book, Beautiful Trouble: A Toolbox For Revolution

The Institute for Local Self-Reliance

The Institute for Local Self-Reliance has a vision of thriving, diverse, equitable communities. To reach this vision, they build local power to fight corporate control. They are a national research and advocacy organization that partners with allies across the country to build an American economy driven by local priorities and accountable to people and the planet. Local self-reliance means that people are able to exercise power over our lives: how we provide for our families, how resources are shared and allocated in our communities, and how decisions made by government, corporations and business affect all of us.

This organization recognizes the biggest challenges in the U.S. today are corporate control and diminishing community power which undermines the strength of our democracy and local economies. For the Institute, local self-reliance is the best answer to these challenges. So whether it's fighting back against the outsize power of monopolies like Amazon, ensuring high-quality locally-driven broadband service for all, or advocating to keep local renewable energy in the community that produced it, ILSR advocates for solutions that harness the power of citizens and communities.

See more and get resources at https://ilsr.org/

WHO Guidance and technical packages on community mental health services

The WHO Guidance on community mental health services: promoting person-centered and rights-based approaches is a set of publications that provides information and support to all stakeholders who wish to develop or transform their mental health system and services to align with international human rights standards including the UN Convention on the Rights of Persons with Disabilities.

The main reference source for all stakeholders is the Guidance on community mental health services: Promoting person-centered and rights-based approaches document which provides a detailed description of person-centered and human rights-based approaches in mental health, examples of good practice services around the world and recommendations for integrating such services into national health and social care systems and services. This comprehensive document is accompanied by a set of seven technical packages focused on specific categories of mental health services and guidance for setting up new services.

This guidance aims to empower governments, policy-makers, health and social care professionals, nongovernmental organizations, organizations of persons with disabilities and other stakeholders, to introduce and scale up mental health services that protect and promote human rights, ultimately improving the lives of people with mental health conditions and psychosocial disabilities everywhere. Find these resources at https://www.who.int/publications/i/item/guidance-and-technical-packages-on-community-mental-health-services

The Importance of Gender Affirming Care for Transgender and Gender Expansive Youth

Growing up is hard enough. For children and teenagers who are questioning their gender identity, the task of taking on commonly experienced milestones of adolescence like puberty can be even more distressing. Read more about helping young people working their way through transition at https://nursinglicensemap.com/blog/the-importance-of-gender-affirming-care-for-transgender-and-gender-expansive-youth/

SumOfUs

SumOfUs is a community of people from around the world committed to curbing the growing power of corporations. They want to buy from, work for and invest in companies that respect the environment, treat their workers well and respect democracy. Barely a day goes by without a fresh corporate scandal making headlines. From polluting the environment to dodging taxes—when left unchecked, corporations don't let anything stand in the way of bigger profits.

In an age of multinational companies that are bigger and richer than some countries, it can be easy to feel powerless. But there is a chink in their armour. The biggest corporations in the world rely on ordinary people to keep them in business. We are their customers, their employees, and often their investors. When we act together, we can be more powerful than they are. Together, our community of millions act as a global consumer watchdog—running and winning campaigns to hold the biggest companies in the world accountable.

Learn more by exploring their campaigns at https://www.sumofus.org/

The Ruckus Society

Ruckus has trained and assisted thousands of activists in the use of nonviolent direct action. They either bring activists to them (at Training Camps or Skillshares) or they go to the people (community-requested tailored trainings). Through these trainings, they help people learn the skills they need to practice nonviolent direct action safely and effectively. These trainings contain cerebral elements as well as physical, classroom-style instruction for action planning, communicating with the media, building leadership and political analysis, and nonviolent philosophy and practice.

Ruckus promotes and teaches:

• Implementation of strategic nonviolent direct action against unjust institutions and policies;
• Organized strategic development and coherent planning to advance campaign goals;
• The establishment of broad coalitions with common objectives;
• Effective methods of media outreach and Internet/Technology activism to inform the general public;
• Respect for all living things and a commitment to the power of diversity.
• In addition to hosting Trainings, Ruckus also provides Action Support at a wide variety of levels (from helping you brainstorm action ideas to pulling off an action for you) for groups who desire assistance with their action campaign.

Their Action Support program goes hand in hand with their Training program, and they love nothing better than helping folks who have trained with them take action in order to build their skills and experience, and most importantly—create positive changes!

Check them out and get involved at https://ruckus.org/

Civics Unplugged

Civics Unplugged (CU) is a nonpartisan 501(c)(3) social enterprise whose mission is to empower the leaders of Generation Z to build a brighter future for humanity. While Generation Z is deeply motivated to contribute to addressing the challenges we collectively face, traditional empowerment structures were simply not designed to equip young people with what they need to understand and address impediments to human flourishing. This is where Civics Unplugged comes in.

At CU, they are creating a new way to empower thousands of civic-minded youth around the world each year to devote themselves to radically increasing the health and resilience of humanity's collective future.

CU is powered by a digital-first team and community of thousands of Gen Z leaders committed to fostering human flourishing around the globe. CU's core team is based in NYC and represents decades of experience across politics, law, education, social impact, tech, venture, pop culture, media, and community building. It's at this intersection of these many domains that the magic of CU emerges.

Read more and show it to the young people in your life at https://www.civicsunplugged.org/

Using Graphic Novels in Education: March: Book One

For those who would like to know more about Congressman Lewis, who is honored in name several times in this book, here's a place to start.

March: Book One recounts Congressman Lewis' youth in rural Alabama and provides a wonderful window into what life was like for Black families in the 1940s and 1950s under Jim Crow and segregation laws. Lewis' first-person narrative allows him to reminisce as he revisits his past, while the prose and art give us the feeling that we, too, are reliving this tumultuous time in American history along with him. Together, we are introduced to Martin Luther King, Jr.'s words and speeches, and we learn of the birth of the Nashville Student Movement and their non-violent struggle to eliminate segregation through their lunch counter sit-ins and their trips to prison and City Hall. We learn of Lewis' first meeting with Dr. King and about the Supreme Court school desegregation decision of Brown v. The Board of Education. We learn about the case of Emmett Till in Money, Mississippi, of Rosa Parks and Jim Lawson and F.O.R. (Fellowship of Reconciliation), the last of which published Martin Luther King and the Montgomery Story, a comic book that deeply influenced Lewis and so many more.

To help readers more fully understand the time period, Lewis, Aydin, and Powell sensitively relate how painful this era was for everyone, without casting aspersions. Lewis narrates the pivotal events in his life through gentle conversation while Powell's art leaves us to interpret and feel their resulting emotions and consequences.

For tips on using this work in education and personal exploration, check out http://cbldf.org/2014/02/using-graphic-novels-in-education-march-book-one/

Farm Aid

On Wed 14, July 2021, The Guardian published a long-form article detailing how the classic American family farms have been gradually bought up by corporations. As the Guardian puts it, "four firms or fewer controlled at least 50% of the market for 79% of the groceries. For almost a third of shopping items, the top firms controlled at least 75% of the market share."

These are the twisted roots of the American AgCo I write about. And it is a devastating scenario for small farmers. They are out-competed by the market power of these large conglomerates, crushed between low returns and high costs. According to the same Guardian article, there has been a near doubling of calls to the crisis hotline run by Farm Aid (https://www.farmaid.org/), as family farms stumble under the debt incurred trying to keep up with behemoths. There have been hundreds of farmer suicides in the last few years, a gut punch to an already tiny percentage of the United States population.

If you know a farmer who needs help, please share the Farm Aid phone line or email with them: 1-800-FARM-AID (1-800-327-6243) or go to farmhelp@farmaid.org

What's happening to little farm outfits is a reminder for the rest of us too: what's on our plate matters, and not just to our personal health. Where our food comes from matters. Buy local, from a farm market or farm stand where you can. If you can't afford to, don't beat yourself up. Consider reaching out to your members of congress to discuss breaking up Ag monopolies. But don't forget: you have the power to impact this situation with everyday choices. We all do.

ACES HIGH

JOKERS
WILD

A Wildcards Playlist, Part 6

- Dope Saint Jude, "Didn't Come to Play". Resilient, 2018
- Leo Justi & Brazzabelle, "Swipe It Off (feat. Zanillya)". Swipe It Off, 2019
- Ndidi O, "Call Me Queen", Call Me Queen, 2019
- Bikini Kill, "Rebel Girl", The Punk Singer (Original Motion Picture Soundtrack), 2015 Bikini Kill Records
- Joan Jett, "Bad Reputation", Bad Reputation (Expanded Edition) 1980 Blackheart Records Group
- The Interrupters, 'Title Holder', Fight the Good Fight, Hellcat Records 2018
- Skinny Beats, "Give It to Me", Skinny Beats, Head Bitch Records 2019
- The Interrupters, "White Noise", The Interrupters, Hellcat Records 2020
- Latashá, "Who I Am", Who I Am, Sugaroo Records 2020
- Hydraulix & Oski, "Nothing Can Stop Me", Disciple, Disciple Records 2018
- Daft Punk, "Harder Better Faster", Discovery, Virgin Records 2001
- Dope Saint Jude, "Go High Go Low", Go High Go Low, Platoon Ltd 2020
- LCD Soundsystem, "North American Scum", Sound of Silver, DFA Records 2007
- Joan Jett & The Blackhearts, Victim of Circumstance, I Love Rock 'N' Roll (Expanded Edition), Blackheart Records Group 1981
- Beastie Boys, "Sabotage", Ill Communication, Grand Royal

Records 1994

- L7 The Band, "Shitlist", Bricks Are Heavy, Slash Records 1992
- Kairo featuring Sha'Ki, "Gr8ness", Round One: Glory, 2019 Offstream Music Group
- Pharrell Williams, "Freedom", Despicable Me 3 Original Motion Picture Soundtrack, 2017 Columbia Music Group
- The Interrupters, "Phantom City", Say It Out Loud, 2016 Hellcat Records
- Operation Ivy, "Bad Town", Operation Ivy, Epitaph Records 2009
- Gaslight Anthem, "Boomboxes And Dictionaries", Sink or Swim, XOXO Records 2008
- Beans on Toast, "World Gone Crazy", The Inevitable Train Wreck, Spin City Productions 2019
- Dope Saint Jude, "Grrrl Like", Kipo And The Age Of Wonderbeasts (Season 1 Mixtape), Universal Pictures Film Music 2018
- Beth Yen feat. THURZ, "Wild Jungle", Wild Jungle, Heatrøck 2017
- Atomic Drum Assembly, "Feelin", Jump In, Island Life Recordings 2007
- Dawn Richard, "New Breed", New Breed, 2021
- Linkin Park, "Points Of Authority", Hybrid Theory, Warner Records 2015
- Crys Matthews, "This Kind of War", Changemakers, 2021
- She Drew The Gun, "Trouble Every Day", Trouble Every Day, Kobalt Music Publishing 2019
- The Interrupters, "Leap of Faith", Fight The Good Fight, Epitaph Records 2018
- Massive Attack, "Massive Attack x Algiers featuring Christiana Figueres", https://www.youtube.com/watch?v=FoBYMAla9_8&list=PL8HyB52xsG8U7PgEy0WQwVyRYkTo7OFIt&index=31, Unit 3 Films 2020
- Phantogram, "When I'm Small", City Of Ommz, Create Music Group 2011
- U2, "I Still Haven't Found What I'm Looking For," The Best Of 1980 - 1990, Island Records 1987
- Joan Jett and the Blackhearts, "Do You Wanna Touch Me", Bad

Reputation, Blackheart Records Group 1980

- Alanis Morissette, "All I Really Want", Jagged Little Pill, Universal Music Publishing 1995
- Edie Brickell & New Bohemians, "What I Am", Shooting Rubber Bands At The Stars, Geffen Records 1998
- Nahko And Medicine For The People, "Love Letters To God", HOKA, The Orchard Music 2017
- Arrested Development, "United Front", Classic Masters, Capitol Records 2002
- Andra Gunter, "Oz The Originator Intro Song", Kipo And The Age Of Wonderbeasts (Season 1 Mixtape), Universal Pictures Film Music 2018
- Gaeya, "Contact", Awakening, Gaeya Music 2020
- Mandy Harvey, "Creep", Nice To Meet You, The SoNo Recording Group 2019
- Jordy Chandra, "Late Night Call", 1AM Study Session, LoFi Publishing 2019
- Grouplove, "Let Me In", The Fault In Our Stars (Music From the Motion Picture), Atlantic Recording Corporation 2014
- Lindsey Stirling, "Stars Align", Lindsey Stirling, Forward Music Publishing 2013
- No Doubt, "Running", Rock Steady, Interscope Records 2001
- My Brightest Diamond, "Be Brave", Be Brave - Single, Asthmatic Kitty 2011
- Halestorm, "I Am The Fire", I Am The Fire, Atlantic Records 2015
- Crys Matthews, "We Must Be Free", Battle Hymn for an Army of Lovers, Crys Matthews 2017
- Blue Öyster Cult, "Burnin' For You", Burnin' For You, Atlantic Records 1981 **Quoted Chapter 16**
- Mystery Jets, "Wrong Side Of The Tracks", A Billion Heartbeats, Mystery Jets Records 2020
- I See Rivers, "We Don't Get More Time," Deep & Rolling Green, Believe Music 2020
- Saunder Jurriaans, "Easy Now", Beasts, Decca 2020
- Corey Hart, "Never Surrender", Never Surrender (Angels) 2020, Saphir Music 2020
- Las Cafeteras, "Luna Lovers", It's Time, Las Cafeteras Music 2013

- Crys Matthews, "American History XIX", Battle Hymn for an Army of Lovers, Crys Matthews 2017
- Lily Allen, "Fuck You", It's Not Me, It's You, Regal 2009
- Janelle Monáe, "Americans", Dirty Computer, Bad Boy Records 2018
- Deap Vally, "Gonnawanna", Femejism, The Orchard Records 2016
- Peter CottonTale, "Pray for Real", CATCH, Kobalt Records 2020
- Rising Appalachia, "Resilient", Leylines, Rising Appalachia 2021
- Switchfoot, "Where I Belong", Vice Verses, Atlantic Records 2011
- Crys Matthews, "Battle Hymn for an Army of Lovers", Battle Hymn for an Army of Lovers, Crys Matthews 2017
- Grouplove, "Ways To Go", Spreading Rumors, Atlantic Recording Corporation 2013
- Aerosmith, "Deuces Are Wild", Big Ones, Geffen Records 1994
- Bon Jovi, "Lay Your Hands On Me", New Jersey, Island Records 2009
- Bleachers, "I Wanna Get Better", Strange Desire, Sony Music Entertainment 2014
- Alanis Morissette, "Guardian", Havoc and Bright Lights, Collective Sounds 2012
- Lindsey Stirling (VenTribe), "We Found Love", Sony ATV Publishing 2012
- Switchfoot, "Love Alone Is Worth The Fight", Fading West, Atlantic Records 2013
- Hedley, "Anything", Anything, Capitol Records 2013
- The Interrupters ft Rancid, "Got Each Other", Fight The Good Fight, Epitaph Records 2018
- Sara Bareilles, "Brave", The Blessed Unrest, Epic Records 2013
- Bon Jovi, "Because We Can", What About Now, The Island Def Jam Music Group 2013
- Delta Rae, "Run", After It All, Sire Records 2015
- Rising Appalachia, "Resilient", Leylines, 2019
- Vienna Teng, "Soon Love Soon", Waking Hour, 2002

Other Books By The Author

The Aces High, Jokers Wild Series
Aces High, Jokers Wild Book 1: The Hands We're Given
Aces High, Jokers Wild Book 1.5: The Boys of Summer Have Gone
Aces High, Jokers Wild Book 2: Call the Bluff
Aces High, Jokers Wild Book 2.5: After Hours Game (A Wildcards Christmas)
Aces High, Jokers Wild Book 3: Raise the Stakes
Aces High, Jokers Wild Book 3.5: Bad Hand (A Wildcards Halloween)
Aces High, Jokers Wild Book 4: Aces and Eights
Aces High, Jokers Wild Book 4.5: Follow The Lady
Aces High, Jokers Wild Book 5: Draw Dead
Aces High, Jokers Wild Book 5.5: Draw Out

Anthologies
Neon Dreams and Nightmares: Mixed Punk Works of Dystopian Futures
Dark Horizons: A Collection of Near-Future, Dystopian, and Cyberpunk Sci-fi: Multi author 5 book box set

JOKER

About The Author

O.E. Tearmann is the author of the Aces High, Jokers Wild series. Their books include strong themes of diversity and found family, providing a surprisingly hopeful take on a dystopian future. Bringing their own experiences as a marginalized author together with flawed but genuine characters, Tearmann's work has been described as "Firefly for the dystopian genre." Publisher's Weekly called it "a lovely paean to the healing power of respectful personal connections among comrades, friends, and lovers."

Tearmann lives in Colorado with two cats, their partner, and the belief that individuals can make humanity better through small actions. They are a member of Rocky Mountain Fiction Writers, the Colorado Resistance Writers, and the Queer Scifi group. In their spare time, they teach workshops about writing GLTBQ characters, speak and plant gardens to encourage sustainable agricultural practices, and play too many video games.